"I can't help you if you don't give me the benefit of the doubt."

"Why should you do anything for me?" Nicole asked. "You don't know me, and you've said yourself that you have more than enough of your own problems to deal with."

"True, but I've also been a cop long enough to recognize when things aren't adding up. Hell, I'm not saying I can perform miracles, or even change anything. But my intention is to help."

She had to look away. "I can't think. Not right now."

"What's holding you back? What are you afraid of?" he asked, taking her clenched hands between his. "If someone carrying a badge did something wrong, we all need to know."

He didn't understand what this would cost her, and she was afraid to tell him. Afraid that he wouldn't believe her; afraid that he would. But every day that slipped by, the trail grew colder.

She pulled herself free. "There's more to this than what I've told you. Something else happened that night...."

"Ms. Myers never fails to give the reader an entertaining story with fresh characterizations and dialogue that sparkles."
—*Rendezvous*

MORE THAN YOU KNOW

HELEN R. MYERS

MIRA®

ISBN 1-55166-504-2

MORE THAN YOU KNOW

Look us up on-line at: http://www.mirabooks.com

Printed in U.S.A.

ACKNOWLEDGMENTS

Special thanks to the following, who gave generously of their time and expertise:

Sergeant Kurt Bjornson, Dallas Police Department, Central Patrol; Victoria Eiker, Dallas Police Department, PIO; Sergeant J.W. King, Dallas Police Department, Homicide; Robert C. Renko, Special Agent OSI, USAF

This is, in the end, a work of fiction, but as much care was given to technical accuracy as possible. It should also be noted that "copspeak" alters regionally; a *radio car* in one area is a *patrol car* in another. I did attempt to remain geographically true, but inevitably breaches will have occurred, some intentional, some not.

One of the disturbing necessities in writing this story was for my female protagonist to take on the role of Everywoman and, therefore, make a good number of mistakes when it came to her actions and reactions in moments of crisis. In good conscience, therefore, I highly recommend the reader also invest his or her time in reading *The Gift of Fear* by Gavin De Becker, Little, Brown & Company, for a reminder of the survival skills that may save *your* life.

To Bradley Grant, a special hug and gratitude for the sharing that planted the first of three seeds that inspired this journey.

And last but never least, to my husband, Robert, who is always my third eye and ear, my ballast through all rough seas, and a fountain of information in his own right—my endless gratitude and love.

*As soon as questions of will or decision
or reason or choice of action arise,
human science is at a loss.*

—Noam Chomsky

‗‗‗‗‗ Prologue ‗‗‗‗‗

It was during the horror of a deep night.

—Jean Racine

Dead on her feet, but trying to be quiet for her brother's sake, Nicole Loring all but tiptoed as she let herself into Jay's apartment. The turnout at Van Dorn's, one of Dallas's premiere auction houses, had been better than anyone had expected, the bidding on many items intense, which was reason enough for her throat to feel as though she'd been swallowing sandpaper half the evening, and her feet to burn like a lit cigarette was inside each shoe. She wanted only to crawl into bed and sleep until noon. Unfortunately, she had to be back at her desk by nine o'clock, alert for a private phone auction. Van Dorn's had acquired a '74 Harley-Davidson motorcycle belonging to a recently deceased Hollywood celebrity, and Nicole had discreetly alerted a handful of foreign collectors interested in motorcycles—collectors most likely to guarantee the firm a tidy commission from the sale. The other crimp in her plans was that for the second night in a row she wouldn't be sleeping in her own bed.

Yesterday her apartment building had suffered an electrical fire. The good news was that the flames were contained to the apartments behind hers. The bad news was, thanks to the design of the connected ventilation system, the toxic smoke and fumes hadn't been. It would be several days before she would be allowed back and, in the meantime, Jay insisted she crash on his couch.

It wasn't necessary to turn on a lamp. Jay had left the kitchen stove light on, which lent the living room a faint glow, something her burning eyes and aching head appreciated. But as she stepped out of her high heels and quietly moved around the room, she wondered if all this conscientiousness wasn't wasted. Jay *could* still be awake. Deciding to check, she set her purse and keys on the coffee table and circled the couch to glance down the short hallway.

His bedroom door was closed. Not exactly what she'd expected. When they'd discussed schedules and routines yesterday, he'd warned her with typical sangfroid that he would continue to keep his bedroom door open and to sleep in the nude. If she'd suddenly developed a terminal case of modesty, or worse yet, penis envy, she was to kindly turn away when en route to the bathroom, which required passing through his bedroom to get to.

After sharing a good laugh, he'd told her about his last visit over a year ago to "The Dungeon," their nickname for the family home, and how he'd shocked their mother into tipping vodka into her breakfast orange juice after she'd burst into his room unannounced to surprise her "J.J." with coffee.

Poor Jay. He didn't know that morning vodka was nothing new to their mother, and hadn't been for a long time.

Suddenly a muffled sound stopped her.

No. That couldn't have been a moan...at least not *that* kind of moan. But then she heard the rhythmic squeaking of bedsprings—a more telling sound.

Her incredulity turned into indignation as another unmistakably sexual grunt was followed by an undecipherable whisper. Good grief! After all those protestations and reassurances he'd made when she'd worried that her presence would be an intrusion, her brother was in there doing it with some girl? Damn it! She should have gone to a hotel after all. Now she couldn't even wash up without embarrassing everyone—or at least herself. This wasn't exactly what she'd meant when they'd argued about her staying here:

"Your life's enough of a mess as it is, your schedule about to become a nightmare. I'll be in the way."

"Don't be an ass. You're the only relative I'm not ashamed to claim. Here I've just spilled my guts about why I need your support more than ever, and you want to run off to a hotel and room service?"

They *were* close. No matter who else came in to and passed out of their lives, they provided a constancy for each other. But this...this was asking too much. Talk about exercising poor judgment. On the other hand, until she knew the details she shouldn't jump to conclusions. Besides, who was she to criticize? At least he had a love life. Hers was nonexistent!

Okay, she decided returning to the sofa, to make up

for one night of poor hygiene, she would indulge in two facials this month—and he could pay for both.

Then again, maybe his friend would be leaving soon. Surely, at some point Jay would remember she was due home? Hopefully he'd already heard her. Something about the way he'd sounded that second time...well, someone had seemed to be protesting in there.

Resigned, she folded an afghan to use as a pillow and lay down in a fetal curl. But no sooner did she close her eyes than the utterances from the bedroom grew more intense. The bedsprings began squeaking faster. When she heard moans become urgent growls and garbled exclamations, she had to press her hands to her ears to keep from yelling herself.

Then, finally, all was silent again. Soon, she assured herself, soon whoever was in there with him would leave. It would probably be less awkward for everyone if she pretended to be asleep...but was Jay going to get an earful once that front door closed!

She shut her eyes to wait.

When Nicole opened her eyes again, daylight poured in around the rubber-lined draperies.

She sprang up and checked her watch. Eight-fifteen. How could she have fallen asleep, let alone overslept.

"I'm dead," she muttered, scrambling off the couch. No way was she going to make it to the office in time.

Slipping pins tugged and pinched in her sleep-mussed chignon as she hurried down the hallway, but she stopped pulling them out the instant she saw that her brother's door remained closed.

She checked her watch again. No, she hadn't read it wrong, and the second hand was working—which meant what?

For one thing, her dear, popular brother had had some night. For another, she must have been more tired than she'd thought if she could sleep through the finale of his little interlude. Knowing he should be up himself, she knocked on the door hoping that at the very least his date was long gone.

"Hey, Romeo! If you're in there, rise and shine. I need to get in the bathroom and then race to work before Max sends a hit man after me."

No answer. She placed her hands on her hips. "Jay, did you hear me? Don't I at least get a peek at the newcomer?"

Her unease growing, she reached for the knob, hesitated, then turned it. It came as no surprise to find it unlocked.

"Jay...?"

His king-size bed stood flush against the double windows and faced the door. Although the drapes were closed, there was sufficient light for her to see. But dear God, she wished she couldn't.

Even as the first wave of nauseating odor assaulted her nostrils, the full horror of the scene registered in her mind. Gagging, she stumbled to the bathroom, and barely reached the commode in time.

1

Three weeks later

Well, everyone can master a grief but he that has it.

—William Shakespeare,
Much Ado About Nothing

Come morning she was going to have one helluva hangover, but at the moment she couldn't find a good enough reason to give a damn.

Nicole took another swallow of champagne, the last one still a cool, tantalizing memory in her mouth. She knew Max had noticed, as he had when she'd gulped down her first few glasses. After three weeks, would this be the night when his patience and concern finally turned to anger? Everyone had their limit. Of course, if he did blow a fuse, she would be quick to inform him that she was doing him a favor by choosing this lesser of two evils. Overindulging in wine beat taking one of those nasty pills her doctor had prescribed for her. Those tranquilizers turned her into a zombie and left her almost brain-dead for up to two days afterward. Better to deal with a hangover and the occasional panic attack. Sure, the champagne was turning her into someone far more mellow than Max liked his cool, efficient auctioneer and trusted right hand to be. So what? The bulk of her responsibilities were over for tonight. She'd earned this.

Tonight Van Dorn's had succeeded in finding new owners for the choicest antiques and collectibles consigned from the Crown estate during this ''by invitation only'' sale. Tomorrow—her hands shook and her stomach twisted itself into a new knot at the mere thought of her schedule—the remaining items would be offered to the general public. This intimate party was Max's way of thanking the most valued of his clientele, and it had been going on for better than an hour. Moments ago she'd adjusted the dimmer switch reducing the lighting in the room—a subtle hint for everyone to finish their drinks and leave. The question was, would she last until they did without making a total fool of herself? The temptation was already strong to turn off everything and shout, ''Get lost, already! Scram! Shoo!'' in her best east Texas drawl. Only her respect for dear Max kept her from giving in to the impulse. He would not be amused...and she would be ashamed. Eventually.

''Not.''

Air, she thought. She needed fresh air before things got any worse. Didn't anyone else notice how hot it was in here? If she could have five, at least two minutes of unrecycled oxygen and privacy, she might hold on to her sanity for yet another day.

Praying that she didn't look quite as desperate as she felt, she signaled her assistant Carlyn, posted at the caviar, to let her know that she was heading for the atrium. She then ducked beneath the lowest fronds of a huge potted palm and circled around Max's beloved bronze centaur. Her destination lay beyond the French doors, but the way was blocked by a pair of Van Dorn's more high-maintenance patrons. The last thing she needed was to be asked to again recite the provenance of the early Modigliani head they'd claimed tonight. Considering the amount of alcohol flowing in her bloodstream, she might end up reciting Rommel's victories in North Africa instead.

It didn't happen. To her relief they merely nodded and stepped out of her way. Moses couldn't have been happier upon witnessing the Red Sea parting.

She attempted what she hoped resembled a serene smile, although bitter thoughts ate at her insides. Like everyone else, the couple appeared oblivious as to what she was going through. In fact, not one of the attendees had given an inkling that they understood her situation, let alone saw that she was coming apart at the seams. Either nobody read anything beyond the society columns in the paper these days, or she was becoming a better actress than she thought. Who would have guessed it? Being related to the Grand Duchess of Pretense and Denial was finally an asset.

Outside she found more plants to maneuver around, as well as a pair of wrought iron benches, then the koi pond with the fountain that was so soothing to listen to. She was glad to discover she wouldn't have to share the New Orleans-style hideaway with anyone else. It was difficult enough to wrestle with the invisible hands attempting to choke the breath out of her; she didn't need the added humiliation of—

"You're beginning to worry me."

The familiar masculine voice had her spinning around and flattening against the brick wall, still warm from late August's afternoon heat. Of all the people who could have followed her out here, he was the most unwelcome. A few weeks ago Nicole would have been better equipped to cope; she could have stared straight through Roman McKenna and walked away like a well-trained ice princess who sincerely believed pit bulls could be dealt with as easily as bores. But this moonlighting cop had developed the most annoying tendency to transform into something else around her, causing her to lose focus when he spoke to her in that gruff, kind way, making it nearly impossible to ignore the compassion-warmed eyes she would otherwise describe as anemic vampire-blue. Earlier he'd tried to talk to her, back when she'd been inhaling her first glass of champagne. She'd had just enough sass in reserve to give him a smile that should have put him on penicillin, and to suggest he go write someone a parking ticket. The set of his strong jaw now indicated that he wouldn't allow a second brush-off. She intended to try anyway, because tonight tenderness frightened her far more than intimidation did.

"How flattering," she drawled. "You should know, though, that when I have a chance to catch my breath after a hectic night, I take it. Don't you think I've earned the right, Mr....*Officer* McKenna? Or am I under house arrest and required to clear every step I take with you?"

His frown deepened. "What are you talking about?"

Yes, he was very good. That befuddled expression looked genuine, but no amount of champagne would let her forget that he was one of *them*. A cop. If he wanted to play games, she would show him that she could hold her own under the most stressful conditions.

"Forget it." She added an indifferent shrug, mostly to stretch the muscles tensing along her shoulder blades. "My mistake—as usual." She pointed toward the party with her glass, spilling a few drops of her drink. "So, what did you think of tonight? Impressive, wasn't it?"

"If you'd been any more effective, you would have seduced me into bidding on something."

That would have been an accomplishment. He could have ill-afforded to open a bid on most of tonight's offerings let alone have stayed in for the fall of the gavel, for when he wasn't securing the auction house, he was a member of the Dallas Police Department. And not, Nicole thought, recognizing the suit that had seen a few too many dry cleanings, a very high-ranking one.

"Don't let Max hear that you resisted me," she replied. "He likes to believe I could sell a kaleidoscope to a blind man."

"I'll keep it our secret…provided you switch with me." Before she could catch on to what he was up to, he eased the champagne flute out of her hand and gave her the tumbler of sparkling water that he'd been holding.

Nicole didn't care for what happened to her insides when his fingers brushed against hers any more than she liked losing her emotional crutch. She arched an eyebrow, hoping the haughty move hid her embarrassment, and that the darkness muted the blush she felt stinging her cheeks. "Charm isn't going to get you any further than the you-Tarzan-everyone-else-Cheetah approach you guys usually use."

Once again his look suggested he wasn't following. "I'm only trying to help. In case you haven't noticed, you've had enough to drink."

"Hardly, if I can still hear you. Thanks for the concern, though."

"You can save the gratitude for after I get you home."

"Pardon?"

"I'm driving you. Now."

"The hell you are." One thing she no longer tolerated was being told what she was and wasn't going to do and when. For the better part of her thirty years she'd been bullied, manipulated and dictated to, and she'd worked hard to escape such control-driven behavior. Too hard to put up with it now, even if the person trying had a legal right to do so. In the wake of her brother's death, her opinion of the law enforcement community had undergone a drastic change, and she was in no frame of mind to believe, let alone trust, any cop. "First of all, I'm not drunk...more's the pity. And second, I'll sleep on the couch in my office before I go anywhere with you."

Roman McKenna set her champagne glass on the brick wall beside them. "I wish I could believe you would, and I appreciate that you are upset. You and your family have suffered a terrible loss. But it doesn't make sense to take it out on the people trying to help you.''

"You hypocritical bastard. How dare you say that to me!''

"Miss Lor—''

"Isn't there *one* of you who isn't an accomplished liar?'' Nicole's hands were shaking so badly now, water sloshed over the rim of the glass and onto her silk sheath. But before she could register the impulse to fling the remaining contents at him, he took the tumbler from her as he had the flute.

"Nicole, hey! Nick—'' having set the glass beside the other, Roman took careful but firm hold of her upper arms "—take a deep breath. Do it!''

She didn't want him touching her. She didn't want him using the affectionate abbreviation of her name as only Jay had. But she was no better at communicating that than she was at coming to terms with her brother's death.

"Please go away.'' Feeling her control slipping, she buried her face in her hands. "Why won't you people let me be?''

"I'm not sure I know what 'you people' means, and I'd like to honor your request. Hell, I'm trying, only…''

Something about the way he abruptly fell silent had her summoning the energy to look up again. What she saw confirmed suspicions that were as disconcerting as everything else going on.

He was attracted to her. It had been evident from

the night he'd started at Van Dorn's. So was the fact
that he didn't want to be. What he didn't, could never
know was, if things had been different, she might have
admitted to suffering from a similar dilemma. With his
riveting eyes and rugged good looks, so different from
the pampered men she tended to meet in her line of
work, he cut an image that was disturbingly physical.
Sexual. Only her grim situation made it easy to remind
herself that they had about as much in common as chili
and chateaubriand.

"Try harder," she replied, hoping she sounded
more haughty than afraid.

His hands tightened for a moment before he released
her. "Done. But I am taking you home. Your boss
already made it clear he would consider it a personal
favor." When she opened her mouth to protest, he
added, "Look at it this way, after tonight you'll never
have to do it again."

"What's that supposed to mean?" His promise
spawned a demon's vision of tomorrow, of some street
person finding her body in a filthy Dumpster.

"This is my last night. I've been promoted to detective. Homicide. The schedule is pretty demanding,
so there's no way I can guarantee Max that I'd be here
when he needed me."

Another bigger-than-his-britches detective. Exactly
what the city needed. But on the heels of that shrewish
thought came an unmistakable sinking sensation.

She was going to miss having him around.

His bland navy blue tie became her focal point as
she moistened her lips. "Well. Congratulations."

As they stood there almost hidden by the white

crepe myrtle fanning out beyond the brick dividing wall, he searched her face. "I wish you meant that."

"Of course you do."

His answering sigh sounded as heavy as the weight on her heart these days.

"Look, can we start over? Get through this without shedding blood? Okay, so you think I'm shit. I'll live with that if I have to. But my conscience won't let you get behind a wheel tonight. Max said it would be all right if you left, and he's having someone bring your purse to the back door. Will you come with me, or do we go back inside and risk you falling face first into the fish eggs?"

What was the point of fighting? He was right. Everyone was right. And she was tired, of everything. Nevertheless, when Roman stretched out his hand, she couldn't quite bring herself to accept it. She did, however, move away from the wall, albeit shakily, and head for the back doors of the atrium, the route that was a shortcut to the rear exit.

Neither of them said another word until they were in his not-so-new black pickup truck.

"She may not be what you're used to riding in," he said in response to her dubious inspection, "but she's a damned good truck."

"I'm not a snob, Detective McKenna."

"Could you try calling me Roman? Too much formality makes me feel as though I should be in a penguin suit. Besides, the detective thing hasn't wholly sunk in yet."

They shouldn't be talking at all. She didn't want to be charmed by the man or to have her curiosity piqued beyond where it already was. It wasn't as though they were ever going to see each other again.

In self-defense, she leaned her head back against the seat, wrapped her arms around her waist, and closed her eyes, willing herself to send the right message before the spinning lights behind her tightly shut lids cost her the contents of her stomach. She tried to focus on happier things, beloved images…peace.

It never crossed her mind to give him directions; as a result, no one could have been more stunned than she was when the truck made a sharp turn, abruptly stopped—and she discovered they weren't merely at a traffic light.

He was parked at her home. Her *new* home as of this week.

"Now what's wrong?" he asked.

She had no idea how she looked, but she felt…about to lose it. "How did you know how to get here?"

"Max told me."

Did he? Or had someone else obliged—the same someone who'd been turning her life into a nightmare ever since she'd found Jay's body?

Before panic could immobilize her, she grabbed the door handle and made a run for it.

2

A thing done at the wrong time
should be regarded as not done.

—Sanskrit proverb

"Nicole? Damn it!"

The woman was beginning to act certifiable. It was only that look of abject terror in her eyes—a look that both troubled Roman and made him feel lower than a worm—that compelled him to take off after her. Fortunately, her strappy shoes made speed impossible.

He caught her before she could get more than a few yards. "Whoa." He meant his hold to steady more than to keep her from running. "Easy does it."

"Let me go or I'll scream!"

"For what? Being chauffeured home? Good point. Have me arrested. I'm likely to get three-to-five for that. Add Max's foresight in giving me directions here, and the judge might tack on another ten to the sentence."

The fight went out of her faster than air from a slashed tire, and she stood there limp, vulnerable. Only her eyes gave away her inner battle to gauge the truth in what he was saying, and her chagrin at the conclusions she'd come to.

"Too much to drink," she moaned, covering her face.

Roman couldn't agree more—and he hated seeing her like that.

Before Maxwell Van Dorn had introduced them, he'd described Nicole Loring as a double threat. Not only did she have better instincts about art than he ever would, he'd declared, but she possessed a naturally classy allure that had his male customers—particularly those from oil rich countries—frequently trying to steal her away from him. At the time Roman thought the comment poetic rot from an older guy lusting after some young skirt. Then Max called her into his office and Roman had been left wondering if the San Andreas Fault had shifted east about thirteen hundred miles or so.

Back when he was a kid, the term "golden girl" had been the cliché for every blonde from California. While he didn't have a clue as to where Nicole originally came from, and "girl" hardly did her justice, she was golden all right. Golden hair that he'd itched to loosen from the severe knot she always wore at work, golden eyes that grief hadn't dulled, and skin… Maybe the less he thought about her alluring assets, the better. At any rate, ever since that first day, he'd been torn between relief that she did virtually everything she could to avoid him, and frustration over how well she succeeded.

Not wanting her to continue looking at him as though he'd just confessed to being Ted Bundy's twin, he released her and rubbed at the perspiration building in the lines running alongside his mouth. Between the humidity, the damned suit, and having to walk on eggshells with the woman, he might as well be in the middle of a nuclear meltdown.

"Look," he began, hoping she was sober enough to follow, "the only ulterior motive I had was wanting to sleep tonight knowing you didn't kill yourself or somebody else on the road." She didn't need to know that his dreams would be full of her regardless: dreams where she didn't end up here, but in his bed under him. Why should she care if, after several months of living his own personal hell, she was all that made it bearable to close his eyes? "But if it'll make you feel better, go call Max and ask him how I knew where to go. First, though, ask yourself how else I could have found this place?"

"That's rich, considering you're a cop."

This constant suggestion that the police were some species of lowlife was getting to him. "Meaning what? No, don't look away. You brought it up. Finish. At first I thought it was one of those chemistry things— you know, when people rub each other the wrong way? But it's the *badge* with you. You hate cops."

"I try to avoid using the word 'hate.'"

"You didn't have any trouble with 'bastard.' Why don't you trust us?"

"Don't patronize me."

"Jesus...lady, I'd have to understand where you're coming from to even try. Does this have to do with your brother? Did something happen with the investigating officers?" The look she shot him spoke fathoms. "No, I don't already know the answer to that. This may blow holes into your conspiracy theory, which is what I'm beginning to suspect we're dealing with, but I don't know anything about your situation beyond Max saying that your brother died recently, and that *you* found him. Dallas isn't the 'one-riot, one-ranger' town it used to be. We deal with a helluva bunch of calls on a daily basis. It's not unheard of for a cop assigned to Patrol not to know about something that's gone down in another department, let alone another branch."

He watched her attempt to process that...then cling to her suspicions.

"Next you'll tell me that you never read the newspaper."

"Not lately. My life is *complicated*. All caps." The mere word was almost laughable to him. "Between it and my job, keeping up with national and international heartbreak isn't at the top of my priority list."

She frowned, then fussed with the ornate clasp on her black leather bag. She had lovely hands, the fingers shaped for a dancer's expressive movements—or to caress an artifact and beguile a collector so that something looked more desirable than it was? At any rate, those hands continued to shake like an alcoholic with the DTs.

"If that's the truth..." she replied slowly.

"Hell, yes, it's the truth. Ask Max. Ask the Boy Scouts who recycle my empty beer cans."

She bowed her head. "I didn't know."

Although he could barely make out what she said, the hint of regret, while no means an apology, was the most welcome thing he'd heard in a long time, next to the news about his promotion. Exhaling to purge some of the tension boiling inside him, he nodded. "Forget it. In my field, losing your cool on occasion is inevitable...but doing it with you makes me feel like garbage."

"Then it should help to know I prefer your anger to being stared at all the time."

Interesting that she'd noticed. Her honesty pulled a corresponding truth from him. "I stare because you're like nothing I've ever seen before." Clearing his throat, he glanced around. "Now I'm going to check the grounds and make sure everything's okay. Then I'll get out of your hair once and for all. By this time next week, you won't even remember my name."

She blinked as though he was speaking in another language. "Everything is fine here."

"It's too dark. And what with those hedges blocking your neighbor's floodlights, as well as most of the streetlights, unless you tell me you have a pet rottweiler lurking in the bushes, I think it's wiser if I have a look around."

"That's not my house."

He'd gotten no more than two steps toward the stone two-story on their left. When he turned around, Nicole gestured half-heartedly to the separate garage with the rooms above it that the truck's headlights illuminated. "That's where I'm living. Max didn't explain?"

"He gave me the street address and said to pull into the driveway instead of parking out front."

She appeared somewhat reassured by that. Almost pleased. Go figure, he thought.

"I only moved in a week ago. Goldie—my land-lady, Mrs…Mrs. Gilman—is out of town."

Roman considered the dark windows above the two-car garage. Because of her job and the way she dressed and carried herself, he'd assumed that the whole place was hers. She fit the Highland Park-Turtle Creek image. But unlike the miniature castle of a house, the garage was a spartan box framed in white vinyl siding. Worse, the unlit stairs leading up to the rooms were an invitation for a mugger looking for an easy target; a tipsy, exhausted woman trying to balance herself on sexy but treacherous high heels wouldn't stand a chance.

"You should turn on the outside light when you're going to be home after dark."

She frowned at the stairway. "I thought I did."

That decided things for him. He returned to the truck and grabbed his flashlight from the glove compart-ment. Then he reached inside his suit jacket and drew out his .38.

Nicole's eyes widened at the sight of the Smith & Wesson handgun. "What's that for?"

"Companionship. Go on up. Careful on those stairs."

By the time he circled the grounds and inspected everything, she had made it inside without breaking her neck. Holstering his weapon, he climbed the steep stairs, gave the flimsy storm door a look of disgust, and snorted at the glass panes on the upper half of the inner door. For someone so easily spooked, she sure did a good job undermining her own safety.

Upon entering, he found Nicole had poured herself

another glass of wine and was half through it. Between emotional and physical exhaustion, and the effects of the liquor she'd already consumed, she looked about two gulps away from passing out.

"Everything appears okay outside. You want to look around in here before I go?" He scanned the combination kitchen-dinette area that opened to the living room, as much for security reasons as to keep his gaze off her.

"Why? The door was locked and—" she flicked a hand toward the small mountain of boxes in the middle of the floor that confirmed her new resident status "—how would I know if everything's the way I left it?"

Roman pressed his lips together and checked the coat closet thinking, terrific. She jumps at the sight of her own shadow, and assumed because her door hadn't been forced open that no one had been in here. Typical victim-in-waiting.

Her bedroom presented another psychological head scratch. Not for its shoe-box size, but for the bare mattresses and the stark armoire that was the only other piece of furniture. Nothing at all what he expected of a connoisseur of fine things; in fact, it looked as though she'd moved in today.

He looked under the bed then inspected her closet, frowning that it, too, seemed...mysteriously empty. He saw a half dozen suits in there, and a few other separates, plus three pairs of shoes. As his senses dealt with more amber and vanilla, he concluded that the fire he'd heard employees at Van Dorn's talking about must have really done a number on her wardrobe as well as most of her other possessions.

Sympathetic, he entered the pristine white bathroom and came face-to-face with a pair of black lace panty hose draped over the shower stall door. Not needing the reminder that one of his most recent fantasies was imagining her shapely legs wrapped around various parts of him, he got the hell out of there.

He found Nicole balancing herself against a kitchen cabinet while alternately slipping off her shoes and tugging hairpins out of her chignon. The empty wineglass stood precariously close to the edge of the counter.

Sweet heaven, he thought as a pin pinged against the linoleum floor and molten gold tumbled well past her shoulders. He'd never apologized for liking to look at women, but none had ever left him feeling as though he'd taken a hit from a stun gun the way this one did. If only she'd waited two more minutes for him to leave. He hadn't wanted to see what a silk waterfall looked like, to discover how much younger and fragile she seemed this way. Too damned desirable for her own good.

"You're, ah—" he swallowed, his mouth impossibly dry "—all set."

By her expression, he knew that she'd forgotten he was still around, and as she glanced toward the door, he wanted to oblige her, but his feet refused to budge. What else could he do but look his fill?

"Did you check that light outside?" he thought to ask.

Without replying, she went over to the switch. When

nothing happened after she flipped it twice, he joined her, reaching outside to make sure the bulb was screwed in snugly.

It wasn't.

"Well, there's your problem. It must've...worked itself loose." He took his time tightening the thing, then called himself an ass for trying to make the simple task seem like brain surgery. "Sometimes that happens."

Intent on saying good-night and getting the hell out of there, he spun around.

As his upper arm struck her breast, she gasped and recoiled. Certain that if he didn't stop her, she would back straight into those boxes, he grabbed her. That was a different kind of mistake—one his body thoroughly approved of.

"Did I hurt you?"

Although plastered together from chest to thigh, she continued trying to massage the spot. "L-let go."

"If I do, you'll back straight into those boxes."

"You're too close. I can't..."

Breathe? Think? Neither could he; nor had he ever wanted any one so badly. That's why when he saw the pain in those glorious eyes replaced by awareness, he lost the battle with himself and lowered his head.

It was like stepping off a cliff, only in slow motion. It took forever to reach her, to learn how it felt to have her lips against his, only to discover it was everything he'd wanted and feared.

At the sound of the rest of the hairpins in her hand hitting the floor, he had a flash image of Fourth of July fireworks. When she wrapped her arms around his neck, it became Thanksgiving, Christmas and his birthday all at once. It didn't matter if it was mostly liquor and grief that was making her cling to him; she felt too good to allow common sense a free kick at his conscience.

With a groan, he locked his arms around her and drew her closer yet.

"Well...shit."

The man standing below in the deepest shadows of a live oak tree watched in disbelief as the man upstairs kicked the inner door of the apartment shut. Swearing again under his breath, he reached for a cigarette and lighter.

He would've bet anything that bitch would send Rent-A-Cop home carrying his balls in his hands. But, no, she seemed to be enjoying herself as much as he was. Maybe enough to go at it hot and heavy for the rest of the night. Was his luck staying in the sheer crap zone or what? It went to show you could never assume you had anyone figured out, especially not a broad.

To think of all those irritating tears she'd shed for her brother, and that righteous attitude he'd put up with when she wasn't yammering over the guy.

He pocketed the lighter and blew a stream of smoke into the humid night air. "Oh, yeah, I got your number, babe."

At least he wouldn't have to worry about her causing any trouble tonight. A good thing, too. He had enough people busting his chops without any help from the Ice Princess inside. It would relieve his mind, though, if he could be sure that what was going on in that apartment was a one-nighter. He didn't need Rent-A-Cop getting too involved with this female, getting any heroic ideas, maybe sticking his nose where it didn't belong.

He circled the building to get a protected but advantageous view of the bedroom. The mini-blinds were down and closed, but he would have been able to tell if they turned on any lights.

The windows remained dark.

He snickered. Could be he'd given Big Tex too much credit. Maybe they weren't going to get it on after all.

The snap of a twig had him reaching for his gun even as he spun to his right. Although his night vision was good, he couldn't see more than shadows on shadows, thanks to the dense foliage. But seconds later, just as he was about to shrug off the noise as some critter skulking around, he heard a scrambling sound, then the dull thud of hurried footsteps on sod.

"Ooh," he crooned. Yes, indeedy. He had himself a varmint, all right. The two-legged variety. "My favorite."

Determined to find who it was, he took off in eager pursuit.

3

One cloud is enough to eclipse all the sun.

—*Thomas Fuller*

She had grown to hate mornings. No longer a fast riser, gone was her ability to bounce out of bed and cheerfully face whatever the day offered. Lethargy had taken possession of her like some alien being; it had fastened itself to her skin, invaded every organ in her body, and impregnated her brain with seeds of equally ugly moods. The second she remembered last night, those seeds shot fingers with claws from one end of her skull to another, and blinding pain had her regretting wakening at all.

Sobbing, she twisted around and stared at the empty side of the queen-size bed. So much for hoping it had all been a bad dream. There on the other pillow was the indentation of his head; the indentation of his body remained on the rumpled sheets. She didn't remember putting sheets on the bed, but what came too readily was the recollection of strong arms, urgent whispers and hot bodies.

She sobbed again as she rolled back onto her stomach and buried her face in the pillow. How could she have done it? With a virtual stranger no less!

"I'll never touch champagne again."

But as she made that vow, she knew she would give a good deal for something even stronger right now to kill the foul tastes in her mouth and to mute the fierce pounding in her head. Hang what the experts said; hair-of-the-dog remedies were proving to be her most sympathetic friends.

Knowing she had no choice, she eased herself up into a sitting position and stared at the clock until what she saw made sense. Six-twenty. Dare she hope that he was gone? After listening for several seconds and not hearing anything, she threw off the sheet and eased out of bed.

Since she often slept in the nude during the warmer seasons, the revelation that she was wearing nothing but lace top stockings didn't hit her until she saw herself in the bathroom mirror. Shock had her spinning around too fast, and she had to grip the doorjamb to keep from stumbling. She gripped tighter as she spotted her clothes scattered around the floor.

The place looked as though she'd done some kind of striptease. Or else she had ended up on the losing end of a wrestling match.

Once again she suffered a flash of memory—strong hands, impatient and bold, moving over her...her own uninhibited response. Oh, God. Could she just die and get it over with? What he must think. This time her drinking had exposed far more than her vulnerabilities, it had made her want. Too much. She understood crav-

ing the oblivion the wine had provided, even forgave
herself for succumbing to it, but a quickie with a cop?

Muttering a choice expletive, she turned back to the
sink and tried to avoid direct eye contact with the rav-
aged figure in the mirror. She failed. Wild hair and
raccoon eyes were her reward for last night's reck-
lessness. Disgusted, she fumbled for the bottle of
Scope mouthwash and filled her mouth with the green
concoction, grimacing at the sting that countered any
hint of agreeable mint taste. Gagging, she spit into the
ivory bowl, only to repeat the process until confident
that her breath wouldn't peel the paint off the walls.

"Shower," she dictated through bruised senses. She
turned on both water taps in the stall and stepped in
without waiting for the temperature to regulate.

The initial icy assault was brutal, but effective. If
she wanted to get through the rest of the day, she
needed a clear head, and this was the fastest way to
achieve that. There was work to do, and not all of it
at Van Dorn's.

Once the water warmed, she stripped off her stockings and reached for the sponge. The loofah did to her
body what self-loathing did to her mind, and by the
time she stepped out of the stall, she was groaning for
a different reason. At least she was clean, though, and
feeling a bit less of a tramp. She just wished she could
remember if they'd used some kind of protection last
night, but at this point she couldn't even recall how it
had felt to have him inside her.

At least she would never have to see Roman Mc-
Kenna again. And for her own peace of mind she
would buy a home pregnancy test kit after work, even

though it might be a little soon to guarantee accuracy. Surely she couldn't be *that* unlucky?

But what were the chances of a cop having AIDS and not telling her?

What if he doesn't know whether he does or doesn't?

She pressed her palms to her eyes and willed herself to stop her mental self-torturing. Everything would be all right. If it wasn't...well, if it wasn't, she would deal with that later. In the meantime, she had more pressing things to worry about.

At ten minutes after eight, she unlocked the rear entrance to Van Dorn's. It was later than she'd planned on getting here, but there had been Goldie's house to check on, mail to put out...she'd decided Goldie's precious African violets would have to wait until this afternoon, though. The time-consuming task of calling then waiting for a cab because her car remained parked here had convinced her to deviate from Goldie's detailed, handwritten schedule. If the damned plants died, so be it. The way her head and stomach still felt, she wouldn't live through the day anyway.

Behind her on Fairmount, traffic remained thick with city-bound workers, people with cellular phones pressed to their ears as had been the case with her moments ago when she'd rescheduled a luncheon meeting. She was glad the store didn't open to the public until ten. The rest of the staff and warehouse crew would start arriving between eight-thirty and nine, and that left her with enough time to make coffee and browse through several newspapers, check voice mail and faxes in peace and quiet.

As she entered the dark building, she could hear her office phone already ringing. Certain that it was Max, she ran the last steps to the red-on-red room and snatched up the antique receiver.

"Checking on me?" Hoping she sounded more like her old upbeat self, she dropped the armload of Dallas, Houston and New York papers that had been waiting outside onto her glass and wrought iron desk.

"You're late. How do you feel?"

Despite his machine-gun delivery and gruffer than usual tone, Nicole knew how relieved Max was that she'd shown up at all, and silently thanked whatever guardian angel had directed her to him that rainy, unencouraging day seven years ago when she'd been job hunting. A first-generation American born to a Scandinavian father and Jewish mother, Maxwell Van Dorn had been weaned on a diet of business, politics and society from the moment he stopped tugging on the family corgi's tail to spend hours on end sitting under his father's desk, listening as the senior Maxwell negotiated estate sales. Married for thirty-one years to sculptress Rebecca Simone, they had no children, much to their regret, which perhaps explained why he acted like both mentor and parent to her.

"Ten thousand apologies for worrying you, O Great One," she said, meaning it more than her dry tone implied. "But I wouldn't have been more than a minute or two off my schedule if I hadn't had to call for a cab. Ahem."

"Ah, but as your ally, my wife, has often pointed out, 'You have to be breathing to bitch, darling.' Re-

assure me and say you sent the good shepherd Mc-
Kenna home with his head intact last night?''

That was one part of the evening she didn't want to
talk about. "Let's just say we both learned a few
worthwhile lessons in human nature and are the wiser
for it.''

She could almost see Max's ears perking up.

"How provocative. Are you saying he made a
pass?''

"You're impossible.''

"No, I'm an old married man who's not too repressed to admit he thrives on titillation. Besides, I've
been noticing him watching you. There was lust in
those world-weary eyes. Truth be known, I'm glad
he's got his promotion. Who needs a brooding wolf
like that skulking around his prize lamb?''

The Bloody Mary Nicole gulped down for breakfast
threatened to do a reversal. "Aren't we in rare form
this morning? I'd rather talk about the fifties furniture
you want to build a show around. Are you sure we
want to pick up that small collection from the museum
that's closing in Cleveland? My hunch is that it's still
too soon for any sizeable focus. I made a few calls
and what interest there was seems less enthusiastic
than we'd been led to believe.''

"Mmm. I tossed the idea past Rebecca and she
agrees with you—at least for this region of the country.
That's it then. Let's let our competition in California
have it.''

"Good.'' At the sound of the back door opening,
she leaned over to see which of their employees was
the first to arrive. When she saw how wrong her as-

sumption had been, she lost track of what Max was saying. "Sorry. The...the coffee machine is doing something strange, I'd better go check."

"I'll be in by eleven. Remind the kids I'm having lunch sent over at eleven-forty-five."

He always did the day after a good sale. But at the moment, Nicole couldn't have cared less if he'd announced he was divvying up the business between the lot of them. "Will do. Have to run!"

She barely had the receiver back on its cradle before Detective Wes Willard appeared in the doorway of her office.

At five-nine and with the narrow face and body that was consistent for a small-boned man, he didn't appear to be anyone's idea of threatening; in fact she'd seen his mirror image selling shoes and men's fragrances at boutiques a number of times. But one morning in his presence had been all that was necessary to make Nicole understand how deceiving looks could be.

As usual his round eyes—so bright and yet opaque—gauged and labeled. Some might have called them intelligent eyes. They made her think back to college in Nacogdoches and the rodents she would occasionally see in the early morning hours while jogging around the Stephen F. Austin Arboretum. They'd been cunning creatures whose bite could threaten a deadly case of rabies. She suspected a person could suffer worse from the likes of Detective Willard.

"I saw your car outside all by its lonesome," he said in lieu of a greeting. "Thought it the gentlemanly thing to check on you."

"Turning over a new leaf, are we?"

He looked pleased at the uneasiness she couldn't quite hide despite her scornful words. "Determined to keep misunderstanding me, I see."

"Oh, no, Detective. Everything about you comes through loud and clear. As long as I pursue the truth about my brother's death, you plan to turn my world inside out."

He ran a caressing hand down his tie. Like his brown suit, the patterned navy-and-gold silk reflected quality, as did his linen shirt, the cuffs of which sported real gold. He apparently believed in the old theory that clothes made the man…and in shutting down any case that even hinted at something sleazy or wasn't cost-effective to ensure his upwardly mobile career.

"Right. In fact I'm such a monster—" he shifted his other hand from behind his back "—I worked overtime to return this to you."

Nicole recognized the leatherbound notebook right away. It was the address book she'd given Jay a few years ago after he'd lost his second and most promising position with an up-and-coming architectural firm. He'd been talking about doing some work on his own. The book had been part of a desk set meant to help him set up a home office. He never did follow through with his plans, but apparently he'd liked the gift enough to use it for personal information.

She took it, careful to avoid any physical contact with Willard. "What a surprise. I wonder if I'd still be waiting for this if I hadn't shown up at Homicide yesterday?" He hadn't been pleased when he'd walked in to find her talking to one of the sergeants requesting its return; however, he'd succeeded in convincing his superior officer that he had a valid reason for continuing to keep it. Strange that he should be returning it now. She hadn't expected to see it for some time. If ever.

"I told you," he replied, "just as I explained last week—and the week before that—I planned to get it back to you as soon as I was through checking out the people in there. People you yourself requested I talk to."

Oh, yes, she'd asked, demanded and begged that horrible morning in Jay's apartment, once she'd realized Willard meant to reduce her brother to nothing more than an embarrassing statistic. He'd shut her down, humiliated her, did everything but call her a mental case. Nothing she said had changed his mind, or the report. As far as Detective Wes Willard was concerned, Jay was dead due to his own stupidity.

And yet he'd taken the address book.

"So," she replied, a new wave of bitterness rejuvenating her sarcasm, "what new conclusions have you come to regarding the 'case that isn't a case'?"

"None. But I have finished making sure we have a record of who your brother knew and socialized with in case some other poor jerk gets himself in the same bind—no pun intended. You heard me tell Sergeant Braxton that's all I wanted. Believe it or not, building a character profile on cases like this could help us save a life down the road."

She believed that well enough; that's why yesterday she'd offered to wait for him to photocopy whatever he wanted. But she didn't believe him. No, Detective

Wes Willard had something else on his mind, and that scared her to death.

She paged through the book to avoid having to look at him.

"What the hell do you think you're doing?"

"Making sure all the pages are there."

Willard snorted. "You're a real piece of work, you know that? Why don't you do yourself a favor and take a lesson from your parents? Seems they knew their son pretty well. You, on the other hand, are living in denial. Now I know this has been a painful tragedy for all of you, but it happened, and the sad fact of the matter is that while it's not all that common an experience, it's less unusual than we'd like. What you should try to remember, though, is that it's over."

"Then why won't you leave me alone?"

"What on earth do you mean?"

She heard the change in his voice, subtle but noticeable. If she looked up, he would be smiling. She didn't want to see it, see him laughing at her.

"You keep showing up wherever I am," she replied. "You interrogate whomever I talk to. When I go back, people won't speak to me anymore. They're afraid."

"Yeah, of *you*. And maybe they should be. That's what keeps bothering me about this whole thing. You. Trying so hard to put a different spin on this. Why? You want to know what I think? I think maybe you've got something to hide. Maybe you kept something back about what happened that night."

It was all Nicole could do not to shiver. He was

both right and dead wrong. Which was it? Had he found out something?

"What about it, Ms. Loring? Is all this talk about murder to keep the spotlight off you? Maybe your baby brother wasn't the only one with a taste for the kinky. Maybe you two were a team and you're afraid the media's going to get wind of that."

"You're despicable."

"Bet that kind of press would throw your oh-so-respectable parents into a real snit."

She wanted to scream. She wanted to shove the man out of the building and into oncoming traffic. "Get out," she replied coldly. "Get out and leave me alone!"

"Nicole?" a cautious voice called from the back of the building. "Nicole are you in here?"

Once again Willard stroked his tie. "Guess that's my cue to turn down your kind offer for coffee and make tracks. You know what they say about three being a crowd. Until next time——" he nodded to the notebook "——you're welcome."

Nicole stood there as he backed out of the room and remained rooted there when Carlyn Teal appeared in the doorway.

"Hi." The younger woman pointed with her thumb over her shoulder. "Who was that? He just gave me the nicest smile."

"No, he didn't."

Carlyn laughed briefly, her expression confused. "What?"

"He's pond scum masquerading as a human being." Realizing she sounded too intense, Nicole shook her head, refusing to be pulled down further into Willard's pit. "Forget it. It's nothing. He's nothing. Come on, let's get some coffee." The aspirin she'd chased down with the Bloody Mary weren't doing anything for her. Maybe caffeine would.

As she put down the book and approached the door, instead of getting out of her way, Carlyn touched her arm. "I wish you'd let someone help you. We all hate to see you continuing to suffer. Maybe, now that you've moved and once you finish unpacking, a few sessions with a therapist would help you see there was no way you could have anticipated Jay's suicide."

It was all Nicole could do not to scream. Everyone had been so quick to buy into the story Wes Willard had suggested she and her parents use to explain Jay's death. Most especially her parents, who saw what happened as one embarrassment and disappointment too many. What, they'd decided, was suicide compared to what Detective Willard had pronounced as the truth?

Fighting the choking grip frustration and anguish had on her throat, she patted Carlyn's hand. "I'll be fine. I just need a little more time that's all."

"Promise?"

"When have I ever lied to you?"

4

*Life belongs to the living, and he who lives
must be prepared for changes.*

—Johann Wolfgang von Goethe

After years of driving on Hall to Central Patrol, Roman felt strange heading for Main Street and the aging municipal building. It stood out from under the shadows cast by Dallas's geometric skyscrapers, aging but rich with a history unparalleled in the city—from much of the country for that matter. Oswald was first held there after Kennedy was shot, and it was where they initially incarcerated Ruby after he silenced Oswald. Roman had been all of four months old at the time, but he'd experienced a bit of what the assassination had meant to the country while doing his stint in the marines. While waiting for a bus at the Port Authority building in New York a guy had struck up a conversation with him, eventually asking where he was from. When he told him Dallas, the guy's whole demeanor had changed. "That's where they kill presidents," the man had sneered. "How can you stand living there?" Roman had wanted to ask him how he could stand having such a fucking empty skull, but having already learned a lesson or two about the human race, he'd simply walked away from the jerk. He had, however, actually seen the cells on the top floor of the building. There, surrounded by peeling green paint and exposed piping he'd smelled what could only be described as dead air, and had left quickly feeling as though he was escaping purgatory. He hoped they wouldn't insist on another tour today. All he wanted was to do his job, and most of that would take him out of this building.

He'd come early enough to miss the worst of the commuter traffic and as he passed the lot filled with unmarked cars, he remembered how the guys at Central Patrol had taunted him about what he had to look forward to. It was no secret that when it came to budgeting, detectives' vehicles were at the bottom of the list. So much for job prestige, the guys had joked before promising to give him a lift whenever they found him stranded on the side of the road in his broken down piece of junk. Truth be known, though, Roman didn't give a damn about status or prestige, and from what he saw in the lot, the pickings looked okay to him. He was even willing to make a few repairs himself if necessary because he'd always liked messing with cars. Of course, if he got caught that would probably earn him more razzing, but so be it. He'd never been a time-card puncher, and emptying someone else's dirty ashtray or paying for a quart of oil out of his own pocket wasn't going to faze him either.

After checking in with personnel, he made his way to the third floor and presented himself to Lieutenant Dave Waldrop, a friendlier version of his former marine drill instructor. The granite-jawed giant seemed genuinely glad to see him, not only because the department was in the midst of summer vacations, but these days Homicide simply had hell filling positions.

"Did personnel show you around or are you already fairly familiar with the place?" Waldrop asked.

"I can find my way around, sir."

"Good, then—hold on. I need to deal with this."

"This" turned out to be a problematic report filed by a detective named Diaz, who appeared at the door and was motioned inside by the lieutenant. Waldrop introduced him to the shorter man, and Diaz responded with a firm handshake, but kept eye contact to a minimum. Roman knew better than to take it personally. When you were about to get an ass chewing, the smaller the audience the better.

"Joe, great job locating this guy," the lieutenant said, passing over the computer printout he'd been holding. "But are you sure everything here is as thorough as it needs to be to help the D.A. get a conviction?"

Right then and there Roman decided working here was going to be okay. Waldrop wasn't the kind of guy who fed his own ego by disemboweling his people. Even Diaz looked more disgusted with himself than annoyed at having to redo a report, and quickly took the copies and cleared out.

Waldrop motioned Roman into a chair. "Sorry for the interruption. But having made it this far, you already know that these days we have to be better secretaries than cops. That's harder on some of our Hispanic people who in many cases haven't had the same quality of education as others did. But ready or not, we have to work around that due to the ever-increasing Spanish-speaking population." Waldrop's voice bore no inflection to indicate his personal opinion about the matter; he simply stated what was a fact of life they had to deal with. Smoothing a hand over hair more salt than pepper, the senior cop took his own seat behind his desk and eyed Roman. "So. All those incentives they dangled before you couldn't convince you to stay in Patrol."

"I guess if I was wholly interested in paychecks and retirement benefits, I'd have chosen a different field of work to begin with, sir." What he didn't plan to admit was that he'd wanted to be here since he was a boy, due in part to his neighbor Fred Runyon, who'd been a detective. Old Fred had been one cool dude as far as Roman was concerned. His hero, back when he believed in such things. But he knew better than sharing such sentimental rot, even though Waldrop had a picture of John Wayne on his wall otherwise filled with degrees and citations.

With a nod, the lieutenant continued. "I heard about your little girl. Sometimes life really sucks. The fact that you could achieve what you have in spite of your personal crisis says a great deal to me about how you're going to work out here."

Roman wanted to stay away from the subject of his heartbreak. Meggie's situation could reduce him to a blubbering jerk faster than a TV evangelist could ask for money, and that's not what was needed or expected of him here. "My personal problems won't affect my job performance, sir."

"Uh-huh. And next you'll be willing to show me

that you don't bleed when stabbed or shot. Look, son, I'll say this only once, and then we'll drop it. When the shit hits the fan—and it does for all of us at some time or other—it will be all you can do to hang on. Just know we'll be ready to cover for you." He tilted his head toward the long room filled with thirty-something desks. "We may get competitive around here at times, but we know when and how to support each other."

Before Roman could think of a suitable reply, the lieutenant signaled to someone else at the door.

"Here's your partner. Tucker carries almost fifteen years of experience in this department on those lumpy shoulders."

As the disheveled man shuffled into the office, he abandoned the struggle with his half-knotted tie to wrap a bear-size paw around Roman's hand.

"Ralph Tucker. How's it going?"

He had a child's mischievous eyes in a face that was as disproportioned as it was animated. But Roman had been around long enough not to be taken in by the slow, good ol' boy smile that dimpled the guy's Pillsbury Doughboy cheeks. "Good to meet you," he replied.

"Ralph, you look like crap," the senior detective muttered. "And you don't smell much better. Have you been sleeping in your car or did your youngest upchuck breakfast on you on your way out the door?"

"Aw, the washing machine busted the other day and there's been a delivery problem with the new one. Figured I'd help out Shirl by stretching the laundry some."

"Sure, spoil *her*. She only has to suffer with your ass a few hours a day. We get you the rest of the time. Go find a clean shirt and some deodorant before you start a mass exodus out there." To Roman he added, "He may not seem it at the moment, but Tucker's a bloodhound. He'll work the smallest lead until he finds what he's looking for. Don't ever ask him to skip a meal, though. And when he does go home, there's always another mouth to feed and a new appliance to buy, eh, Ralph? How many kids've you got now?"

"Still holding at six, sir." He shot Roman a wide grin. "All boys."

Without having met her, Roman pitied Shirley Tucker. If all of her kids took after their big lummox of a father, she was probably a medical miracle. He remembered how Glenda had suffered giving birth to their Megan. To endure that six times…?

"Do they have a discount day named in your honor at the grocery store?" he asked.

Ralph rubbed the tip of his ski-sloped nose with the back of his hand. "Not yet, but I have a standing ten-percent discount with the dentist." He asked Waldrop, "Want me to introduce him to whoever's out there?"

"Go ahead. I'm due up in the chief's office in a minute. McKenna, good luck. If you have any questions, for God's sake ask. It'll cut down on mistakes."

"Understood, sir."

Ralph proved as congenial as a party hostess, as funny as a veteran stand-up comedian, but as Roman had been warned, none of that diminished the man's impressive knowledge of the department and everyone in it. After being swatted by the secretary for snooping in her lunch sack, he ushered Roman around the room giving him a thumbnail sketch of each detective's track record—usually paling to his own. Of course only six of the twenty-five in the Crimes Against Persons, Homicide Section, were in right now, so that made it a relatively brief tour. The other seven on the first shift were out, either preparing for court or working cases. The twelve who manned the second ten-hour shift would be here by five o'clock. They worked a four-day week, and a rotating two-person team were on call for the off-hours. By the time Ralph led him to their desks, he'd also invited Roman to dinner and asked to borrow ten dollars.

"My wife's birthday." His dimples deepened. "Gotta pick up a cake and some flowers on the way home."

"Then you might need twenty." Roman reached for his wallet.

"Best not overdo it. She'd only get suspicious."

The main room was arranged in three rows of desks set in pairs that stood face-to-face. Theirs was in the farthest corner of the almost windowless room. Each had a computer monitor identical to those at Central Patrol and the other branches. Computers had streamlined operations in many positive ways, but while most of the cops he'd met liked the reduction of paperwork that came with being able to call in reports, when you had hands the size of Ralph Tucker's, fishing out information could turn keyboards into a natural enemy.

"Used to jam these things up so bad, I'd get frustrated enough to wanna sail 'em through a window, and you can't imagine what I did to the central system.

Then Rita saved my life," Tucker said, wiggling reddish eyebrows as he glanced toward the entryway where the department secretary sat. "Told me I needed to think of each key as a woman's nipple. Touch light. Treat 'em with respect." He sat down before Roman's keyboard and stretched his arms like a pianist preparing to play his piano. "Now the only problem is I'm horny all the time. Shirl always knows when I've been stuck in the office too long."

Roman wanted to listen to that like he wanted a finger wave. Tucker's comments only reminded him of what, rather *whom,* he'd left only a short while ago.

"There we are." Ralph typed in the appropriate password on Roman's computer. "And here's the tie that binds us," he drawled, as a list of cases appeared on the blue screen.

"Please, Tucker." A man wearing yellow suspenders and carrying his suit jacket draped over his left forearm approached and slowly lowered himself onto the chair beside Roman. "No romance before I have something in my stomach."

Ralph chortled with pleasure. "Let me introduce you to the department's granddaddy. Roman McKenna, Isaac Newman." Ralph nodded toward the detective with the basset hound face, who looked to be in his late fifties. "Sir Isaac to those who know and love the old fart. He's a sweetheart, but has no sense of humor before his morning tea and scrambled egg sandwich on white bread. Ulcers," he added in a false whisper.

Ignoring him, Newman set his green coffee mug and cellophane-wrapped sandwich on his desk. Roman guessed he hadn't smiled since the Miranda ruling took effect. But there was something kindly in his dark brown eyes that had Roman suspecting little kids loved crawling up onto his lap.

"Where's—" Ralph twitched his nose "—Willard?"

"Dining with Ross Perot, what do I know?"

The silver-haired detective's weary expression suggested he was as tired of trying to keep up with his partner as he was listening to Tucker's nonsense. On the other hand, the news had Ralph beaming.

"Hey, McKenna, looks like you're bringing me luck already. Here, you take over."

Deciding to stay impartial until he knew what was going on, Roman remained silent as he took the seat Ralph abandoned and then used the computer's mouse to move the cursor down the list of files on the screen. To anyone paying attention it would look as though he was merely checking on how many active cases they had—and he was. But he was also looking for more.

Unfortunately, he found only one listing beginning with L and it wasn't Loring, which meant Ralph Tucker hadn't been the detective on record for Nicole's brother's case. He hadn't been the one to put that look of fear and loathing into her beautiful eyes.

But that also meant Roman would have to check the master list to learn who the bastard was.

Max Van Dorn had told him that it was a homicide detective who'd been the first to appear at Jay Loring's apartment. Not unheard of, but unusual. The guy must have been in the area, heard the call on the radio, and had responded faster than anyone else. Roman would need time and privacy to locate the report.

Of course, if he was smart, he would keep his nose out of this. Nicole Loring could turn into an unhealthy preoccupation. Call it the sixth sense you developed in this line of work; the air around her all but hummed with bad vibes, just as *she* did sex appeal. However, his conscience wouldn't let him forget about her; nor would his curiosity. If only he hadn't behaved badly last night.

He'd crossed a professional line. Now all he could do was remember…how she'd felt in his arms, the taste of her, the way she'd reached for him. Even the memory of her scent was doing dangerous things to his head. Everything about her was like a craving that wouldn't let go.

So, who? Which of these guys had it been?

He was glancing around the room when Tucker's phone rang.

After a few grunts, Ralph said, "We can be there in—" he checked his watch "—make it twenty minutes. Give me the address again. Good. Stay put. We're on our way."

As his partner hung up, Roman lifted both eyebrows. "What's up?"

"Time to saddle up and ride, pard. We've got smoke signals on the Spango case." Before Roman could ask, Ralph provided the background. "Forty-two, white male, divorced, gay. Shot outside his coffee shop on Oak Lawn shortly after ten p.m. It happened almost two weeks ago, and I've had holy heck finding anyone who would admit to being on the planet let alone in the area—and you know Oak Lawn on a Friday night. Thought I was going to have to write this one off as a random robbery-homicide, though I knew in my bones it was a hate crime, victim being shot in the head and nuts and all. But,'' Ralph added, pointing to the phone, ''that was a guy who says he was driving by and saw it happen. Tried to forget it, didn't want to be involved, but couldn't do it. God bless consciences. Just when I think this world has become totally overrun with sociopaths, I find me an honest to goodness human being. You may have to hold me back, Mac. If this guy's for real, I may be tempted to lay a wet one on him.''

Shaking his head, Roman followed him to the back exit that led directly to the stairs. The door swung open as Ralph was reaching for the knob and a dark-haired man in as much a hurry as they were jerked to a stop.

''Won't do you any good to try and sneak in, Rat Boy,'' Ralph said, loud enough to be heard at the elevators—or the lieutenant's office if he'd been in. ''Everybody knows you're late. What were you doing? Playing footsie with a councilman's wife at some United Way breakfast?''

Although the well-dressed detective was at least a half foot shorter than Ralph, that didn't keep him from shooting him a look of contempt. ''F.U., Tucker, and may all your sons grow up to be TVs.''

Roman was interpreting the abbreviation for transvestite when the man's gaze locked with his. To his surprise he saw a flicker of recognition and...amusement? He told himself that he had to be wrong. They'd never met before that he could recall.

"Willard," Ralph muttered, as the man continued past them without further comment. "Be glad introductions have to wait for another time."

"That's the guy you mentioned before? Newman's partner?"

"A gin-u-whine, card-carrying prick. If I spend more than ten minutes at a time around him, I start having fantasies about forcing rodent poison up his nostrils."

"Any particular reason I should know about?"

"Just one. I hate apple-polishing weasels, and he's the queen of them all. Dresses like he's already an alderman or something—but don't think his aspirations are aimed that low." Ralph ignored the elevator and began trotting down the stairs, forcing Roman to follow. "It won't surprise me at all if one day he becomes mayor, or congressman. But if that happens, that's the day I pull up stake and truck my brood out of Texas."

His venting didn't stop until they were at the olive green sedan they'd been assigned for today. He tossed the keys at Roman. "D'you mind?" he asked, drawing out an electric razor from his suit pocket. "I've gotta shave."

Roman said he didn't and once Ralph gave him the address that was near Love Field, he circled to the driver's side.

"While we're at it, you got any pet peeves I should know about?" Ralph asked, once they were settled inside the car.

"Not that I can think of. You?"

"Shoot, with the size brood I have, I could be my own republic. It's easier to just go with the flow, man.'' He lifted the battery-operated razor to his chin and then hesitated. "Heard about your little girl. Cryin' shame.''

"Yeah.'' Roman keyed the ignition and listened to the engine stutter, cough, then rumble to life. "I guess if there's anything I'm hesitant to talk about it's that.''

"Sure. But since we'll be spending most of our days and nights in each other's pocket so to speak, I want you to know that I'm here if you ever need to talk.''

"Thanks. Remind me to get your home number and I'll give you mine. You don't have to worry about me not being there in a crunch, though. I'm not welcome down in Houston—that's where my daughter is. The only time I'll disappear is if the call comes from the hospital.'' His throat tightened on those last words, and he focused on backing out of their parking slot.

"I hear you,'' Ralph replied. "It would be the same for me.'' He switched on the razor. "Now about our boy Spango...''

5

None knows the weight of another's burden.

—*George Herbert,*
Jacula Prudentum

By the time they called it a day, Roman felt as though he'd worked a double shift. A rush of starts and stops had followed their first appointment, which, though promising, wasn't going to lead to a quick arrest unless the perpetrator walked into the municipal building and turned himself in. After that appointment there were various people to track down on another case, witnesses' stories to confirm, leads to check out. In the end Ralph was apologetic. As they'd parted he said, "This was as frustrating a day as I've had in a while. Hope you don't think it'll always be like this."

"You mean all that running and coming back with almost empty pockets?" Roman shrugged. "I figured it wasn't too bad. We weren't called to a new crime scene."

"Amen to that. You sure you don't want to come home with me?"

Roman asked for a rain check. Once Ralph left, though, he changed his mind about returning to the third floor and studying the computer files so he didn't have to ask Ralph an endless stream of questions at every stop. He'd taken in enough new data today to sort through. Besides, something had been building inside him since this morning, and he needed to take care of it.

When he turned down her street and saw her car only a few hundred feet in front of him, he told himself it was a sign that he was doing the right thing. But as he followed her into her driveway, he knew his presence was going to upset her. The look in her eyes alone as she stared into her rearview mirror could have been that of someone who'd just found out they'd had unprotected sex with a carrier.

"You don't have to panic," he said, as he exited his truck and approached her. "I won't take more than a few minutes of your time."

"I have to be back at work in less than two hours," she replied as though she hadn't heard him.

Her words were as stilted as her body language was stiff; nevertheless, that was better than what he'd expected. At least she hadn't run at the sight of him— or worse, drawn out a gun.

"I remember." She had that other sale tonight for the general public. If asked—which wouldn't happen—he would tell her that she didn't look ready for it. Concerned someone was on the other side of the hedge and might be eavesdropping, he stepped closer. "Look, I don't blame you for being embarrassed, or angry, but I'm trying to tell you that you needn't be."

Her distress turned her cheeks a deep pink, a shade that matched her suit. It didn't ease the shadows under her eyes, though, or hide the weight loss that he could now attest to as accurately as her gynecologist.

"Easy for you to say," she muttered. "Unfortunately, I can't remember enough to decide one way or another."

"That's because nothing happened."

She frowned, her disbelief almost as palpable as her distrust.

Aware he had to give her more if she was going to believe him, he shrugged hoping it hid his own complicated feelings. "Yeah, sure, we kissed. But things didn't go much further than that."

"Excuse me. I know you were in my bed. Those sheets you so thoughtfully put on gave you away."

"Look, I was beat and concerned for you. So I made the bed and crashed beside you for a few hours. Clothes on."

"While I, short on musical skills to sing you a lullaby, performed a striptease?"

He rubbed the whiskers beginning to roughen his jaw. "Actually, you announced that you slept in the nude and if I didn't like that, I could go—well, suffice it to say you didn't allow me much time to argue."

"Sounds as though I was quite the lady."

"You were hurting. I know what that's like. I have a daughter battling leukemia...and losing."

"Dear God. I had no—I'm sorry." She didn't say anything more for several seconds, she simply closed her eyes and pressed the hand with her keys to her chest. As grateful as he was for the reprieve from her scorn, Roman realized she was in another kind of emotional quandary and that it would be up to him to get them through this.

"You need to get out of this heat. Could we finish this conversation upstairs?"

There was no reason for her to agree, and he didn't need to spill his guts to her, someone with no room in her life for additional trouble and heartache. He certainly had nothing to offer her. But when she offered a brief nod and led the way up the steep stairway, he didn't hesitate to follow.

By day her apartment was steeped in soothing shadows thanks to the mature oaks framing two sides of the building, yet because the air conditioner was obviously set higher while she was at work, it was almost uncomfortably warm. Roman stayed just inside the front door as she put down her purse and adjusted the thermostat.

Just as the cooling unit kicked on, she asked, "Would you care for a drink?"

"That's not necessary."

Outside, her gaze had barely skimmed his; now it lingered and softened. "You look like I feel. What'll it be?"

"Beer if you have it."

"Is Moosehead beer okay? I experiment so that I can recommend different brands when we're meeting with international guests."

"Fine."

He thanked her again when she handed him the green bottle and watched her pour herself a glass of chilled white wine. From the looks of the label it cost about three times more than what came in the jugs he and Glenda used to pick up for parties they'd attended. Not exactly a reassuring reminder of the gulf between her lifestyle and his.

"You don't have to drink that standing."

"Are you sure?"

Her gaze met his again before skittering away like a moth confused by too much light. "I'm not sure of anything anymore, except for what I said before. I am sorry. About your child, I mean. Why are you still sane?"

"Who said I am? Some days it's all I can do not to drive my car into one of those concrete walls on Central, or drive off one of the higher overpasses to finally escape thinking about what she's going through. What she'll have to go through before it's done."

"What's stopping you?"

"The thought of who I'd land on, who I might hurt in the process. There's enough pain in this world without me adding to it."

"Have you shared any of this with your wife?"

Posed quietly, even gently, the question didn't hide that she remained confused and embarrassed about last night. "You think I would have touched you if I'd been married?"

"You wouldn't be the first man to conveniently forget that small technicality. And life's tragedies have a way of tempting people to do things they normally wouldn't."

"Glenda and I are divorced."

She held his gaze for several seconds before lowering hers. "I see."

"I wish you did. But then I'm not sure *I* understand

it completely. At any rate, I can't fault her for tiring of being married to a cop, even though she knew better than most what she'd been getting into. Her father had been on the force, too," he said in response to her quizzical look.

"Obviously she loved you enough to take some risks."

"What she wanted was to get out of the house. I knew it, but told myself the end justified that. What I resent is her changing her mind after we'd had a child together. I resent her taking away my daughter because she'd cultivated greener pastures. Most of all I resent her lousy timing." He rubbed his thumb against the moisture coating the bottle, disgusted at the barely constrained anger he heard in his voice. "She and her surgeon husband live in Houston," he said more calmly. "That's a long haul for me, even if I could manage it every weekend. And, as you can imagine, my work makes that impossible. The only positive thing in all this is that Glenda's husband has contacts, which ensures Meggie getting the best treatment. Unfortunately, it's not good enough."

"Meggie. Short for Megan?" When he nodded, Nicole offered a slight smile. "That's a lovely name. How old is she?"

"Five."

She didn't reply, but closed her eyes and shook her head.

He liked her for that, her decision not to say the socially correct thing, although he knew her capable of it. It allowed him to be honest, too. "Look, I only told you so you'd understand that nothing I said last night was a line. Damned if I know what it was, but…I apologize for adding to your pain.''

Her eyes filled. "You're a nice man. I'm sorry for having missed that.''

"Not that nice. I couldn't keep things professional between us.'' Remembering, he gulped down more of his beer.

"Well, I don't know anyone else who would have watched a woman behave as I did and not take advantage.''

"Call me old-fashioned, but if I make love to a woman, I prefer her to remember she'd enjoyed it.''

Her coloring deepened. "Make love…now that may be laying it on a bit thick.''

"Do you think it would have been simple screwing between us?''

Doubt returned in her eyes, and for a moment he couldn't swear that she was breathing.

"Why are you doing this?'' she whispered.

"Maybe I'm a glutton for punishment. Hell, I don't know. I guess I just don't want you remembering me as one of the more regrettable episodes in your life.''

"I think you're making that impossible.''

Good. He wanted to leave with something, if only to know she would remember him as much as he would remember her. "And will you be all right?''

She intercepted the concerned look he shot at her glass. "This will be all I have tonight. I swear.''

"I'm glad to hear it, but I meant more than the drinking. I meant the situation with your brother. I'd listen if you wanted to talk about it. If not tonight—''

"I'm afraid I've developed an allergic reaction to the police."

Once again he heard bitterness underscoring her restrained words. "Would you mind expanding on that a bit? What is it about me, about us, that immediately sets off alarm bells in you?"

"I happen to believe that you all stick together, cover for each other, that sort of thing."

"Cover what?"

"If I knew the answer to that, do you think I'd be jumping at the sight of my own shadow? All I know is that my brother did *not* do what the police insist he did the night he died. Either on the record or off."

What the hell...? "Do you have any proof to substantiate that?" He saw her mouth tighten and the warmth in her eyes extinguish faster than a lit match going under a waterfall. "Nick, all I know about what happened is what little Max told me. Your brother hung himself, you found him, and it's tearing you apart. I swear, that's it. That's all I know."

For an instant she looked ready to leap at him and rip out his throat. As the air conditioner cranked away pumping chilled air around them, Roman thought it couldn't begin to compete with the frigidity that had settled between them. Then she collected herself.

"Does the term *AEA* mean anything to you?" she asked at last.

As with the military, law enforcement was a bastion of codes and abbreviations, and that particular one had him hoping he'd heard incorrectly, or that his first guess was exceedingly wrong. "Come again?"

The wine in her glass began to slosh around like a

choppy sea. Shades of the same thing that had happened last night, and it was a sure sign that she was reaching an emotional edge.

"Autoerotic asphyxia. Carrying sexual gratification beyond the norm."

"That's what I was afraid you'd meant. You're sure that's what the medical examiner concluded in your brother's case?"

"No. That's what the *detective* who arrived on the scene said. And his conclusions were soon echoed by the others. 'Accidental asphyxiation due to perceptual distortions while attempting sexual stimulation.' In other words, we're supposed to believe that my brother's favorite way to get his jollies was to tie a plastic bag over his head and handcuff his hands behind his back. But to protect the family's reputation, we were *allowed* to tell the press that it was a simple, unimpressive hanging-suicide, which is not only as insulting to my brother as the other conclusion, it's insane!"

Even as he watched her clasp a hand over her mouth to fight back sobs and warned himself about what he might be getting into, Roman put down his beer and stepped closer. "Tell me who headed that investigation. You remember, don't tell me you don't."

"The gift would be to forget him. The name's Willard. Detective Wes Willard."

6

Unnatural deeds do breed unnatural troubles.

—*William Shakespeare,*
Macbeth

Nicole studied Roman's face looking for deceit and cunning, but unless she'd suddenly lost her ability to read people, she decided she could safely assume her news hadn't taken him by complete surprise as she'd suspected it might a brand-new detective.

"You know him," she said.

"We ran into each other today, literally. And I should add—before you throw that wine at me and order me out of here—it was for the first time." Roman frowned. "You're sure that's the guy?"

"Detective Weston Willard. It's not a name I'm likely to forget."

"Well, hell."

"Don't tell me. He's the most distinguished member in the department, right?"

"I don't know, but...he's the reason you hate cops?"

"I'm not comfortable answering any more of your questions, Detective McKenna," Nicole replied.

It wouldn't take a 1-900 call to a psychic to figure out that he was sorry he'd asked the question, maybe even sorry that he'd come over. But to Nicole's amazement he stayed put.

"You're suggesting that your brother's investigation was botched...or worse?"

The concern and reluctance with which he spoke didn't make the underlying question easy to answer. In the end she hedged, too. "You're looking troubled, Detective."

"There was something about the way he looked at me this morning...I had a hunch he knew me. But as I said, we've never met before. That doesn't mean he couldn't have seen me on patrol some—"

"Oh, my God."

"What?"

"He saw you at Van Dorn's."

Roman shook his head. "He never came in. Not while I was on duty."

"No, he would make sure he wasn't spotted."

"You think he's stalking you?"

His uneasy tone put Nicole in fast retreat again. "I meant what I said. I don't think we should continue this conversation."

"What if I told you that my partner's not wild about him, either?" he asked.

"His sergeant likes him well enough. At least he gave him the benefit of the doubt yesterday when I went down to the station for the third time to get back a piece of my brother's property. No matter what my argument, that there were letters I needed to write, calls I needed to make to notify Jay's friends and business associates who might not have been informed yet, Detective Willard had been countering with a reason for keeping Jay's address book. First he'd been tied up with other legitimate cases that had to take priority, the next week he was running behind schedule because he'd been testifying in court. Finally when I went in and approached a Sergeant Braxton about the matter, pointing out that I'd settle for a chance to photocopy the thing, Detective Willard appeared and suddenly came up with the story that he was profiling 'people like my brother.'"

Roman winced. "I guess you were glad to get out of there after that."

"Very. And I left without Jay's property."

"Well, I haven't met Braxton yet, and I know glitches happen and so do delays, but my hunch is that you'll have that book back soon. He just wasn't going to chew out one of his people in front of you."

"As a matter of fact, Detective Willard returned it to me this morning. At least, that was the excuse he used for dropping in at Van Dorn's well before business hours," Nicole said.

"That's why he was late arriving at headquarters. Did he explain how he managed to finish up so quickly?"

"My experience with the man is that explanations aren't his strong suit. He either orders or accuses."

Roman inclined his head in a way that said he had gotten the same impression. Then his expression grew uncertain. "I'm glad things worked out for you, but...listen, what little I know about autoeroticism is that it's considered pretty much an experimental thing among young, white heterosexual males. That suggests to me that maybe Willard wasn't wrong to want your brother's address book in case someone your brother knew is also into that sort of thing.''

Nicole didn't want to hear that. ''The idea that my brother participated in anything so—so grotesque is as outrageous as the suggestion that we say he'd hung himself! I wholly disagreed with my parents' decision, and I'll never forgive them for releasing that statement to the press.''

''Hold on a second. All I'm trying to say is that it's possible Detective Willard is concerned about anyone else making a similar gruesome mistake.''

''Haven't you been listening? I found his body. Whatever happened,'' she continued heatedly, ''was done *to* him by whoever else was in that room.'' Before he could voice the surprise she saw on his face, she added, ''No, he wasn't alone. *Yes,* I heard her!''

''You were *there?*''

She nodded and briefly shared her version of what had happened that night. ''That's why when Willard said the handcuffs were on backwards, I knew what I was dealing with,'' she added.

''Backwards? You didn't say that before.''

She shot him a resentful look. ''Maybe for good reason.''

Although he worked his jaw, Roman let that one pass. ''Keep going. You told Detective Willard of your own suspicions?''

''And he dismissed or reacted scornfully to everything I said. When I persisted, he called me hysterical.

He said it would have been impossible for anyone to get out of the apartment without waking me."

"It is an amazing story."

"I was exhausted!" she snapped back. "Thanks to that fire, I'd just been through two days of insanity, while maintaining my normal work schedule. Almost everything in my apartment was either smoke damaged or ruined, as a result, when I wasn't racing to rebuild my wardrobe, I was on the phone with my insurance agent. I fell into a deep sleep and, like thousands of other people, it has always been difficult to wake me the first hour or so after I drift off." Her expression grew tormented. "Don't you think I wish I stayed awake? I'd give anything for another chance to have the sense to follow my instincts. But I didn't...I *didn't.*"

She covered her face with her hands fighting the tears that kept wanting to come, no matter how often she cried herself to sleep. She had to stay strong because she had to get back to Van Dorn's. She had responsibilities. Oh, God, more than anyone knew.

"Here."

She reluctantly raised her head to see Roman close, offering her the last swallow or two of wine in her glass. When he saw how badly her hands were shaking, he helped her hold it.

"You're in no shape to work tonight," he said, as she wiped her lower lip afterward.

"I have to."

"Then I should go. But—" his look was apologetic "—can you tell me the rest? There is more, isn't there?"

"Yes," she replied wearily. "He started grilling me as though I was a suspect, asking me about my relationship with my brother, his schedule, his work, his friends, our childhood…he got ugly when I told him that I'd had enough and was going to report him. He went from aggressive to mean, and he began suggesting disgusting things about our relationship. He even said if there was a murder, I would be the number one suspect."

Roman stepped back to lean against the opposite wall. Even the muscles in his face went slack for a moment. "It was a lousy thing to say, but logical."

"I don't give a damn. I know what I know."

"Do you realize what you're suggesting?"

"Saying. I'm telling you that my brother was killed not twenty feet away from me, and the man who was supposed to do something about that insisted I write the experience off to bad luck…or else."

She had to sit down. But it was Roman who pulled out the dinette chair for her, and he helped her get there. She didn't know she was crying until he was pressing tissues into her hand.

"Damn it!" she ground out, hating this latest loss of control. "Damn, damn, damn! I thought I'd cried all the tears I had in me."

"It's okay."

"No, it's not. It doesn't get me answers, or justice, and I can't afford to do this now when I have to stand before dozens of people in a few hours."

Roman squatted before her. "It would take a helluva lot more than a red nose to ruin this face, Nick."

As he wiped a tear from under her eyes, Nicole

leaned back in the chair to escape his touch. "Why do you call me that? Only Jay called me that."

"You two were especially close, weren't you?"

"We might as well have been twins. There was less than a year between us." What might have been a sob came out as a choking laugh. "When we were older and understood the biological connotations of that, we used to joke about it. My parents aren't the demonstrative type, not to us, and certainly not to each other. We never did figure out how we were conceived, let alone what kept them together."

"Sounds romantic," he murmured, a faint crook at the corner of his mouth.

"That's not a word we heard in our home."

"Rough childhood?"

Nicole shrugged away the almost gentle question. "Depends on how well you handled rigidity and ridicule in an otherwise privileged environment. I coped better than Jay did, but this is still the South where in certain families different things are expected from sons than from daughters. I got through my teens without getting pregnant or otherwise maligning the family name, so I can look forward to my father agreeing to walk me down the aisle of a church if I wish. Provided he approves of the groom."

Roman was silent for several seconds, and then said carefully, "I know you're pressed for time, but can you tell me specifically what you think happened? I can't help you if you don't give me some benefit of the doubt."

What a temptation that offer represented. She had no choice but to question it. "Why should you want to do anything for me? You don't know me, and you've said yourself that you have more than enough of your own problems to deal with."

"True, but I've also been a cop long enough to recognize when things aren't adding up. Then there's the pain I see in your eyes. If someone doesn't reach out to you soon, you're going to crash. Hell, I'm not saying I can perform miracles, or even change anything. I might even end up agreeing with Willard—"

"What a confidence-winning remark," she drawled.

"—but my intention is to help. Definitely help."

The husky words were like a caress across her lips. The tenderness in his eyes embraced her. It was a dangerous combination. "Because you want to go to bed with me?"

"I'd be a fool and liar to pretend otherwise," he said gruffly. "But considering what we're both going through, I know that would be a huge mistake. Does that reassure you at all?"

"Nothing about you reassures me."

"Nick."

She had to look away or he would have her reaching for him. "I can't think. Not right now."

"What's holding you back? What are you afraid of?"

Did he have any idea what he was asking?

Roman took her clenched hands between his. "If someone carrying a badge did something wrong, we all need to know."

He didn't understand what this could cost her, and she was afraid to tell him. Afraid he wouldn't believe her; afraid that he would. But she also knew she was floundering. Losing precious time. For every day that slipped by, the trail grew colder. Maybe it was already too late.

She pulled free to ruthlessly wipe at her tears. "There's more to this than what I've told you. Something else happened that night, something that even Detective Willard doesn't know about. Something too special and important, which proves Jay wouldn't have played any crazy, sick, sexual games." She swallowed hard at the blockage in her throat. "You see, Jay just found out that he was a father. He'd taken custody of his infant son earlier that evening."

7

Circumstances alter cases.

—Thomas Chandler Haliburton,
The Old Judge

Roman exhaled with a silent whistle, then rose to put some distance between them. He needed a second to take in what she'd just told him: to step back emotionally and see the whole picture she was painting. The image refused to hold. It was simply too bizarre, too horrific.

"Please tell me, I misunderstood. There was a baby in the apartment while all this went down?"

"He had to be. When I phoned just before the auction that evening, Jay had him. He had his son."

"He said so?"

"And I heard baby sounds."

Roman nodded, but his insides churned with growing revulsion. "And then you arrived at the apartment, and heard what you heard. Where was the child then?"

Nicole gestured helplessly. "I assumed he was in the bedroom with them. That's where Jay told me he planned on keeping him."

"How old a baby are we talking about?"

"A week? No more."

If the bastard had tried for the big one with the kid in there, Roman was glad Jay Loring was dead. It would save him from beating the crap out of the perverted—

You don't know that's what was going on. You don't know anything for certain yet, Slick.

He rubbed at the day's growth of whiskers along his jaw collecting his thoughts. "Back up for me. Was your brother married? Divorced?"

"Neither. The baby was the result of a one-night stand. He barely remembered the mother when she materialized on his doorstep the same day I moved in."

"Did you meet her?" Please say yes, he prayed.

"No. I'd already gone to work when she arrived, but he called me right after she left." Her gaze turned inward and her expression grew tender. "I'll never forget how he sounded. He went from panicked to excited and back again."

Roman thought of the evening Glenda told him that she was carrying Megan. They'd agreed to wait before starting a family, but over the holidays her birth control prescription had run out and she'd been too busy to make a doctor's appointment to get the thing renewed. They'd figured it was the New Year's Eve celebrating that had done it. Happier times. They seemed a lifetime ago.

"So this woman shows up out of the clear blue," he said, to get them both back on track, "and says what?"

"That she'd given birth to their child, but she couldn't keep it. She made it clear that if he didn't want his son, she would be forced to give up the baby for adoption.''

''He believed her?''

''Definitely. From the way Jay described her, I gathered she was a nice, but naive girl who'd gone to Gregor's with friends one night and got in over her head. Gregor's is where Jay was working,'' Nicole said when Roman raised his eyebrows. ''He'd become a bartender while waiting for a better opportunity to develop. And before you ask, yes, I do think he'd gotten a bit too used to the money, as well as the party lifestyle. I'd been worrying that he hadn't said anything about looking for a better position for a while. That's why, after the shock wore off, I thought this baby could turn out to be the best thing that ever happened to him. Force him to take his life more seriously.''

''Spoken like a sister who loved her brother.''

''I'm not trying to put a fairy-tale spin on this. Jay had his weaknesses. He enjoyed his creature comforts and was prone to look for the easy way out. But he was never a welfare bum.''

Roman thought about the club. It was a popular place located in Deep Ellum, a part of the east section of downtown that had been dying for years, but had experienced a rebirth thanks to artistic iconoclasts and entrepreneurs willing to risk the higher crime rate in the area for a chance at the American dream.

''I know the place,'' he said. ''It's considered one of the hottest spots around town, if you can afford it.''

''You're asking me if the girl belonged there, and I

have to assume so. Jay said she was an SMU student—a rather shy and sheltered one.''

"Not too shy," Roman replied. "She went home with him and had unprotected sex."

Nicole sighed. "That's what it all comes down to, isn't it? I remember him mentioning several times that females outnumbered males three to one there. Some girls were flat-out determined not to leave alone, and at places like that the bartender is almost as much a celebrity as the band."

"If your brother's bone structure was anything like yours, I can appreciate the attention he got."

Nicole lowered sable lashes that looked almost too lush to be her own. "What I'm trying to say is that while what happened wasn't an isolated case, he remembered this girl because she'd been abandoned by her friends for exactly the reason I'd mentioned. He felt sorry for her and basically kept her at the bar with him until closing when he'd planned to take her home. Obviously, that's not all that occurred. But the point is, once the initial shock wore off, he believed the child could well be his. After she showed him a photo and presented medical information, there was no doubt of it. Despite his Hispanic coloring, the little boy is apparently the spitting image of Jay."

"You didn't see the picture?"

"No. She only had the one and asked to keep it. Can you blame her?"

"A photo and paperwork can be manipulated." Or used for blackmail down the road.

"I understand, but Jay was convinced. Which is not to say he was ready to take on the responsibility of raising a child on his own. It was only after the girl explained how she couldn't, *wouldn't* be able to keep the infant, that if Jay didn't take him, she would be forced to give him up for adoption, that Jay made his decision.'' She shrugged. ''I don't know what else to tell you. He asked for a day to buy a few things, and the following afternoon she brought the child. I was at work. When I phoned just before the auction that evening, there was a difference in Jay's voice. He was...how can I explain it? He hadn't sounded so happy in ages.''

''And when you arrived at the apartment?''

Once again the color drained from her face, her voice went flat. ''His bedroom door was closed. I can't tell you what went through my mind. Here I'd been excited to get home and meet my new nephew, and...''

Roman knew she wanted to stop there, but pushed. ''What happened in the morning when you finally woke?''

''At first I was in a panic because I'd overslept. Then I remember thinking that surely the baby wouldn't have overslept, too. A child that young needs food, diaper changing—''

''You're sure the bedroom door was still closed?''

''Yes.'' She began shaking again and gripped her hands together in her lap. ''I knocked, and when no one answered, I opened it. He was lying there on the bed with that horrible plastic bag over his head and another over his...his...''

When she couldn't finish, Roman had to guess, although this wasn't a subject they'd spent much time on in class. ''Penis?''

She nodded quickly, but avoided eye contact. "I became ill. But after...I mean before I called 911, I knew I had to go back in there. I had to get the baby. It should have struck me sooner, but the shock—I couldn't think for a minute. That's when I discovered there was no one else there. No evidence whatsoever that there ever had been a child in that apartment."

Roman didn't want to cause her more pain, but knew the questions he had to ask next, and so he drew nearer, once again squatting before her and taking her hands with his. He felt he read her better when they were closer. It was as if his nearness blocked some self-defense mechanism in her.

"Why didn't you tell Willard about the baby?"

"Oh, what difference does it make? You won't believe me anyway."

"I'll try. Something had to have happened besides the fact that you had an immediate negative reaction to the guy."

She made a brief derisive sound. "You see? You're already thinking like a cop. Methodical. Logical. Whatever is intellectually unacceptable to you must be an automatic lie. Well, I lived this, and there was nothing logical or sane about what happened, or how I felt, or the way things went afterward."

"You didn't tell him," Roman reiterated quietly.

"I couldn't!" she cried. "I intended to, even began to. My God, I was frantic. I kept thinking at any second I'll wake up and this will have only been a nightmare. Or that a neighbor would knock on the door and it would turn out that Jay had asked them to watch the baby. And all the while my mind is racing, reminding me that I had to call our parents. How was I going to tell them? How was I going to tell them about the baby that wasn't here? And then...Detective Willard's demeanor changed, the immediate conclusions he jumped to...it was all wrong.''

"Wrong how?''

"Too fast. Too sure. I couldn't believe what I was hearing, and the more I tried to correct him, to explain, the more I felt his animosity. Then when he suddenly did a whole personality reversal and in a sickeningly sincere way suggested we say it was a suicide, I don't know, I just shut down inside.''

"That's not a good enough excuse.''

"It's not an excuse!'' She jerked her hands free and almost knocked him over as she retreated to the farthest end of the kitchen. "People are almost as much my business as art is. I have to read faces, pick up on interest and intent, read through the veneers of disinterest and even aloofness. In other words, I need to be sensitive to a con when I see one, and when that cop walked into my brother's apartment he made my skin crawl. Every instinct inside me shrieked, 'Don't trust him!' And surprise, surprise, each time Detective Willard's path crosses mine, those alarms sound louder and louder. So don't tell me—what are you doing? Don't.''

It was wrong, completely unprofessional, but Roman cornered her in the V of the counter and put his arms around her, held her despite her struggle to break free.

"McKenna!'' she cried in a tortured whisper.

"I'm sorry. I'm sorry for pushing, for the hurtful

questions, for all of it. But I had to hear everything, Nick. Because what you're suggesting means I should have called my superior officer ten minutes ago.''

"With what? I only know what I saw, what I felt.''

"You withheld information. If there is a child—''

"Of course there is, but I have no proof!''

"Where's that documentation Jay told you about? Surely the baby's mother passed that over when she gave him the child. And what about a birth certificate?''

"I don't know. What do you think I've been doing every minute I'm not at work? Looking for answers, clues, anything! Do you know what it's like to try to find a child you've never seen, let alone can't openly talk about? That's what I'm up against, living in fear that Willard is going to find out about the baby. Obviously he suspects something, because he hasn't left me alone.''

"Has he threatened you?''

Her smile was cold, mocking. "He's too smooth for that. He drops by. He happens to be where I am at lunch. He shows up when I'm at the apartment complex trying to find out when I can get the rest of Jay's things out of there.''

"After three weeks, and the manner of death uncontested? Why haven't they let you have them?''

"The management office says the police haven't given them a release yet. When they call, Detective Willard is conveniently out.''

No wonder she'd been acting the way she had, scared of her own shadow. Hunted.

She must have seen the conflict in his eyes because

she began trying to free herself again. "Forget it. It's not your problem. You've been tolerant and kind, but you have enough on your own plate to deal with."

He stopped her by locking his mouth to hers. To keep her there, he framed her face with his hands and used his lips, teeth and tongue to make sure she understood that no matter what she saw on his face, she shouldn't assume she knew what was going on under his skin.

Finally, forehead to forehead, the two of them all but panting, he muttered, "Understand now? Walking away from you doesn't seem to be an option, so I'm doing the best I can to understand and believe."

"Which makes you either dense or too sweet for words." She traced his lower lip with her fingertips. "Can't you see that I'm trying to let you off the hook?"

"Wait until you're asked."

He bit one finger lightly before kissing her again. By the time he lifted his head again, she was relying on him to keep standing. He liked that, to know he had the same effect on her that she had on him.

"I have to get back to work, McKenna."

"I know. Make me a promise first—do nothing until you hear from me again."

As expected, she looked doubtful. "That's no small thing."

"You have to give me a chance to catch up and find out what I can."

"All right," she replied slowly. "But not long."

"Not long."

"And be careful."

Because he knew if he stayed this close he would kiss her again, Roman stepped back to put some space between them. "I will. Believe me, Nick, I know what this is costing you."

"Dear God, I hope so."

8

We boil at different degrees.

—*Ralph Waldo Emerson*

Roman stopped for a six-pack and a burger on his way home, and thought it a miracle that he made it without busting a tab on at least one of the cans before entering his stuffy apartment. His current homestead was on the wrong side of Central Expressway, the scenery unimproved by dusk's blurring of details. The red brick buildings built in the fifties resembled abandoned military barracks, and while the place was no slum, no one could argue about the ongoing challenge to beat the roaches to whatever was edible inside. That was why he preferred to eat out or to pick up something on his way home. The rent did make it possible for him to send a bigger monthly check to Glenda, though, and the hope that he was somehow making things a little easier for Meggie kept him from succumbing to disgust and moving. He would have slept in his pickup and saved all the rent money for his little girl if the demands of his job, the need to get decent rest and look halfway presentable, weren't so important. Not that Glenda needed or wanted his money. Her fancy-schmancy doctor-husband was taking care of what expenses Meggie's insurance didn't cover. The only way Roman had convinced her to accept the checks he sent was by suggesting she buy their daughter gifts with them—stuffed animals, balloons, flowers, a VCR and videos...anything to help Meggie try to forget her pain and the treatments during those times when he couldn't get down there to do it himself.

That's what he'd been reduced to—a surrogate Santa Claus.

Upon entering his minuscule cave, he hung his jacket over the back of the bar stool in the kitchen, aware he had to wear it several more times before he could afford to get it dry-cleaned again. Then he put the six-pack of Miller beer in the refrigerator, taking out the last cold can on the otherwise empty top shelf.

He gulped down half before stripping off the rest of his clothes. Once down to his jockey shorts, he turned on the TV, took another swallow, and settled on the unmade sofa bed.

The air conditioner kicked on, blurring more of the background noises—traffic from Central, but mostly yelling neighbors who were an odd mixture of calcifying Anglos and newly married Hispanics. Tonight the lot of them sounded as though they were hard of hearing. So much for being impressed with having a cop in their midst. At least he hadn't been burglarized yet; however, he wasn't planning on making any improvements, either. The TV and microwave were ancient, bought from a fellow cop who'd been divorcing and was in need of cash for attorney fees. The only other things of value he had beside his gun were his three suits, and even they would raise eyebrows in places lit with more than a forty-watt bulb.

He took another swig of beer and checked his watch. It was too late to call Houston. Meggie would be asleep by now, and Glenda wouldn't thank him for disturbing them.

With no great enthusiasm he reached for his dinner. As he unwrapped the burger and squeezed two tubes of ketchup onto his fries, his thoughts inevitably boomeranged back to Nicole.

His initial visit to check on her, to apologize for letting things get too personal sure hadn't gone as planned. The woman was like the most habit-forming narcotic. God help him if she was playing him for a fool. Sure, his instincts told him that she was legitimate, but her story...hell, he'd never heard of anything so nuts.

Concerned that he might forget something, he lunged off the bed to retrieve his notebook. This was one story he had to keep straight.

Minutes later, he frowned. Not at his messy handwriting, but at the facts of the case. They remained incomprehensible, as confusing as they'd been the first time he'd heard them. A man who had everything to live for was dead. A baby that he couldn't prove existed was missing. And a highly respected detective in the DPD was behaving in a way that could cost him his career.

Why risk all that?

Why make it up?

Roman wondered which question would bring him

closer to the truth of what happened that night…and who did he trust to get the answers?

Any way he looked at this, there was one fact that stood out. Because Jay's apartment was on the second floor—he'd made sure to find that out before leaving Nicole—after having killed Jay Loring, the perpetrator would have to have walked past Nicole that night. With the kid no less. The baby couldn't have made so much as a chick's peep, and anything and everything that had belonged to the infant—hell, there had to have been at least one dirty diaper, or how about formula? All of it had to have been removed at the same time. Who could be so thorough, so cunning? Most important, could Nicole really have slept through it all?

The cold french fry he put in his mouth tasted like wood. He swallowed it and it dropped like a whole tree trunk to the pit of his stomach.

Willard's report had to hold some answers. He also needed to find out who the hell J. J. Loring was, aside from the harmless, charming man Nicole had described. Roman thought of what she had supplied as she'd walked him out to his truck…

The double J stood for Jay Johnson. Jay being his and Nicole's maternal grandfather and Johnson their paternal grandfather, both long dead. So were their grandmothers. What aunts, uncles and cousins remained were scattered throughout the country, and unless there was a funeral, the families preferred contact be kept to the exchange of Christmas cards. Apparently, Mrs. Loring excelled at that. She and Doctor Loring, a professor of philosophy and humanities at the University of Texas at Tyler—who, Nicole had added dryly, possessed little of his own—lived in one of the stately homes along the city's famed Azalea Trail. "Snobs," Nicole had drawled with a sardonic smile when he'd asked for a translation.

Nicole had lent him a picture of her brother and Roman studied it now. As he'd expected, Jay's photogenic, blond good looks had matched his sister's. Small wonder he'd been popular with the opposite sex. A graduate from the University of Texas at Austin, he'd also apparently been more successful at finding tennis and golf partners than people wanting him to build their office buildings or luxurious homes. In fact, from the little Nicole had said in that department—or rather hadn't said—Roman guessed the guy had been somewhat bitter about his failed architectural dreams and had chosen to live life on all eight cylinders, racing toward nowhere in particular.

Regardless of what she might want to believe about the baby putting a new resolve in the guy, maybe Loring panicked and opted out before his adoring sister and everyone else found out how inept he really was with relationships.

He would have chosen a damned easier way to do it, Ace. Besides, there's still the matter of the kid.

The phone rang. Half hoping it was Ralph telling him that they had an emergency so he could focus on something else, he picked up the receiver.

"Yeah?"

"It's me."

Glenda. A reality check all right, but of a different order.

Immediately tensing, he set the can on the night stand. "What's happened?"

"Do you mind not doing that? You chew me out for not keeping you informed, and when I do, you lose it before I have a chance to say two words."

It was the same song and dance she always put him through, her way of getting back at him for forcing this accommodation from her, yet still small change in comparison to what he wanted or thought he deserved. "Okay, Glenda, so I expect the worse these days, so sue me for what you don't already own. How's Meggie?"

There was a pause and then a deep sigh on the other end of the line. "She's finally asleep. It was a rough day."

They were all rough. Although he'd been denied permission to be there for most of the procedures, he'd done his own research to know the treatment of leukemia in children got ugly.

"Tell her that I love her."

"I do regardless of whether I talk to you or not."

"I'm trying not to take anything for granted."

That was another thing she used to complain about—unfairly as far as he was concerned. Looking back he found it incomprehensible that she'd ever dated him, let alone agreed to be his wife. She'd liked almost nothing about being the daughter of a cop, and not much more about being married to one that had been just starting his career. Roman wondered if life with Super Doc was an improvement. Doctors' schedules sucked, too. On the other hand, the prestige and money could make things more palatable—like the sugar coating on a nasty pill.

"Since this isn't going to be one of our better conversations," Glenda said after a prolonged silence, "let me tell you what's going to be going on that you need to know about."

The few bites of food he'd managed threatened to lurch up from his stomach. Although he mentally prepared himself for bad news from Houston every day, his gut had its own idea of how to react to his daughter's tragedy. "Go ahead."

"We've decided to take her to Disneyland before…before she grows any weaker."

It was something Meggie had wanted to do ever since he'd taught her to say Pluto, or in her case, "Pootoh." The week he knew he'd worked enough overtime to pay for the trip, Glenda had hit him with the news that she was leaving him for the asshole doctor she'd met who was about to take a better position down in Houston, leaving him and taking his daughter with her. Ever since, Meggie had been too ill or undergoing some new treatment to attempt the vacation. That Glenda and Meggie's doctor thought it was okay now confirmed what he'd been trying not to face from day one.

"Roman? Are you there?"

"Yeah." But he wished he wasn't. He wished he'd never met Glenda because then his baby would never have to have gone through this hell.

"I'm assuming your promotion will make it impossible for you to see her off?"

No invitation to join them, not even a lukewarm

one, despite the reassuring knowledge there was no way in hell he could afford such a trip, regardless of whether or not he could get the time off. As a result, it was tough repressing all of his bitterness. "The trick to keeping your job the day after making detective is to show up for work more than once. If you could hold off a week or—"

"There isn't time."

He closed his eyes. "I know. I know."

"Look, you don't have to worry that she won't have the proper care. Josh is coming along."

"And is Dr. Wonderful borrowing a friend's jet to fly you over, or did I underestimate his success and your ambition by overlooking that he owns his own corporate toy?"

Glenda's frigid silence came over the line loud and clear. "Could you try to remember this is about Meggie? Think of her for once, instead of taking cheap potshots just because you're feeling sorry for yourself!"

He wanted to snarl back, "Believe it or not, I can be bitter over being screwed by you and grieve for my daughter all at the same time." Instead, he pinched the bridge of his nose and prayed he could restrain himself long enough to get through the call. "When are you leaving?"

"Saturday. Josh says we can't afford to delay."

He hated the guy for stealing his family, but he couldn't deny his reputation in the medical community. "Is the trip wise at all?"

"We've made arrangements to see that she doesn't overdo it."

If will alone had anything to do with it, Roman knew his ex would pull it off all by her feisty little self...or someone would answer for it. The days when he'd misconstrued Glenda's petiteness for fragility, were long over.

"All I'm asking," she continued, "is that you call her tomorrow so she can say goodbye."

"Why are you making it sound as though I never call?"

"Because you rarely do when she's awake or not in treatment."

Because he never knew when any of that was scheduled, and the times always changed before he could memorize what little information Glenda shared with him. "You give me a specific hour, Glenda. I'll happily pull off the highway to use a pay phone if I have to, but I'm not a mind reader."

"I've given you times. You've ignored them."

"No. Never. But I can't call if I'm responding to a signal code or in court. Hell, why do you bother with the pretenses if you're intent on turning me into the bad guy?"

"That's it!" she snapped. "I don't have the energy left to deal with your anger. Friday, Roman. After three in the afternoon, but before six. Or better yet forget I called, I don't give a damn."

As the line went dead, Roman swore and slammed down his receiver. It wasn't enough of a purging, though, so he crushed his barely touched burger and fries between his hands and thrust the whole mess back into the sack, then stormed to the kitchen where he rocketed the remains into the trash container.

Anger? Fuck, yes, he was angry. He'd *loved* being a father; had worked damned hard to be with Meggie every minute he could, even to the point of refusing invitations out with friends—something that didn't go over well with Glenda at all. That's what really ticked her off, he thought bitterly. Not his attitude now, no; it was that she knew that no matter what, she would never obliterate the bond he and his daughter shared. And as a result, Glenda would never be free of her own guilt.

Still swearing, he took out another beer from the refrigerator. If he'd known she was going to do this tonight, he would have let the machine take the call.

"Shit." He kicked the trash can and sent it into the refrigerator.

Satisfied that McKenna was settled in for the night and that Ms. Ballbuster was tied up with another gig at Van Dorn's, Wes Willard relaxed somewhat. He'd had an anxious moment or two earlier when McKenna had shown up at Nicole Loring's, but apparently the woman had set him straight by letting him know that whatever he'd gotten a taste of last night was to be a one-shot deal. It had been a grim-looking McKenna who had driven past him a while ago. Just to be sure, though, Willard had followed him to this dive of an apartment complex.

Willard lit a cigarette and checked the clock on the dashboard of his car. The delay had him running late, and that wasn't a good thing. You didn't keep certain people waiting.

He drove swiftly back across Central, to Highland

Park, past mansion after mansion with their manicured yards and gated estates locked up tight for the night. As he neared his destination, he reached into his pocket for his cellular phone and quickly punched in a number.

After only one ring, came a terse, "Yes?"

"I'm two blocks away. Meet me out front."

"I told you never to come to the house!" the man on the other end of the line whispered harshly.

"Yeah, well, it couldn't be helped. You want what I have or do I find another buyer for it?"

The man hesitated. "I can't pay you until tomorrow."

"You're good for it. But it'll be double the usual rate."

"That's outrageous! Why?"

"You'll see. Do I stop or keep driving?"

After another slight hesitation, the man replied, "I'll take it. But for heaven's sake be quick about it. I have guests arriving in a matter of minutes."

Willard smiled to himself, but didn't bother replying. Disconnecting, he dropped the phone on the passenger seat, and picked up the boxed videotape beside it.

As he approached the house, one of the farthest from the road, he saw a figure illuminated by the soft landscape lights hurrying down the circular drive. Identifying the man in the dinner suit, Willard killed the car's lights and rolled down his window. He stretched out his arm, but didn't quite stop. The older man had to jog not to miss him, and when he grabbed the box, Willard held on a few seconds longer.

"Bastard," the man whispered furiously.

Chuckling, Willard let go and accelerated. By the time he turned on the car lights again and looked in his rearview mirror, the street was empty, the image of the neighborhood as refined as ever.

If only people knew the truth, he mused. Of course, it was in his best interests to make sure they never did.

9

*Compromise is but the sacrifice
of one right or good
in the hope of retaining another—
too often ending in the loss of both.*

—*Tryon Edwards*

Nicole woke to the ringing phone. She knew of only one person who would do this to her, and she wasn't ready for her.

"Yes, Mother?"

"Oh, good, you're up. I wanted to catch you before your father comes downstairs. You know the UTT faculty reports today for the fall semester, and he likes to be punctual."

How typical. There had been no "Hello, Nicole, how are you today?" nor a "Sorry to wake you, dear." When and if her mother's thought processes ventured beyond herself or her momentary agenda, they rarely stretched further than her husband and his position at the University of Texas at Tyler.

"Well, by all means, let's not upset him on his first day back as a member of the gainfully employed." She saw no reason to hide her sarcasm. Those years of compromising her own beliefs, not to mention her needs, to be "the good daughter" were behind her. "What can I do for you?"

"I have to know if you're still coming this weekend." There was no hint in her mother's voice to indicate she'd perceived any change in Nicole's mood.

This weekend. With all that was going on, she hadn't given it much thought. "That was the plan, unless something else has come up?" She accepted that she had to get out there, but she didn't want to go. If it wasn't so damned important, if she could count on her mother to collect what she needed, and mail it to her—but that was a childish fantasy.

"No. Your father wants this over with. I'm planning on getting groceries today, and I wanted to know if you're still on that silly diet?"

"I'm not on any diet, Mother." The suggestion irked as much as her idea that removing Jay's possessions from the house was something to be "over with." "I'm simply not eating sweets for breakfast the way you and Father do. Coffee and a piece of fruit and toast will be fine for me. But I can pick up that myself on the way in."

"Did I say anything about not getting it? I simply don't want too much in the house. You know how your father overindulges and then complains about indigestion."

Yes, Nicole knew. As disciplined as he was professionally, he tended to be compulsive when it came to food, and her mother manipulated, controlled and contrived to keep him in a respectable suit size—when she wasn't encouraging him to gorge himself into a heart attack. But Nicole doubted this was really a call intent on pinpointing her current eating habits.

"What's actually on your mind, Mother?" She sat up and shut off the alarm button on her clock. It was due to go off in ten minutes anyway. "You aren't changing your mind about letting me have some of Jay's things, are you?"

Heaven knew it wouldn't be the first time either of her parents had gone back on their word. That's why—despite a dire need to catch up on much needed sleep, questioning more of Jay's neighbors, and the people who worked at the club—it was important to get to east Texas. Even as Jay's body was being carried down the stairs of his apartment, her father had begun cursing his "worthless hide" and regretting the day he'd learned they had a son. "By God, the minute we get home, you start packing his things," he'd roared at his wife. "I want every sign of him out of my house!"

"Heavens, not me," her mother replied now. She sounded as though she was cupping her other hand around the mouthpiece. "But you know your father. I swear my nerves can't take much more. He's suffering such mood swings."

Nicole thought her mother was crediting the man with too much range, and if there was any suffering being done, it certainly wasn't by Dr. Jason Loring. He'd stayed consistently dour and acerbic for the thirty years she'd known him, except when they'd shown the gall to challenge his behavior toward them. Then he stretched all the way to nasty. Not in public, though...oh, never in public.

"Why don't you buy him his favorite cheesecake.

If you're lucky he'll eat himself into a seizure, have to go to the hospital, and you'll be able to get some rest until I get there and relieve you of your burden.''

"Don't start, Nicole. He's still your father."

If she'd had the energy, she would have laughed at the sudden about-face in her mother's attitude. Once, it used to frustrate and hurt Nicole to no end that a usually reasonable, intelligent person could behave with such stunning inconsistency, one minute confiding personal intimacies and flaws about the man she'd married as if Nicole were her sister and not her daughter, and then berate her like some stern headmistress when Nicole responded honestly to her own bad experiences with the man. Now, however, with her scarred heart safely bandaged and out of reach, she was merely opting for efficiency. Because the sooner her mother got to the point, the sooner Nicole could hang up.

"What I was thinking was that you should come tonight instead of Saturday," her mother continued. "Then you can get up early and load what you want while your father has his golf game."

"Why don't I skip sleeping altogether, and work through the night? Then I could be gone before dawn, and he would never have to remember that he'd had *any* children."

"Do you have to turn everything into a melodrama? Our hearts were broken by what happened. But J.J. did this to us, not vice versa."

"He died, Mother. That's all he did. The rest is conjecture that you're accepting without giving him the benefit of the doubt. How do you do that, assume the worst about him, and still face yourself in the mirror every morning?''

''The police came to those conclusions, not me. And let me remind you, young lady, I also raised that boy. He wasn't the saint you want to paint him.''

''Who is? But nothing he did, or rather didn't do to please you and father, deserves what you're doing to his memory. How can you make such intellectual leaps? The police chose the easy way out, don't you see that?''

''He was always strange,'' her mother said vaguely.

Nicole gripped the phone. ''Complicated. Troubled. Not perverted.''

''I did not use that disgusting word, and I didn't call to discuss a closed subject.''

''That's the point. It *isn't* closed. Something terrible happened, and until we uncover the truth, Jay's death will always haunt us.'' Surely her mother believed that in some lucid corner of her mind that alcohol hadn't already saturated. ''At any rate, I can't come earlier. I have commitments at work that will keep me until late, and what with my continuing search for the baby—''

''Oh, for heaven's sake. Nicole, you're *not?*''

She'd confided her secret after Detective Willard had left the apartment, but not surprisingly both of her parents had rejected the idea. ''I told you I would keep looking until I found him.''

''But that nice detective…what was his name again?''

''Willard.''

''The one who came to pay his respects again after

the funeral? I thought it was something like Waterford or Winston?''

"It's Willard, like the rat in the movie."

Once again her mother responded with disapproving silence. "What I'm trying to point out," she said at last, "is that he would have mentioned a child if there had been one. He would have offered to help."

Nicole shivered as she remembered how she'd seen Willard coming up the stairs of Jay's apartment and had sweated blood afraid her parents would say the wrong thing in front of him. "There *was and is* a baby."

"Some Mexican's child we can't be certain was his?"

It was the closest thing to an admission or acceptance that Nicole had heard yet. "Jay was sure. And what difference does the baby's ethnicity matter as long as he's healthy?"

There was a muffled sound on the other end of the line, then her mother whispered, "Your father's on his way downstairs. Please, Nicole. Enough. I need you here tonight. How often do I ask anything of you?"

"That's a joke, right?" Ever since she could remember her mother had been using or manipulating her love, and, sympathetic to what she'd thought her mother had to endure with their father, Nicole had been there for her. Until she'd realized that it was all a veneer to get her own way. Until she'd seen how her mother used her husband, too, used everyone in a classical pattern of codependency.

"What, dear?" her mother said, away from the phone. "Oh, it's only Nicole. What were you going to tell me, Nicole? I have to finish getting your daddy's breakfast.''

Never had Nicole called her father "Daddy." She would have choked on the word. Jay had tried it a few times early on, but he'd been cured quickly. And did her mother believe her father so dim-witted as to buy the false cheerfulness in her voice? Then again, he probably wasn't even paying attention. As long as he got what he wanted when he wanted it, he didn't pay attention to what anyone did.

Wanting desperately to get off the phone, Nicole relented. "All right, Mother. Tonight. But that means I'll leave Saturday morning."

"Don't be silly. We barely see you these days, we need to do something special. But we can talk about that when you get here."

Her mother hung up before she could reply.

After taking a slow, steadying breath, Nicole did the same.

"No, Mother, we won't talk," she said to the white telephone. "We'll discuss the weather, your latest effort to get your name in the paper, the weather, you'll gossip about the neighbors, the women in your various clubs, the weather... Oh, the hell with it."

What made her think she would ever get that relationship, any of her relationships—she amended, thinking of Roman McKenna—straightened out?

Work. Work was what she excelled at. Relieved to have come to one conclusion without having to take two aspirin, she headed for the bathroom and a shower.

10

*He who peeps through a hole
may see what will vex him.*

—Spanish proverb

Roman arrived at the station a good hour early and, as expected, found he had the department pretty much to himself, since most of the second shift had already called it a night, and the lingerers were preoccupied with their own concerns. It created exactly the opportunity he'd been hoping for.

After introducing himself to the two yawning men nearest to his desk, he settled down with his coffee and breakfast-in-a-muffin that he'd picked up on the way over. A tap on one key removed the fish swimming across his computer screen, then he typed in the correct access code.

Finding Jay Loring's case was easy, nothing like in the old days when you had to deal with file drawers and hundreds of folders, any of which could be misplaced or hidden at another desk. And the results of snooping in someone else's workspace never changed. It put a mark on a relationship that followed you.

His pulse kicked up a notch when he found what he

was looking for. To settle down his overzealous fingers, he took a moment to unpack his breakfast and take a sip of the tongue-burning brew. Before him was the first dozen lines of Jay Johnson Loring's filed report.

"Something in there that I can help you with?"

Ice water down his back couldn't have been a less pleasant surprise, and Roman hoped his hand didn't shake too much as he put down the foam cup. "Hey, Wes Willard, right? You're early."

"So are you. And that's not your case."

Easing his chair around, he saw that Willard was dressed every bit as sharp as yesterday, and he was not smiling. This was exactly why Roman would have preferred having Ralph's seat, which faced the main entrance.

"Yeah, I know, but I was going to brief myself on one of Tucker's cases—" he glanced back at his desk, frantically looking for the list of names "—Loftis. That's it. Only I saw this name, Loring, and realized I knew the guy's sister."

"Small world."

The excuse was weaker than spring ice, but Roman knew Willard had to accept it, or make a scene. "What brings you in this early?" He took a big bite of his sandwich to avoid having to think of something else to say too soon if Willard's answer was brief.

"Court this morning. I like to work ahead."

Willard slipped off his jacket. His suit made Roman feel like his own had come from some garage sale.

"How do you know the sister?" Willard's gaze split him in vertical halves. "You two date or something?"

Roman managed a self-deprecating laugh, but wanted to kick the smart-ass's chair out from under him. "Yeah, right. She's way out of my price range."

"You never can tell. Sometimes the most high-maintenance types can surprise you. Look at her brother." Willard nodded at Roman's computer screen. "No one would have guessed him to have a taste for the perverse. So who knows? A big strapping cowboy like you might be the change of pace she's looking for."

The bastard knew. Somehow he knew.

Roman pretended to miss the reference to the case. "I have a sick daughter. I'm not much interested in dating these days. Anyway the only reason Ms. Loring gave me the time of day was because it was my job to be a shadow around Van Dorn's. I guess you've been thorough enough to know I moonlighted over there for a brief time?"

"Well, you're probably better off not putting your neck on the chopping block," Willard replied, ignoring the question. "The short time I had to deal with her was no picnic. She called me at all hours of the day, kept insisting her brother was murdered, that I was repressing evidence..." He checked the shine on one of his gold cuff links. "When none of that worked, she even tried coming on to me in an attempt to coerce me into making more of the death scene than there was."

It was all Roman could do not to ram the computer keyboard down Willard's throat. "Sorry to hear that. She'd seemed a nice lady."

"Which just goes to show you that looks can be

deceiving. That's why I'm keeping an ear to the ground in case I find out that maybe her brother wasn't the only fruitcake in the family.'' As though warming to Roman, Willard added, ''We haven't had a chance to talk yet. How's it going so far?''

Small talk was preferable to discussing Nicole and her brother, but Roman doubted Willard said anything without a reason. ''No complaints.''

''Bet partnering with Gomer's a different experience than anything you've done so far.''

''Actually, I think I lucked out,'' Roman replied. He would let the prick think what he wanted of him, but he wasn't about to compromise his relationship with the person designated to watch his back. ''The lieutenant's right about him being thorough and tireless.''

Willard showed no reaction to that. ''You were over at Central Patrol before coming here?''

''On foot downtown at first. Then I paid my dues in a squad car, until I aced my exam.''

''How did you hear about the Van Dorn job?''

''The guy who had it before me had to quit and recommended me.''

''So you missed young Loring's grand exit?''

''Yeah.'' Didn't Willard realize that he was starting to sound fixated?

''Too bad. Maybe you could have helped me out with Miss High-and-Mighty. Not too many of us would stand for someone trying to burn us for doing our job. Ungrateful bitch should be happy there wasn't a leak to the press about what really happened. Her oh-so-proper family would kick her butt so hard for that, she would leave a wake on the Gulf.''

Roman frowned pretending to have missed something, and used the mouse to read farther down Jay Johnson Loring's report. When he got to a description of the death scene, he sat back in his chair. "Ah. Now I get it."

"Welcome to the real world, cowboy."

Roman pretended to be uncomfortable by what he'd read. "I once answered a 911 call for what turned out to be an experimental S-and-M party gone out of control, but nobody died."

"*Really.* Recently?"

"What? No. Glad I didn't have to take this call."

"I've seen lots worse. I figure she cleaned up some before calling it in. Families do that, you know. The shame's more than they can handle."

Roman had to force his eyes off the screen. "Understandable." At Willard's snort of disgust he shrugged. "I'm simply making an objective observation."

Willard suddenly smiled. "So you are."

As he strode out of the room without so much as a "See you," Roman exhaled with relief, but still called himself several variations of a jerk. Because he'd just made an enemy, and because of all the people he could have ticked off in the department, it was Willard.

"Ah, Nick," he murmured under his breath. "This is not good. Not good at all."

11

*Much hath been done,
but more remains to do.*

—Lord Byron

"Are you swamped?"

Nicole wanted to laugh at the girl peering into her office, but she was afraid it would end up sounding hysterical. She needed to call two collectors whose work by an increasingly popular southwestern artist was going up for sale next week, but, nonetheless, had unrealistic reserve prices. She smelled hanky-panky going on between those two to inflate prices. Also, one of their best forgery sniffers had found a dubious signature on a painting, and she wanted to arrange for a second opinion before it went back to the owner. Then Max wanted her to walk through an estate with him in Fort Worth as soon as possible to see if handling its liquidation would be worth their while. There were numerous other chores and situations to delegate if she was going to get out of here at a decent hour today, and she was already regretting her promise to Roman about doing nothing until she heard from him.

Mentally shifting all that aside, she motioned Carlyn

into her office. "What's put that frazzled look on your face?"

"I shouldn't bug you, but I need a break. I mean, I came this close—" she put her index and thumb together "—to damaging the clasp on a stubborn Cartier bracelet. Could I possibly talk you into taking a breather? Maybe going out with me for lunch?"

Nicole had intended to spend her lunch hour talking to Max about the upcoming jewelry sale. But Carlyn was her protégée and she hadn't invested the time she had in the girl to lose her now. She owed that to Van Dorn's as much as she did to herself.

"Okay. Sure. Any preferences?"

"That corner place on McKinney with the blue awning? Their salads are always great."

Nicole nodded in agreement thinking it funny how she could never remember its name, either. She glanced at her Rolex watch, last year's Christmas gift from Max. "Why don't we go now? That's one of the first places to get crowded."

Carlyn's relieved nod told her that this was the right thing to do, and within five minutes she was skirting around one of McKinney's quaint streetcars to get to the old house-turned-restaurant that served breakfasts, lunches and snacks virtually around the clock. The inner decor was somewhere between New Orleans romantic and New England rustic, and they opted for a table in the plant-adorned atrium. Familiar with the menu, they ordered their favorite grilled chicken salads and—after only a slight hesitation on Nicole's part—chardonnay. Then she leaned across the glass and wrought iron table in order to keep from being over-heard.

"Should I guess that this is about your fiancé and not work?"

Carlyn, a dead ringer for Jennifer Aniston, made a face as she unwrapped her silverware from its protective linen napkin. "How embarrassing to be an open book."

"What's Dennis done now?"

"Oh, Nicole…he's changed his mind about waiting to start a family, about me working, about everything. Suddenly I feel as though I went to bed engaged to Barbie's Ken, and woke to Michael Keaton's character in *Pacific Heights*!"

When she was excited or in a hurry, she often used film references as a shorthand; however, it painted an adequate picture for Nicole. As for Dennis Frame, he was an appealing guy—at first glance, she amended, thinking of the few times they'd met. An up-and-coming attorney, he worked downtown, wore only the best suits, ate in the best restaurants, and socialized only with people who might be useful down the road. There was nothing earth-shatteringly new or criminally wrong with that; unfortunately, life wasn't a recipe wherein if you chose certain ingredients, you were guaranteed perfect results. Dennis refused to see that, and tried to program everything the way he did the laptop computer he dragged virtually everywhere he went.

"What are you going to do?" Nicole didn't want to think about her own dilemma if Carlyn announced that she was giving notice.

"I haven't gotten that far. Right now I'm trying to psyche myself into putting some food into my stomach and keeping it there. Does that tell you how scared I am?"

"Do not add a pregnancy to this."

With perfect timing, the waiter brought their wine. Despite her hesitation in ordering it, Nicole reached for her glass faster than Carlyn could.

"Bite your tongue," the younger woman whispered. "I'm just wound to the point where I can't keep much of anything down—which Dennis insists is a dead giveaway that I'm bulimic. Have you heard enough yet?"

She most certainly had, but Nicole offered a supportive smile as she sipped gratefully at her drink. What people did to people they professed to love. What people *tolerated* from people they wanted to love. "Go on."

"Then there's my mother, who thinks I should see a therapist, since no one in their right mind would risk letting such 'a catch' slip through her fingers. She doesn't care that he's making me miserable, and— Just tell me how he could have changed so much in such a short time."

"Are you sure he has? Maybe *you're* the one who's changed."

"You mean I've been living in denial all this time?"

Nicole knew better than to coddle. For all her anxiousness at the moment, Carlyn was made of tougher stuff. "When you're not the one falling in love, you tend to see things from a different perspective."

"But I've always despised people who go around with rose-colored glasses surgically attached to their brains," Carlyn replied, frowning.

"So you're fallible. Welcome to the human race. What I can't do is tell you that it's okay to split with Dennis. Not only aren't you ready to decide that, if you make a hasty decision now, you'll start doubting it the minute you don't have a date for some Friday night."

"Never mind Friday. How about the minute I tell my parents that all the money they've already dished out on my gown and the reception was for nothing?"

Money. All her life Nicole had noticed how it complicated everything making people avoid decisions they should have made and make others they shouldn't have. "The Carlyn I know will tell them if it's necessary, and pay them back if she decides her feelings for Dennis don't go as deep as she thought."

"You're joking, right?"

"Believe it or not, it feels rather good to keep your actions honest. The rest—including how your parents will react—doesn't matter."

Carlyn eyed her with a mixture of curiosity and admiration. "Sounds as though you're talking from experience."

"I know about parents and making yourself sick from trying to please everyone."

Carlyn slumped back in her chair. "I guess I have more serious thinking to do."

"The good news is that the ring you're wearing isn't a wedding band."

Her friend eyed her with new respect. "How do you

do it? You're going through hell yourself. In fact I felt guilty coming to you with this. How are you holding it all together and still able to act as though my silly problem matters?''

"Are you sure I am?" Truth be known, Nicole yearned to gulp down her wine and tell the waiter to bring the rest of the bottle.

Carlyn didn't reply right away because the waiter returned with their salads. When they were once again alone, she discreetly wiped her fork in her napkin. ''No one is condemning you for the few times you've indulged in a bit too much bubbly. The consensus is that the rest of us would have been at a rehabilitation clinic by now if we'd been in your shoes.''

And they didn't have a clue as to how bad it really was due to Willard being clever and discreet, and her own care in keeping her problems from interfering with her work. Nicole wiped her own fork, then smoothed her napkin over her lap. ''You give me too much credit, but thanks. I am trying to remember that when what's happening to you becomes self-destructive as well as disruptive, that's a sure sign that you've lost it.''

"I hear what you're saying, but I'm afraid I'm nowhere near as brave as you are.''

Nicole understood that kind of self-doubt. ''I've developed a litmus test of sorts that might help. The next time you think you don't have the guts to do something, ask yourself what you're going to lose as a result—not tangible things, the important ones. It's amazing how clear decision making becomes.''

"Even if those decisions aren't what anyone else wants to hear?"

A feeling of sadness overcame Nicole. "They probably won't be."

"You see? That triggers the weenie in me. At the same time my life feels like a patchwork of accommodations. First there was school to get through and having to please my parents...then came Dennis. When is it time for me?"

"When you decide you value your own opinion most of all." This was a late bit of wisdom Nicole was only now fully comprehending. "Freedom costs, babe."

"With all due respect, your lack of a social life scares me. It did even before I saw what a mess my life was becoming."

"It would have rattled me at twenty-six, too."

"Four years makes that much difference?"

Because her young friend looked so skeptical, Nicole knew better than to try to explain. Besides, there were some parts of her life that remained sensitive. "You tell me in four years," she replied instead.

Carlyn shot her a droll look and for a minute they concentrated on their food.

"What about kids?" Nicole asked on impulse. "Do you see them in your future?"

"Not for a long, long time. You?"

"No, but...a friend of a friend found herself in a situation and I realized that sometimes those decisions are out of your hands."

"You mean like falling for someone who already had children? Hmm..." Carlyn frowned and slowly turned her dinner roll into bread crumbs. "I don't know. I guess my answer would have to be that it would depend upon the man. Heaven knows, I wouldn't want to meet him tomorrow."

"What if you already know him, and it was his nephew or niece, a cousin maybe that he was suddenly forced to take charge of?"

"That's an awful stretch." Carlyn thought for another few seconds and shook her head. "I seriously doubt I could do it. It would be difficult enough to deal with my own."

Once Nicole had believed the same thing. In fact, she had looked forward to being a coddling aunt who spoiled her nieces and nephews rotten, then sent them back to her brother. But if she ever found Jay's son, there would be no going home for him...and more than likely no one to stroke her back as she stumbled through teething, the measles and whatnot.

"Are you okay?" Carlyn asked, looking more concerned.

"Sorry," she replied, forcing a reassuring smile. "I guess I'm having second thoughts about adding to your depression."

"No! I appreciate everything you said. In fact, I think I know what you're trying to tell me...and what I have to do."

It might end up breaking her heart, Nicole thought, aware of the weight of her own. But it wouldn't cost her her sanity. Or worse. That's one thing that made their situations so different, and what left Nicole feeling almost envious of her younger friend.

12

*Advice…those who want it the most
always like it the least.*

—Earl of Chesterfield,
Letter to his son, January, 1748

"Where do you wanna eat?"

They were driving down R. L. Thornton, heading back to town and Roman couldn't help but shake his head over Tucker's question. Everyone was right. No matter what, Ralph's thoughts never wandered far from the subject of food. They'd driven all the way out to Decatur to question a witness in an older case, so productivity-wise, they didn't have much to show for their morning; nevertheless, his partner had his priorities in neat order.

"You choose," Roman told him. "I'm game."

"Good. I need some calories and grease to lift my spirits." Tucker pointed to the exit they were approaching. "Take Inwood. We'll see what's happening at Sonny Bryan's."

The barbecue restaurant was an institution with many Dallasites; almost as much as Texas Stadium, a few miles behind them. Roman stopped there himself on occasion, but the real reason he went along with the choice was so they could talk away from anyone they were likely to know.

The lunch crunch had yet to begin, and as the two of them entered the low-slung building with its smoke-and-barbecue stained windows and smudged everything else, they immediately drew in the smells of mesquite-cooked beef, pork and beans. Seating came in the form of school-style desk-chairs, and a number were occupied with staff from the hospital down the street, as well as various blue-collar types from the warehouses and small industrial shops in the area. But once Roman ordered himself a chopped beef sandwich and iced tea and Tucker got himself a mixed plate with extra cole slaw and potato salad, they were able to find an empty corner and settled into their ungainly seats.

As he peppered his mountain-chain of salads, Tucker made sounds similar to a salivating bullmastiff. The effect of that heavy seasoning had Roman thinking of what you dug out of a cat's litterbox, and he averted his gaze trying to decide how to pose a certain question to his partner.

After swallowing a huge forkful of the blackened goop, Tucker shot him a sidelong look. Roman had yet to touch his food.

"Something bugging you?" his partner asked.

Roman wondered how much of his inner tension was written on his face.

"Yeah, it shows," Tucker said as though he'd voiced the thought. "I walked into the department this morning and you looked like some of the stuff my wife finds in the refrigerator's vegetable bin at the end of the summer. Also couldn't help noticing Willard was sitting there as though someone had tied his shorts in a knot.''

None of that helped his appetite, but it worked as an invitation to talk. "I guess I've got a problem.''

"My pa used to say, 'If you've got only one, you need to give advice, not hang around looking like some sorry panhandler.'''

"It's a rough situation.''

"Spit it out.''

Roman couldn't. Not in the way Ralph wanted him to. "What do you think of the department's shrink?'' he asked instead.

His partner almost choked on his iced tea. "Hell, son, if you need a head doctor after two days on the job, we'd better talk to the lieutenant about a transfer, not some mind jockey.''

"It's not about me.'' Yet, he amended silently. "It's about someone I know. Someone who needs help.'' If she was telling the truth. Even more if she isn't. He saw Tucker begin to speak and added abruptly, "Don't ask me to name names. I can't do it, and I can't explain why not.''

Ralph eyed him shrewdly. "Don't think that's quite fair, pard, considering Willard knows.''

He was right. If things got any more complicated or messy, it would be Tucker's butt in the wringer along with his because everyone would assume he knew. "Hell,'' he muttered.

"Don't apologize.'' Ralph sucked the tender meat off a rib bone. "Regret's about as useful as a stiff pecker on death row.''

"If it had been strictly about me, I wouldn't have said anything so asinine. But she—"

Ralph almost sunk into his food. "We're talking about a woman? Just shoot me now and save my family grief. Here, use my gun—" he shifted to offer access inside his jacket "—that way they might believe you were doing me a favor."

"C'mon, Tucker. This is tough enough without adding the bullshit. Besides you're married. You're supposed to respect women."

"I do—the one I've got. You on the other hand already know your lady friend's a magnet for trouble. Even after Shirl threw that hot iron at me and I had to get those sixteen stitches in my ass, I never thought—"

"Stitches from a hot iron?"

"From beating a hasty retreat through the sliding glass door—that was shut tight. Don't look at me like that, it's all relative," he added, wagging the naked bone at him.

Maybe at another time he would have thought the guy a candidate for a padded cell, but at the moment Roman appreciated his humor, just as he did the gesture. "Do you know about any of Willard's cases?"

"Some. The question is, why do you?"

"I know a member of the family in one. The deceased's sister. Have you heard about the AEA case?"

Ralph grimaced. "Barely. I was just glad I didn't get the call. Surprised Willard did what he did for the family, though. Fill me in."

Roman told him—everything except the part about the baby. "So now she's trying to find some evidence, find someone who might have seen anyone leaving the apartment that night.''

"Like I said, Willard's a publicity hound,'' Tucker replied slowly. "It doesn't add up that he'd pass on an opportunity to get the kind of press an AEA case would bring. You whisper politics in that boy's ear, he almost comes. Of course, the rest of your story doesn't quite gel, either.''

"It's not my story.''

"Yeah, right. What's missing in this story of yours, Mac?''

A heavyset man was about to take the seat directly across from them. They both glared at him, and after a double take, the man quickly moved to the more crowded side of the room.

"Later,'' Roman replied. "Right now I need to talk to an expert about this autoerotic crap.''

Tucker picked up a slice of his Texas toast and began sopping up sauce as though the last two minutes of conversation hadn't happened. "Stay away from the police shrink,'' he said at last.

"Why?''

"Because that line about confidentiality they always use on you is bull. I know somebody over at Baylor Hospital who's a better bet.''

"You're sure? He's good?''

"He'll see you go home knowing more about that stuff than the fools who do it.''

Roman nodded. "That's what I want. I appreciate this, Ralph. And as soon as I'm able, I'll explain the rest.''

"Oh, I already know. *Its* got legs up to her dimples

and eyes that would give a blind man whiplash.''
Tucker sucked sauce off his thumb. ''Just promise me
you'll watch your ass.''

''I will...and for the record, she doesn't have dimples.''

''Like your dick noticed.''

13

When faults are scrutinized, the relationships cease.

—Indian proverb

It was past ten o'clock Friday evening when Nicole turned off Broadway and made the little zigzag through side streets to her parents' two-story home. As she'd feared, all of her efforts were for naught and she'd gotten a late start after all. The traffic on I-20— most of it probably heading for the gambling boats across the Louisiana border—had made the drive all the more tedious. Not even the knowledge that she was out of reach of Detective Willard for a while cheered her. Sure, she was grateful for the reprieve from feeling like a fly caught under an overturned glass, but each mile put her that much farther out of reach of Jay's child. It was like some tremendous betrayal, regardless of how important the reasons.

Her parents' house was the second from the corner in a neighborhood about fifty years old. The two-story, white brick looked deceivingly welcoming with its landscape lights and the exquisite crystal lamps glistening in the wide windows. But Nicole knew only too well how few guests had ever crossed their front threshold because her father didn't like strangers invading his domicile. That was why she'd always preferred the place by day—when he wasn't there. How her school friends had envied her; she never did explain that what they were envying was a shell, nor told them that to her the house had always felt more like a boarding school than home. She'd been too ashamed of her anger and pain.

As she parked in front of the two-car garage, she wondered if her parents were even home. Except for those lamps timed to go off at midnight, the interior seemed dark, and no light was on in the master bedroom. Then she spotted a movement behind the sheer dining-room draperies. They parted and she saw a slender, fair-haired figure peering out. By the time she collected her small weekend bag and made it up the stairs, her mother had the front door open.

"I was beginning to think you were going to let me down," Lorraine Loring said, offering her cheek.

At fifty-four the petite woman in violet silk remained striking, if slightly brittle around the edges. They shared the same multitoned blond hair; however, her mother's was now more silver than blonde. "Ash, darling," her mother insisted to anyone brave enough to mention it. To add to the more youthful look she kept it permed and sprayed in the same sexily sophisticated style Grace Kelly had worn in *High Society*. God forbid that the world should forget how she and the late actress-turned-princess had shared more than a faint resemblance. But regardless of how stubbornly she kept that one style, time was making itself known, allied by gravity, which pulled at the sparse flesh covering her slender bones. Since her mother's idea of exercise extended only as far as rubbing assorted creams into her skin, gravity was winning. Not too fast, but winning nonetheless.

Nicole mechanically provided the obligatory kiss, and tried not to dwell on the sad truth that she felt nothing from the act. "I told you my schedule and that I would be late."

"You could have called to reassure me."

Her mother liked reassurances—and rarely gave any in return. "Check your machine. I had two delightful conversations with it."

Her mother glanced over her shoulder as if just realizing they had an answering machine. "We couldn't put off dinner with the Martinsons any longer, and it went on and on," she said, dragging the n's and rolling her eyes. "But how can you tell the dean of your school that you're bored numb and want to go home? Well, come in before every moth in east Texas gets inside. I swear they see my drapes and salivate."

Maybe the out-of-towners, Nicole thought dryly, but she doubted the rest were that hard up. Her mother's heavy-handed use of potpourri and scented sprays— her attempt to cover the effects of her smoking— would suffocate anything with lungs smaller than a blimp. Nicole knew that she would be reaching for an allergy pill before long herself.

"Was the food good?" she asked, politely. "Where did you go?"

"*Their* country club. Do you think Buddy Martinson is going to miss an opportunity to show off? I ordered the cheapest thing on the menu to make my point, not that it did me any good. Buddy insisted we all have the endive salad to start. It was fabulous. I really have to find out their recipe for that dressing."

"So it wasn't a totally unpleasant evening?"

"What can I tell you, your father loathes talking school business after hours, and restaurant food always gives him indigestion. And how can you enjoy yourself when all you see is question marks in your hosts' eyes? Thank goodness they have just enough breeding not to have brought up Jay."

Nicole understood. It was shades of the same for her at work, but in her case, she knew it was because her internal emotional battle was taking a toll on her and people were noticing. Her parents were like those robotic beings in *The Stepford Wives*.

Good grief, you're starting to reason like Carlyn.

"I take it Father is already in bed?" She tried not to sound too hopeful about that.

"Where else? He took his usual dose of pink poison and I can already hear him snoring like a bull elephant with sinusitis. Of course, in the morning he'll tell me that he didn't sleep a wink, while I'll be the one with four pieces of luggage under each eye." Her mother headed for the dining room. "I was about to have an aperitif to numb my nerves. I'll pour you one."

Just the thought of whatever syrupy concoction her mother was into this month made Nicole shudder. Unlike her, she disliked sweet drinks and her mother knew that. "A last cup of coffee sounds better." She set her things on the bench seat at the foot of the stairway. "I'll make it."

"Caffeine at this hour? You'll be pacing all night like a zombie."

"No, I'll be working."

"On what?"

"The reason I'm here, Mother. To sort through Jay's things. You did say you wanted to get them boxed and out of here."

"But you can't do that after driving all the way from Dallas. I know for a fact that whenever I get back from shopping there, I'm useless for two days afterward."

Shopping, Nicole thought sardonically. She should try working. "I appreciate the concern, but I'm fine."

"Absolutely not. I won't hear of it."

"Excuse me, but I think I'm a little old for you to dictate to."

Her mother stared at her as though discovering a new species of weed in her yard. "Why are you being difficult?"

"I don't see that I am," Nicole replied, with the unflappable professional tone she used on difficult clientele. "You asked me to drink with you, I declined. Now you're getting upset. If there's something going on that you haven't told me about—"

"Don't put this on me, you're the one with the attitude. I sensed it the moment you came in." Clucking her tongue, her mother refilled her delicate stemmed glass, already half empty. "Do what you want then, you will anyway. You're just like your father, all aggression and stubborn will. I don't know why neither of my children inherited something from me. You two might as well have been adopted."

Amazing, Nicole thought as she stared at her slender

back. No matter what, the woman managed to turn herself into a victim of some kind. "Mother, Jay's death has all of us stressed out, but I'm only trying to get done what you yourself wanted, and I'll need time to sort through everything in order to decide what I want to take with me, let alone box the rest for you. You needn't worry that I'll disturb you."

"That much you're right about, but only because I took care of things myself this afternoon."

"You what?"

"I hired a boy." Her mother nodded beyond the bar. "It's all out in the garage."

Nicole didn't know what to say. The idea seemed a violation to her. "How could you let a stranger go through his things?"

"He's not a stranger, he sacks my groceries. And all he did was open drawers and shove things into boxes. Besides, I had to do something after your father's latest explosion. I meant to spare you this, but if you must know, on Monday he phoned and caught me tearing up while I was vacuuming in there. The dust in that room...I have no idea where it comes from. If I don't thoroughly clean the place every week—"

"What did he say, Mother?"

"He bellowed. You know what that means. He bellowed, 'That's it. Get that pervert's crap out of this house or I'll do it myself! I'm sick and tired of closed doors. This is *my* house. I paid for everything in it including that goddamned door and I want it open!'"

Nicole sighed silently. There was the real problem. Her father had never allowed them to close their bedroom doors when she and her brother were growing up. It hadn't been so bad when they were young, except when they'd had to listen to their father's tirades at their mother; but as they'd entered their teens, privacy had become more important. However, whenever they'd asked for permission, they'd gotten another earful: accusations that they had something to hide, of being "dopers and deadbeats." "You think I'm going to kill myself working for a bunch of parasites?" he would demand. As a result, until the day she moved out, she was forced to either dress in her closet or in the bathroom, where a closed door was allowed, but the lock dare not be turned.

"Why am I not surprised?" she murmured now. Needing a moment to absorb this news, she retreated to the kitchen and decided to make tea instead of coffee. Hot tea always soothed her.

Shades of bronze, copper and yellow spawned an inviting aura as she circled the center island. It always amazed her that her mother could create such inviting environments, while what went on inside them was complicated, dark and depressing.

Relieved that at least the saucepans remained where she remembered, she took out one and quickly filled it with a cup of water from the bottled offerings in the refrigerator to avoid the horrible tasting tap water. As she set the electric range, her mother came in, her liqueur glass in one hand, the inevitable cigarette in the other.

"Everything is labeled," she said to Nicole, as though suddenly recalling good news. "It's not as though you'll have to unpack and start over."

"Fine."

"You're angry."

"As the man said, this is his house. You have to toe the line."

"Don't be snide."

Nicole raised her hands upward. "What should I say? Give me my lines, Mother, and I'll repeat them back to you. That's how much I want to avoid any more ugliness."

"I don't need you patronizing me. Since you're determined to have this attitude—"

"Attitude? My brother was murdered! I'm an aunt, but I don't know where my nephew is, or if he's even alive—"

"Not that again." The fine lines around her mother's mouth deepened as she pressed her lips together. "I'm going to bed."

Her mother slung back the crème de menthe left in her glass like a pro, and stubbornly went through the motions of rinsing out the glass and drying it. Then she carried it into the dining room.

Nicole listened until she heard the master bedroom's bathroom door shut. Sighing, she turned off the stove heat. She no longer wanted the tea, either. She wasn't even sure she had the energy left to get through the evening.

At least there was a good bet that her father wouldn't appear to turn this into a true melee. Except for his stiff performance at Jay's apartment and the funeral, he'd let it be known that he wanted to avoid her as much as she wanted to avoid him.

"Welcome home, Nicole." Shaking her head, she went to switch on the garage light.

Roman stood in the doorway and stared in disbelief at the empty bed. No, he thought, his heart slamming against his chest. No! He'd gotten the room number wrong, that's all. It had to be!

"Excuse me, but you shouldn't be here."

He looked down at the hand on his arm and then at the face staring up at his with confusion and disapproval. "She's...gone?" was all he finally managed to get out.

The nurse glanced into the room and realization lit in her eyes. "You mean Megan? No, her doctor okayed her to leave earlier than they'd originally planned for their trip. She and her mother and father have gone to Disneyland."

"I'm her father."

To her credit, the nurse recovered well despite a deep blush. "Excuse me. I meant her stepfather. Is there something I can do for you? Would you like to come back to the nurse's station and I'll get you a cup of coffee, while I check their itinerary? I'm sure we have a number where they can be reached."

"How long since they left?" Maybe he could catch a taxi to the International Airport in time. It was way across town and traffic remained congested despite the hour, but with luck—

"Oh, I'm sure they're in California by now. They left right after noon."

It was almost midnight now. He'd been so pleased to be able to catch the last flight down once he found out the shrink Ralph had recommended couldn't see him until next week. He'd planned to spend the night in Meggie's room watching her sleep and then returning to Dallas once she boarded her own flight in the morning. It had cost him, too. He'd used his badge at Dallas Love Field, letting the ticket agent at the Southwest Airlines counter believe he was on emergency police business. Now he had to wait at least another six hours before he could catch a flight home. And for what? To scare himself half to death and then depress himself for the rest of the weekend?

He looked at the Disney stuffed toy he'd found at the airport gift shop, and the balloons. Feeling a fool, he handed them to the nurse. "Find someone who might want this."

"That's very kind of you, but why don't I share the balloons and save the dog for when Megan gets back?"

By then she'd have seen the real Pluto, would be inundated with her own souvenirs that her mother and Dr. Wonderful no doubt would buy for her. The unappealing picture had him shoving his fists into his pockets. "Do whatever you think best."

Without saying goodbye, he walked away. He had to get out of there. Frustrated and sick at heart, he was afraid he would end up sitting down on the floor and crying like a big baby, or else breaking every window in the place; the level of violence and self-pity was competing that strongly for control of him.

Could his life get any more dismal?

Nicole worked until four in the morning. Then she lay down on the sofa in the sunroom until she heard her father leaving for his golf game just after six o'clock.

Once safely alone again, she headed to the kitchen to make the coffee she'd denied herself last night, and found her mother popping aspirin into her mouth and washing them down with tomato juice. At least she assumed it was plain juice. Seeing her own behavior reflected back at her made her wonder—and wince.

"I swear I have bought that man every contraption invented," her mother muttered between sips, "and he still snores enough to wake the dead back in Richmond."

Not for anything would Lorraine Loring let it be forgotten that her people were true Southerners. Like a dowry brought to a marriage, Nicole could recall she most often raised the issue when she needed to silence her multi-degreed and pompous husband, whose own family tree was as vague as print from carbon paper.

"I doubt I was able to get ten minutes of rest last night," she continued. "I'm so tired my head feels as though it could roll off my shoulders."

"Have you eaten anything aside from dinner last night?" Nicole asked.

"I do not have a hangover."

Knowing better than to offer any advice, Nicole put on water to boil and retraced her steps to the bathroom by the utility room where she'd left her purse before lying down. She dug out her toothbrush and toothpaste and proceeded to brush. A minute later her mother's reflection joined hers in the mirror, a refilled glass of juice between them.

"I'm prepared to discuss whatever's bothering you now."

Removing the toothbrush from her mouth, Nicole replied, "No, you're not." She rinsed and met the bloodshot, naked eyes in the mirror, not so different from her own. "You want to address. Discussing anything scares you to death."

The tendons along her mother's neck stretched and flexed as she raised her head, trying to match Nicole's height. "You think I don't know what contempt you feel for your father and me? You don't approve of us. You think you're better than everyone."

Nicole quickly brushed her hair back into a ponytail. "Actually, I think I'm a neurotic mess, a person who is better at her work than in living. But at least I'm honest enough to admit when I've tied one on."

Her mother arched her neck even more, her manicured fingers tracing both actual lines and suspected ones. "I have allergies, that's all. I've asked the girls at my salon and they agree with me."

"In that case—" Nicole plucked the cigarette out of her mother's free hand, dropped it into the commode, flushed, and turned on the overhead fan "—smoking aggravates the condition, and if you don't care about that, how about a little consideration for what your secondhand poison is doing to my throat and lungs?"

"Oh, you, you, you! When did you become so selfish, Nicole?"

The scene was almost laughable, except that it reminded her too much of planes spiraling out of control toward earth. Zipping her cosmetic bag, she wiped the hair from the sink and counter.

Why she had believed this trip could be achieved in a civil, even compassionate manner, she didn't know. Unable to think of any reason to continue trying, she collected her bag and sidestepped past her mother. "I don't know that I am. But I do know how to save you from having to endure any more."

Accepting that she would have to get her coffee elsewhere, she dug her keys out of her purse and grabbed up her overnight bag.

Her mother followed like an aggravated terrier. "What do you think you're doing now?"

"Leaving. I have what I want in the car."

"For heaven's sake. Just because things don't go your way is no reason to run."

"Mother, please note, I am walking out. And the reason is that I prefer not to be your source of morning mental calisthenics."

Her mother followed her out to the garage and to her car. "You're going to upset your father. You didn't even say hello to him."

That was almost amusing. "He'll be so relieved, he'll probably offer to take you out to dinner again."

"At least do something with your hair and that face. You can't drive all the way to Dallas without makeup."

Ordinarily she wouldn't think of it. Like it or not, she was Texas born and bred, and that meant putting as much care into her appearance as she put pride in her career accomplishments. But she had the chords of revolution vibrating inside her, and if that meant risking being seen without at least two coats of mascara and the rest of the war paint she kept close, so be it.

Meeting her mother's arched gaze, she slapped on her sunglasses. "I'll call you if I find out anything about your grandson."

Her mouth set, her mother walked away, retracing her steps into the garage. Without a look back, she punched the garage door button, and disappeared inside.

Before the door lowered completely, Nicole had her car backed out of the driveway. Oddly enough, while the censure, the absolute rejection, should have hurt, instead of the slow internal bleeding she'd experienced so many times before there came the oddest sense of relief.

"Son of a gun," she murmured, as she left the old neighborhood in her rearview mirror. "Well...okay."

14

*Friendships begin with liking or gratitude—
roots that can be pulled up.*

—George Eliot,
Daniel Deronda

Roman was coming back down the stairs of her apartment when Nicole pulled into the driveway and parked beside his truck. His watch told him it was barely past nine-thirty, and her expression through the windshield said, "This had better be good."

Slowing his pace, he made it to the car just as she climbed out. He shoved his hands deeper into his pockets, a bit shaken to realize how glad he was that she'd shown up. "More bad timing, huh?"

"Is something wrong?"

"Just thought I'd stop by."

Despite her sunglasses, he could feel her gaze moving over his face and knew she was taking in the night's growth of whiskers, hand-mussed hair and rumpled suit. No doubt about it, he looked like a bum, and he didn't blame her for her wariness.

"Were you on a case all night?"

He considered letting her believe that, then shook

his head. "In Houston. My flight got in only about an hour ago."

"Megan...?" she whispered.

"She's all right. They took her to Disneyland. I'd gone down to see her off, but they left earlier than originally planned."

"Oh, no."

"It doesn't matter." He was lying through his teeth, but her sympathy was too sweet and made him want much more. Too much. "What about you? You're up and at 'em early."

"I've been to Tyler. My parents' house. An equally abbreviated trip."

He could see that maybe she'd left in considerable haste. Although the squeaky clean look made her appear more approachable and younger, she also seemed emotionally whipped. He would bet anything that behind those tinted lenses her eyes were red, and not merely from a lack of sleep.

Could she possibly be dreading having to retreat to her barren apartment as much as he was his?

"Want to go have breakfast, brunch or whatever and talk about it?" he asked.

Her lips parted and her movements were jerky as she gestured to her designer jeans and black, belted tunic top. "Really, I'm grimy from working and...I couldn't, no. But thank you."

"Sure." A part of him had expected her to decline; nevertheless, he felt the rejection in a place that didn't need the added blow. "Guess I'd better go then." He took a step backwards. "Just wanted to check in and make sure everything was okay here since we didn't get to touch bases yesterday.''

She glanced back at the garage apartment, then the house. "Thank you. That was very—"

"Forget it." He didn't want polite but rudimentary words, either.

His hand was on the truck's handle when she said, "I could make something."

He paused. "You don't have to."

"I'll have to check what's in the refrigerator, but I'm fairly certain there's enough to make something brunchy."

She was obviously as surprised at extending the invitation as he was in hearing it. "Are you sure that's what you want? To deal with pots, pans..." *Me.*

"We'll find out. At any rate, I'm too keyed up to rest yet, and I am rather sick of my own company. Would you mind me tacking on a fee, though?" She nodded at her car. "I could use help carrying those boxes upstairs."

Short of getting rid of a corpse, she could have asked for anything. "It's a deal."

He waited for her to get her small suitcase and purse, then collected one of the boxes before following her up into the dark apartment. While she lowered the thermostat, he set his armload beside the last of the boxes in the middle of the room and shrugged out of his suit jacket, deciding no machine could work faster than his sweat glands.

As he was hanging the jacket on a dinette chair, he caught her sidelong glance, and despite the sunglasses guessed what she was looking at. He eased off his shoulder harness and placed it and his gun on the same seat. "Better?"

"Sorry. It's the reminder, that's all."

"I understand."

She moistened her lips. "Will you want coffee or…?"

"Coffee would be terrific."

During his next several trips to the car, she achieved her own impressive progress. By the time he was stacking the last box she had the place smelling like a popular restaurant in the middle of its busiest hours.

He wandered into the kitchen and sniffed at the aromatic steam rising from the wok. "Look out…onions and peppers."

"You don't like Mexican food?" She froze, spatula hovering over the wok. "I would have sworn it was the safest bet."

Safe in more ways than one, he thought, eyeing the number of onions in the pan. Did she think he needed reminding that all she was offering him was a meal? "I would say that you're cooking for a human garbage disposal, but having witnessed my partner in action several times now, I'll merely claim to be the guy most likely to use the heck out of silverware."

It was the right thing to say. She even managed a brief smile that eased the tension around her mouth. "You won't need much. I'm making fajitas. How's the new job going?"

He edited himself because he didn't want to ruin the moment. "Interesting. Different. Demanding."

"I imagine. But it sounds as though you like your partner."

"Yeah, Tucker's a mess. Ralph Tucker, married, six sons."

"Oh, my."

He liked her soft laugh. "Listen, before I offer to help, mind if I wash up?"

"Of course. I think I left the bathroom decent."

And she had, which was a pity. He wouldn't have minded feeding his fantasies by eyeing a piece of her sexy lingerie draped somewhere.

Once he'd washed several hours of dust and grime down the glistening sink, he returned to the kitchen. Nicole had moved on to sautéing strips of lean beef.

"What can I do?" he asked, rubbing his hands.

"Plates and silverware." She told him where he could find everything. "And the coffee's ready. Help yourself."

By the time he had the yellow crockery set on the green place mats, the silverware on cheery sunflower napkins and coffee poured into canary yellow mugs, she was mixing the vegetables into the beef and warming the tortillas.

"I'm sorry I didn't have enough fresh vegetables for a salad, but that's usually what I run out of first."

"You're joking, right? This is great."

When she turned off the heat, he carried the wok to the table. She followed with the tortillas, and for the next several minutes conversation was limited to descriptive sounds and sentence fragments, as each took a steaming tortilla and filled it.

"Mmm..."

"Good."

"Coffee, too."

"Fresh ground helps."

By the time he was reaching for a second helping, Nicole was sitting back in her chair and watching with a bemused smile on her face. He didn't stop what he was doing, his stomach wouldn't let him, but he did raise his eyebrows in query.

"I'm surprised, that's all."

"At how fast I'm wolfing down your food? You shouldn't be, you're a great cook."

"No, at how glad I am that you were here when I pulled in."

He could see that. Now that she'd removed the glasses, it was easier to read the remnants of hurt and grief and bone-deep fatigue in her eyes. But there was warmth returning there, too; also, the tension had eased around her mouth, and she wasn't quite as pale as before. "Look out, Loring, you might swell my head."

She didn't reply, but there was a hint of a smile around her lips as she sipped her coffee.

"I don't mean to ruin the pleasant ambience," he continued, "but did you tell your parents that I was going to try to help you?"

"They don't want to know. My family is...we're like a foundation with so many cracks, I think it's time to accept that a This Property Is Condemned sign is in order."

"Are you sure? Sometimes the shock of an unexpected death can turn families around, bring them closer."

"When I arrived at the house, my mother was drinking. When I left this morning, I'm fairly certain she'd picked up where she'd left off. I don't know what shape my father was in. He'd arranged for the earliest tee-off at the golf course, and the truth is I was relieved.''

Roman nodded as he chewed, and took his time swallowing. ''My father was a sloppy drinker and a bully. How my mother stood him for the ten years she did, I don't know. The last day of his life, he split my lip for being late for dinner. It didn't matter that I had a paper route and it was pouring buckets. If he hadn't gotten killed later that night in the same storm, I'm pretty sure I'd have killed the son of a bitch myself, eventually. That's just so you'll understand that I know what it's like to despise your own flesh and blood and to be ashamed of having been put in that position in the first place.''

With a faint sigh, Nicole set down her mug. ''What a pair we are.''

He knew she was insinuating that he'd proved her point why any attraction between them had to be repressed, and he agreed that the odds were against them. However, that didn't make the cravings any less intense. ''The good news is that my mother married our neighbor, who was a widower. Fred was a cop, and he enjoyed a brew occasionally, but he showed us all how you could control it and not let it own you.''

''He's the reason you joined the police force.''

''He was the best.''

'' 'Was?' ''

''He died in his sleep almost two years ago. My mother sold the house and moved to Arizona to live with my sister. They're closer than I am to either of them.''

Nicole's gaze moved over his face. "You haven't quite forgiven her for staying with your father as long as she did, and for forcing you to endure all you did."

"Forgive, yes. Forget, no." He pointed with his fork to her plate. "You should try to eat a few more bites. You were doing better a few minutes ago."

She ignored that. "May I ask you a personal question?"

"I thought that's what this was all about."

"Why didn't your ex-wife tell you that they would be leaving earlier?"

He abandoned his plate for a moment and, leaning his forearms on the table, met her curious gaze. "I told you before. As far as she's concerned, she married the wrong guy the first time around, and because I'm the only one she's ever confessed that to, I'm now the enemy."

"That's ridiculous. And yet…I understand what you mean."

"Good. Then it's your turn. Why did you go to Tyler if there's so much tension between you and your parents?"

She told him about their decision to clear all reminders of her brother from the house. "I knew if I wanted to be able to have something to pass down to his son, to show him pictures, yearbooks, Jay's sports awards…I didn't have a choice."

Roman was concerned that she remained so sure about the baby, but he admired her intent. "They don't know about the girl your brother was involved with?"

"Know about it, don't believe it, and they've made

it clear that if it is true, a bronze-skinned grandchild isn't anything they'll want publicized.''

"Have you given much idea to how you'll cope if you do get him?''

"It's safer not to.'' She lifted one shoulder. "I keep from having an anxiety attack by telling myself that I'll be able to face that when it happens. In reality I'm not even sure I'll be living here. A baby isn't what Goldie agreed to when she invited me to take this place.''

She told him about her landlady who was on one of her lengthy vacations: how the childless widow had used Van Dorn's to sell things from her husband's estate and how she had become a regular at their sales because art took the place of family to her.

"Moving here meant breaking my lease,'' she concluded, "and there are days when taking care of Goldie's house can be a handful. But that also helped me keep sane.'' She nodded to the living room. "Unfortunately, my apartment suffered more damage than I'd first guessed—in case you're wondering at my lack of furnishings.''

"I admit I was,'' Roman replied. "Even though I knew about the fire, I thought this place was a bit spartan for a woman heavily into art and antiques.''

"Max said I was due a minimalist phase.''

About to quiz her about that and her relationship with Van Dorn, the ringing phone stopped him. When Nicole ignored it, he said, "It might be important.''

"It isn't.''

Something about the way she suddenly lowered her

lashes to hide her eyes from him had him rising and crossing to the bar. Not only was the recording playing out, but the message light was blinking.

"You haven't listened to your messages, either, have you?"

"I doubt there are any," she replied quietly without turning around.

At the beep, there was silence...and finally the sound of someone hanging up. Getting an odd feeling about the call, Roman pushed the message button. There were three other calls since she'd been to Tyler. They all were like that.

"When were you going to get around to telling me about this?" he asked.

"It's probably just some kid messing around. As I was moving in, Goldie warned me that she caught the teenage boy next door watching me with binoculars."

"Uh-huh. Are we talking thirteen or nineteen?"

"I didn't ask."

"And why don't you have caller ID?"

"Because I've never needed it." Squaring her shoulders somewhat, she rose and carried her not quite empty plate to the sink, scraped the remaining food down the drain, and hit the garbage disposal switch.

Roman was glad to have to wait until she shut off the motor; he needed the time to check his temper. "Okay," he drawled once it was quiet again. "Let me ask you this. Will you lend me a couple of your pillows?"

"You are not going to sleep on my couch."

"And first thing Monday, you're going to order caller ID."

She set down the plate hard enough for it to crack. "Do not do that. My father always ignored me as though I was invisible, or worse yet as dumb as a cow."

"I'm not your father, and I am staying. If it's the kid next door doing this—and I can see you don't believe it is—then I'll talk to him. But if it's Willard or someone else, I don't want you tucked away back here all by yourself."

"So I'll get a gun."

"And end up shooting me. I don't think so."

She wrapped her arms around her waist. "A cop wouldn't use his own phone, McKenna."

"I'm not suggesting he would. Maybe I'll find a pattern in the way he uses pay phones. Maybe it's not even Willard. The point is we don't know *anything* yet because you kept it a secret." He took a deep breath to calm down. It didn't work very well, and for one good reason. "Ah, hell. I should have known."

"Known what?"

Roman shot her an apologetic look. "Willard caught me reading your brother's report."

Nicole slumped against the counter.

"I know, I know, I should have told you, but I thought I'd explained things away enough to—" The look on her face filled him with shame. "You're right, I'm full of it. What I don't understand is if he has something to say, why doesn't he approach you directly instead of leaving this potential trail."

"Because it's more fun to drive me slowly out of my mind." Muttering an epithet, Nicole strode to the refrigerator and drew out an open bottle of wine. She had a glass half full when she stopped, set down the bottle and covered her face with her hands. "God. I'm turning into my mother."

Roman gave up trying to keep his distance. Stopping directly behind her, he began gently massaging her shoulders. "No, you're not. You recognize the impulses. You stopped." There was little difference between her muscles and her slender bones, she was that tight. Sensing she was also seconds away from crying and would hate herself for that, too, he decided to redirect her agitation.

"Come here."

Before she could figure out what he was up to, he had her facing him and captured her mouth with his. It required being careful—his beard would be brutal on her sensitive skin—but he wanted to be careful with her, just as he wanted something fiercer. Just as he wanted to drag her to DFW and buy two tickets to some tropical beach, where they could do this and more in the surf until the sun rose again.

"Damn you, McKenna," she whispered when he finally let her catch her breath.

"I think you're too late." He stroked her high cheekbones with his thumbs and pictured her arching under him, those lashes lifting and their gazes joining as he buried himself deep, and then deeper inside her. Beautiful woman. Brave woman. How could she think he wouldn't attempt anything necessary to help her, regardless of how it left him feeling? "Better now?"

"No, but let me go and I promise to put back the wine."

"Good. I don't want any lethal weapons in your hand while I tell you the other news."

She stiffened. "I don't think I like being handled by you any more than I care for Willard's tactics."

He supposed he deserved that, but as he released her and put some space between them, there was no denying the stabbing sensation under his ribs. "Then I'll try to be quick. I've found someone, a psychiatrist at Baylor, to talk to about AEA."

"But I told you, Jay didn't—"

"Can you prove it? No. Could you look at the police photos and point out possible irregularities, maybe outright errors that would justify reopening his file?"

She turned her head away toward the windows, only the blinds were shut. It didn't seem to matter to her, though; her gaze was turned inward. "How did you find this person? Can he—is it a man? Can he," she continued when he inclined his head, "be trusted?"

"Tucker says yes." He raised his hand to silence her before she could start at him again. "He's my partner, Nick. We put our lives in each other's hands. Hell, I had to be straight with him."

She continued facing the windows, but the fight visibly drained out of her. "When do you meet?"

"Monday, right after my shift."

"But that's two days from now!"

"The time will go fast enough," he replied, not believing it for a second.

"And then what? You'll be ready for a pop quiz on sick sexual games? It's close to a month since Jay's baby was taken. Any lead has to be colder than death at this point, and wasting time talking to someone Jay didn't know, about a lie someone else fabricated, only adds to the confusion."

"Or I may learn something valuable we haven't considered. Damn it, Nick, at this point, we don't even know the sex of the person we're supposed to be looking for. Have you thought about that? The probabilities change. If it was a guy in that room, it's not likely that he would still have the baby. But could a woman kill while a child was in the room? If so, why? Who was she? Should I start looking for the baby's mother? Hell, that badge in my jacket pocket says I should even be suspecting you!"

For a split second Roman expected Nicole to slap him. He would have stood there and taken it if only out of guilt for saying all he had, especially that last part, since regardless of what the books said, he had only to use his eyes to know better than to include her in any possible list of suspects.

"My God," she whispered. "Is there nothing you people won't do or say?"

"Think what you want, that's the way it's done," he replied grimly. "It's rarely, 'There's a body. There's the murderer. 'Night everybody, see you in the morning.' My gut says to talk to someone about the death scene, so that's what I'm going to do. Until then,

I'm going to go through those boxes with you. Come Monday, I want to go into that shrink's office knowing Jay almost as well as you did. Are you going to help? Not me, but your brother and his child?''

Her eyes filled, but she retained her composure. "All right. But there's just one thing," she said, her voice flat. "You don't touch me again. I've already been fucked by the police. It's not going to happen twice.''

15

...And take upon 's the mystery of things,
As if we were God's spies...

—William Shakespeare,
King Lear

Once Dr. Stanley Bender knew what Roman wanted, he refused to continue their discussion in his office. Pushing up the already rolled sleeves of the plaid shirt stretching across his jelly roll middle, he suggested dinner someplace private.

"You like pizza? We can go to my apartment and order in. I'm a regular with this local place, and the delivery service is excellent. That way we won't have to worry about being disturbed."

Roman wondered if he'd missed something. Had Tucker set him up to teach him a lesson?

"If you want pizza, I think there's a decent place a few blocks from here." After a bitch of a day, and an equally grim weekend, he didn't need some guy making a pass at him.

"We need Internet access. That'll be the fastest way to grasp what you want to know. Wouldn't suggest that for everyone. It'll be pretty raw stuff even for a homicide cop. But you seem like someone who has his feet planted fairly well in reality. You should be able to handle it.''

The guy talked fast for someone whose job it was to listen to other people and thoughtfully analyze what they said; and along with giving silent thanks for having been mistaken about the guy's sexual persuasion, Roman hoped the doctor hadn't been wrong about him.

Stanley Bender's apartment was barely three miles away, in the back half of the second floor of a building that looked like two berry boxes fastened together by aluminum gutters. On the edge of a ritzier neighborhood, the landlord must have recognized he was sitting on a gold mine, and that improvements were a waste when a juicy offer for the land would eventually be forthcoming. Stan's rooms seemed to reflect his awareness of that—or of a life devoted to his work. His apartment was nothing more than a storage locker for years of data; the D.A's offices didn't look more cramped. The wall space that wasn't covered with steel file cabinets and cardboard boxes was filled with bookshelves of every size and style. Clearly Bender was as much a bookworm as a pack rat, and added shelves rather than yield one bit of precious information to the Dumpster out back.

There were three desks set in a large U in the middle of what should have been the living room. The damned thing looked like a mission control of the mind, Roman mused drolly. ''You're serious about your work,'' he said, watching as the psychiatrist ran his finger down the memory list on his phone and punched in two digits.

"Lots of people needing help out there." Stan paused and then said into the mouthpiece, "Yeah, this is Stan. Howie? Hey, how about two of the usual as fast as you can? You're the best, man." He hung up and motioned Roman to pull up a second office chair to the computer and detoured to the kitchen. "I hope you like veggie pizzas. I don't eat meat, but they put those exotic mushrooms on them, so I guarantee you'll think you're dining on filet mignon."

Fungus and grass pizza. Resigning himself to another stop at a burger biggy joint on the way home, Roman said politely, "Sounds interesting."

"Ah, I hear a skeptic. That's okay. I love making converts. White or red?"

"Excuse me?"

"Didn't Ralph tell you? I'm an amateur winemaker."

Tucker had failed to mention that. And now, not only was he going to be fed yard refuse, but he was about to have to wash it all down with communion grape juice. "I guess he forgot to pass that on."

"I'm working on a modest table red that I'd really like your opinion on, but I have a cheerful white if you'd prefer."

"The red is fine, though I should warn you, I'm no expert."

The eager-to-please man was back quickly, his thick glasses reflecting the computer and fluorescent lamps and obliterating his eyes as much as illuminating his wide grin. It struck Roman that he was enjoying this. Apparently, Stan's private life didn't include a wife or girlfriend—at least not the live-in kind—and hadn't for a while if one judged his somewhat oily, too well-fed body against what he knew of Dallas women's tastes. But at the same time there was an energy in his eyes that spoke of intelligence and relentless curiosity.

The goblet he passed to Roman was finely carved crystal. The liquid inside was bloodred, bright. He tasted it and found himself surprised.

"I'm impressed."

"Not too bitter?"

"As I said, I'm no connoisseur, but I taste a nice...am I crazy or is it nuts?"

Stanley beamed. "Pecans—we are in Texas. But don't get me started on my secret passion or we won't get anything else done tonight." He took a sip himself and gestured to the computer. "How deep do you want to go? Pick up from where you left off at my office."

Roman liked the way the guy moved so easily from small talk to being a professional. "This is off the record, okay?"

"Talk to Ralph. I'm the original soul of discretion. Or to be more accurate, I'm an invisible man, if you can believe it," he added, arms akimbo. "People tend to forget me as quickly as they leave the hospital."

"Somehow I doubt that." He nodded to the rest of the apartment. "You live alone? No wife or kids to worry about overhearing anything?"

Although he confirmed that with a nod, there was a shadow of regret in Stan's smile. "Guess you could say that I do better straightening out other people's lives than my own."

"The loneliness doesn't get to you? I don't mean to

sound nosy, but I'd feel better knowing who I'm talking to."

"Sure. I have my black holes. At nine I was wrapped from neck to ankle in plaster—don't ask or you will be here all night," he added with a half groan, half laugh. "But what happened also inspired me in a way."

Roman nodded, but also felt sorry for the guy. "How did you come to know Ralph?"

"Oh, Ralphie and I grew up together. He was a neighbor when my grandparents resettled us in the Oak Cliff area. I liked him because he never made fun of me even though it was obvious I was what the kids today call a geek. So what's your problem, Mac? You don't mind me calling you Mac?"

"That'll work." Roman knew there was no easy way to break into the subject and decided to just dive in. "A friend lost a member of her family about a month ago under pretty disturbing circumstances."

"You identified it as AEA. You're sure?"

"That's how it appears on what I've read on our computers. Autoerotic asphyxia, right? We barely addressed it during training."

"Names." Stan shrugged, unimpressed. "You know what I've heard the military boys call it? 'Death by misadventure.' The government never ceases to amaze me with their skill at using euphemisms. The services, particularly the air force, do have the greatest number of occurrences, though, what with all those young, strapping adventurous boys. What we're talking about is death occurring via masturbation, but unusual masturbation in that it involves various components." Stan gave him an owlish stare. "Am I getting warm to what your reports described?"

"You are if what we're talking about includes a scenario with plastic bags."

"That's one variation."

"Then I should add that the family is having problems with the official conclusions."

"Careful words. And complete bullshit." Stanley's reply was as gentle as his smile was mocking. "I appreciate your respect and caution, but—correct me if I'm wrong—what you really want is to shut up the family, am I right? You guys don't want to deal with a slander suit. At the same time, this isn't the kind of thing that's easily understood by the public at large, and you need to keep it quiet."

"Actually, the family chose to call it a suicide. Hanging."

"Of course, because next to pedophilia, I would say AEA is the most disturbing kind of sexual behavior for your average John or Jane Doe to grasp."

"Okay, but two things," Roman said. "First, you're drawing the wrong conclusions about my part in this. I came to this situation after the fact, and regardless of the badge, I am here on behalf of the family."

Stan raised curling eyebrows. "Interesting. Well, angels of mercy come in all sorts of manifestations. Who are you soft on, the mother, sister or aunt?"

"You're being a smart-ass, Doc."

"Placate me. I work sixteen hour days, and when I get home, the most I have to look forward to is a few pieces of moronic E-mail."

"It's the sister."

"Uh-huh. And she can't handle the idea that her golden-haired, blue-eyed brother could be accused of doing anything so outrageous."

"How did you know what he looked like?"

"It's the profile—although by no means exact. Participants cross all cultures and socioeconomic levels, but they tend to be in their early to mid-twenties, and if it's any comfort, rarely gay."

"I don't know that she cares about that at this point."

"He didn't add insult to injury by dying in her house, did he?"

"His apartment. She was the one visiting."

"Odd. Usually, this is a behavior that's carefully hidden. Apartments aren't known for having soundproof walls."

"That's one of the things that leads me to agree with her conclusions. She heard it happening, only at the time, she didn't know what she was hearing. She'd worked late and assumed he had...company."

"And received a nasty surprise in the morning, eh? You might want to give her my number if you sense down the road that she's not progressing through the stages of grief very well. Tell me, was she tempted to 'sanitize the scene' as you guys put it? That's common with family, removing the bindings, the bag from over the head—"

"Listen, why the bag over the genitals?"

"Did he do that? Interesting. Could be the added sensation. We are talking about someone with an extremely healthy sexual appetite. He's craving the ultimate erotic experience. This is a form of solo S and

M if you will. Pain blending with pain. But my edu-cated guess is housekeeping. Maybe he knew he was pressed for time, and didn't want a large clean up job afterward. It's crucial to remember that these people always plan to survive this." Warming to his subject, Stan leaned forward in his seat. "Would you like to know some of the history behind the practice?"

"I guess I'd better."

Stan swung his chair toward the monitor and began typing. "For written authentication, we have to go back at least as far as the Marquis de Sade, and there are also reports that in the Eskimo culture strangulation was long part of their sexual experience."

"Maybe that explains why I've never been tempted to move to a colder climate."

Stanley chuckled, but continued to type as fast as a court stenographer. "There was a particularly interest-ing prison story I remember. Old England, mind you, not this modern day post-Kennedy-Judge Sarah Hughes-every-inmate-gets-a-TV pandering. This jailer discovered that during hangings men experienced or-gasm soon after their breathing was compromised. In-trigued, this guy tried it himself—with the help of a female inmate to assure his safety, of course." He shot Roman a sidelong look. "He must have enjoyed it con-siderably because he supposedly experimented a num-ber of times before something went wrong."

"Fatally wrong?"

"Oh, yeah. And that's frequently how the younger ones die these days. Something goes wrong because they've underestimated what they're doing. And it's such a private, solitary practice, there's no help to bail 'em out.''

Roman thought of what he'd read in the police report. "This guy didn't try to hang himself, though. He was found prone in bed."

Sighing, Stan leaned back in his chair. "Stop me if I'm going too deep into the science of asphyxia, but you actually have four options. Neck compression, oxygen exclusion, the obstruction of the airway and compression of the chest. Follow me so far?" When Roman nodded, he continued, "If this guy was lying in bed with a plastic bag over his head, I'm guessing he died of strangulation caused by some binding around the neck."

"A leather belt."

Stan stroked three layers of jowls. "I don't know...ideally, you're aiming for a slow increase of pressure. If he'd fastened the thing all at once, it seems to me that it would be too much too soon. By the time he secured his hands...how did he do that?"

"Handcuffs."

"Oh, well. Well, well, well."

"You're losing me, Doc."

"Those are an invitation for trouble. Where was the key?"

"In his hand."

Stan pointed at him as though making his point. "You see? The poor bastard thought he could get free but misjudged his air supply."

"Not exactly. The cuffs were on backwards."

Stan removed his glasses and took his time cleaning the lenses with his tie. When he put them back on he nodded to the screen. "I'm going to go onto the Web and find you enough reading material that by the time you're done, you'll know more than you ever wanted to know about the subject. Then we'll eat and you can ask me what you don't understand or what doesn't fit." He nodded to McKenna's glass. "Drink up and I'll refill it. You're gonna need the sustenance."

One thing Roman had to say for Stanley Bender, he read people well. By the time Roman had sifted through twenty minutes worth of data on the various forms of asphyxiophilia, he wasn't sure he could handle any pizza, and although he appreciated the wine, he wanted a stiff scotch more.

But when the doorbell sounded, he rose first to answer it, wanting the break from the screen and its compelling yet twisted stories. Besides, he felt the least he could do was take care of the bill and tip. Stan thanked him and disappeared into the kitchen again to refill their glasses. When he returned, he also carried an entire roll of paper towels.

Once seated, he balanced one of the two boxes on his lap and happily folded back the lid. "So? How're you doing?" he asked, then took a large bite of thick gooey cheese and vegetable concoction.

McKenna decided to dampen his taste buds with more wine first. Warily eyeing his own pizza, he replied, "There are some sick people out there."

"Yup. But that's what keeps me in business."

"What do you tell a relative like that airline pilot?"

"The one who strangled himself while attached to the bumper of his car after the chain got wrapped around the rear tire?"

"And the guy who attached hot wires to his genitals and then submerges himself in water?"

Stan nodded and chewed, chewed and nodded. "You hope, of course, that they're not the ones to find the body."

"And?"

"And try to remember that this was a choice inside an obsession. In a way these people aren't unlike alcoholics or drug addicts. It's compulsive, but with a difference. You don't see the signs when the urge builds. I'm afraid the best, maybe the only thing for the family is to let go."

"'Let go. Let God.' Do they have a therapy group for this shit the way they do everything else, Doc?"

"Eat, damn it. You're getting emotional."

Roman grimaced one last time then took a bite to get it over with. Surprise had him glancing at Stan.

"Ah-ha. Ah-ha. You see?" Stan's full red cheeks resembled waxed McIntosh apples.

Roman shook his head, unable to believe it. Then he took another bite. Belatedly, he checked the name on the box thinking he might share this experience with Nick one evening. Fat chance, he thought seconds later. The way she'd looked when she'd turned in Sunday night, he would be lucky if she let him near her again.

What a weekend. He didn't blame her for lashing out; she was under attack from all sides and it made sense for her to see his invasion of her space as another form of assault. Still her words had stung, stung more because he'd obviously been wrong about the attraction between them. Or at least hers didn't go as deep or eat at her the way his did. It didn't matter if that was wiser, and better for both of them in the long run. It felt like a knife in his gut, and he'd been dealing with a few too many of those lately.

"Where're you at, Mac?"

Stan's kind question had Roman refocusing on the computer screen. "This would be a perfect way to hide a murder, wouldn't it?"

Stan caught up with his mental gear-switching. "That's the sister's opinion? She's in shock, and the closer they were, the deeper the hurt and denial. Let me ask you this, did they find other paraphernalia? Pornography, videotapes, sex manuals?"

"Nothing like that was in the report, and she didn't say anything about that. Of course, she hasn't been allowed back in there, except when she'd gotten his burial clothes." That was something he hadn't had a chance to check on. Why hadn't Willard let the tape be removed on the door yet? "If there is that stuff in the place, what does it mean?"

"That she definitely didn't know her brother as well as she thought she did. Of course, that's the case if he was just experimenting for the first time, too. But what I'm saying is that an experienced guy wouldn't have been likely to get the cuffs on wrong, so if you don't find anything else in the apartment, that could be a partial clue."

"What about the belt? Wouldn't he have needed help securing it around his neck?"

"Not necessarily. And once he realized the mess he was in, he would have panicked, started hyperventilating. Everything in the neck would begin expanding making the fit tighter. I am surprised he was found in bed though. You say she heard this happening?" When Roman nodded, Stan frowned. "And she wasn't disturbed?"

"I told you, she thought he had a lady friend with him. It was unexpected and upset her—" Roman didn't want to tell him the real reason why if he could avoid it "—but short of knocking on the door, she didn't see what she could do."

Stan had stopped eating a while before. Now he lowered the half-eaten slice into the box. "No. That's wrong."

"What do you mean?"

"If a guy's hanging and he blows it, you find him where he was hung. But unless this guy was tied to the bed, he would have been fighting with everything he's got to get free. That means trying to bust through a window, anything to attract attention, because he knows he's only got seconds to save himself. Not only wouldn't his sister have mistook those sounds as sex, the autopsy records would indicate massive bruising all over his body from the violent end."

"Jesus."

And Willard, acting as though he was experienced in this kind of death scene, had accepted it on face value. He hadn't had the place dusted for fingerprints, hadn't collected evidence.

"Oh, my God."

"Hey, Mac...what is it? Mac?"

Willard. *Willard.*

"Man, you're scaring me."

Roman couldn't speak at the moment, but if he could he would have admitted he was scared, too. And in way over his head. If he'd doubted it before, he didn't now.

16

What shall I do? say what. What shall I do?

—*William Shakespeare,*
The Tempest

As was typical of Van Dorn's routine, there was no auction on Monday evenings; in fact, due to the success of recent sales, their inventory was low and it would be a while before they had another event. Taking advantage of the lull, Nicole left early and stopped to pick up a few things at her favorite gourmet grocery before heading home.

As they had all day, her thoughts drifted frequently to Roman. She guessed he was meeting with that doctor at Baylor now, and despite herself, she wondered how it was going? How long before he got back here? There had been no more calls over the weekend, and she'd tried to convince him that he needn't spend another night on her couch, but he'd disagreed. She figured the bed at his apartment had to be pretty awful to tolerate the torture of scrunching up his big frame to fit her ivory leather couch...and the change in her attitude toward him.

It had been a strange and awkward weekend, mostly

her fault; but at the time she'd felt justified for saying what she had. She didn't like how he'd assumed control and was making decisions, treating her like some brainless twit, thinking all he had to do to keep her in line was give her one of those mind-searing kisses.

But their time apart had given her an opportunity to put things in better perspective, and she knew he must think her an ungrateful bitch and a nut. She'd given him no evidence, nothing to support her feverish accusations, yet he stayed on. So patient with his own life in hellish turmoil.

By the time she got home, she decided she should apologize, at least for the crude language. She'd reacted out of fear as much as anger, mostly because he'd stirred things inside her long repressed and, in a way, wholly new to her. The timing for that could hardly be worse.

It took her two trips to carry the "few" purchases upstairs. After she put everything away, she changed out of her suit into a cooler, silk lounging outfit. The state of her wardrobe had her shaking her head anew. She'd bought enough business clothes to get by until her life was on an even keel again, but her around-the-house wardrobe wasn't exactly the kind of thing you wore when you were serious about keeping an interested man's mind off sex. As she carried her hamper of laundry to the main house to use Goldie's machine, she hoped that by the time Roman did arrive, he would be too tired from his long day to notice.

She unlocked the back door, shut off the alarm and stopped in the washroom to load the machine. That done, she went to get the mail. She was lingering in the doorway to take advantage of the better light while sorting bills and letters from bulk advertising when the phone rang. She crossed to the entry table to answer on the closest extension.

"Goldie?" a woman all but yelled into the phone. "Is that you?"

"No, this is Nicole Loring, the housesitter. Who's calling please?" Most of Goldie's friends and business contacts knew she was out of the country, but considering how old this woman sounded, Nicole guessed she'd forgotten.

"She's not back yet? I was sure she said she was returning today."

"Two weeks from today. But I talk to her several times a week. Can I pass on a message?"

"Ach. Two weeks! Yes, it's here on my calendar. You'd think I would look before dialing, but it's been so busy without Goldie. Everything is on my shoulders when she's the organized one. I'm Dolly Friedman, maybe she's mentioned me?"

"Mrs. Friedman, of course. You and Goldie chair the entertainment committee for the children's clinic." Over the years Goldie had shared her entire life story with her, and anything else that was on her mind.

"That's me. The cupcake lady they call me. Goldie sings and plays on the piano—a little Broadway, some songs from the old country—but I can't carry a note, so Goldie decided that's what I should do. Listen, sweetheart..."

As Mrs. Friedman got down to the reason for her call, a movement out of the corner of her eye had Nicole turning back to the glass storm door. A young man had opened it and was leaning inside. He was no taller than her and lean like a dancer with a face to match, but his strong shoulders and muscular legs suggested he was used to more physical work. His jeans and white T-shirt, which contrasted starkly against his bronze skin, told her that he was definitely not one of the neighbors. Probably an employee with one of the companies that did the yard work in the area, Nicole decided. Then again, everyone on this block used Green Mansions, and they weren't due until tomorrow.

There was also something about the intent way he stared at her...

"Excuse me," she began the instant he stepped completely inside. Why on earth hadn't she set the lock on the storm door? It wasn't much of a deterrent, but— "Stop right there! Who are you?"

"Miss...you alone?"

"Hello?" Mrs. Friedman sounded confused. "Are you talking to me, dear?"

"No, Mrs. Friedman." Nicole spoke firmly, hoping it would warn off the intruder. "Hang on. Sir—" she pointed at the man and lowered her voice, reaching for her most authoritative tone "—out. You don't just enter a house uninvited."

"Talk." His English was obviously minimal, no surprise there, and he motioned anxiously as though trying to tell her to end the call. "Alone."

She could only imagine what he had on his mind. "Out. Now! Or I call the police."

His eyes widened with alarm. "No-no!"

Muttering something in what she assumed was Spanish, he fumbled with the door and beat a hasty retreat. Relieved, Nicole could only stand there and gape.

"Hello? Hello! Are you there, dear? I'm calling 911 if I don't hear the young lady again! Hello!"

"Mrs. Friedman, it's all right." Nicole pressed a hand to her racing heart. "Everything's fine. The silliest thing just happened, but it was obviously a misunderstanding. He had to have been at the wrong house." That's the more logical explanation, Nicole told herself. "Now what were you asking me to pass on to Goldie…?" They continued with their conversation and a few minutes later, she said, "All right, I will. It was lovely talking to you. I hope we get to meet, too. Absolutely. Soon. Bye."

"Mercy," she breathed after hanging up. Could that woman talk. When Goldie and her friend got together, there was probably no getting a word in edgewise.

What a day this was turning out to be after all, she thought as she returned to the front. She locked the storm door, then set the inner door's dead bolt.

As always, she checked the rest of the house, then put her washed clothes into the dryer, once again grateful that Goldie had extended the invitation to her to use her facilities. That done, she settled at the little table in the kitchen where she wrote the checks for the bills that had come in.

Finally, her clothes dry and folded in the basket and the mail for tomorrow on top, she reset the alarm and let herself out the back door. It was dusk and down the street she heard a dog barking, disrupting the otherwise serene evening. Maybe the guy who'd scared the heck out of her was still looking for the right party, she thought wryly as she balanced the basket on her right hip and sorted through the keys to find the one to her apartment.

Only steps from the house, she heard the unmistakable sound of rapid steps behind her. But before she could begin to turn, a bare, bronzed arm came around her neck and slammed her back against a rock hard chest.

Caught off guard, the basket flew out of her grasp, and Nicole was vaguely aware of mail and lingerie flying every which way. Strangely enough, the sight reminded her of the white doves that flew out of the stadium at the Olympics opening ceremonies.

Oh, God! she thought with renewed horror. It was him! The man at the front door hadn't left. It hadn't been an innocent misunderstanding.

She wanted to ask him why? To explain he didn't need to do this, that she would give him money, whatever he wanted. But she could barely breathe, let alone speak. Then he began dragging her backwards, completely shutting off her air supply.

"Shh. No fight. Help."

The thought that she was about to get raped was an ice bath, but a shock that launched her into action. She began beating and clawing at his forearm with renewed energy, kicking with her feet. Unfortunately, her feminine slip-on sandals had little effect on him; they didn't even provide the slightest traction on the slick grass, instead sliding off during her struggles.

To her horror, he easily hauled her past Goldie's beloved pink dogwood. Within seconds he would have her in the tall shrubs and then there would be no hope of any passerby spotting her. Why wasn't that kid next door playing Peeping Tom now!

She tried to scream again, used her short nails to claw at her attacker's face, tried to slow him down by forcing him to bear all of her weight.

As he grunted and wrapped his other hand around her waist to lift her off her feet, lights briefly illuminated them.

A truck was pulling into the driveway. Roman! Dear God, Roman...

Hope shot through her, rejuvenating strained and weakening muscles. As she sensed her attacker having second thoughts, she tried a feint, lunged forward with all her might and then backwards just as violently. It pushed him off balance and broke his hold.

"Roman!" she screamed. Then she was falling.

She slammed onto the ground, first with her back, the air rushing out of her lungs, followed by a brutal blow to her head. Agonizing pain blinded her. Her body jerked from head to toe as though taking a tremendous electrical charge.

"Nick!"

What a sweet sound, she thought in some dazed corner of her mind. But she couldn't have replied if she'd wanted to.

Roman suddenly appeared over her, his gun drawn. "Are you all right?"

She managed to wave him on, but the "Go" in her mouth stayed there.

"I'll be back," he muttered. He touched her cheek briefly—and was gone.

If she'd had the strength, she would have begged

him to take her with him. The foolish impulse spoke eloquently of how scared she was of being left alone again.

Stop it, Loring. You're alive. What is it Rebecca says? You have to be alive to bitch.

Sanity returned, and the fiercest of the pain subsided. Nicole gingerly tested her ability to move. The experience wasn't pleasant, but she slowly forced herself to sit up. Nothing was broken, but by morning she had a hunch every bone and muscle in her body would feel as though it had been pummeled. As for her head—she felt the back of her skull—no blood, thank goodness; however, a nice lump was already forming.

With a sigh she slowly took in her surroundings. Her lingerie was scattered everywhere, as was Goldie's mail. Who knew where her keys had landed. She had to find them.

Ignoring the nauseating roll of her stomach at her slightest move, she eased onto her knees. The ground seemed to dip and rise, dip and rise. Nicole took several deep breaths to keep from vomiting.

Keys. She had to focus. But it was so dark, she couldn't see!

Inch by inch, she explored the thick carpet of grass. Every move sent a scream of protest through her body and a steel rod through her head. The instant her fingers made contact with metal, she gripped the keys and slumped back onto the grass in relief. But she knew that at the rate she was going, it would take at least a half hour to collect everything else, and dreaded the thought of having to carry everything upstairs.

Fortunately Roman appeared from around the corner

of the house. Breathless and looking a bit disheveled himself, he holstered his gun and hurried to her.

"Hell, I'm sorry. He got away."

Stopping before her, he bent at the waist, his loosened tie hanging past his knees, the open V of his shirt. Nicole had never seen a more beautiful sight, and she refused to take her eyes off him.

He seemed to have a similar affliction. "I saw him get into a car. Too far and dark to get a plate number." He crouched before her and began to reach out, then checked himself. "Are you hurt?"

Yes, she thought, her heart felt as though it was being fed through a meat tenderizer. But to him, she said, "Nothing serious." Of course, if she didn't lie down soon, she was going to humiliate herself by being sick in front of him. Barely stifling a groan, she massaged her back. "I don't understand this."

"I take it you didn't know him?"

"No. I thought he was one of the gardeners."

In as few words as possible, she told him what had happened. By the time she finished, she was shaking more than ever, and from what she could see of his face, he looked as though he was wearing a steel mask.

"Damn it to hell," he growled. "I have to phone this in."

"No!" Nicole grabbed his arm to just below where he'd rolled up his sleeves. "I couldn't deal with being surrounded by police again. Not tonight."

"Nick, that guy was going to rape you—or worse!"

Earlier she would have agreed with him, but now that she'd had time to think... Since when did rapists linger, as this one had? Since when did they keep asking to talk? "I don't think so, and you won't either once you think about it. It's too much of a coincidence."

Roman swore again and reached for her. "Can you bear my touch long enough for me to help you stand?"

That kick to her conscience hurt almost as badly as the knock to her head. "Roman. What I said the other day...I should never have been so hateful. Not to you."

"Forget it." He all but lifted her to her feet himself. "Do you need me to carry you?"

"Of course not. I'm fine."

But the second he let go of her, she swayed on her feet.

"Yeah, you're perfect," he muttered, and swept her into his arms.

"McKenna! Now I am getting dizzy."

"Close your eyes."

"My things..."

"I'll get them later."

"You'll kill us both trying to carry me up those stairs."

"That's a joke, right? At this point you can't weigh one-fifteen."

He was a pound low, but she knew it would be childish to point that out to him. So she did as he'd directed, since the dizziness didn't go away, and tried not to dwell on their closeness, that she wasn't wearing a bra, and that his left hand was close to finding that out.

"Did you eat today?"

"Yes."

"What?"

She eyed his intimidating profile. "It's understandable that you'd feel like interrogating someone, but I'm really not up to this. Could I have a rain check on the official butt chewing?"

"Consider it a promise."

At the top of the stairs, he insisted she put the keys in his right hand, and shifted her so he could unlock the door. Once inside, he carried her straight to the bathroom, where he set her onto the vanity.

When he flipped on the light switch, she moaned and tried to cover her eyes. It didn't matter that the lights were behind her over the vanity mirror; at this point, anything would have been too bright.

Roman took hold of her wrists and forced them down. "Let me see."

"I need aspirin."

"Let me make sure you don't have a concussion first." He tilted her head back and studied her eyes. Whatever he did or didn't see did nothing to ease his frown, but he was impressively, wonderfully gentle as he started easing hairpins out of her chignon. Dropping them onto the counter, he eased his hand into the tumbling mass and tested the bump at the back of her head.

"Ow!"

"That's an egg a sacked quarterback could sport."

"Aspirin and an ice pack, McKenna, and I swear I'll listen to your jokes tomorrow."

"I'd be happier if you'd let me take you to Emergency."

"Try it and I won't be the only one admitted."

She could sense an explosion building in him, but

to her surprise, he slowly exhaled. He did, however, place his hands on either side of her, the move bringing them nose to nose.

"Nick, honey, you could have been seriously hurt. Possibly killed. Don't you realize yet that would matter to me? Give me a clue as to what if any of that's sinking through that wonderfully thick skull of yours."

"You saved my life."

"Thank God, I got here when I did. Are you sure you're not hurt anywhere else?" he asked, his relentless gaze moving over her. "You're as white as that outfit, minus the grass stains."

He looked over her shoulder into the mirror, then eased up the back of her tunic top. Whatever he saw had his breath catching and slowly expelling in a raspy moan. "How long had you been fighting him?"

How long was the War of the Roses?

Nicole knew what it meant when her survivor's humor kicked in—she was close to turning into a puddle of tears. Wanting to avoid that, knowing it wasn't wise, that Roman would have every right to slap her down as she had him the other day, she whispered, "Could you just…could you do me one more favor?"

"I'll try."

"Hold me?"

A muscle flexed along his jaw, then he scooped her up off the vanity and into his arms as though she was a child.

She wrapped her arms and legs around him and buried her face against his shoulder. It didn't matter that he'd forgotten about her back and was crushing her to him like crazy. It was a good hurt because she felt safe now and very much alive.

He carried her out of the bright bathroom and into the blissfully dark bedroom where he simply stood and rocked her from side to side, his face buried in her hair.

"Better," she said, exhaling shakily.

His only response was to press a kiss against the shoulder exposed by the wide, slipping neckline of her top.

Her skin tingled from the intimate caress. Her breasts did, too, from the heat and fierce pounding of his heart. It had been so long since she'd felt this feminine and cherished.

"You need to get into bed," Roman said after a small eternity. "Do you think you can manage while I go back out, get your things, and lock up my truck?"

"Sure."

"When I'm done, I'll make you some soup and toast so the aspirin won't eat straight through your stomach."

He eased her down onto the ivory bedspread. Brushing a strand of hair from her cheek, he whispered, "I'll be back," and left.

Once he knew McKenna had given up the chase, Willard went after the maroon '64 Chevy Impala. He could have stopped it right away for the broken left taillight, but waited to stick the cherry strobe on the dash until he knew they were close to a vacated shopping center. When the car pulled in, he eased his BMW beside the driver's door and lowered the front passenger window.

"*¿Qué lección necesita hoy?*"

"I need no lesson today."

"Then why the fuck are you sticking your nose where it doesn't belong, *chico?*"

The younger man turned away to look out the windshield.

Willard stared at his profile. He was a good-looking kid. A moneymaker. But he'd been trouble from the day he'd taken him under his wing. That was the problem with using the Mexicans. They either thought they were in damned no-fault California, or acted as if they believed Texas would be returned to the mother country any minute.

"Well, if that day comes," Willard drawled, "the one thing you can count on is that your share of the pie will be the same puddle of piss you had on the other side of the border."

"*¿Qué?*"

"That's right, play dumb. I'll bet if I asked if it was you hanging around here in the dark last week, you'd answer the same way. And I know better than to ask what you said to her. For your family's sake, you'd better pray she's as much a loser as you are."

"*¿Qué?*"

"I'll spell it out for you." Willard picked up the .38 resting on his thigh and aimed.

17

The only way to get rid of
a temptation is to yield to it.

—*Oscar Wilde*

When Roman exited Nicole's apartment, he paused at the top of the stairs and gazed up at the night sky. They were too close to downtown's bright lights to see many stars, but he didn't need them to feel grateful tonight.

She would never know how he'd debated going to his own place instead of coming back here. He'd known how unhappy she'd been about having him around; it had been enough to tempt him to give her one night's peace. But certain as he now was about Jay's death, and his continued concern about those hang-up calls she was receiving, he'd figured he couldn't risk it. He'd been almost too right.

What he'd seen upon his arrival would stay with him for the rest of his life. But who the hell was that guy? Had he been the one making those calls? The timing was too much of a coincidence not to put him at the top of the list of suspects. Only what the hell had been his motive? It couldn't have been a fluke;

otherwise, why would a yard worker, who inevitably sticks out in this neighborhood like a stray mutt would at the Westminster Dog Show, target a woman for rape, yet leave his car blocks away?

It didn't make sense—unless rape hadn't been his motive. Roman thought of the few words Nicole said he'd spoken. "Alone...talk..." And why had he been so polite at first, then violent when he jumped her later?

Desperation.

About what? That she'd rejected him? Couldn't make her understand him?

That he would be seen with her.

Damned if that didn't make some sense. But, again, *why?* Who would recognize him around here? The hairs on the back of his neck tingled as he scanned the area. No, he assured himself in the next moment. If there was someone out there, he would have known it the moment he stepped out of the place, perfect target that he was standing there.

One thing was for certain, he and Nick needed to talk, but it would have to wait. She was in no shape for that tonight. Come morning it would also be a good idea to call Tucker and ask him to cover for him for an hour or so.

Roman exhaled and gripped the wrought iron railing to flex and roll his tense shoulder muscles. Morning...a long time away, and that only added to the ache in his loins.

"Down, boy," he muttered, and rubbed briskly at his thighs. Then he started down the stairs.

Try as he might, though, he couldn't forget one

thing. How she'd reached for him. Held him. What she'd said to him Saturday, the arctic chill that had almost made air-conditioning unnecessary in the apartment over the rest of the weekend, all that was history. As he scanned the yard, studied the deeper shadows beneath each tree and behind every shrub just in case, another part of his mind still felt her against him. The power of that, and his arousal, floored him. Not only was she out of his realm of experience on a social and economic level, but she'd grown model thin, and he'd never been turned on by toothpicks. Or so he thought.

After retrieving his jacket from the truck, and the flashlight from the glove compartment, he locked up and went to work collecting Nicole's things. Mostly lingerie, he noted after uprighting the woven straw basket. He scooped up the filmy stuff scattered around him. Most of it was silk. Sensual. Just what he needed.

When he was sure he had it all, as well as the mail, he returned upstairs and placed the basket on one of the dinette chairs, the mail on the table. Then he went to work looking for some canned soup and bread.

About ten minutes later, he carried a tray into the bedroom, only to stop in his tracks.

Nicole hadn't completely succeeded in getting into bed. She'd undressed all right, slipping out of everything but a pair of panties; however, whether from pain or weakness—he could only guess—she'd stopped there, curling into a fetal position on the edge of the mattress where she'd either passed out or drifted off to sleep.

Hoping it was the latter, he set the tray on the bathroom vanity and crossed back to her, felt her forehead and checked her pulse. "Nick…come on, honey, wake up for me."

It took some coaxing, but her eyelashes finally fluttered and lifted. When she looked at him, however, there was no reassuring sign of recognition.

"How do you feel?"

She licked her dry lips. "Tired. Dry. Do I have the flu?"

"Not the flu, sweetheart." He checked the lump at the back of her head and was relieved to find that at least it hadn't grown any larger. "Let's get you under this sheet. Will you let me do that for you? Nick, look at me. Who am I?"

For the space of seconds he saw a panic build in her, and a corresponding fear gripped his gut.

"I don't…McKenna? McKenna, I think I'd prefer a hangover."

What a little scrapper she was. "Been there myself, babe. I'll bet your head feels like it's got a heavy metal rock band playing in there." Stretching, he drew down the bedspread and tugged the sheet from under the pillow. "Once we get you comfortable, you'll start feeling better."

Once again he scooped her up, moving her higher on the bed. In the subdued light, with her long hair teasing his arm, pearl and diamond studs glistening in her ears, and her sleek body almost as lustrous as those pricey concretions, she was every bit a fantasy.

As much for his sake as hers, he quickly drew the sheet over her, then tried to adjust the pillow where it would hurt her the least. "How's that?"

"Aspirin."

"Food first."

He brought over the tray and eased down beside her setting it on his lap. I'm guessing you like New England clam chowder, since that's the only kind in your pantry, but I hope your stomach can handle rubber fish."

Nicole eyed the soup and closed her eyes. "I have enough lumps already, thanks."

"Atta girl. Keep up that feisty spirit."

"Please, McKenna. It'll take too much effort to chew."

"Then we'll stick to the liquid. Open." He spooned a bit into her mouth.

Nicole did try, but it took swallowing three times to get the trickle of nourishment down. "I don't think this is going to work, Doctor," she muttered when she could speak again.

He could see that for himself and broke off a corner of toast. "Try this instead."

She had to work at that, too, her stomach clearly revolting. But Roman remained persistent. After he got almost a half slice into her, he tried a few more spoonfuls of soup.

"Enough," she moaned. "Now can I have the bloody aspirin?"

He felt the corner of his mouth twitch. "You sound like Max."

The mention of her boss had her eyes widening. "Oh, no! He's scheduled a meeting tomorrow that I can't miss."

"Wanna bet? At best, you'll do well to make it to the bathroom without upchucking your tonsils."

"You don't understand. This is something we've already postponed once."

"Tough. Better yet, he can handle the meeting by himself." Roman knew she didn't have a clue as to how bad she'd been roughed up. "Nick, you may be trying to avoid facing this, but I've had just enough psychology to know you're on the edge of an emotional meltdown. When I walked in here a few minutes ago, you had to struggle to recognize me. If you don't give yourself time to adjust to all that's happening in your life, you won't be dealing with merely blank moments, you'll be minus your entire identity. Maybe for weeks, maybe for months."

"If that's an example of your bedside manner, the sooner the better."

He was afraid for her, but she was right: his knee-jerk reactions were inflicting their own damage. He rose and picked up the tray. "I'll get some ice for your head and that aspirin."

He continued nursing her throughout the night. He gave her the tablets, helped her sit up to get them down with water, held the ice pack so that she didn't have to stay rock still or deal with her pillow getting soaked once she fell asleep.

As for sleep, hers was fitful. When she wasn't moaning from the pain, she was writhing to free herself from the grips of a nightmare. Throughout it all, Roman bathed her feverish face with a washcloth, checked her for progressive signs of concussion and held her when she was in the midst of a bad dream.

At around three in the morning, things leveled off and she settled down. Exhausted, he stripped to his briefs and settled beside her, hoping for a few hours of rest himself.

The next time he opened his eyes, he found her staring at him. Straight off he could tell this was a stronger Nicole and that she had something on her mind, so he remained silent to wait for her to share what it was.

"You never told me about how it went with your meeting."

He was afraid she would remember that sooner rather than later. "How's the head?" he asked, hedging.

"Working."

"Be glad." He checked his watch in the glow from the bathroom light. "There's still another hour or so until daylight." He rose on his right elbow and touched her forehead. It was cool. "Need a drink of water?"

"No."

"Then go back to sleep."

"Something's changed."

"Yeah, your hat size has temporarily increased a notch or two. Close your eyes."

Instead, she slid her hand up his chest, letting it rest over his heart as though trying to get a read on him that way. "You don't have to keep anything from me, McKenna. I'm better."

"Sure you are."

"Please."

With a sigh, Roman shifted closer and drew her into the curve of his arm. "Let it be for now."

In reply she kissed the spot where her hand had

been. Then she turned her head and touched her lips to his nipple.

Roman pressed his head deeper into his pillow. "Nick, I'm not saint material. And I'm really not in the mood for a cold shower."

"Then don't take one." This time she circled him with the tip of her tongue. "Kiss me instead."

"I don't want to just kiss you, damn it. I want to bury myself inside you." He caught the hand exploring his chest hair and slid it down over the full length of his arousal. "Deep."

She repeated the motion on her own. "That's what I want, too."

He clenched his teeth together and fought the surge of hunger that ripped at his insides like claws.

"Don't you understand why? Because while I was fighting that man, I found myself thinking, 'Roman will never kiss me again. We'll never make love.' If we had, if only once, whatever happened afterward...I could have endured it."

"Don't say that."

"I need you to know."

"You're dreaming again," he said for his benefit as much as hers.

"Would that make it easier for you? Then pretend I'm dreaming. Pretend that in the morning, I won't remember any of this." She circled him with her fingers. "As long as you don't forget."

He sucked in a sharp breath at her gentle but effective touch, and shifted so he could see her eyes. They were clear, evenly dilated, a beautiful gold. "How in sweet heaven could I?"

With that he took her mouth with his, invaded the warm interior with his tongue and put into the kiss what he knew he would never allow himself to put into words. His excruciating care soon had the muscles in his arms quivering as he struggled to save her from his weight, and left his heart pounding as though he'd run a 5K race. Yet the kiss went on and on…until he had to touch more of her. But because he didn't trust his hands to be gentle enough, he used his mouth, caressing her cheek, the graceful length of her neck, the elegant slope of her shoulder.

Need provoked him into brushing aside the sheet, then he glided his hand over her breast. The instant swelling, the tightening of her nipple and tension in the rest of her told him a great deal, but he had to know more. Watching her face, he continued his journey noting the sharp dip of her waist, the subtle swell of her hip, the satin-smooth length of thigh, and back up between them to where silk stopped him.

The brush of his fingers had her catching her breath, a sound as arousing as the tiny jolt that shook her body. Later, he thought, if the world allowed time, he would ask how long it had been for her. But for now he knew enough.

Stroking her again, he lowered his mouth to her breast, tracing his tongue around and around the aureole, fascinated by the texture changes, relishing the way she arched toward him when he licked up the delicate peak and drew her deeper into his mouth. All the while he explored the increasingly hot, dampening silk that kept her out of his reach.

"Before we say goodbye," he murmured, returning

to her lips again, "I want one night to do this properly. Will you promise me that?"

"What's so *im*proper about tonight?"

"The fact that I should be pistol-whipped for touching you when I know you're weak as a kitten. Believe it or not I am going to be more careful than I ever have been with anyone in my life."

"Sounds devastating," she replied, sounding anything but grateful. "I hope I live through it."

He understood, knew he could talk himself blue in the face and she wouldn't comprehend that it would cost him to protect her. "Promise," he said, before nipping at her lower lip, exposing a hint of the passion burning inside him.

She sucked in a quick breath. "Anything."

Even as an anticipatory shiver rushed through him, he rolled off the bed and reached for his pants. When he found what he was looking for, he dropped the foil packet on his pillow and hooked his thumbs into the waistband of his briefs. As he saw her gaze shift from the shiny thin square to him, he stripped and climbed back onto the bed.

"No, I don't."

"Don't what?"

"Do this often. If you look closely, you'll see that's a pretty worn wrapper."

He proceeded to remove her last stitch of clothing the way he had his—without false modesty or pretended shyness. For regardless of his belief that they were destined to ultimately go their separate ways, on some level he understood that she belonged to him, in the same way a part of him would always be hers.

"I wasn't going to ask."

"Because you're too much the lady. I'm doing some wondering, too, only I won't ask, either. Not tonight, and not for any gentlemanly reasons."

"Why then?"

"Because it wouldn't matter anyway. I want you too much."

"Be careful, McKenna. You're starting to sound seriously romantic."

"I don't know about romantic, but I am serious." Once again he ran his hands up her legs, to the nest of curls that could have been golden thread. Uttering a low sound of approval, he stretched alongside her and palmed her. "I'll bet every inch of you tastes like something the sun kissed."

Before she could respond, he claimed her mouth again. Then there were no more words, just the caressing, exploring and provoking that soon had her trying to draw him over her.

"I want to feel all of you," she whispered against his lips.

Nevertheless, Roman resisted, knowing she was in no shape to bear his weight. "This way," he said, easing them both onto their sides and sliding her leg over his hip. Then he wedged his leg between hers and thrust the tip of himself against her moist heat.

Nicole's lips parted, and meeting his steady gaze, she took the condom from him. They continued watching each other as she put it on him, and he thought her touch as sensual as anything he'd experienced with other women. It was because of the way she kept looking at him, he realized; her lovely eyes said that she got as much out of this simple act as he did.

"Now," she said on a sigh when she was done. "Let's not wait anymore."

As slick as she was, he knew he still had to be careful, but he slid into her with one smooth thrust—and had to close his eyes. "Sweet—" He didn't want to curse. But it was good, too good. He had to fight the temptation to roll completely on top of her and race them both to an urgent release. "I think we're in trouble, Nick."

"I think we knew that from the beginning."

True. He'd struggled with that knowledge, to avoid contact with her until the night Max shot him a look across the room that said, "Save her, damn it."

Now who was going to save him?

Knowing better than to think there was an answer, or more accurately not caring if there was one, he locked his mouth to hers, swallowed her satisfied moan and worked toward earning another, any delicious sound he could. And slowly, slowly, he increased the rhythm and pressure of his thrusts, his mind willing, *"Come with me…come with me."*

The swelling promise built, too quickly to bring her all the pleasure he wanted for her. The way she tightened around him was wildly stimulating, too. When he felt her breath catch and the tremors inside her begin, he was already there himself.

Cushioning her against him, he let the last few intense strokes rush them both into release.

18

Now comes the mystery.

—Henry Ward Beecher

They fell asleep wrapped around each other, and it was Nicole who woke him over an hour later by trying to ease free. Roman instinctively tightened his arms.

"Where do you think you're going?" It still seemed fairly dark, although he belatedly remembered there had been some mention of rain in the forecast for today.

"One guess. It's also time for you to get up or you won't have time for a shower. Give me two minutes."

He let her untangle herself from his limbs, but saw the care with which she moved. "Will you make it?"

"Not gracefully, I'm afraid. I don't suppose you'll be considerate and close your eyes?"

She was sweet...and proud. "Concern before consideration."

"That's what I thought."

Moving as stiffly as someone wearing a body cast, she eased to a sitting position, assimilated herself, then inched her way to her feet. Roman almost winced watching her.

"Nick, honey, you're scaring me."

"I'm beginning to appreciate why football players get paid so much."

With hands extended like a sleepwalker, she made her way to the bathroom. Roman held his breath, torn between wanting to carry her so she wouldn't have to suffer and dragging her back into bed. He settled for what he sensed she needed at the moment. Gentle humor.

"If it's any consolation, that's one perfect-ten tush. Black-and-blue spots and all."

Her idea of a middle finger more resembled a royal wave, and once the door was shut, he rolled over to bury his face into her pillow to grin, but also to groan with renewed desire. However that lasted only as long as it took for his conscience and common sense to kick in.

Yielding to this hadn't been the most brilliant thing he'd ever done, and the lack of sleep, along with the amount of stress building around them left him feeling less than a hundred percent, but damned if he was going to regret making love with her. Just the thought of how it had felt made him want her again. He did, however, have the brains left to know that was out of the question. What he had to concentrate on was how she would take the news he'd refused to share with her last night.

Wanting to make things as easy for her as possible, he dragged his sorry butt out of bed and went to put on the coffee. When he returned to the bedroom, she was there, too, wearing a short white robe and moving with slightly more agility. An attempt to con him, he suspected.

"Tell me you're not still planning on going in today."

"I have to. But thanks for the concern. A little coffee, a lot of aspirin, and I'll be a new woman."

"I'm calling Max."

"Don't you dare!"

"Give me one good reason."

She began to speak, then her gaze dropped. With a muffled cough, she looked away. "I can't argue with you when you're like that."

He understood at once, but was it his fault that his briefs hid nothing? "Honey, I've been 'like that' since the day we met. If you'd ever looked below my tie, you'd have noticed." Muttering at her stubborn insistence to risk her health, he strode to the bathroom. On the other side of the closed door he heard...

"I noticed."

Chuckling despite himself, he reached for the water taps.

Ten minutes later he was back in the kitchen slipping his gun into its holster, but leaving his jacket on the dinette chair. When someone as indifferent to fashion as he was noticed how his appearance looked worse than ever since he'd begun staying here, he was in no hurry for Nicole to see the full effect until absolutely necessary.

A glance at his watch told him that he had exactly thirty minutes to drive to his apartment and change—if he kept what was about to happen brief.

"Thanks," he said, as she pushed a yellow mug

across the counter at him. "Smells good." He wanted a moment to simply look at her, not only because a part of him still couldn't believe this gorgeous woman had wanted him, but because within seconds, she could also loathe him for wearing the badge that would forever symbolize deceit and betrayal to her. "Regrets?" he murmured over the brim.

She used both hands to keep her mug steady, but her eyes were luminous. "That would be slightly tacky, wouldn't it, since it was my idea?"

He scratched at his freshly shaved jaw. He'd had the nerve to borrow one of her throwaway razors. Not enough, though, to ask if he could bring over some clothes until this was over. "Was it? You can't know how hard I was bombarding your psyche with my strong power of suggestion."

Her lips curved, if only briefly. "No regrets, McKenna. No matter what."

So she was beginning to read him better, too. He sipped more coffee and debated on how to begin.

"Try starting with the bottom line." Her amber gaze remained direct. "I know you don't want to hurt me. That's why, regardless of whether I agree with you or not—"

"Oh, you'll agree with me. Or rather, I now agree a hundred percent with you."

She paused, and it was only the slight wobbling of the mug that gave away that she understood the innuendo. "What did you learn specifically that convinced you?"

"Stan's—Dr. Bender's input when I described the scene that morning. I'd always been bothered by it, but not sure why. In fact, I'd almost had myself convinced it was simply the bizarreness of it. He made me understand that unless you knew what to look for, you wouldn't recognize the obvious.''

"I think you're going to have to spell out the specifics for me.''

"There isn't a doubt in my mind that Jay was murdered.''

She put down her mug and came to him, wrapping her arms around his waist. Roman did the same, locking her to his pounding heart and kissing the top of her head, then her forehead.

"Thank you,'' she whispered after several seconds. "I've been feeling so alone, even beginning to accept that maybe I was losing my mind.''

He closed his eyes and stroked his cheek against her hair. "My problem is dealing with how much danger you're in.'' By every law of logic he knew, she should be dead, too. That one ugly truth was a cold, dense dread filling his lungs.

"And Jay's baby.''

He hadn't allowed himself to go there yet. Now that she insisted, he shook his head. "I want like crazy to believe that your brother had a neighbor or somebody take the child.''

"He wouldn't have done that. You don't hand away a newborn that you've just discovered was your own flesh and blood.'' Nicole met his gaze again. "Besides, that would have meant the sitter would have been expecting the baby to be picked up, and when that didn't happen, he or she would have come to the apartment or gone to the police. No, the baby was there.''

Roman forced himself to picture Meggie in such a situation. The image had his throat tightening. "I know," he croaked.

As though she could read his mind, Nicole slid her fingers under his tie to stroke his heart. "You're the last cop I should have happened to."

"Hey." He took hold of her chin to give her a stern look. "You think I'd want to miss being looked at the way you look at me?" Because the question also brought home the fragility of their relationship, he kissed her.

She immediately wound her arms around his neck. As she opened to him, what he'd meant as a brief, fierce assurance of his presence in her life became a soul-searching, body-melting, oral intercourse.

Wanting to fill his hands with her bottom and grind her against his instantly aroused flesh, he tore his mouth free and buried his face in hair. "God...this is nuts."

"My fault," she gasped. "I wanted to get your mind off things if only for a moment."

"Yeah, well, if I told you where it went and what I want right now, you wouldn't stop blushing for a week." He forced himself to let her go. "I have to get the hell out of here, and we haven't covered everything yet."

Nicole handed him his mug. "Willard."

He couldn't decide what impressed him more, her skill in recovering her equilibrium or her ability to follow his thoughts so well. "Something about him, at least about his actions in your brother's case, reek. I think we may find our answer in Jay's apartment."

She frowned. "While I've believed he's botched this from day one, you're intimating at something else, aren't you?"

Before he could reply his pager sounded. Roman plucked it off his belt and read the message. The number had him reaching for the phone. "It's my partner."

He dialed Tucker's cellular number. "You're at it damned early," he muttered the instant they were connected.

"Would have told you yesterday, but the news came late. It's my turn in court. I was going to leave you with a mountain of calls to make in the interim, and then I intercepted this one eighty-seven. We have a male Hispanic about twenty-three at a deserted shopping center. He was found in a maroon Chevy. Looks like a gang-style execution to me. How fast can you get here?"

Roman couldn't believe what he was hearing. "Right away, but...did you say a maroon Chevy? Maybe a '64 sedan? Two door?"

"Bingo."

"Is he wearing a white T-shirt and jeans? Hair kind of long?"

Ralph was silent a moment. "You're getting downright spooky, partner."

Instead of explaining, Roman met and held Nick's gaze. "Give me the address. I'll fill you in once I get there."

When he hung up, Nicole said, "You described the man who attacked me."

"He's been found a few miles from here. He's dead, Nick."

19

*Mischiefs feed
Like beasts, till they be fat,
and then they bleed.*

—Ben Jonson,
Volpone

It looked as though half of Central Patrol had shown up to check out the crime scene, and Roman received several waves and a few smirks as he parked beside Tucker's dust-covered station wagon. It was nothing compared to what he expected from his partner once Ralph noticed he still wore the same suit he'd had on yesterday.

"What's the latest?" he asked, upon joining the taller cop at the driver's side of the Chevy.

Tucker didn't take his eyes off the gloved forensics specialist bagging trace evidence. "Not as much as I'd like. Just let the cleaning lady who found him go." He pointed with his notebook toward the street. "She was walking to her bus stop and spotted the vehicle at approximately five-fifty. The car was here by its lonesome, seemingly abandoned after rolling into this light post. More curious than worried, she approached on the passenger side, saw the victim slumped forward and to the right of the steering wheel with a single gunshot wound to the head. Concerned citizen that she is, she pulled out her cellular—''

"Say what?"

"I swear on Shirl's diaphragm."

"You'll have to do better than that."

"Point taken. But the fact is everybody's carrying a phone these days."

"Okay, okay. You really believe she saw all that in the dark?" Roman glanced around. There wasn't a working light on the lot, and the nearest streetlamp had to be at least a hundred yards away.

"She carries a flashlight. And Mace spray. Also a knife. The woman," Tucker drawled, his dimples deepening, "is the 007 of domestics. Our boy, here, could have used her protection. He'd apparently forgotten your number."

"It wasn't that kind of an acquaintance," Roman replied just as dryly. "Or a long one."

"Somehow I'd already figured that out." Tucker made a ninety-degree turn and for the first time took note of Roman's attire. Although he was only fractionally more presentable himself, he bowed his head and rubbed the back of his neck. "Did you and Stan have a fruitful evening together?"

"Can it. Focus on this...when I saw this guy for the first time at dusk yesterday, I was pulling into Nicole Loring's driveway, and he was dragging her into the shrubbery."

"Son of a bitch. How is she?"

"Bruised and upset. Not easily defeated, though."

"Spoken with exactly the right professional reserve. Well, if this doesn't shrink wrap the world…"

"I chased the guy for a few blocks, then he hopped into this car he'd parked by a service truck."

"So he wouldn't stick out in the neighborhood." Tucker turned back to the vehicle. "I didn't think this was random, but you're sure putting a strange twist on things. Fletcher tells me the lack of powder burns on the victim's temple and the trajectory of the bullet would indicate the shooter was about six to eight feet away and relatively on the same level as gorgeous George."

"Someone sitting in another car," Roman said, mostly to himself. "You're right, it could have been a rival gang thing."

"Sure, sure…except that he jumped your lady." Tucker glanced at him again. "She didn't know him? Couldn't recall having ever seen him before?"

Roman didn't bother making noise about the possessive tag. Besides, it was true in a way. Until he could assure Nicole that she was safe, she was his concern, even if he wouldn't allow himself deeper claim. "He'd tried to get into her landlady's house a few minutes earlier." He shared that part of Nicole's experience, as well.

"Huh. Easily intimidated, wasn't he?" Tucker played with the change in his pocket. "Do we discount attempted robbery? Rape?"

"I do now."

"Not so fast." Tucker waved his notebook at him. "We didn't find a driver's license in his wallet, but I did find some kind of ID card that says he works—

worked at a health club off Hillcrest. It identifies him as one Angelo Aguirre. The DMV didn't have anything on him, and surprise-surprise, the address listed doesn't exist.''

"What are you asking? Maybe Nicole knew him from that health club?" Roman looked at the address on the card in the plastic sample bag Tucker held up for his perusal. "If she was a member of one, she would use a facility closer to where she lives and works. My guess is she can afford any of them."

"We'll check it out nonetheless. Look at him. The guy's a stud muffin. Maybe not the kind of boy toy a rich girl would want hanging around for the long term, but for a change of pace...?"

"Goddamn it, Tucker."

Ralph studied him for several seconds. "Why don't you tell me what old Stan had to say?"

Roman glanced around to make sure they wouldn't be overheard, as much to check his temper. The number of uniformed cops had thinned somewhat and those with a reason for hanging around were either moving back the growing number of onlookers, directing traffic, or guiding the wrecker truck that had been called to the scene. As for the technicians working in and around the car, they were wholly focused on their work.

"Jay Loring was murdered," Roman said tightly. "And Willard's got some serious questions to answer, the chief one being why the body didn't show evidence of a guy struggling like a maniac once he knew those cuffs were on backwards. His report indicates Loring was just lying there like day-old bait fish. Not even his neck wounds were consistent with what the situation would have demanded.''

This time Ralph was the one to glance around. ''Do you know what you're suggesting?''

''I'm not wasting my breath suggesting anything. I'm stating a fact. Willard's report is bullshit. The only person likely to believe that shoddy piece of police work would be a first-day student at the academy.''

''We'd better table this conversation until we have more privacy,'' Tucker said to the space between his size fourteen shoes. ''While no one would be more tickled than me to see that piece of slime finally fingered for something, accusations about another cop—'' he shot Roman a grim look ''—are not received well.''

''Right now all I care about is giving Nicole the aid she should have gotten from us in the first place. She's been out there all alone for weeks, Ralph.''

''And if it gets out that you're being rewarded for your conscientiousness with an invitation into her bed—'' as Roman began to protest, Tucker gripped his arm ''—I'm on your side, pal. Get your brains out of your balls. Or do you want to go through what your lady has been dealing with?''

He was right. Like it or not, Roman knew patience was the key. Every step from here on had to be above reproach. Nodding, he drew a deep breath and focused on the dead man. ''What do you need me to do?''

Once the technicians were through, the body bagged and transported, and the wrecker was hauling the car away, Roman and Tucker headed downtown to report in. Considerably late, Tucker headed for court; for his part, Roman found the department more than half empty, but he was relieved that two of the missing were Willard and Newman. At least that allowed him to phone the apartment and when Nicole didn't pick up, he dialed Van Dorn's.

"It's me," he said, as soon as she answered.

"Are you all right?"

Although it did something to him to hear the warmth and relief in her voice, he wasn't happy that she'd gone in to work, after all. "Never mind me, how are you? Tell me you had someone drive you in?"

"Carlyn did. Don't lecture, please. I wouldn't have felt any better staying at the apartment."

Maybe it was best that she be around people who knew and cared about her. "That's something, I guess. Is Max there yet?"

"Just now."

"I want you to go tell him. Everything."

She hesitated a moment, then said, "This is about the dead man, isn't it? He is the one from last night?"

"Yeah."

"My God. What does that mean?"

"It means you go into Max's office and you tell him."

"Not everything."

"You need his understanding and protection, and for that you have to give him your trust. From here on out, I don't want you alone in that place. Anywhere for that matter. If you want, I'll talk to him about getting one of the guys from the warehouse to follow you home and hang around until I get there."

"Roman, you're scaring me."

"That's the idea. This guy was shot in the head, Nick, and it was no random thing. He did something he either was or wasn't supposed to. We have to go with the assumption that included getting to you."

"Was he murdered because he didn't kill me?"

"Either that or for attempting to talk to you. Isn't that what he said to you? 'Talk.'"

Nicole gasped. "Someone was afraid of exposure! Oh, no...Roman, if only I'd understood! Instead, I jumped to the wrong conclusion and—"

"You did exactly the right thing under the circumstances. Don't beat yourself up about it."

"But he might have known where the baby was."

She was right there, however, Roman couldn't let her dwell on that. When the lieutenant signaled him into his office, he knew there wasn't time to reassure her. "I have to go. Try to hang on to the belief that what's happened opens doors, not closes them." He didn't know if he believed that himself, but she didn't have to know that at the moment. "Go talk to Max, Nick. I'll be in touch."

"All right. Be careful."

"Always."

But as Roman headed across the room, he wondered how many risks he was going to have to take to get to the bottom of this mess, and who else was going to get hurt along the way.

20

*Blessings never come in pairs
and ills never come alone.*

—Chinese proverb

"If I wasn't so relieved to know you're all right, I'd fire you." Max gripped Nicole's hands within his and shook them in frustration. "Why couldn't you have told me this from the first?"

"I had no proof. Besides, what could you have done?"

"I'd have been a friend. Pardon me for the naive assumption that would mean anything to you."

With a chest-deep growl, he shot to his feet and paced from one end of the dark-paneled office to the other. Nicole watched knowing better than to attempt to deprive him of his tirade. Max enjoyed his image of himself as benefactor and sage. Not only did he look like a Byzantine prince surrounded here in a room full of gold-framed art and artifacts—personal treasures he'd "saved" from the auction block, but that Rebecca refused to have at the house—he played the part to the hilt.

"This is what we're going to do," he said, slicing

the air with his left index finger. "I'm going to call the security firm I used before I started hiring moonlighting cops—and remind me to call the Chief and tell him what I think of—"

"Max, I told you, you can't say anything to anyone."

"Okay, okay. But later when this is over, you'd better believe I'm going to get vocal. I don't make the campaign donations I do because I like to eat bad banquet food. I expect my staff to be safe in this city. Anyway, leave it to me," he continued more calmly. "By noon you'll have your own full-time bodyguard."

"Absolutely not."

"This isn't a debatable issue, Nicole."

"Then I quit."

Max swore. "Why are you being so stubborn?"

"Stop yelling." Nicole massaged her temples where pain seared every time he thought of something else to roar about.

He grew immediately conciliatory and attentive. "Poor darling. Let me pour you a brandy. No, tea. I'll page Carlyn and have her make you some of that hideous green stuff."

"I'm fine. Just...sit." She patted the gilded armchair he'd abandoned several times to vent or wax sentimental. "Let me try to explain that I'm not being stubborn, but practical. Roman's staying at my apartment once he's off du—"

With a sarcastic grunt, Max interjected, "I'll bet he's made sure he doesn't sleep on the couch, either."

"Behave. What I'm trying to tell you is that I

wouldn't be opposed to having someone here for all of us, but otherwise—"

Max's phone buzzed and Nicole glanced at the console. His second extension was flashing. "That's for me. I had my calls transferred over here."

It turned out to be the management company at Jay's apartment complex. They'd been pushing to get the police tape removed because it had been making the other tenants uneasy, and apparently they'd just received the release.

"Finally," she replied, wondering if the spiral of bad news was about to slow. She asked a few pertinent questions, then thanked the young woman on the other end and hung up.

"Good news for a change?" Max asked, hovering close like an oversize raven.

"Detective Willard has given permission to clear out Jay's apartment. Isn't that convenient timing? They've given me until the fifteenth, but when I call the furniture leasing company, I think I'll tell them that I'll start removing his personal things today, so they can pick up the rest no later than the end of the week. In fact, I'd like to start right now if that's okay with you?"

From Max's expression, she might as well have announced she was off to teach lacquering to the Japanese. "And how do you plan to accomplish that, by crawling on all fours? When I tell you that you're in no condition to cope here, that doesn't mean I'm going to look the other way while you finish putting yourself in a hospital from—"

"It has to be done, Max."

"Not today it doesn't."

Hadn't he listened to anything she'd said? "There have to be answers in that apartment. Some explanation. Why else would Detective Willard keep us out of there for so long?"

"Well, if there is, don't you think he would have found it himself by now?"

"Then why hasn't he backed off?"

"Oh, for heaven's sake..." Max circled his desk and reached for the phone. "I can see reasoning is going to be useless. I'm calling Darnell in the warehouse. He has the biggest set of shoulders in the place, and even if you don't have any trouble, at least he'll get the damned packing and loading done for you."

Nicole relaxed against the chair's tall back. "Thank you, Max. You really are taking this well."

"The hell I am. The only reason I'm doing this is because I refuse to speak at your funeral!"

Touched and properly chastised, Nicole let Max have Darnell collect a number of boxes from the warehouse, then drive her home to change. By the time the former college football star drove them to Jay's apartment, she'd reached Roman, who pulled into the apartment's parking area only moments after they did.

"You shouldn't be dealing with this right now," he said after climbing out of the navy blue unmarked car.

"How could I wait?" She introduced him to Darnell, glad that the younger man's size seemed to appease him somewhat. "Where's your partner?" she added.

"In court. He should be out soon."

"And you should be working the case from this morning."

His answering look reminded her that he was, but when he spoke he merely replied, "I wasn't going to let you go in there without someone who knew the score."

Grateful, she ripped off the tape on the stairs and then climbed them to repeat the process for the strips across the door. Then she unlocked the dead bolt.

As she stepped inside, she found herself holding her breath, afraid to draw in any reminder of what she'd experienced here. But there was no stopping the memories.

Nothing looked different. Although something terrible had happened here, everything looked the same—the rented furniture, the big screen TV, complicated stereo unit, spotless kitchen... At least the smells were gone. When she went to the bedroom, she understood why.

The mattress had been removed leaving only the box spring. All evidence that someone had died here was gone. How was that possible when the place had been locked up?

"Don't," Roman murmured near her ear.

"You don't understand. They've removed it. How can they remove evidence without permission?"

She felt Roman's hesitation. "It's not evidence if there's not an acknowledged crime. The manager probably got a special release for health reasons," he added.

That made sense. But then was the mattress all that had been taken?

Steeped in paranoia, she shook her head. What she needed to do was work. The sooner she was finished, the sooner she could get out of there.

She gave Roman a reassuring look over her shoulder. "We'll be fine. You go do what you have to do."

"I want to check around the complex first."

She knew better than to protest what she suspected was nothing more than baby-sitting, but not wanting to say anything in front of Darnell, she nodded and instructed the warehouseman to start bringing the boxes upstairs. After Roman left, she began emptying the bedroom closet of clothes, checking all of Jay's pockets before folding things and packing them away.

She had Darnell mark the boxes for the homeless shelter she'd decided to donate the bulk of her brother's belongings to.

Halfway through the top rack, she reached for a sports jacket and found a matchbook from somewhere called Velvet's in its pocket. It didn't surprise her that she didn't recognize the name; considering the gaudy black-and-pink cover, she doubted it was an establishment she was likely to be interested in. However, when she asked Darnell, an unabashed night owl and club devotee, he didn't know the place, either. What bothered her more was that Jay apparently did—and he'd never been a smoker.

"Oo-ee." Darnell whistled quietly after lifting the flap and passing the packet back to her. "This might explain things."

Inside Nicole saw a handwritten message in red ink. *Would love a repeat performance sometime.*

A suggestive comment, but one she refused to read

anything into. What she wanted to know was who had written it? There was no signature.

"I have to show this to Roman," she said, hoping he hadn't left the complex yet. "I'll be back in a minute."

Before she could reach the front door, she heard a sharp knock. Amused that they must be intuitively sending each other messages, she reached for the knob. "I was about to come looking for you," she said, tugging open the door.

Wes Willard smiled at her through mirror-lensed sunglasses. "What a delightful thought. I'm glad I was able to save you the trip."

Everything inside her chilled. "What do you want?"

"I'm on my lunch break and thought I'd stop by to make sure everything is going smoothly for you. When I gave the okay to clean out the place, I figured you wouldn't waste any time getting over here."

Although he was a strong reminder that she was nowhere near one-hundred percent, Nicole lifted her chin, wishing she could slam the door on his smug face. "Do you have a problem with that?"

"Not at all. I'm glad to see that you're finally putting this unfortunate episode behind you and moving on."

"No thanks to you."

With a slight shake of his head, he stepped toward her. She had no choice but to back up, which allowed him access inside.

"How long do you think it will be before you're

done?'' he asked, stepping over the yellow tape she'd dropped inside the doorway.

"Why? Thinking about assuming the lease?"

He slipped off his glasses and met her scornful gaze with unsmiling eyes. "Amusing. But my tastes run a bit more on the—" he glanced around "—refined side."

"Really? Police must be paid better than I thought."

"You would, considering the one you keep company with. Where is our big strapping cowboy? I saw the unmarked car downstairs…"

She was momentarily stunned that he knew they'd been seeing each other, but quickly recovered and gestured outside, hoping she seemed fairly indifferent. "Not far. If you'd like to speak with Detective McKenna—"

"Did I say that?"

"What did you say, Detective?"

"Apparently nothing that's impressed itself on you thus far." He took another step toward her.

Nicole had no choice but to take another back. "Please don't come any closer."

"Why are you getting all defensive?"

"You're intentionally trying to intimidate me. And if you come any nearer—" she added when he took yet another step "—I'll scream."

"You okay, Nicole?"

Bless Darnell. Nicole shot the muscular giant a grateful smile. "Thank you, D—"

"Do you make a habit of eavesdropping on what's none of your business, boy?"

The speed with which Willard turned on the young

man shocked Nicole and from the way Darnell's dark eyes widened, it would seem he was taken aback, too.

"Ah...no, sir."

"Show me some ID."

"I didn't do nothing."

"I'll be the judge of that. Do it, boy."

Darnell dropped his gaze to the floor, his expression grew closed. Fortunately, Nicole had grown up in a home where prejudice and double standards were common, and she wasn't as easily cowed.

"Don't move, Darnell." And with no small disdain for Willard, Nicole added, "You're out of line, Detective. If you don't leave immediately—"

"What the hell's going on?" Roman stepped into the living room.

If Wes Willard was unhappy with his appearance, he covered it well. Easing around, he gave Roman what could only be called a smirk, rather than a smile.

"Well, well. The cavalry cometh. Small world, Mc-Kenna."

"And getting smaller. Hope you're not claustrophobic, Willard."

The senior detective chuckled and slipped his hands into his pants pockets. "That's right, Big Tex, stand tall for the pretty lady. Unfortunately, the posturing is unnecessary. I only stopped by to make sure Ms. Loring wasn't having any problem with the management allowing her in here."

"Thanks for explaining that," Nicole replied. "I'd have hated to have misunderstood your intent."

Willard narrowed his eyes before sliding his gaze to Darnell. "Just advise your friend that in the future he should address the police with the same respect he would his mama.''

"You're done here, right, Detective?" The slow drawl left Roman's voice, being replaced with a decided edge. "Miss Loring won't have to endure any more *official* visits?"

Willard slid on his glasses. "As far as I'm concerned. It's been closed from day one." Without another word, he left.

The three of them stood there until they heard his car door slam and the engine start. Only then did Darnell exhale noisily.

"Jeez Louise, was he real?"

Nicole exchanged looks with Roman. "I'm afraid so."

"In that case, I'd carry me a couple vials of blood around for insurance, Miz Nicole, cause that's one thirsty ghoul. For a second, I thought he was gonna haul my black ass to jail."

"I wouldn't let that happen, Darnell," she assured him. "But thank you for what you did. Why don't you start bringing the full boxes in the bedroom to the company truck. I need a minute with Detective McKenna."

"Sure thing."

When he was heading downstairs with the first box, Nicole met Roman's equally concerned gaze. "You've made an enemy of Willard. I didn't mean for that to happen."

"It couldn't be helped. When I saw the way he was treating you two…" He shrugged and extended his arms. "Come here."

Although she didn't think that was smart, either, she

stepped into his protective embrace. It amazed her at how balanced the world became once he drew her close and she felt his strong heartbeat joining with hers.

"Are you okay?" he asked, his lips brushing her temple.

She murmured something unintelligible. "I don't know if I'll ever be okay again. If you hadn't come back when you did, I don't know that I could have contained the situation. He didn't like Darnell being here."

"That's exactly why I don't want you alone at any given moment. I did a quick survey of this building and there isn't anyone home on this side. You'd better believe Willard already knew that."

"But what did he want? Surely he wouldn't try anything in broad daylight?"

"I'm beginning to suspect he doesn't think the way you or I do. What I intend to find out is how he unloaded his partner to get over here. At any rate, he knows he can't pull anything again without being put under the same screws he uses on people."

"Somehow that's not very reassuring. There's something extremely...cunning about that man." Remembering the matchbook, Nicole drew away. "I need to show you something." She drew it out of the pocket of her jeans and passed it over.

Roman's expression went from surprised to frowning.

"You know the place," she said, unsure whether to be pleased or worried.

"The question is where did you find this?"

"In one of Jay's pockets. How low do I have to sink my imagination?"

He didn't answer right away, partly because Darnell came through to collect another box, but also because he took his time to open the flap and read the message inside.

"Doesn't leave much to the imagination, does it?" he said, once they were alone again.

"That's not a woman's handwriting," Nicole replied. At Roman's dubious glance, she pointed to the letters. "Look at the bold strokes, the pen's tip leaves a stark, wide imprint. If this is a woman, she's over sixty and on the Forbes and Fortune five-hundred list."

"At Velvet's? It's a dark hole-in-the-wall down in the industrial section, Nick. Rumor has it that it caters to people into...well, let's call it alternative life-styles."

Despite the cautious words and his sympathetic expression, Nicole was thrown. She'd thought Velvet's was, at worst, maybe some topless club. "No. Not Jay. I don't know how he came to have that, but my brother was no more into cross-dressing or homosexuality or anything like that than he was into putting plastic bags over his head."

When Roman merely stood there watching her, she felt the rush of shame and embarrassment, an unexpected and barely containable anger that had her spinning away to take refuge in the bedroom. She needed space, to calm down and think of a rational explanation.

Roman followed. "Nick..."

Needing to purge the angst and panic threatening to

overwhelm her, she tried to slam the closet door. But the carpet kept it from giving her the sharp report and reverberating walls her emotions craved. Without thinking of how childish it would make her seem to him, she struck out at the top row of videotapes on the waist-high case beside the TV.

The whole row went flying in various directions, some crashing to the floor. A few burst open and plastic cartridges tumbled out. But that's not all.

A shower of bills spilled from one of the boxes, as well.

Roman picked up one of the crisp green slips of paper. "Hundreds." He held it up to the light. "And it looks authentic."

There had to be thousands of dollars there. As Nicole took in the scene, all she could remember was how often she'd offered to co-sign a note to help Jay start his own business. She had even planned to write him a check for his next few rent payments so he would be able to prepare a proper nursery for the baby. That he had let her chatter on, knowing he had a stash of his own... She turned back to the rest of the boxes left on the shelf.

"Don't, Nick."

Ignoring him, she eyed the offerings. The money had fallen out of a false cover for *Casablanca*, an all-time favorite of his. Remembering the other film he watched frequently, she snatched up *The Fountainhead*.

The lid popped open eagerly and more money sprang out. She dropped it and reached for a third box, this time *The Treasure of the Sierra Madre*.

Roman grabbed her wrist. "No more."

"Let go," she whispered. "I want to know how much there is, how big the lie gets."

"To what end? You're the only one who'll suffer."

"I'm fine." She pulled until he released his hold, and then resumed opening boxes. "Just fine." It became her mantra, two words she repeated over and over to keep from breaking into hysterical laughter, or tears.

There were four boxes in all. Not enough to begin a business on his own, true, but a considerable nest egg.

Once Roman took the last box away from her, he shoved it along with the rest of the money into the canvas bag he found in the closet. Then he led her out of the apartment.

"Anything else up there can damn well wait," he muttered.

Nicole barely heard him. Emotionally finished, she thought she did well to make it all the way to Darnell's car before collapsing.

21

Poor intricated soul!
Riddling, perplexed, labyrinthical soul!

—John Donne,
LXXX Sermons

There was nothing like an unconscious woman to reduce men to stumbling incompetents. Even knowing the cause as he did, Roman thought he did well to catch Nicole before she cracked her head open on the bottom stair. Darnell proved less useful.

"What's wrong?" he asked, racing over to them. "She have a stroke? A heart attack?"

This was definitely about the heart, Roman thought in the one corner of his mind where alarm bells weren't going haywire. To the younger man, he replied, "Just one blow too many."

"Should I call 911?"

"Hell, no." How did he think her nightmare had started? He tucked the bag under his armpit and swept Nicole into his arms. "Get the back door of my car. Then lock up tight upstairs."

Once he had her lying down in the back seat, he turned to Darnell who'd returned to watch over his shoulder. He acted like a stray pup. "You're going to have to explain this to your boss," he said. "There's no way she'll be able to go back to the office today."

"Oh, man...I was supposed to take care of her. He'll have my hide."

"This was nothing you could have prevented. She'll be okay once she gets some rest. Tell Max that I'll call him from her place, and that I need him to send over Carlyn as soon as he can. Now go!"

"What about those boxes?" Darnell asked, pointing to his half-loaded van.

"Do you know where she wanted them taken?"

"Yeah, I guess."

"Then do her a favor and drop them off on your way."

That seemed to make Darnell feel better. "You tell her, okay? Tell her I did it right off."

Roman drove Nicole home, and once he had her in her own bed, he phoned Dr. Stanley Bender. To his relief the psychiatrist answered his own phone.

"Mac, Mac." Stan sighed after listening to Roman's brief recap of the situation. "You realize, of course, that I should tell you to bring her to Emergency."

"They'd only contact her parents, who are the last people on the planet she needs in her face right now. Look, Stan, she may have a few lumps and bruises, but it's her emotions that have suffered the real injury, and I don't want just anyone messing around with those."

"I don't know whether to call you a flatterer or an arrogant bastard. I also must be nuts to consider a house call, but what the heck. I'm free until two o'clock. Give me directions.''

After concluding his conversation with Stan, Roman called Max, who also peppered the phone line with adjectives once he learned Roman refused to take Nicole to the hospital. However, he calmed down somewhat once assured that Dr. Stanley Bender had an M.D. attached to his credentials.

"Okay, Max, I'll update you as soon as he leaves," Roman said at the end of their conversation. "But you have to send Carlyn over as soon as possible. I have work to do, and there's no way Nicole can be left alone. Fine. Send Darnell, too. That's probably a wise idea. I appreciate it.''

Quickly hanging up, he jerked his tie loose, as well as the top button of his shirt, and went to check on Nicole. Although she lay as he'd left her, he thought her coloring had improved somewhat.

"Nick, honey, can you hear me?'' He'd already loosened her hair, and now stroked it. "You've got to open your eyes for me, babe, or you're going to have one scared cop on your hands.''

She didn't exactly do that, but her lashes fluttered and she did turn slightly toward the hand he rested against her cheek.

"Someone's coming over to check you out. He's the doctor I had the meeting with last night. You'll like him.'' He gabbed on, not paying attention to half of what he said, but was reassured whenever she gave the faintest hint that she heard him.

Minutes later, he heard Stan's heavy step outside. Relieved, he hurried to let him inside.

"I'm grateful," he said, stepping back for the winded man.

Looking warm, but otherwise unflappable, Stanley patted his shoulder. "Don't mention it. But when was the last time you took five, Mac? You look twice as rung out as you did yesterday. Keep it up and your friend's not going to be the only one in need of help."

Roman raked his hand through his hair. "It's been a bitch of a morning."

"So I gather. Sit and breathe for crying out loud. Is she in there?" he asked, pointing to the door that was leaned shut. "I'll be back shortly."

Roman would have preferred to follow in case Nicole needed reassuring, but Stan vetoed the idea and shut the door behind himself. It left Roman feeling as useless as he did when he listened to Meggie on the phone as she described how grueling her day had been. And because he could almost see the black hole his emotions wanted to spiral into, he went down to the unmarked car and got the money to redirect his thoughts.

He'd just finished inspecting and counting it, then tucking it away in what he hoped was a safe spot when Stan emerged from Nicole's bedroom.

"How is she?" he demanded, trying not to read too much into Stan's somber expression.

"The good news is that she's not catatonic, and from what I can tell she has every reason to be." He shook his head, but his expression held admiration. "She's a surprisingly strong lady, isn't she?"

"She was convinced she needed to be there for her brother, to give him what their parents couldn't or wouldn't. What worries me is that she has to be feeling betrayed, and the more she digs, the deeper that betrayal seems to go. What did she tell you?''

"Not much. Consciousness isn't a condition she holds in high value at the moment. I'd consider a prescription for a tranquilizer to guarantee the uninterrupted rest she needs, but considering the fall she took yesterday, I'd prefer not to induce sleep. In fact, although I don't see any dilation problem in her eyes, it wouldn't be wise to let her stay under for long stretches. Treat her as though she has a mild concussion. Wake her every hour or so, then start stretching that out if she seems to be responding well. I'd also like you to get some food into her as soon as possible. Chicken broth would be a good start, and I'm not talking the canned stuff. The soul reacts better to the real thing.''

"Do you moonlight as a Jewish mother?'' Roman asked, bemused.

"Whatever works.''

"Well, I'm not much of a cook, but a friend of hers is coming over to stay with her. I'll see what she can do.''

Stan didn't seem altogether happy about that. "You're leaving?''

"I'm on duty. I have a murder case only hours old that may be related to this,'' he said nodding to the bedroom. "I have to go. But I'll be back as soon as I can, and I'll check in regularly.''

"See that you do. She'll need to talk, and yours is the only name she's spoken so far.'' Stan scratched the tip of his nose. "At the risk of getting too personal, *are* you what that lovely lady needs?"

Roman ignored the tightening in his chest. "No. But I can't abandon her, either. Not in view of what's going down."

"Honorable. However, I think you're overlooking something critical, something as important as your professional dedication. You see, when I look into your eyes, there's a member of the walking wounded looking back at me." Stan shook his head. "A cop with his own considerable baggage is no prize candidate for any budding romance, but he's downright dangerous for a woman as vulnerable as Ms. Loring. Be careful. For both your sakes."

Roman's thoughts once again drifted to last night—or rather this morning—and how perfect, but undeniably wrong it had been. Just as he knew it was wrong now to want like crazy to go to her, hold her, seek his own oblivion inside her.

"You're not telling me anything I don't already know," he said wearily.

Once again Stan patted his shoulder. "Then I'll get out of here and leave you to it."

"What do I owe you?"

The psychiatrist waved away the question. "You're still on my IOU to Ralph. But down the road, try to get her to call me. I know I mentioned it the other day." He glanced back at Roman. "I'm politely insisting now."

"I hear you, and I'll do my best."

No sooner was Stan out of the driveway than the Van Dorn van pulled in, followed by a canary yellow compact. Darnell and Carlyn. Roman directed them to leave him room to get out before escorting them upstairs.

"She's resting, but I need you to wake her every hour or so and to talk to her for a few minutes. Carlyn, how are you with boiling chickens?"

She stopped midway up the stairs. "Dead and defeathered ones, I hope? I can't even bring myself to order lobster at a restaurant."

"The doctor wants her to have homemade soup. Obviously, I can't do that, and I was hoping you'd volunteer or know where we can find some."

The blonde did an about-face and headed down the stairs. "See you later, Darnell."

"Wait a minute!" the big warehouseman cried. "I can't cook!"

"Calm down. I'm only going to the market."

"Nothing doing. You make a list and *I'll* get what you need."

Roman let them settle the matter between them. Then when he tried to put two twenties by the list Carlyn was making, he was surprised how she waved him off.

"Max anticipated that and gave me plenty," she assured him. "It's his way of buying frequent progress calls."

Once Darnell was on his way with list in hand, Roman asked Carlyn, "Do you think you can hold the fort until he gets back?"

She listened intently as he dictated a list of don'ts, particularly about opening the door to anyone, even if they said they were the police and flashed a badge.

"I'll admit that you're scaring me a little," she said at last. "But I don't think you'd leave us if you thought we were in any critical danger."

"You've got that right." His instincts told him that for the present, any danger Nicole was in would come from inside herself.

By the time he got downtown again, Ralph was out of court.

His partner listened to a recap of the morning while chomping on the last of the three hot dogs he'd picked up outside the courthouse. "Tell you what, pard," he said, licking mustard off his fingers, "I can vouch for you that Willard had the time to be where he shouldn't because I saw Sir Isaac waiting to testify outside the courtroom down from mine. But I don't like that he knows you're suspicious of him. From here on, you'd better act as though you're expecting someone to draw a bead on you at any moment."

"I'll be careful. Any new thoughts about our latest stiff?"

"Well, that money sounds like a fine incentive for him to have been stalking Nicole."

"If he knew about it. The one connection, the only connection I can make at this point is that he was Hispanic and so was the mother of Jay Loring's baby."

Ralph studied the monitor screen on Roman's desk listing the minimal information they had so far on Angelo Aguirre. "There's also the small technicality that no Deep Ellum bartender saves forty Gs mixing strawberry daiquiris and drawing drafts."

"Meaning you don't think it or Loring was clean."
Roman didn't, either.

"You said Nicole knew exactly what boxes to reach for?"

"Turns out they were his favorite films."

"A filing system for himself or a sure way for her to find the cash in case something happened to him?"

Roman nodded slowly, warming to the latter part of that guess. "She would be less likely to simply box and give away his favorite videos. Wish he would have added a tape of himself explaining what the hell this was all about. How could he let her stay in his place and not be aware of the danger he could be placing her in?"

"Maybe he did and y'all haven't found it yet."

Roman met his partner's gaze. "I took her keys to the apartment."

Reaching around him, Ralph cleared the screen. "Then let's haul ass, pard."

It was a good hunch, but the apartment offered up nothing more useful regarding Jay Loring's secret activities when he wasn't working at Gregor's. Disappointed, Roman checked his watch and told Ralph that he needed to get to a pay phone so he could check on Nicole. His pager also brought the news that Glenda had tried to ring him.

"We're close to the health club," he added. "Let's head that way and then finish up by dropping by Velvet's."

"Works for me," Ralph replied.

They stopped on Hillcrest at a gas station and convenience store where Ralph went in to buy himself a soda and snack, while Roman telephoned Nicole's apartment. Carlyn answered, informing him that the soup was coming along nicely, and that Nicole had been a bit confused by seeing her there, but had quickly gone back to sleep after obediently reciting her name and a few other pertinent facts.

"Max called," the girl added. "He wanted to stop by on his way home, but now that I've seen what shape Nicole is in, I convinced him to wait a day or two. Don't be surprised, though, if this place resembles a florist shop by the time you get back. He knows how much Nicole loves flowers and he'll probably inundate her with them."

The bit of information reminded Roman of how much he didn't know about Nicole, and even though he wanted to ask Carlyn what her favorite blossom was, he didn't want them to become the source of too much gossip at Van Dorn's. Instead, he thanked her for all she was doing and asked to speak to Darnell.

"Anything to report?" he asked the other man.

"Everything's fine."

"Make a point of casually going outside every once in a while to check around. If you feel even slightly suspicious about anything, you have my pager number. Call me immediately."

"You bet."

Once Roman and Ralph were on their way again, Ralph asked how things were going. He was chewing on a huge piece of ugly pink peanut brittle between sips of soda, as though he hadn't eaten all day.

"So far so good," Roman replied. "I just wished

I'd asked Nicole if her brother had been a member of this club."

"We'll find out."

The health club was another few miles up the road in the back of an older shopping center. Whether it was the hour or the facility, traffic inside was minimal and Roman and Ralph had some difficulty finding someone to come out of one of the offices to speak to them.

"Damnation. We could load a couple of these machines into the car and be out of here for all the attention anyone's paying," Ralph muttered.

"See anyone who looks like a janitor or assistant trainer down any of those hallways?" Roman asked, searching himself.

"Not even that. No wonder business sucks." Ralph circled a counter and went to a glass-walled office where a man sat behind a desk chatting on the phone. He pounded on the door and called, "Police!"

Within seconds the flustered man was at the door. "What's going on?" he demanded looking from Ralph to Roman.

Ralph flashed his badge and introduced himself and Roman. "We need to ask you a few questions regarding an Angelo Aguirre. Does that name ring a bell with you?"

"No," the man replied, barely glancing at Angelo's ID. "Now if you'll excuse me, I'm in the middle of a business call."

"Look again. Please," Ralph added, with no hint of his usual sense of humor. "The reason we're asking is because the guy's dead and this card says he worked here. By the way, who are you?''

The budding yuppie turned as pale gray as his shirt and stared at the laminated identification. ''Uh…Guy Franken. Manager. And that could be…okay, sure. It's Angel.''

''Well, Angel was found shot in the head this morning. When did you last see him?'' Ralph asked, narrowing his eyes as though considering this man as his chief suspect.

''Oh, listen, you're barking up the wrong tree. See, he hasn't worked here in months.'' Guy Franken shot Roman a look that was a clear appeal for understanding.

Roman asked, ''He quit?''

''Not in any formal sense. He just stopped coming.''

Roman nodded to the ID. ''Were you aware that address doesn't exist?''

''I'm not…I don't know.''

''Would you mind checking your records? A phone number or next of kin's address would also be very helpful.''

After a slight hesitation, Franken said, ''I'll see what I can do.'' He led them to an office two doors down that was unoccupied. ''You'll have to excuse me if I'm not as quick at locating things as my secretary is,'' he added opening a file drawer. ''She and most of the staff are still on lunch break.''

That won a droll look from Ralph, whose expression said he thought the place was two steps away from bankruptcy court.

"In what capacity did you employ Mr. Aguirre, Mr. Franken?" Roman asked.

"Oh, he did a little of everything, I suppose. Swept up, helped in the laundry room, maintained the rest rooms... Actually, delegating tasks wasn't something I involved myself with. That would have been Ms. Vansell's department."

"And she's out to lunch?" Ralph asked, as though not believing any of this.

"No, she's at her chiropractor's." Realizing what he must have inferred, he glanced over his shoulder and added, "A nonwork-related injury. Here we go."

He drew out the thinnest of files and flipped over the one sheet inside, reading with a deep frown that barely aged his youthful face. "That's the only address I had for him, and I don't see a phone number. But here. Here's a listing for emergencies...a Feliciana Arroyo. Says she's the sister. I'll write down the address and phone number, but if the other address was a phoney, I don't know how much luck you'll have with this one."

"Helpful and brilliant, too," Ralph drawled minutes later as they left the building. "Well, I wasn't expecting much, but no wonder Angel walked from this dump. No matter what else he ended up doing for a living, it probably beat playing token slave here."

"And things are about to get more cheerful," Roman said handing him the slip of paper before heading for the driver's side of the car. "Look at that address."

Ralph read and twisted his rubber face into yet a new variation of grimace. "Why us? We'll be lucky to get out of that neighborhood with our engine intact, let alone the damn tires. Lock and load, pard. I'd rather we don't become some gang inductee's initiation."

The address for Angel's sister was miles south and east of the health club, beyond an older industrial section of town. In a small residential neighborhood, hidden by decades old oaks, at the end of a narrow street cramped with matchbox-size dirt-stained cottages and filthier yards, the Arroyo home had one benefit—an overgrown ligustrum hedge that also hid it from Military Parkway's busy four-lane traffic.

Roman parked parallel to the half-dead cedar in the front yard and eyed the black-and-white dog sitting under the cinder block front porch. The terrier mix mongrel reminded him of the mutt in the old *Our Gang* series.

"What are the chances of it biting?" he asked Ralph.

"Better ask what are the chances of it having rabies," Ralph replied.

It turned out that they got more attention from the neighbors than the dog, who announced them with a few rather bored yaps and scurried deeper into the shade of the porch. In contrast, almost everyone who was outside along the street stopped what they were doing to watch them, and many a flimsy screen door opened as those inside were warned of the *gringo policía*.

"Maybe I'd better stand out here and keep an eye on things," Ralph said. "You speak any Spanish?"

"A few phrases." Roman hoped it was enough to tell whoever was inside that a relative was dead without causing too much pain...and to tell if they were lying when asked some necessary questions. But when he knocked on the screen door and heard a soft keening from somewhere in the house, he had a feeling his concern about the language barrier might be too little too late. *"¿Hola...? Perdón, ¡hola!"*

He tried the screen door and found it was unlatched.

"Hold it. You aren't just going in there?" Ralph called in a loud whisper. He nodded to their audience. "You've only got at least three dozen witnesses."

"Someone's crying."

"You prefer to hear her scream rape or worse get a belly full of .12-gauge pellets? Knock again, damn it, and stop scaring the bejesus out of me."

"Wait. Here she comes," Roman said hearing footsteps.

He turned back to the door as a young woman in a skimpy tube top and cutoffs almost as brief shuffled toward him. Her mass of black hair was scooped up in an untidy ponytail, and her face, although young with impish features was red and puffy from weeping.

"Buenas tardes, señorita. Ah...¿habla inglés?"

He all but sighed in relief when she offered a minute nod, rigid as it was.

"I'm Detective Roman McKenna with the Dallas Police. Miss Arroyo is it? Miss Arroyo, has someone from the department already been out here to tell you about...?"

"No one comes. The neighbors tell me my brother is dead. Why you come now? You are no longer needed."

Roman didn't blame her for her resentment, but he needed to try to explain if he had a hope in hell of getting her to listen to any of his questions. "You have our deepest apologies, Miss Arroyo, but we didn't know about you until—well, no more than a half hour ago. Perhaps you weren't aware that your brother was driving without a license in a vehicle that had falsified records. We only had an employment card to go by, and the health club where he worked some months ago had you listed as the person to contact in case of an emergency."

Around twenty-one and no pushover, she listened to his explanation without any visible reaction, except to occasionally sniff, and when he gestured with his hand to signal he didn't know whether to apologize again or what, she shook her head as if rejecting it all. "Now you are going to tell me that you don't know who killed him, either."

"I'm afraid we don't. Not yet. But maybe you could help us find out. Do you know what your brother was up to since he quit working at the club?"

"No."

"No idea how he made his living, who his friends were?"

"No."

She was one little hardnose, that's for sure, and Roman didn't want to be rough with her, but she wasn't giving him much choice. "Ma'am, we know your brother was in this country illegally. If I ask you for some ID, would you be able to come up with the appropriate paperwork for yourself?"

"I was married to an American. I have as much right to be here as you do."

That explained the difference in names. "Is your

husband around? Maybe I could ask him a few questions.''

"He's dead.''

The Irish had a saying about bad luck, "If I bet on the tide, it wouldn't come in.'' Roman figured that was about the extent to his streak today. Exhaling, he bowed his head. "I'm sorry, *Mrs.* Arroyo, but I'm feeling a little desperate myself. You see, I saw your brother last night when he was still very much alive. He was running away from a lady he'd attacked outside her home, and that lady is a friend of mine who also lost her brother recently. I'm trying to understand why, Mrs. Arroyo. Why he was—''

"Get out.''

It might only have been shock, but he sensed he'd hit a nerve. "What if I said the name Gregor's?'' he asked more quietly. "Does that mean anything to you?''

"No, and if you don't get out of here now, I'll start screaming!"

Because it was exactly what he'd heard Nicole say only hours ago, he grimaced, but raised his hands in surrender. "All right, then. Thank you for your time, ma'am.''

He started to walk away and heard what was probably her latching the worthless hook latch. Fully intending to follow Ralph to the car, he experienced the strongest impulse to ask one more question.

He glanced over his shoulder. "What about Velvet's? Ever hear of it?''

22

The desire of the moth for the star,
Of the night for the morrow,
The devotion to something afar
From the sphere of our sorrow.

—*Percy Bysshe Shelley*

When Roman walked into Nicole's apartment again, he was far later than he'd intended to be, more tired than he wanted to think about, and he'd forgotten the flowers. The last he noticed as soon as he saw the long-stemmed roses on the dinette table and the huge colorful arrangement on the bar. He could only imagine what was back in the bedroom. The apartment was lit by candles on the bar giving a depressed rather than romantic appeal. Some of that came from Carlyn's and Darnell's unhappy expressions as they stood at opposite poles of the apartment. Roman suspected they'd discovered they didn't like being cooped up together with little to entertain them. If so, they were probably less happy with him.

"Sorry," he said, turning on the outside light and leaving the wooden door open. He thought it might improve their mood to have the hint that they could

leave whenever they were ready. "I really did try to
get back here sooner than this. How is she?"

"Sleeping."

The one-word summation was provided by Darnell,
who was already striding toward him—or rather escape. "I'll see y'all."

"Thanks for everything, man." Roman held out his
hand. "I know it was a long day."

The gesture took some of the sullenness out of the
younger man's expression. "Hey, Mr. Van Dorn says
I get paid overtime for this. Guess I can't complain."
He cast a last glance toward Carlyn. "Too much."

"Be careful with the speed limit. Now that it's getting dark the HP police will be suspicious of vans,
even those with familiar logos."

"If I'm stopped, I'll tell 'em to call my man, Detective McKenna."

"Just don't use that as an excuse for speeding on
Central."

Finally grinning, Darnell even said good-night to
Carlyn as he let himself out.

"How are you doing?" Roman said, ready to hear
her side of things.

"Don't worry, Detective McKenna, we're fine. It's
simply that—"

"Roman."

She smiled shyly. "I was only going to say that it
was easier for me. I knew what to expect what with
Nicole still trying to get moved in here, while coping
with everything else. Darnell only saw that there
wasn't much to do. I think he was also disappointed

that he didn't get to scare off anyone except the florist delivery boys.''

"That's what the bulk of policework is—waiting and waiting.'' He glanced back at the closed bedroom door. "When was the last time you wakened her?''

"Six. And the bad news is that I got all of a cup-and-a-half of soup in her today, only because when she mentioned being thirsty I tried to feed her broth. But I must say this last time, she actually sounded closer to her old self.''

"I meant what I said to Darnell,'' he told her as she collected her purse and the jacket to her suit. "I appreciated you two being here for her.''

"That's what friends are for. Actually, this makes me feel like a real friend. Until now I've considered her more a mentor. Seeing her vulnerable and hurting these past weeks…'' Her eyes filled and she didn't finish.

"I understand.''

"Listen—'' Carlyn paused before him "—I'm going to go pick up a few things for her. Sleeping stuff. She's been running a fever now and then, and I had to change her twice. That's how I found out that her nighty wardrobe is…well, with Darnell being around, and—'' she glanced away, embarrassed "—okay, let me just say it. I saw the extra toothbrush and razor in the bathroom and figured this won't be your first night here. I put all your stuff in the first drawer so that Darnell wouldn't see them. Not that he hasn't made his own observations.''

Roman had assumed the topic would come up eventually, and for Nicole's sake he wanted to stem any harmful gossip. "I'm temporary, Carlyn."

The young woman studied his face and offered a gentle smile. "If you say so. But if you ask me, she deserves someone solid in her life."

Solid, there was a joke. In that case, he definitely didn't qualify.

"What time do you need me to be here in the morning?" she asked, breaking into his thoughts.

"Would six-thirty be asking too much?" He'd stopped at the apartment on the way over and picked up a change of clothes knowing that his hours would be an imposition for anyone, especially an engaged young woman with a job that didn't require her to be at work until mid-morning.

"I'll be here."

Roman followed her out to make sure she had no problems, then he returned inside, locked up, and gratefully stripped down to his slacks. Wanting a beer like nobody's business, he first detoured into the bedroom.

The instant he sat down on the edge of the bed, she roused. He told himself that she would have done so for any interruption, but the way she virtually curled around his thigh had him wanting to scoop her up and settle her on his lap.

"How's it going?" he murmured, leaning over to brush his lips across her forehead. He was glad to find it much cooler than before.

"What time is it?"

"Closing in on nine. Does your head hurt?"

"Not anymore. I think someone's packed it full of cotton balls while I've been sleeping."

"You needed the rest. Can I get you anything? Carlyn said you didn't eat much today."

Nicole blinked, and slowly brushed her hair back. "Carlyn...I remember." She gazed around the room lit subtly by the bathroom night-light and eyed the flowers on both nightstands and her armoire. "McKenna, tell me that you didn't do this?"

She gave him too much credit. "It's Max. He wanted to spoil you."

She remained silent and Roman knew she was fighting the fog to remember. Everything.

"The money..."

"It's safe. No need to worry about it tonight."

"How much is there?"

"Nick, that's not important right now."

"How much?"

"Forty."

Her eyes widened. "Thousand? My God..."

"Maybe he didn't believe in banks."

"He did. I'm the beneficiary of two accounts, both with modest balances, hardly enough to cover his funeral expenses." She stared off into space. "I gave him money to dress well for interviews, offered to cosign a note..."

"Maybe he took out a loan with someone else."

"How? By putting up both kidneys as collateral?"

"He could have won a few ball game bets."

"Not Jay." She covered her face with her hands. "Don't try to make me feel better, McKenna. I have to stop hiding from this."

"So he didn't stay on a pedestal like some of those gold statues you and Max sell. You don't have to bury all your good memories along with the bad—which, I should add, you don't know are true yet."

She struggled to sit up. "You're right. Besides, I'm stronger than this."

Roman smiled for the returned hint of her spirit, even as his tongue grew thick at the picture she made in the ivory negligee, whose champagne lace strap slipped off one shoulder. "That's what Stan thinks, too."

"Stan who?"

"The doctor who visited you earlier."

"Your psychiatrist friend. Was I rude?"

"Apparently he didn't think so." For his own sake, he replaced the strap on her gown.

"My family has an aversion to psychiatrists... probably because we know we need them so much. My mother would die if she knew— God. How am I going to tell her any of this, or my father for that matter?"

"You're thinking too much, Nick. Lie back down and try to get a little more sleep. If not for yourself, do it for me. I think Carlyn put you in that thing to drive me nuts."

She shot him a tolerant look. "McKenna, you are so full of it. I'm about as appealing as a bag lady."

"You think?" As she settled against the pillows, he followed, and despite his good intentions, he kissed her exposing a modicum of feelings and concern for her. "I've never kissed a bag lady that way," he murmured, his lips lingering near hers.

Nicole stroked his cheek. "You're going to do it, aren't you?"

"What?"

"Finish breaking what's left of my heart."

Not if he could help it.

Her words were like a kick in the gut, reminding him that he'd added to heartbreak today and ticked off more than a few people. Hadn't Feliciana Arroyo slammed that door in his face for being an insensitive ass? And hadn't Ralph cussed up a storm when, due to him insisting on heading over to Velvet's, they'd been slow in receiving a tip and, therefore, too late to stop a reluctant prime witness in an upcoming trial from running? Least forgivable was that in all the commotion he had for the first time forgotten that Glenda had called early this afternoon.

Not wanting to burden Nick with any of that, he tucked the bedsheet under her chin. "Go to sleep. I'll have a beer and shower and turn in myself."

He downed half the bottle of the cold drink before he let himself dial Glenda's home number. Hoping she was the one who answered and not his replacement, he frowned at the card in the arrangement on the kitchen counter. He'd assumed all the flowers were from Max. Who the hell was Cameron?

"Hello?"

"I'm sorry I'm late."

"Of course, you are, Roman," his ex-wife replied, sounding more fatalistic than angry. "Never mind. I only called to let you know we're back."

"How did it go?"

"She had a blast," Glenda said, some tenderness

warming her voice. "I hadn't seen her so happy in ages."

"Did she get to see her Pluto?"

"Yeah. She has a picture for you."

"Did she hold up well?"

"We had to strap her in her cart to keep her from running after everything that caught her eye. And in the end she didn't want to leave."

Roman closed his eyes, grateful she'd been allowed that experience. "Good. That's good. What about now? How's she feeling?"

"She seems very much at peace. I don't know," Glenda added with a forced laugh. "Maybe we should have taken her sooner. I think it's made a world of difference."

Behind his lids, his eyes began to burn. He knew she was lying, and that she was asking him to participate in the lie. "Sounds like it," he replied, then had to clear his throat. "Okay, listen, thanks for being tolerant about the hour. Can I call there in the morning to talk to her?"

"Yes, here. I'll tell her to expect you."

Glenda hung up without saying goodbye, and Roman thought it was just as well. They both knew it was because they were closer to the toughest goodbye they would ever have to face, and neither of them had the courage to admit it to the other. He even forgot about making a big deal over the wasted trip down there. None of that mattered anymore. What did was that somehow he had to get down to Houston again to hold his baby while she still knew it was him.

He thought back to the time when the only way she

would go to sleep was when he lay across her baby bed with her and told her several stories about the constellations outside her bedroom window. She would lean her head against his shoulder, her tiny honey-and-gold curls tangling in his arm hair, and he would call her Little Meggie Mermaid.

If he closed his eyes, he could hear her delighted giggles again...smell her baby shampoo. But these days those memories came accompanied by a sharp pain in his chest.

Swallowing against it, he blew out the candles beside the flower arrangement, then stood there in the darkness. It didn't help. It certainly didn't ease his grim hold on reality...the knowledge that tomorrow was coming. Ready or not. Like the final chorus in the children's hide-and-seek game.

Ready or not.

23

Never glad confident morning again!

—*Robert Browning,*
The Lost Leader

It was tempting to lie there and pretend to sleep on. But Nicole had always had too much energy for her own good, and the second time Carlyn started withdrawing after checking on her—the digital clock on the nightstand flashed 8:30 in red—she called out hoarsely, "Don't go."

Carlyn spun around, a smile of pleasure brightening her pretty face. "Welcome back to the land of the living. How do you feel?"

"Like something rejected by my garbage disposal." She eased up to a sitting position and carefully adjusted a few pillows behind her. "I do, however, seem to remember you taking awfully good care of me yesterday. Thank you."

"Don't mention it. Ready for coffee and something to eat?"

"Shower first."

"Need help?" Carlyn asked, stepping closer as Nicole slid her feet to the floor.

"No, but you could be a bigger help if you moved some of these flowers into the other room. I think I'm being anesthetized by them."

"I was afraid of that. We're running out of places to put them. As soon as people hear you're under the weather they ask Max how to get flowers to you. There are a few more vases in the bathroom."

"That's awfully kind of everyone, but for pity's sake call Max and tell him to put out the word that I'm fine before I have to commit myself to the Betty Ford Clinic."

With that she took aim for the bathroom on legs that wobbled like overcooked spaghetti. She didn't re-emerge until she'd shampooed her hair twice, and had scrubbed off every skin cell that wasn't firmly attached. Unsure of what she was ready to wear, she put on the white terry robe on the back of the bathroom door, and rewrapped her hair in a towel before venturing out in search of coffee.

"Darnell!" she cried upon seeing him. Carlyn hadn't mentioned that he was there, too.

He whipped off stereo earphones and rose from the couch where he'd also been reading the paper. "Hey, look at you. You feeling better?" He rushed to pull out a bar stool for her. "Come sit."

"A personal maid and a valet-bodyguard, this is...very interesting."

"You want juice with your coffee?" Carlyn asked, ignoring the comment and quizzical look. She swept an arm toward the refrigerator. "We have orange, cranberry, mango-banana and grapefruit."

Nicole murmured her thanks to Darnell as she sat

and rested her elbows on the counter, her chin in her palms. "Opening a juice bar?"

"It was more of a matter of me not drinking soda, and Darnell being a bottomless pit. Thought we might as well fill him with something that's good for him. Especially since Max is footing the bill while we're here."

Enough was enough, Nicole thought. She could and would happily pay for her own caretaking. "Hand me that phone, Darnell," she muttered, stretching for the machine that was out of reach.

Carlyn crossed her arms, completely undaunted. "Don't waste your time. That is unless you want to hear Max's blistering baritone as he grills you about every swallow and bite you've taken in the last twenty-four hours, and what the doctor said...?"

Nicole made a face. Max *would* ignore her protests, then lecture her for being up already. Who needed that?

As Carlyn slid a mug of coffee at her, Nicole settled for taking a careful sip. "Mmm, wonderful. And no juice, thanks. Nothing exotic to eat, either," she added as Carlyn opened her mouth to speak. "Maybe some toast and a soft-boiled egg?"

Her friend accepted that as being better than nothing and went to work. Nicole turned to Darnell.

"Do you know if anyone checked Mrs. Gilman's mailbox for the last two days?" When he shook his head, she asked, "Would you? Thanks."

Once he was gone, she noted Carlyn's secret smile. "What?"

"Merely admiring the smooth moves of a master. So what did you need to ask me in private?"

Nicole didn't waste any time. "How did Roman seem to you this morning?"

"Ah. I thought so." The younger woman put two eggs in a saucepan of water and set the heat-resistant glass on the stove. "Quieter than usual and extra tired. Did you two have a squabble?"

"No. I woke when he first came in, but I don't remember anything else."

That wasn't entirely true, however. She was acutely aware that despite that luscious kiss, he hadn't slept with her last night, and from what Carlyn just said, it didn't sound as though he'd gotten much sleep at all. Why?

Had he figured out where all that money had come from and was afraid she would ask? Maybe he'd had more reason to worry about her safety and had stayed up to keep watch throughout the night. But then wouldn't he have said something to Carlyn and Darnell, and wouldn't they be more somber?

The card on the exotic bouquet beside her caught her attention. She leaned closer and frowned. It wasn't from Max as she'd assumed because many of the flowers were personal favorites. It was from Cameron. Oh, dear. Cameron.

If Roman had seen this and, despite what she'd said to him about breaking her heart, drawn certain conclusions...

God, listen to you. He's taken on your problems at the risk of his own job—not to mention on top of ev-

erything that goes along with having a critically ill child—and you're wondering if he's in a jealous snit?

"I'd like to help if I could."

Nicole realized she'd been so lost in her private thoughts that she'd forgotten Carlyn was standing there observing her all the while. She quickly shook her head. "You've already done more than you should have been asked."

"That's a joke, right? You've never collapsed before, what did you expect?" Carlyn dropped two slices of bread into the toaster and pushed the lever down. "Darnell told me about yesterday. He said that this other detective came to your brother's apartment and acted real weird. Darnell was scared to death that he was going to pick a fight with him as a reason to arrest him. When he mentioned the detective's name, I recognized him as the guy who came to Van Dorn's last week. Was it?"

Nicole didn't want to appear standoffish, but she couldn't drag another person she cared about into this nightmare. "Don't ask me anymore questions, Carlyn. When I can tell you, when *I* know what's going on myself, I'll explain. I promise."

She started to shake her head again, and a blinding pain behind her eyes had her gasping, then covering her face with her hands.

"What's wrong?" Carlyn was immediately at her side.

She had to wait until the needle driven through her skull melted into a dull throb. "I don't know. Hopefully, I just woke too abruptly, but…oh. My purse. Could you—"

"I know where it is," Carlyn replied, already hurrying to the bedroom. She returned quickly and placed the leather bag on the counter. "Tell me what to look for and I'll get it."

"The prescription my doctor gave me back when...damn." Reaching for the purse herself, Nicole inadvertently knocked it over spilling the contents everywhere.

"Stay put," Carlyn said. "I'll get everything."

But the pain had receded enough for Nicole to want to help and she eased off the stool to fumble with the several items closest to her. She saw the small plastic container with the pills under her wallet, but what had her staring was the small black book that was to its left.

"Well, you're looking right at them and didn't know it." Carlyn shook the small bottle that she'd scooped up, along with the wallet. "Nicole...?"

"That isn't mine."

Carlyn frowned and read the label. "It says so right here."

She wasn't referring to the pills. It was the notebook, and she was trying to understand what it had been doing in her purse. Granted, she'd had some trouble with her memory lately, but she knew the contents of her purse, damn it. The notebook didn't belong there.

Carlyn handed it to her, and she slowly, reluctantly paged through it. She had to do that twice because the majority of the pages were blank. The few that had something written on them listed initials and addresses that made her shiver—not because she recognized them. She didn't. Oh, a few addresses seemed familiar, but what left her shaken and chilled was the handwriting.

It was Jay's.

How had this found its way into her purse?

_____ **24** _____

Coming events cast their shadows before.

—*Thomas Campbell,*
Lochiel's Warning

"There may be no mystery," Roman said that evening. "You really could have forgotten that Jay gave it to you."

It had been a long day for Nicole. She'd had to recover from the blunder of speaking in front of Carlyn, to appear convincing when pretending she'd subsequently recalled putting the notebook in her purse herself. Then for the rest of the day, she'd hidden in her room swallowing aspirin every few hours instead of the sedative she'd been tempted to take for her headache so she would be lucid when Roman returned. And after all of that she had to listen to this?

Sitting on the same stool she had that morning, she wanted to throw the damned thing at him. "Excuse me. I did not forget, and I didn't put it in my bag!"

"Nick, if anyone has a right to make a mistake, it's you. For the last few weeks you've been under a helluva strain. Maybe you inadvertently picked it up thinking it was your address book."

Cops. Sometimes they were more reluctant to use the muscle in their skulls than scientists. "I repeat—I did not *forget*. And I know what I do and don't put in my purse. My address book is in one of those thick organizers. As I said, I didn't know about that—" she nodded to what he held "—until I knocked over my bag and everything fell across the kitchen floor."

"Yeah, but, Nick...you've been digging around in your purse for a month and you didn't notice it before."

"Listen, buster, I have not waited all day to share this with you, only to be criticized for not acting like your idea of a 'normal' woman."

"Could we keep the sarcasm down to a minimum. You're not the only one who's had a long day."

He was right in that respect. It was her anxiousness that had her growing impatient. She drew a deep breath. "I apologize. But please don't patronize me."

He studied her for a long moment, until, finally, he inclined his head. "Maybe I did make it sound that way. I'm sorry, too."

When he used that deep, gruff tone with her, she all but melted inside. Not smart when she was trying to follow his lead tonight by keeping her own distance.

"Did something happen that you need to talk about?" she asked, still wondering what had changed in the last twenty-four hours.

"It's what didn't happen." Roman took another deep draw on the beer he'd opened for himself, then he removed his jacket and gun as was becoming his routine upon arriving here. Of course, the gun stayed within reach. "We spent most of the day chasing down

people for a few older cases. Ralph's still acting like
a bear with a thorn in his backside over the witness
who skipped—not that I can blame him, since it means
the D.A. will have to accept a plea bargain on what
should have been a clear-cut murder-one conviction—
and I didn't get to do squat on your brother's case or
Aguirre's.''

"Why can't you do some of the investigating on
your own time?''

"It's not possible.''

"Why not?''

"I have to get out to Velvet's. Flash around Jay's
picture...and Angelo's. Ask if anyone remembered
seeing either of them. Then go to Gregor's and hope
to find someone who saw Aguirre with your brother.''

"Exactly. Go do it.''

"And leave you here by yourself? Not likely.''

"I'll go with you.''

He had begun to lift the bottle to his lips again and
froze. "Twenty-four hours ago, you were practically
comatose. Before that you were a hairbreadth away
from a concussion. Carlyn tells me that you've been
fighting one helluva headache all day, and you still
look as though a ten-mile-per-hour wind could knock
you over. How do you figure that I'm going to take
you to some dive, let alone a yuppie club where the
noise level is enough to shatter a healthy person's ear-
drums?''

"But if it would help...''

Roman shook his head and drank.

"I feel much better," she insisted. "The worst of
the headache is gone, and I'd much rather be doing

something constructive than sitting here driving myself crazy speculating.''

"Listen to me. I can't take you to Velvet's. You're a lady, damn it!'' he snapped when she continued to stare owlishly at him.

Nicole relaxed, and smiled. "That's sweet, Mc-Kenna.''

A rumbling sound rose from his chest. "Now who's patronizing whom?''

"Seriously. I'm touched. But I have seen naked women before. And men for that matter.''

"This isn't like art class, Nick. This is...''

"Exotic dancing?''

"Try raunchy.''

She found it amusing that he wouldn't meet her gaze as he spoke. "Well, we're not talking about hiring someone to do a lap dance, are we?''

"And what if some woman propositions you?''

"It's a gay club?'' She might not be able to explain how Jay had obtained all that money, but she did know about her brother and his sexual preferences.

"I'm sure they have some employees and patrons who swing both ways.'' Roman's tone and expression said he wasn't at all pleased at having to have this conversation. "But what I'd meant was S and M. Low-key in comparison to some cities—Dallas's strong religious community still has a heavy influence on local politics—but the place gets its point across to draw and keep the clientele it wants.''

"I thought you'd said you'd never been there?''

"I asked a cop who works that part of town. Believe me, you don't want a tour.''

"So I'll stick close to you."

"Nick...there's a stubborn streak in you that's giving me a serious pain."

Nicole refused to be baited. "That's your conscience because you know you have to do this." She eyed the book he'd been flipping through. "Those people in there have to be identified and checked out."

"These are business addresses. I'll have to do that during regular hours."

"All of them?" She had thought one or two were, but hadn't been sure about the other four.

"Definitely. And this one here at The Crescent doesn't even have any initials, just an address."

Yes, she'd recognized the stunning hotel-condo-office complex's address on McKinney. "Why do you suppose he left them off? And what does that '22k C.' mean at the front?"

"I don't know. Why does anyone do anything evasive?"

"To hide the obvious."

"That's what I think, too. Now all we have to figure out is, what would be obvious to you if you saw certain initials and that address."

Startled, Nicole looked from him to the flowers. No, she thought. It was a coincidence, that's all. One had nothing to do with the other.

"What?"

"Nothing. I was only trying to guess when Jay slipped this into my purse."

"That last evening after you'd returned to Van Dorn's. It had to be then. Did you carry an evening bag like you usually do to those special events?"

"You noticed that? I'm impressed."

His look told her that there wasn't much about her that he missed. "Where did you leave this bag?"

"On the sofa table behind the couch, right in line with the doorway, and my suitcase was in the front closet." Nicole stopped, experiencing another of those awful moments that chilled her to the bone. "Wait! You think he knew someone was coming over."

"He wouldn't have hidden this among your things unless he was concerned someone might try to take it away from him. And I think he kept it in the first place for insurance—and that if something happened to him, you would need it."

"Dear God. It's too much to take in...and what about the baby coming? Under the circumstances, wouldn't he have postponed whatever meeting this was?"

"The boy was already there," Roman replied with conviction. "Remember? You spoke to Jay and heard baby sounds."

"Of course. But if he was that concerned...surely he would have tried to get him out of there?"

"What if there wasn't time? Maybe whoever he wanted to hide this from showed up unexpectedly. Granted, your suitcase would have been a better choice, but the noise he made putting it in there would have been pretty obvious to someone on the opposite side of the door."

Nicole moaned and gazed up at the ceiling. "What were you doing, Jay? Where did all that money come from?" With a decisive sound, she slid off the chair. "I'm going to change. You can't check those addresses without knowing where Velvet's and Angelo Aguirre fit in."

Roman put down the bottle, pocketed the little notebook and took hold of her by her arms. Resignation made his face look older, but there was still a shadow of intimacy in his eyes. "I know your wardrobe's cut way down these days, but wear slacks if you can, and a blazer. Dark colors. And a minimum of jewelry."

"Am I pretending to be a nun looking for a lost lamb?"

"No, my partner."

For all of her determination to act confident, the truth was that Nicole had never been in a topless club before and had no idea what to expect. She'd reasoned that having traveled through Europe, New York and, of course, New Orleans, she had seen enough of the periphery of those cities' darker sides not to be too shocked. However, walking into Velvet's made her realize there was a difference between peeking into a window or open doorway, and walking straight through the middle of that world.

Darkness, smoke and a body-vibrating primitive beat assaulted them the moment they entered. After several seconds, Nicole's eyes adjusted enough to see Roman standing before a booth with a sign that listed the cover charge for admittance. When he reached into his pocket, she thought he was planning to pay it, but then she saw the middle-aged redhead lose the "come hither" smile. Her heavily made-up eyes shifted to Nicole and back to Roman and her dark bronze lips formed the question, "What do you want?" although Nicole never heard the words.

Roman flashed Angelo Aguirre's ID. Not surprisingly the woman, compressed in a lace and velvet top that did terrifying things to her enormous breasts, immediately shook her head. The next thing Nicole knew, Roman was leading her through a maze of tables and bodies, one instant shockingly close, and the next vanishing in the blinding effects of the strobe lights.

Waitresses brushed by them wearing the tiniest strips of leather between their legs and little else…unless you considered thigh-high leather boots, elbow length leather gloves and leather face masks clothing. A few wore rings clipped to their nipples and sported various other pierced parts that had her struggling not to wince. One girl wearing a vest with circles cut out in strategic places waited until Nicole met her gaze and blew her a sultry kiss.

"The trick is not to make eye contact unless you're seriously shopping," Roman said as they reached the bar.

"You'll pay for that."

"You're in the right place to try without attracting attention."

Ignoring her discreet cough, he signaled the nearest bartender. Nicole used the time to scan the room. There were a few men around who looked as though they'd come here straight from the office, but by and large the mostly male crowd was tough to pinpoint, crossing every age group and professional background, and there were enough women scattered about to change her opinion about who frequented these places.

But she did draw one conclusion—she and Roman might as well be wearing patches that said "DPD."

"What'll it be?" An unsmiling bartender faced them across the counter. He didn't look at them now that he was close; rather, he placed two coasters on the damp counter and busied himself with things like emptying ashtrays and filling snack baskets.

"Two Millers," Roman said.

Once the man went to the cooler, Nicole leaned toward Roman. "I'd be happy with water."

"You don't drink the water in places like this, and you won't be here long enough to touch the beer. Relax."

As the bartender placed two bottles before them, Roman brought out a twenty-dollar bill and set the photograph of Jay on top of it. "Ever see this guy in here?"

"Nope."

The man flipped the photograph off the bill and made change. When he tried to leave, Roman gripped his wrist, then brought out Angelo Aguirre's ID.

"How about him?"

If she hadn't been paying close attention, Nicole would have missed the flicker in the man's gaze. But there was no mistaking the brief glance he shot to the stage.

"No. Enjoy your beer…Detective."

He moved down the bar to take care of another customer and Roman shifted Nicole's bottle closer to her—an excuse to get nearer, she realized as his elbow rubbed hers.

"Check out the dancers, particularly the one with the ponytail."

She'd already noticed the two young women dancing up there. Well, more like gyrating, she amended, noting that the pole in the center of the floor was almost a sexual partner. Both females were dark, exotic-looking creatures with terrific bodies that glistened with sweat under the hot lights. However, Nicole knew better than to guess Roman was asking her to critique their performance skills.

Ms. Ponytail was the fiery one. She watched the girl bend back, back, until her hair—the thick mass had to be an extension, she concluded—all but caressed her calves. As for her taut nipples, they had to be iced or whatever the girls did backstage to create such a visual lie.

When the dancer swung her face near her partner's crotch, Nicole leaned toward Roman. "I'll give her an eight for navigational skills, but what do you want to bet she spends a good chunk of her tip money on a chiropractor?"

"That's Feliciana Arroyo. Aguirre's sister."

Nicole refocused on the stage with renewed interest. "How do we get her to talk to us?"

"Follow me, but say nothing."

There was a narrow hallway off to the right of the stage that led to the dancer's dressing rooms. As they started down it, they came upon a huge man who apparently guarded the girls from would-be pests. The guy had enough tattoos on his arms to convince Nicole that she never wanted to see the rest of his body, nor was she about to joke that gray hair wasn't all that intimidating in a bouncer.

Their song done, Feliciana and her partner stepped off the stage to a smattering of applause and one or two whistles. Aguirre's sister had already spotted Roman. Nicole saw fear in her dark, starkly lined eyes as she approached them.

"How long did you think it would take?" Roman asked mildly, when she was within earshot.

Recovering with impressive speed, she tried to brush past them. "I have nothing to say to you."

"We can talk here or downtown, Feliciana," Roman told her.

The young woman whispered something to the tattooed giant. It had the man exaggerating his straddled stance across the hallway and he stared harder into Roman.

Unimpressed, Roman flashed his badge and murmured, "And what will we find in your file down at the station, old son?"

That had the bouncer reaching back to grab Feliciana before she could make good her escape. He drew the stumbling girl back in front of him and forced her to face Roman.

"Ow! Donny's gonna hear about you handling me and feeding me to the pond scum," she snapped.

"He pays me to watch his ass before yours," Tattoo replied.

Sensing a combustible hostility, Nicole was impressed when Roman calmly reached into his pocket and brought out the matchbook.

"This doesn't have to be painful," he told the hostile dancer, flipping open the matchbook. "I'm just trying to help this woman resolve a mystery. This was found among her brother's belongings. You know about painful discoveries, don't you, Feliciana?"

The woman seemed to ignore what he held before her, but said, "Do you have any idea how many men come through here with their tongues hanging out begging for a little attention? What do I know or care if someone made the guy an empty promise?"

"Not so empty. He's dead...like your brother."

That wiped the sardonic smile off Feliciana's face. "Get away from me, and stay away!"

Nicole couldn't help it, the moment the younger woman tried to flee again, she reached out. "Please. I don't believe your brother meant any harm when he attacked me. Maybe I did at first, but not now. All I'm trying to understand is what he was trying to tell me."

"Nothing. And if you're smart, you'll forget about what happened."

"That's impossible."

Jerking free, Feliciana swept back her damp bangs. "Look, I can't help you."

"I think you could," Nicole replied, "but you're scared. You needn't be. We can protect you."

"Yeah, right. You two want to help? Go away."

As she started another attempt to leave, Roman stretched out his arm and blocked her way. "Not the right answer."

"Don't you get it?" she spat. "I'm not talking. And if I were you, I'd worry about my own back instead of trying to scare me."

"Thank you for the warning, Feliciana. But if you

really want it to mean something, you'd tell me who I should be watching out for."

"Up yours."

Wrenching her arm free, Feliciana darted down the hall, and this time the aging bouncer let her pass. When Roman tried to followed, though, the huge man shoved him against the wall.

"That's enough," Tattoo muttered.

Nicole could see an unmistakable violence appear in Roman's eyes. "Don't!" she cried, then began pulling him away. "Let's go, McKenna. Please."

He went, but reluctantly.

"We should have gotten more information," he said, once they emerged into the humid night air.

"You learned that Aguirre's sister works in the club and that she probably knows who wrote that note to my brother. That's quite a bit for one night."

He shot her a sidelong look. "That's not how it works. The idea is to get everything, and as fast as possible to get the vermin off the streets."

"And how did you plan to do that? By introducing Tiny Tim's testicles to his tonsils? Somehow I don't think that would scare Feliciana into talking."

"Maybe not, but now we have to worry that she'll run."

"Why? She didn't give anything away."

"Her brother's dead. So is yours. And odds are they were killed by the same person. Now she was seen talking to us. If you were her, exactly how much more incentive would you need to haul ass?"

Put that way, Nicole almost felt sorry for the girl. "Maybe we should go back inside...?"

"Forget it. She was probably out the back door before we made it to the front."

"But if she runs…maybe she knew the mother of Jay's baby. What if Jay lied about the student story, too. God, McKenna, what if she's the mother of his child?"

"With that figure? Then she deserves to be the cover model on the next nursing mother magazine."

Nicole stopped in front of her sedan—the only other concession she'd insisted upon tonight. "How can you make jokes about this?"

"I wasn't— Okay, I was. It's cop black humor, our survival mechanism." When she failed to respond, Roman lifted then dropped his hands. "I'm not the kind of man who says the politically or socially correct thing, Nick. By the same token, I'm willing to use brawn if someone is sticking their nose where it doesn't belong. I'm sorry if that doesn't meet with your romantic image of a hero, but I don't have the time or energy to be a role model for your ideals. Maybe you'd better remember that in the future."

Good God, she thought. Not only was he more upset about her interfering than she'd first guessed, but she was right about her earlier hunch, as well. He was warning her off.

Wondering what was going on, she got into the passenger side of the car. Roman slid in behind the steering wheel.

"You can give it a rest, you know," she said, as he pulled out onto Industrial Boulevard.

"What's that supposed to mean?"

"I'm not looking for promises or commitments from

you or any man. And if I was, hopefully I'd have the sense to choose one with fewer problems than I have.''

Although Roman worked his jaw like a stone crushing machine, they didn't speak again until they were at Gregor's. As he flashed his badge to the parking valet and insisted her car be left up front at the door, Nicole knew his temper hadn't abated one bit. That compelled her to glance back at the handsome youth with an apologetic smile wanting the boy to understand Roman's mood had nothing to do with him.

''Knock it off,'' he growled, steering her through the front door.

''I'm not doing anything.''

''Well, do less of it.''

Inside the hostess immediately recognized Nicole, and appeared as embarrassed by her presence as curious. ''How are you?'' she said, in that singsong voice that always had Nicole cringing as though hearing nails on a chalkboard.

''Taking one day at a time,'' she replied with a forced smile.

This svelte brunette had been one of Jay's flings: one that had ended as soon as the woman had attracted the attention of an ex-Dallas Cowboys football player. In fact scales were visible in her expertly made-up dark eyes as she inspected Roman.

''We've all been so worried about you,'' the hostess continued. ''I've been meaning to call I don't know how many times, but things have been incredibly hectic here, so that I'm dead to the world until noon. Then I have to cram a life into the few hours before I rush to work...''

"I understand." Nicole glanced at Roman wondering how he wanted to be introduced. He resolved the question by taking hold of her elbow.

"We're only here for a few minutes," he said, cutting off the chatter. "The bar will suit us."

He propelled Nicole in that direction.

When they were safely out of earshot, Nicole braked. "As grateful as I am for the escape, you don't have to take out your annoyance with me on her."

"You enjoy listening to condescending bitches?"

Things didn't get better when they reached the bar. The bartender on their side had been no friend of Jay's, and was in fact the first to buy Willard's yarn about Nicole being a head case.

"Don," she said, her reluctant greeting barely audible over the roar of the music and crowd noise.

He delivered a stiff nod and then eyed Roman. "What'll it be?"

Roman didn't bother ordering anything; he simply drew out his badge and Angelo's ID. "Ever see him around?"

"No."

"That answer would be more convincing if you looked at the picture first."

Don did, barely. "No." He shifted his gaze to Nicole. "I don't want any trouble. Detective Willard said I should call him if there's ever any trouble again."

"This has nothing to do with Detective Willard," Roman replied before she could. "I'm investigating my own case, and who I come in here with is my business. Am I making myself clear?"

"Okay, okay. But I still don't know the guy. I swear

I would tell you if I did, it's no skin off my nose. Look around you—he doesn't fit in here.''

That much he had right, Nicole thought eyeing the crowded dance floor. It was packed with young professionals and affluent student types. About to tell Roman that this was a mistake, she was surprised to see him flip Jay's picture on the counter beside Angelo's.

''But you do know him, right?''

''Is that your idea of a joke?''

''Just answer the question.''

''You know I do. We worked together.''

''Good. Then you would know if you ever saw these two together, even for a short period of time?''

''Never.''

''See how painless that was?'' Roman turned to Nicole. ''Let's go.''

He led the way out. Fortunately, the hostess was showing someone to their table so Nicole didn't have to suffer the embarrassment of her seeing their abrupt departure.

She held her tongue until they were back in the car and he was turning onto McKinney. ''You are taking me home, right?'' she asked tightly.

''That's the idea. Unless you don't think you've had enough?''

As he braked for the red light in front of The Crescent, Nicole stared straight ahead at the rounded building glistening and regal in the glow of a robust moon. The dual reminder of the place had her frowning.

''Now do you understand what a mistake this was, Nick?''

''What? Oh. No, forget about it.''

"I shouldn't have said what I did earlier," he continued, his tone heavy with fatigue. "Not that way, anyhow."

She cast him a sidelong glance. "But you meant it. You are trying to scare me off."

"Yeah. It's the right thing to do."

"Ah. So?"

"So that doesn't stop me from wanting you." His gaze locked with hers. "So who the hell is Cameron?"

25

*Hope deferred maketh the heart sick:
but when the desire cometh,
it is a tree of life.*

—Proverbs 13:12

For a moment Nicole thought he'd taken to reading her mind. But then she realized his question had nothing to do with their location. Nevertheless, she had reason to hedge. The name was one that triggered so many mixed emotions in her.

"Cameron...?"

"The flowers. Don't play dumb, honey, it doesn't suit you."

With all that was going on in both of their lives, he still wanted to know? The thought more frightened than flattered her. Did either of them see what they were doing to each other?

"Ah, hell," Roman moaned. "Forget it. I shouldn't have asked."

As quickly as the light turned green, so had, apparently, his willingness to speak from a deeper part of his heart. Nicole could only try to catch up.

"It's not so much the question. It's just the irony of

the moment," she replied, and nodded to the stately building they were passing. "He keeps his office there. Cameron Carstairs. He's a customer of Van Dorn's, an entertainment lawyer with a passion for beautiful things."

"You being one of them?"

She glanced at his grim profile. "Yes. He's made his interest clear, but we're not lovers, and we're not going to be. For one thing, I wouldn't feel right about jeopardizing Max's relationship with such a valued client. For another he's married."

"And somehow I get the feeling that's not all."

"No. Most importantly, it's because he bears a striking resemblance to someone from my past."

"Your grandfather?"

"No, my first love."

Roman didn't say anything for several seconds. Then he said quietly, "I'm sorry for the attitude. I guess being eaten up with jealousy takes some getting used to. Just do me a favor and don't tell me that you were Lolita's age when this happened."

"No, I was twenty-one and taking a master's course in Italy. Marius owned a lovely little gallery near the school I was attending in Florence and if you would have told me that from the moment I walked in there and heard him try to explain to a customer the immediacy yet versatility of gouache versus the enslavement that can occur with oils—" She shook her head. "You don't know what I'm talking about, do you?"

"I understand attraction." He stopped for another red light. "Was he married, too?"

"I'm afraid so. With two sons my age. That was

the difficult part for me, and what finally drove me back to the States.''

''You're not over him.''

''I still miss him, miss our conversations. But I think it's different when you part because of circumstances aside from the relationship. Are you over your first love?''

''You mean Glenda. You're not going to think much of me for saying this, but I'm beginning to realize that what I loved was the idea of having a family of my own more than her. Small wonder she left me, huh?''

''There's more than one kind of love.''

''But a woman wants and deserves passion. She wants to be cherished for who she is.''

''Don't men?''

''I think we tend to be cowards. It's easier to go off to war or take up bungee jumping than to deal with our emotions.''

''You're no coward, McKenna.''

He pulled into her driveway and shut off the engine. ''So why am I afraid to ask if there's been anyone serious since Italy?''

''As a matter of fact there has.'' She met his piercing gaze. ''Quite recently. And if you asked him, he would say I have a bad habit of being attracted to men unsuitable for me.''

''Not tonight, he wouldn't.'' Releasing his seat belt, then hers, Roman took her hand and brought it to his lips. ''Tonight he would simply say, 'Come upstairs. Let me hold you until you fall asleep.'''

''Is that all you want?''

He tightened his grip. ''Come upstairs.''

How strange, Nicole thought, to feel such an incredible intimacy with him one moment, and the palm-wetting angst of a virgin relationship in the next. Wholly aware of Roman close behind her, she led the way to her apartment. As he locked up, she wouldn't even allow herself to check her answering machine. There was something strange, yet magical going on here tonight, and she wanted the chance to play it out.

"Would you like a beer or...?"

"You." He came straight at her. "I only want you."

He barely got the words out before locking his mouth to hers. The energy of it, of the way he crushed her to him, spoke of a hunger that matched her own and left her shaking as though they were standing in a walk-in freezer. When he streaked his hands to her hips and pressed himself into the juncture of her thighs the sharp pleasure had her whimpering into his mouth.

Rigid, he broke off the kiss to force her head against his shoulder. "Damn it, you're not up to this."

"I'm all right." This time she slid her hands to his buttocks. "It's just the intensity of it..."

She didn't need to finish explaining, the jolt wherever their bodies touched said it all. It was enough to compel Roman into seeking another kiss, and while he was plumbing her mouth with his tongue, he freed her hair from its ponytail. That done, he initiated a less patient assault on her clothes. Whether it was the riveting desire in his eyes, or the way he kept discovering ultrasensitive spots on her body, she didn't know, but she'd never gotten so wet so fast. Upon discovering that, Roman sucked in a sharp breath and sank to his knees.

Her legs grew weak from the slightest brush of his whisker-rough cheek, then his lips against her thighs. When his tongue began its bold assault at her throbbing core, it was all she could do to fill her hands with his hair to keep from slumping over. It wasn't fair, and it was no small shock to learn how quickly he could make her lose control.

Even before she began to recover, he rose and backed her to the nearest surface—the kitchen counter. Only after he lifted her and she felt his breathtaking penetration, did she understand he had his own limits of endurance.

Tightening her arms around his neck, her legs around his waist, she welcomed his fierce invasion, wanting to savor this impossible fullness. But driven by his own need, he gave her no time to adjust to him, thrusting quickly and then again, and again.

Her control slipped a second time. Yet it was his climax that ultimately ignited hers, fired by the erotic sound of his sharp gasps, the momentary rigidity then shudder of his large frame as he lost the fight with himself.

As his semen shot deep into her, she pressed her face against his shoulder, buffeted by the new spasms rocketing through her.

It must only have been a minute, but it seemed a delicious age that they stayed like that listening to each other's breathing go from frantic to simply spent. Then Roman pressed a kiss to the side of her neck and carried her to the bed.

Because she wouldn't let him go, he laid her down and settled carefully on top of her bracing the bulk of his weight on his forearms. "Are you all right?" he asked. Passion lingered in his voice and in his gaze. "I wanted you too much. I'm sorry."

"I'm not."

"You may be within a few weeks."

He was referring to the fact that he hadn't used protection this time. Although she knew the risk was real—she'd stopped taking the pill some time ago—she couldn't summon the concern she knew their carelessness deserved.

"It will be all right," she told him. It had to be. Not only would it be beyond cruel to force him to deal with becoming a father now of all times, but how could she consider giving birth, let alone raising a child, when she would already have the responsibility of a child if—*when* they found Jay's son?

Roman must have seen something in her face, because without another word he pushed himself off the bed and disappeared into the bathroom. She let him go. She had to. They'd already let down too many guards as it was.

Wondering how and when this torment would end for both of them, she curled into an unhappy knot and listened to the sound of water pounding the tiles in the bathroom.

26

By doubting we come to the truth.

—Cicero

The sound of water pounding on the tiled roof of the fast-food restaurant did little to relieve Roman's headache; nevertheless, he didn't resent the midday shower. Dallas at the end of August was usually a time for talking about what you could fry on asphalt, and for wondering how much water it would take to close the ever-widening cracks in the black earth. The pain in his head had to do with looking at a growing list of clues and not understanding why they refused to connect to make a comprehensive story. He knew he would have been experiencing the same results regardless of the weather.

"Give it a rest," Ralph said before taking another drag on the straw in his thick chocolate milk shake. "There is such a thing as trying too hard. Ever hear of the old saying, 'A man who sees everything sees nothing'?"

They were sitting in their unmarked car outside a burger joint on Lemon, the downpour causing a flash flood off the roof of the eatery and creating a four-inch river of water across the parking lot and into the street. He appreciated that Ralph was back to being his old talkative self, but wished he would just finish eating his lunch. His partner didn't understand that it was Thursday, the end of another week, and it would be damned tough to return to Nicole tonight without something new and encouraging to tell her.

"You heard the lieutenant," he replied. "As far as he's concerned, the Aguirre shooting takes low priority because he was a nobody and illegal on top of everything else. So unless I confided that this guy attacked Nicole and how his sister dances in a club, and that Loring just happened to have a matchbook from the place, he's not going to allow me to keep working this case. On the other hand, if I do tell him, he'll ship my butt back to Central Patrol faster than you can recite your kids' names because I didn't report all I know sooner...particularly about Willard."

"Aw, did you have to mention Rat Boy? You'll ruin my appetite." It didn't, however, stop Ralph from tipping back his head and pouring french fries into his mouth. "How's Nicole? Did she ignore you and go back to work today?" he added, chewing.

"Yeah." Roman had followed her in himself, after trying and failing to make her take one more day off, then—because she was earlier than usual—he'd waited to make sure she'd locked herself in. She'd decided that if she needed to move the forty grand into a safer place, the best bet would be Van Dorn's vault, and to do that she needed Max's permission. The only other piece of good news about her decision was knowing that if she was with Max, she wouldn't be checking out the addresses in that damned black book.

God, between worrying about her and Meggie, he was going to be gray before he was thirty-six.

"Listen, we're going to pass The Crescent on our way to the jail," he said, pocketing his notes. "What do you say we stop for a second and check out that one address there? It won't take a minute to scope out the directory."

Ralph crushed the empty fry box and dropped it into his lunch sack. "Sure, it will. You know full well that if you find the listing, you'll want to go up and have a look at the guy. Then you'll decide what's the harm in asking him a few questions. I'll be lucky if you don't tackle the poor bastard, and threaten to make him eat that bit of cow leather if he doesn't confess everything he knows."

"It's not like your perp is going anywhere." They had finally gotten DNA evidence from the labs to connect a con awaiting trial on an assault and battery case to a six-month-old murder of an old man in the same apartment building.

"Johnson's not the only SOB we have to talk to this afternoon, and we did stop at that complex by the Galleria to check the address there."

They'd been driving back from Addison, for pity's sake, which was the only reason Ralph had agreed to stop. "What help was a vacant office? If we had hung around to wait until the girl in the management office returned from her doctor's appointment to find out when the leaseholder moved out and if she'd release a forwarding address—"

"I would never have made it back to court in time."

"Defense got another delay anyway," Roman muttered.

Ralph scowled back at him. "Ten minutes. If the suite number is still good, you find out who's in there and we're on our way, until we have more time."

"Deal."

This was the one he'd really been curious about anyway because of the lack of initials. Feeling better, Roman waited impatiently for Ralph to finish his drink and drive around to the back where he could lob their sacks up into the Dumpster.

"What did you think about Sir Isaac's announcement this morning?" his partner asked after making the shot.

Isaac Newman had stunned everyone by coming in and announcing that he'd changed his mind about taking early retirement. Roman didn't blame him. "Could you stomach working with Willard until you were sixty-five?"

Ralph shrugged as he zigzagged through the Turtle Creek area. "They've been together for some time. He had to have been used to the guy by now. Why quit when you've only got another fourteen months to go?"

Roman picked up on the sly note in his partner's voice. "What? You think something happened?"

"The old man's wife has health problems. He needs the extra money."

This was interesting. So was the fact that Willard had been all but invisible lately. And that was why, when Ralph pulled into The Crescent's courtyard parking area, Roman thought he was imagining things when he spotted Willard coming out of the building and tipping the valet who'd been watching his BMW, parked at the door.

"I'm going to kick myself in the ass if he spots us," Ralph muttered, braking behind a Cadillac.

Fortunately, the rain intensified even more and Willard had his hands full avoiding a cab, let alone seeing anything across the courtyard.

"See what you would have missed if I hadn't talked you into coming here?" Tucker drawled as Willard exited via the entrance gates.

Relieved and hopeful, Roman almost smiled at the joke. "Do you think it's possible he's just been in to see our guy?"

"Sure would be sweet, but...nah. Too much the coincidence. He's probably here schmoozing some honey's loaded daddy." Tucker grinned evilly. "Then again, I'm not the biggest believer in coincidences."

With adrenaline kicking up his pulse, Roman nodded to the front of the building. "Drop me off so I don't become a lightning rod."

"Watch yourself inside, too."

Roman leaped from the car and hurried into the building. He had to shoulder past a handful of executive types staring through the glass doors as though it was acid that was pouring down out there rather than rain. Wiping a few drops of moisture from his face, he scanned the elegant lobby in search of the directory. He spotted it by the elevators.

Suite 409 was on the fourth floor, but he wasn't prepared for the corporate name above the suite number.

"I'll be damned."

Roman pressed the elevator button for the upper floors, aware that he had enough wings beating inside his gut to get there on his own power. Once on the fourth floor, he followed the directional arrows to the right and strode down the hallway eyeing the rain and flashes of lightning beyond the floor-to-ceiling windows. But he was thinking of Nick and hoping to heaven that she'd meant what she'd told him last night. At least the part about Cameron Carstairs.

The attorney's office was behind an enormous, ornate wooden door that probably cost more than Roman had doled out for his entire wardrobe. Beyond it, in a small but pricey waiting room that quickly announced Carstairs didn't come cheap, sat the receptionist.

The attractive but brittle brunette—she could have been the twin of the hostess at Gregor's—gave him a cool smile. "May I help you?"

He could already tell she was gauging him and coming to negative conclusions, so he adopted a little attitude of his own. "Is he in?" Roman asked, glancing beyond her. He saw people moving about, but could tell from the size of the suite and the activity that this wasn't a large operation. A staff of four, six at most—still impressive for an entertainment lawyer in Texas.

"Do you mean Mr. Carstairs?"

"Who else?"

"Do you have an appointment, Mr....?"

"McKenna. Detective McKenna."

The receptionist sat up straighter. "Excuse me, I didn't realize—is this an official visit?"

"I'd simply like to ask Mr. Carstairs a few questions."

"He's at Las Colinas right now with a client, however, if there's an emergency that he needs to know about... This isn't about anyone in his family, is it? Mr. Carstairs is terribly devoted and protective of his family."

Roman couldn't wait to share that one with Nick. "As far as I know, the family is fine," he replied. "When will he be back?"

Deceptively soft brown eyes studied his for another moment before she replied, "Actually, he was due twenty minutes ago. I'm assuming the weather's delayed...why, here he is."

In his early sixties, Cameron Carstairs struck Roman as the kind of man comfortable in ties and ascots, someone who preferred pocket watches over the wristband kind of timepiece, and who probably never touched a cognac under thirty years old. As they stood eye-to-eye, he could have been intimidated by the silver-haired man with the smiling eyes of a cunning fox. Jealousy and protectiveness saved him.

"Mr. Carstairs, Detective McKenna, DPD. May I have a minute of your time?"

The lawyer's tanned, barely lined face held its polite countenance. "Marlene, what time is the senator's plane due in?"

Smooth, pal, Roman thought. But he wasn't about to get wide-eyed and goofy over a name-dropping social climber. He would get his five minutes if he kept all of Dallas's Who's Who waiting.

"Three, sir."

Carstairs extended his arm toward the hallway. "I'm yours for that minute, Detective. But I warn you, traffic is grim around town. I'll have to time you."

"Fair enough."

The power jockey's office reeked masculinity and an appreciation for fine things. No surprise; Roman already knew the bastard's taste in women. He allowed himself only a brief scan of the room so as not to look too interested or impressed, and wondered if Nick had been responsible for finding some of the violent sea paintings on the wall, the plush suede furnishings or the sculpture pieces on the bookcases and his desk. As he tore his gaze away from a crystal nude torso, he decided it best to let that question go.

"Can I offer you coffee, Detective?" Carstairs asked, hesitating by his chair.

"No, thank you. I have other appointments myself, so I won't keep you."

Apparently the attorney approved of that answer. He sat on the edge of his desk and although he folded his arms across his chest, his expression was disarming and accessible again. "Then tell me, what brings one of Dallas's finest to my door? Not that I don't represent some passionate people. But I do hope no one's done anything rambunctious at a party or driven away from a fender bender."

"Actually, this is about a mutual friend. You know Nicole Loring, don't you?"

"Why...I do. Nikki's with Van Dorn's. Marvelous establishment that has added a great deal to Dallas's art-loving community. Dear Lord, I'd heard she'd had a tough time of things what with her brother's sudden death. Is she all right?''

He spoke in a modulated voice that could sound at once soothing, and at the same time condescending. Roman knew if he had to listen to it during an entire courtroom cross-examination, he would lunge across the witness stand and grab the guy by his throat.

''She could be better.''

''You say you're also a friend? Then you may be aware that I extended my assistance to Nikki several times, most recently through Max Van Dorn.''

''She's received your flowers.''

Something in Carstairs's eyes flickered. Sharpened. ''Good. Good. They're a mere token, of course, but— excuse me, I thought another detective had handled Jay's case?''

''Detective Willard.''

''That sounds right. He seemed quite experienced and thorough.''

''I'm sure he is, but there have been some developments since he concluded his investigation.''

''Really. I'd believed Nikki's collapse was due to the stress of losing Jay. Are you saying there've been other problems?''

''Did you know him?''

''No.'' Carstairs bowed his head. ''But Nikki spoke of him often.'' Carstairs sighed, then impaled Roman with shrewd gray eyes. ''Forgive me, Detective, but I'm still missing the point for your visit.''

''I need to know how long you've had your practice at this location.''

"Well, that's certainly no mystery. Three years. Why?"

"Because your address is listed in a book Jay Loring kept that he slipped into his sister's purse the night he was—the night he died."

To his credit, Cameron Carstairs managed to remain as still as some of the busts adorning his office, but Roman could have sworn that he'd lost a bit of color under his tan.

"This address? Why would he do that?"

"That's what I'm trying to find out."

"I wish I could offer an explanation, but like you, I'm completely baffled."

"That's entirely feasible, but I had to ask." Roman rose. "Thank you for your time." As he opened the door, he paused. "Oh, one more question. Does 22k capital C mean anything to you?"

27

Eternity was in that moment

—*William Congreve*

"I can't believe you asked that. How could you? How dare you!"

This wasn't the response Roman had expected when he broke the news about Carstairs to Nicole that evening. Excited and ready to brainstorm motives with her, he could only stare in disbelief at her indignation. "Wait a minute," he said, setting his hands on his hips. "You're offended?"

"Of course, I am. Do you realize what you've done? Cameron Carstairs has spent at least twenty-thousand dollars with Van Dorn's in June alone!" she snapped. "I don't want to guess what he's meant to the firm since he began doing business with us. Good Lord, Max will have a stroke if he hears about this. What am I saying? He probably already knows you've accused a valued client of heaven knows what, and no doubt the only reason I haven't heard the explosion yet is that Rebecca has taken him to Emergency!"

Tucker's reaction when he'd returned to the car after leaving The Crescent had been much more welcome.

But the shock and displeasure on Nicole's face made his partner's gleeful backslap vanish from his mind.

"Maybe you don't get it." He reached for patience despite the fatigue that pulled on him, the result of juggling two lives these past weeks. "The address Jay listed at The Crescent belongs to Carstairs's firm."

"You must have made a mistake."

"Then why did your brother only write down the address and not Carstairs's initials the way he did on the others? You didn't recognize the suite number when you first saw it, did you?"

"Why should I? Invoices are sent to his home."

"That's what I guessed. Those initials would have gotten your attention. Jay was hiding them from you in case you happened upon the notebook. He never wanted you to see it unless absolutely necessary. If you had, his game—or Carstairs's with you for that matter—would be up. Jay knew about Carstairs's interest in you, didn't he?"

"I told you we were close. Why shouldn't I have confided something like that in him?"

"I'd answer that if I knew when and how he'd come to know Carstairs."

Nicole paced in a circle around the kitchen, rubbing the back of her neck. She'd removed her suit jacket minutes ago, and ever since Roman had been fighting to keep his mind on business and not how sexy she looked in that cream-colored lace-and-silk chemise.

"You're not thinking Jay was into blackmail, are you?"

With that wounded expression on her face and that incredible skin, she looked like a violated novitiate hanging on to her faith for dear life. He hated what he had to do, but Roman rested both hands on the counter that separated them and leaned closer. "I have six people who all belong to something called The 22k C. Does that stand for thousand or for karat? And what does that C mean? In any case those folks were of major interest to Jay. So far I've only been able to check on one other guy on the list. Unfortunately, he recently moved. I'll find him, though. In fact, I talked to the management office late this afternoon and got his new address. One thing I don't need any more evidence to draw a conclusion on is that all six are affluent."

"So naturally that money had to come from Jay blackmailing people."

"Did I say that?" Roman replied. He was, however, relieved that she'd jumped to the same conclusion he and Tucker had. "But let's not forget you were damned upset when you first saw his stash."

She bowed her head. "It was a shock, that's all."

"Bull. However, for argument's sake, we'll play it your way. So where the hell did the forty grand come from?"

"Stop swearing at me!"

"I'm not swearing *at* you, I'm as upset by the situation, what's been done *to* you as you are!"

"You're drawing unfair conclusions."

Roman ran a hand over his face. "Okay, you're scared, and I understand that," he said, trying for a calmer tone. "I'm also aware I don't have all the answers for you yet. But I'm a damned sight closer to finding them than anyone else has gotten. And I'm sorry if this upsets you, but those answers are probably going to be bad news for more people than your brother.''

"Just tell me the rest," she replied, clearly trying to match his restraint. "What did Cameron say?"

He shrugged. "I didn't expect him to open his soul to me straight off."

"Oh, McKenna. You don't have anything except an address. That could implicate...*anyone* in that office."

"Wrong. I have the look on Carstairs's face when I posed the jackpot question about 22k C. For a second I thought he was going to soil his pants."

"That's vulgar."

"Don't pull that Lady-of-the-Manor crap with me, Nick. This isn't the time."

Nicole lifted her chin. "I'm sorry if familiarity is breeding contempt."

"That's not what I mean and you know it."

"I think it is."

Roman narrowed his eyes. "You're not thinking at all. I mention Carstairs and you automatically make excuses for him. Under the circumstances, I have to wonder if you were being entirely honest with me about your feelings toward him."

"I respect him as a professional who's achieved a number of accomplishments. You're condemning him based on something I'd confided that never came to fruition."

"Maybe I find it a little hard to watch you defend an asshole who has a wife and three kids, but is clearly continuing to hustle you. Do you really think he's accepted that 'no' you gave him as your final answer? That's not the impression I got today, *Nikki.*''

Nicole strode across the room and reached for her jacket. "I am not doing this. Do you hear yourself? You sound like a jealous teenager, you, who's worked so hard at reminding me that you don't want to want me!''

"At least I've been honest with you. How about it? Could it be you're considering taking him as a lover after all?''

Violence flared in Nicole's golden eyes. Then she burst out laughing...but it wasn't a reassuring sound.

"I deserve this," she declared, as she disappeared into her bedroom. "And how my mother would love it. She always lectures, 'if you lie down with dogs, you get up with fleas.'''

"Knock it off," Roman growled giving chase. "You hear one bit of unsettling news and you run for cover behind your genteel sensibilities. Grow up, Nick. People with money and breeding do conniving things. They *do* hurt and cheat. It's not only us common folk that turn your tidy, exclusive world upside down.''

"Oh, please! That chip on your shoulder is growing by the minute. Every chance you get you throw my background and success in my face, even though you know better than most how hard I've worked to get here!''

"I'm not attacking your success, damn it. My problem is with your absolute conviction that I have to be wrong about your pal!''

"Has it occurred to you that I've known him a little

longer than I've known you? That should count for something.''

"So should being the guy you *do* let in your bed."

She spun around, her eyes huge in the dimmer light. Haunted. "What's really behind this determination to humiliate me?" she asked in a near whisper. "Is it because of all the women who could have broken through your iron-will and make you forget to protect yourself, it was me? Well, you can stop worrying that your precious seed is alive in my body. I started my period this afternoon.''

He could have been on an elevator where someone had suddenly severed the cables. His insides plunged and plunged, until he felt hollowed out. That's when it struck him—how right she was. How terrified he'd been that she would draw him into a world he knew he could never bear again. The world of parent. Of being Daddy.

"It's for the best," he said quietly.

"You're telling me."

He wanted to go to her, to hold her, but he knew he'd lost the right. "How do you feel? I don't mean about not being— I mean...do you have cramps? A backache?"

"No, McKenna, nor is my behavior tied to PMS."

"Believe it or not, that didn't enter my mind. I was concerned for you dealing with that on top of everything else."

"What might help is if you'd leave."

"You know I can't do that," he said gruffly.

"I'll lock myself in Goldie's house. If her alarm

system gets triggered, it will bring the entire Highland Park Police Department.''

"No."

"Please, McKenna. The money is locked away. Willard hasn't come near me since—"

"He was there today."

She frowned. "Where?"

"At The Crescent. He was leaving as we were arriving. I have a feeling that within the next few days it's all going to start making sense, and when it does, I want you as protected from it as possible."

As expected, Nicole was shaken. "I don't understand any of this any more, and I'm not sure I want to. All I want is to find the baby. What can any of what you're talking about have to do with that poor child?"

"I don't know."

"And I don't know how much more I can take. Growing up, we endured hideous fights between my parents. I promised myself I would never behave that way with anyone I cared about."

"This was my fault. I wanted to provoke you."

She searched his face for several seconds. "Would trying to teach me to hate you somehow make it easier for you to walk away?"

He didn't get to answer because his pager sounded. Sighing he tugged it off his belt and checked the message. "God, no," he whispered.

On weak legs he hurried to the phone and dialed the number he'd memorized long ago. He could hear Nicole following him.

"What's wrong?"

"Houston."

"Oh...Roman."

"It's me," he said, upon hearing Glenda's voice. He listened, heard the words he'd been hoping against hope would never be spoken, and when his ex-wife finished, he barely managed, "I'm on my way."

As soon as he hung up, he faced Nicole. "Meggie's slipped into a coma."

"I'll drive you to the airport."

"I can't think."

"We'll stop at your apartment," she said. "Pick up some clothes for you."

"Nick...damn it, I don't need to be worrying about you driving around Dallas in the dark."

"Then let's get you out of here before it gets any later, and I'll spend the night at Max and Rebecca's."

Hoping that she wasn't just telling him what he wanted to hear, he relented. "Max's. That's better. That may work."

She got him to Love Field within an hour. At the curb, he tried to thank her, but the words wouldn't come. He wanted to crush her against him, but he knew his composure was weakening fast.

"Go," she said softly. "Just call me when you can."

Like a sleepwalker, he forced himself out of the car. The last thing he heard before slamming the passenger door was her whispered, "God be with you all."

God, he thought bitterly. *Yeah, right.*

28

The friends thou hast, and their adoption tried,
Grapple them to thy soul with hoops of steel.

—William Shakespeare,
Hamlet

"You were right to come."

"I should have insisted you move in here the moment this whole bloody mess began."

Nicole gave her hostess and host a grateful smile. It was well past nine o'clock and the three of them were sitting in Rebecca and Max's living room. For the last few minutes she had been explaining her reason for being there—leaving out a few things, including the ugly scene with Roman. Of course, if Rebecca's keen inspection was anything to go by, the older woman suspected something vital was being omitted.

"You'll stay as long as you want," Rebecca told her.

She and Nicole sat together on the green suede couch, and Rebecca took hold of both of her hands as she spoke. The warmth and strength from each talented finger was as much a grounding as Rebecca's dark eyes were a magnifying glass to the soul.

Max grunted his affirmation from the thronelike chair that faced them. "Rebecca's been wanting to get her hands on you for weeks now. Said you needed some nourishing and mothering, bless her curry-loving heart. You'd best give her her way before she nags my ear off."

It was pure nonsense, and Nicole knew it. The two of them were besotted with each other, and far from being a nagger, Rebecca was one of those rare women who spoke only when she had something to say. For a natural conversation hog like Max that was virtue beyond any other.

"Well, I promise not to be underfoot too much. I intend to finish getting the last of Jay's personal effects out of his apartment after work tomorrow." Not only was this a necessity due to the deadline she'd given the management company, but she wanted to look for more clues. "Then I plan to check out the rest of those addresses."

"The hell you will." Max almost spilled the scotch he'd been nursing. "McKenna's right. If anything, the situation's more dangerous than ever. Who knows who would want to get their hands on that book, and what they'd do to get it."

"I'll be careful. Besides, it's almost the weekend. More people will be at the complex. At any rate, doing nothing until Roman gets back is unacceptable. A child's life is in jeopardy. I can't sit by and wait for someone else to find my nephew."

"A newborn child..." Rebecca's Gaelic features grew troubled. "Are you prepared for that kind of responsibility, my dear?"

"I wouldn't even be prepared for a roommate my age. The prospect of one wholly dependent upon me is terrifying. Fortunately, there's been too much going on to dwell on it."

"I'll call Darnell first thing in the morning. He'll go with you or I'll fire him," Max announced, making it clear where his loyalty lay.

Nicole thanked him for the gesture, but added, "Darnell has been through enough thanks to me. You didn't see how Detective Willard treated him. I have a feeling you'd be bailing Darnell out of jail on trumped up charges if Roman hadn't arrived when he did." But because she could see Max was determined that she not be on her own, she allowed one consideration. "I'm thinking of calling Roman's partner. Roman gave me his card in case there was an emergency. Maybe he would be willing to give me at least a few hours of his time. I understand he has a large family. I could offer to pay him."

"I'll pick up any tab," Max said quickly.

"Max, this is my problem."

"Think again. If Carstairs is part of this, as Mc-Kenna believes, it's my problem, too. After all, I led him to you and, consequently, to your brother."

"You don't know that."

"Until someone proves it otherwise, it's the most logical conclusion."

Nicole rubbed her aching forehead wishing all the aspects of this case would stay clear in her mind, let alone make sense. But as it was, the tangled mess was like trying to knit a sweater out of one knotted mass of silk, wool, angora and every other kind of yarn.

"Do you really believe Cameron could be involved somehow? He doesn't strike me as someone who would want to risk the career he's established for himself."

"On the contrary, I've found the more successful the individual, the more it takes to satisfy him. Did Napoleon stick with only France? Was Germany enough to contain Hitler?"

Nicole shivered. "Such friendly comparisons, boss. And yet you let him send me flowers."

"I had the feeling he was one of your favorites." Max shrugged with his mouth. "You always seem slightly more concerned, slightly more attentive to him than others."

How strange...and embarrassing. If Max had picked up on something subtle, how could she accuse Roman of fabricating the suspicions he had?

Rebecca touched her hand. "People are always more and less than what we understand them to be. I've studied the human form for years, and it's the one constant I've discovered."

"But you always manage to focus on the beauty in a subject nonetheless."

"The body *is* a magnificent creation to me, yes. And yet, once I chose not to work with an individual because I was uncomfortable with the energy he exuded."

Nicole found her confession profound, and at the same time disturbing, especially since she'd never met a more confident woman and generous artist. "All right, then...you've seen Cameron Carstairs's photo in the paper. What do you think of him?"

"Oh, intensely charismatic, not a man easily forgotten…and cunning. I'm not surprised at how successful he is."

Nicole was still thinking through that when she excused herself minutes later to make the call to Ralph Tucker.

Not surprisingly, he answered before the end of the first ring. That was because Roman had called from her car phone to let Ralph know he was leaving town, and now Ralph was anticipating a grimmer call.

She was also touched that he seemed genuinely concerned about her.

"I'm fine, Detective, and I apologize for disturbing you at this hour. I'm just settling in at the Van Dorn's as I promised Roman." She then went on to explain the reason for her call.

Not only was he uncomfortable with her intentions, he tried to discourage her. "You have to appreciate there's an ongoing investigation, Ms. Loring. Anything you do on your own could jeopardize what we've already accomplished."

"Please, call me Nicole, and may I call you Ralph? Ralph, I have to get my brother's things out of that apartment. I gave my word to the management office and I didn't give myself a very large time frame as it is."

"That part wouldn't be much of a problem. But the rest…no way. Uh-uh. Besides, if something happened to you, Roman would have my b—head. Ma'am."

Nicole liked him. She pictured him as Roman had described—a big bear of a guy with little midgets of himself climbing all over him. It was a soothing and sane image. "Roman also wouldn't forgive himself if his absence caused someone guilty of something to slip away, would he? All I'm suggesting is the legwork, so that you have the data you need for when he gets back. I promise, I'm not interested in confronting anyone or asking sensitive questions that might compromise anything. What do you say? I would, of course, insist on reimbursing you for your time."

"I'm a cop, ma'am. You can't pay me for doing my job."

"I wouldn't think of insulting you that way, but...to be honest, I'd hoped you might help me get those boxes with my brother's things into my car. Surely you wouldn't be offended by my wanting to pay you for a considerable amount of physical labor that I can't possibly manage on my own? After all, I'd be expected to pay a moving company."

The father of six weakened, and finally agreed to meet her at her place—but not until eight o'clock Saturday morning because he expected that without Roman things would be hectic at the department tomorrow. Thanking him, and extending her apologies to his wife for taking him away from family time, she hung up feeling slightly better. She might not have much hope of getting much sleep tonight, what with her concerns for Roman and his child, but thoughts of Saturday morning would bring new hope on another front. She told herself that had to count for something.

Dressed in worn jeans and a wrinkled T-shirt featuring a watermelon-peel green dinosaur—last year's Christmas gift from his first grader—Ralph Tucker arrived at Nicole's looking anything but the hard-boiled detective. He unfolded himself from an older model station wagon brushing crumbs off himself before extending his hand.

"How ya doing?" he said with a shy smile.

Nicole felt a stubborn crumb or two sticking to his huge, warm hand, but that only made it easier to smile back at him. "Good to finally meet you, Ralph." She glanced at his car, which looked as though a tornado had been trapped inside it tangling children's toys, clothing, athletic equipment and a baby's car seat into one disastrous mess. "I thought we could use my car...?"

That was more than fine with Ralph. His ever-roving eyes had already taken in her outfit—the tunic and pants she'd worn on her last visit to Tyler and agreed it was "too fine" for the peanut butter and jelly remains that were still evident from the kids' last trip in his vehicle. He was a sweetheart, she decided. But not to be underestimated, a conclusion she came to as soon as she saw the bulge of a gun tucked in the back of his pants when he bent to help load the last of the empty boxes into her car.

As she drove to the apartment complex, Nicole filled the silence by asking about his family. She wanted him to relax around her, having the suspicion that like Roman, he saw her as being in a different class and therefore somewhat unapproachable. But by the time she was parking in front of the building where Jay had lived, he'd finished his third story about his rambunctious boys.

"Yeah, they're a handful, but I wouldn't take for

them," he said. Then he grew somber. "I don't know how Roman's keeping it together. If it was one of my kids who was that ill, I'd be nuts."

Nicole shut off the car's engine, grateful that he'd brought up the subject. "I'm dealing with guilt for having taken up so much of his time."

"Don't," Ralph replied. "Oh, I was worried early on, but I think I understand now how he looks at your case. He can't help his little girl, but if he can help you get your brother's baby, he won't feel as useless."

A charity case? She knew that wasn't what he meant, but she didn't feel comfortable that Roman might feel he'd been paying some IOU, either. Nevertheless, she thanked Ralph for sharing that.

They set to work and despite her fatigue and preoccupation, they were done by noon. Relieved though she was that they'd finished so quickly, she was disappointed when they didn't find anything else helpful to the case among her brother's things.

"Don't let it get you," Ralph said when they were locking up and he carried the last box downstairs. "There's plenty to work with, and if we're lucky once we check out the rest of those addresses—"

"Ralph...look." Nicole touched his arm. When he straightened from placing the box in the back seat of her car, she nodded to the woman who'd driven up moments ago and had parked several spaces down. Past middle-aged and frail, the woman struggled with two suitcases, but there was more to concern Nicole. The woman had spotted them early on and was eyeing them as she tried to skirt the area to get upstairs.

"That's Jay's neighbor. I tried to talk to her once, but she acted skittish with me, and the next day she was gone. Do you think she's been away all this time?"

"Let's find out."

Ralph reached into his jeans' pocket and drew out his badge flashing it at the woman. "Ma'am? Detective Ralph Tucker, DPD. Do you live here?"

The woman backed into the stairs' railing, but her attitude resembled that of a cornered terrier. "You don't look like any police detective. I've been interviewed by the real thing and you don't look like them at all."

"I'm off duty, ma'am, and I'm helping Ms. Loring here clear out her brother's apartment. Did you know Jay Loring?"

"I did not. He occupied that apartment. That's all I know."

"Doesn't sound as though you were happy with him as a neighbor."

"As I told that other detective, I simply didn't feel comfortable with what was going on over there."

"And what do you believe that was?"

She shook her head. "Didn't know, don't want to know, ain't gonna guess. You don't bother with strange folks like that. You just hope you'll be left alone, and that the place stays bug- and crime-free."

"In that order?"

"Pardon?"

Ralph scratched the tip of his nose. "You said 'strange,' ma'am. Can you tell me what you meant by that?"

"Nobody seemed to belong with anybody. What did a man in one of those expensive foreign machines want with some trashy girl in a beat-up wreck? That detective understood what I meant. He was appropriately embarrassed of his friends, too."

"His friends?"

"Well, I'm assuming they were. He was here a time or two himself."

Nicole exchanged a shocked look with Ralph.

He cleared his throat. "Ma'am— By the way, who are you?"

"Binnie. Binnie Wagner," she replied with some reluctance. "Now I don't want any trouble, Detective Tucker. That's why I left town. The other detective assured me that everything would be cleared out of there by now and all would be quiet again. That's all I want. I'm no gossip or troublemaker."

"I'm sure he hoped that would be the case, Ms. Wagner, but—"

"Mrs. I'm widowed."

"Sorry, ma'am. This detective…you wouldn't by any chance remember his name?"

She looked offended. "Of course, I do. I assist in the therapy room with stroke victims over at Baylor. If I don't keep track of my patients' names, how can I expect them to remember theirs?"

Ralph leaned forward expectantly. "Well?"

"Wesley. Detective Willard Wesley."

Nicole could barely contain herself until they were back in her car and pulling out of the parking lot. Thus far every clue they'd uncovered had seemed more confusing than helpful. This one was a black-and-white affirmation that all the abuse, ridicule and rejection had an explanation.

"That skunk," she said, remembering the awful time Willard had given her.

"Amen and then some," Ralph replied. "I apologize for any hesitation I had about coming out here with you. You can't know what a gift this could be."

"Oh, yes, I can."

He grimaced. "Sorry. I didn't mean to overlook what this has cost your family."

Nicole thanked him, then asked, "What happens now?"

"We may be on a roll. I say we look up those other folks in that book."

"No, I mean to Willard."

"This will be tough for you to handle, but as far as he's concerned, we wait. We could go to the lieutenant with this, but there'd be hell to pay for it from upstairs where the weasel's worked on some deep friendships, because our Binnie, for all her good intentions and righteousness, can't get Willard's name right. If we don't have all the rest of our evidence neatly stacked, linking him every step of the way to your brother's death, there'll be too much room for Willard to talk himself free. And there's still your baby to find. So far there's not an inkling that Willard knows about him. My hunch is that that's an act. But if we confront too soon, we could still get Willard, but lose your nephew."

Nicole took a deep breath to repress the panic that wanted to overwhelm her. "Are you sure Binnie Wagner's going to stay put long enough for us to resolve this?" she asked.

"No. We just have to hope for the best. We're always aware that no citizen owes us anything, especially when people get hurt occasionally for trying to do the right thing. But it's a good sign that she works in a hospital. Normally, people want criminals locked away all right—until they find out the price they have to pay to do that. Our Binnie, she seems solid." Ralph squinted at the sun. "But I've gotta talk to Sir Isaac."

"Who's he?"

"Isaac Newman. Willard's partner, poor bas— Excuse me."

Nicole bit back a smile. "Ralph, it's okay. Your tongue is going get whiplash if you keep doing that."

Ralph erupted with a brief but loud bark of laughter. "That's a good one. I'll have to use it on my eldest. He comes home from school sometimes sounding like a sailor on a binge.

"Anyway, old Isaac? He's one of us. But he's suddenly decided to retire. I'm beginning to think I know why."

"You mean he might be involved in this, too?"

"Ha, are you kidding? He and Moses shared the same ethics professor. That's what's probably giving him the ulcers he's always complaining about."

"Do you think he could be compelled to testify about Willard?"

"Not without a double barrel load of evidence."

Nicole tried not to be disappointed by that, and turned her thoughts to Roman. She wished he could be here. But more she hoped poor Meggie knew somehow that her daddy was with her, and she thanked heaven Jay's son was too young to know what was happening to him.

She glanced at Ralph, who'd grown silent, too, and caught him glancing longingly at a Whataburger. "My goodness, look at the time," she said abruptly. "After working you all morning, you must be starved!"

"I guess I could eat something if you want."

She had no appetite, but she found she enjoyed filling him up. Or at least attempting to. While he ate, she sipped on iced tea and compared Jay's book to her Mapsco map book to plan the most time-saving route for the next leg of their journey.

Finally, after they dropped off the last of Jay's things at a shelter, she headed downtown to check on the first address on their list.

"What do you think our chances are of getting into the building without signing in?" she asked, pausing before the revolving doors of the tower. The lobby beyond them looked empty.

"I can do it. There's the security guard, over by the elevators. You'd better drive around the block once or twice. Now that Carstairs knows the heat is on, we can't overlook who else may be watching these addresses."

That new possibility of danger jarred Nicole out of her momentary excitement. She thought of Angelo

Aguirre who was dead for having tried to help her. "I understand," she told Ralph. "Good luck!"

In the end she had to make three trips around the block before he emerged again.

"Mission Control, we have contact," he drawled, climbing into her car.

"You matched the initials? That's terrific! Who is it?"

"Another attorney, would you believe. Roy Benedict. Ring any bells?"

"No. What kind of attorney?"

"Afraid that wasn't listed, and the guard was too new to know."

Determined to remain optimistic, Nicole turned north at the next intersection. "I can check out the phone book and see if he has an ad, or call pretending to be looking for representation."

"Not from home, though, or the office. Okay?"

"Understood."

"Until this is over, you 'use your fear as a servant to your intuition.'" When Nicole shot him a startled glance, he shrugged, looking a little embarrassed. "That sounds a little highfalutin coming from me, but it's a quote I like from a guy who wrote the book on getting through stuff like what you're dealing with. This is a no grounder we're dealing with. And—"

"Pardon?"

"A ground ball. A case easy to solve and prosecute."

He definitely had a way of driving home a message,

Nicole thought. "I'll be careful," she replied, and drove toward their next stop.

The address turned out to be a car dealership.

"PJR...*Paxton Russell?*" She couldn't believe it. "He was some sports superstar in the seventies, right?"

"You got it." Ralph surveyed the property and whistled. "This is one impressive spread. I haven't seen so many luxury imports since Shirl sat glued to the TV watching all the VIPs arriving for Princess Di's funeral."

"If appearances are anything to go by, he must have written the bible on marketing your name." Nicole continued down the service lane, until she pulled into a prestigious strip shopping center a few hundred yards beyond the dealership. Parking beneath the shade of an oak tree, she turned to Ralph. "I expected another attorney."

"Just goes to show ya," he drawled.

"But there's a possible connection—Cameron Carstairs is an entertainment attorney, and Russell was a superjock."

"Could be." Ralph reached for her notes on the console between them. "Who's next?"

She was about to start for the Las Colinas area when her phone sounded. Her hand on the gearshift, she exchanged glances with Ralph.

The phone rang again.

"You gotta answer it," Ralph said.

But she didn't want to. She didn't want to find out who was on the other end, even though common sense told her that in all likelihood it was Max who'd insisted she phone in periodically to share her itinerary. She was afraid it wouldn't be Max, but rather Roman.

"We need to know."

Ralph's grim reminder had her reaching for the handset. Then she keyed the activator. "Yes?" she murmured through dry lips.

"It's me."

29

*Death is, to a certain extent, an impossibility
which suddenly becomes a reality.*

—*Johann Wolfgang von Goethe*

Meggie had lost her battle.

Despite anticipating this outcome, Nicole and Ralph fell into shocked silence for several moments, before simultaneously agreeing that it was time to call it a day. The radiant, early afternoon sun made the drive back to her apartment blinding, but neither of them seemed to notice. Nicole knew it was because they were fighting their emotions, and the glare gave them an excuse for having to blink like crazy.

Once at her house, Ralph unfolded his considerable bulk from her car and eyed her across the roof. "You're not planning to stay, are you? I can't leave you here by yourself."

"Understood. Max and Rebecca Van Dorn are expecting me back at their place." Nicole quickly wrote down their number, her home and cell phone number, then passed it to him along with an already sealed envelope. "You can reach me any time at one of those numbers."

Ralph frowned as he fingered the envelope. "This isn't necessary."

"A deal is a deal...and I feel terrible about having taken you away from your family. Especially now."

His dimples deepened as he tightened his lips into the thinnest of lines. "I know this wasn't the time to ask about arrangements, but when you find out—?"

"I'll call you. Absolutely."

He looked as though he wanted to say more, but only shook his head muttering, "Terrible. It's too awful for words."

"At least her suffering is over."

Ralph nodded. "I just want to go home and hug my kids."

"I'll get going so you can."

Grief was so strange, she thought, backing into the street again. At first all you wanted was to be left alone because there suddenly didn't seem to be enough oxygen around for you let alone anyone else. Then you needed company, that warmth that only comes from the pressing of flesh.

She'd driven half a block before braking. "Damn!"

Not only had she forgotten to run up to her apartment for the other change of clothes she'd hung on the entry closet door, she'd left the hospital's number by the phone, as well. She wouldn't be able to find out who was handling the funeral arrangements without them, since it was unlikely that Roman would be answering his hotel phone anytime soon.

She glanced in the rearview mirror. Ralph's station wagon was out of sight; however, his warning echoed in her mind.

"Two minutes," she murmured, shifting into reverse. That was all she needed.

She was breathless from running, as she unlocked her apartment's door, but she did take care to lock it behind her. Not wanting to have to make another return trip, she then went through the apartment to look for anything else she may have forgotten. That's when she saw her answering machine light blinking.

"Oh, Roman, I hope it's you," she said, pressing the message button. She did so want to hear his voice right now, to talk to him in private.

The caller had a deep, masculine voice, all right—but not his.

"Nikki," Cameron Carstairs began. "Cameron here. I talked one of your people into giving me your home number because something disturbing has come up that I really have to talk to you about. Call me at…"

Nicole almost hit the erase button, she wanted to stop from listening that badly. But she knew what a mistake that would be. On a hunch, once the tape rewound, she also grabbed the cartridge out of the machine.

"Replacement, replacement…" She tugged open the drawer beneath the phone to hunt for a blank tape. All the while she fumed at Cameron's nerve. Did he think her such a complete fool to fall for such a ploy?

As angry as she was disappointed in the man, she found the new cassette and slapped it into the machine, then dropped the used tape along with the paper bearing the hospital's number into her purse. All she needed were the clothes on the door and—

She rounded the corner of the kitchen to the living room and stopped in mid step. It was all she could do to hold back a scream.

Willard.

Through the sheer draperies she saw him opening the outer door that she hadn't latched. Knowing it would take him no time at all to break in the other one, she launched herself over to the phone and punched 911.

"This is Nicole Loring!" she gasped, upon hearing the operator. As she rattled off her address, she heard Willard testing the inner door. "Someone is breaking into the garage apartment in the back of the house. Please hurry. Hurry!"

Knowing Willard could get inside, could easily kill her before anyone arrived, she screamed as loud as she could and dropped the phone. Then she ran to the bedroom and slammed the door looking around for what she could place against it. No, she thought, struck by another idea. It would be smarter to get out the back window.

She was checking the distance to the ground when she heard a commotion outside. The sound of multiple voices had her almost sobbing with relief.

Relocking the window, she hurried to the front again.

Two uniformed officers were at the base of the steps, their guns drawn, while Wes Willard was easing downstairs holding his ID and badge up for their inspection.

"Ma'am, are you the lady who called?" the older officer asked.

Nicole nodded, wrapping her arms around her waist. "Yes, I am." She ignored Willard, who turned around to give her a murderous look.

"Is this the person who you said was breaking into your place?"

"Yes."

"Ma'am, he's a detective."

"I don't care if he's the mayor, he was trying to force his way into my home!"

The two uniformed policemen exchanged speaking glances. It was Willard, however, that annoyed her. With a smirky smile to the two officers, he murmured something too low for her to hear and pointed his thumb in her direction.

"Excuse me, officers," she interjected, "but since I'm the one who made the call, I'd like to know what's being said."

Once again the older cop addressed her. "Detective Willard was explaining that he'd come to check on you himself, Ms. Loring. He's concerned that you'd been extremely depressed since your, er, loss."

She was feeling extreme, all right. But if she exposed her true feelings, that would be playing straight into Willard's hands.

Crossing her arms under her breasts, she smiled coldly at the man she loathed. "It's amazing that Detective Willard has any time to pursue *real* cases, what with all the time he's spending preoccupied with *my* emotional stability." To the two patrolmen she added, "Would you kindly wait a moment while I lock up here? I'm due at my boss's. I'm sure you know him, Maxwell Van Dorn?"

As expected, Max's name won dual looks of respect. The older officer holstered his gun. "Sure do, Ms. Loring. Go right on and get what you need. We'll escort you over there ourselves."

It didn't take her a minute to collect her things, but when she reemerged, Willard was gone. There was also nothing in the cops' behavior to suggest that he'd said anything to make the officers doubt her. But she distrusted Willard enough to suspect he wasn't far away. As a result, she was more than grateful when she reached the Van Dorn's circular driveway.

Max was at the door of their two-story Mediterranean-style home, and it was fairly obvious that he'd been keeping an eye out for her. The police waved, but continued on their way cruising the neighborhood.

"Were they following you?" Max asked, the instant he opened her door for her.

There was nothing soft or welcoming about the scowl on his craggy face, but for the first time since Willard appeared at her door, she felt safe. Reaction set in swiftly and with a vengeance, and with her voice trembling, she replied, "Yes. I had to call 911. Oh, Max, I need a drink."

"You're not the only one. I had the oddest feeling—and you know I don't believe in that psychic crap."

Once inside, he called for Rebecca. She emerged from the kitchen, took one look at Nicole, and assumed control.

"Come sit. Max pour something."

"Didn't I tell you?" he said heading for the bar. "She was in trouble. The police were right behind her as she pulled in."

"Poor darling, you're shaking." Easing the purse from Nicole's grasp, Rebecca urged her to put her head down between her knees. "Take a deep breath, dear. That's it. One more."

"I'm fine. At least I will be fine. Give me a second."

Rebecca said to her husband, "Max while you're there, wet a paper towel with cool water. Her hands are like ice, but her head's on fire."

He brought the damp towel and three generous scotches on a tray, quickly grabbing one for himself the instant he set down the tray. With a private smile to her husband, Rebecca calmly handed Nicole hers and then took the wet towel and held it to her forehead.

"Take a sip, dear. Good girl. And keep breathing."

"Reaction," Nicole muttered, annoyed that her teeth clattered against the heavy crystal.

"You're safe now. Whatever was wrong, has passed. It's over."

She was wrong, but her soothing, calm manner had the intended effect. Nicole could feel the tidal wave rushing her toward hysteria receding. But it seemed to take what was left of her strength with it. Certain her spine was being tugged out of her body, leaving her as formless as a jellyfish, she slumped weakly against the back of the couch.

"It began as such a promising day." She needed both hands to hold her glass. To her annoyance, the ice still danced in the amber liquid as though in the midst of some private 7.5 earthquake. "Oh, God. It always starts as such a good day..."

"No, no, no." Rebecca tossed the paper towel on

the tray and quickly slipped one arm around Nicole's shoulders and used her other hand to direct the glass back to her lips. "Don't go there. Focus on today. Now."

That wasn't any better. Her eyes filled with the tears she'd been suppressing for the last hour. "Meggie died."

Max lowered himself into his chair. "Ah, poor McKenna."

"I have to call the hospital. He was in no shape to talk and I need to find out about funeral arrangements."

Rebecca kept her seated. "There's time for that. You take a moment to collect yourself. You've been living on the edge for too long, Nicole. You're losing perspective of when enough is enough."

Wiping away the tears that flowed whether she wanted them to or not, Nicole took a sip of her drink on her own this time. "It was Willard, that's all. He was suddenly there and I knew he was going to k-kill me."

"Holy Mother..." Max leaned forward. "What is this?"

Not taking her eyes off Nicole, Rebecca held up a hand to silence him. "Start from the beginning. Did Roman's partner meet you as planned?"

Slowly, finally, the story poured out of her. It wasn't, however, the smoothest of renditions and she had to back up several times to clarify things. Max swore at the darkest moments and grew increasingly grim, while Rebecca sat like the Sphinx throughout quietly absorbing it all.

"I know I deserved what happened for not following through with my promise to Ralph," Nicole said finally. "But I thought, 'what could go wrong in two minutes?'"

Rebecca dismissed that with a flick of her hand. "It's human nature to expect everything to adhere to our laws of logic. The important thing is that you reacted well. You called for help and those officers got there in time."

"Who the hell gave Carstairs your number, that's what I want to know," Max snapped. "Whoever it is, they're fired!"

"Willard." Nicole managed a wry smile. "I was upset myself, at first. But then it hit me. And when Cameron didn't get a response from me, he must have told Willard, who came to his own conclusion about how best to handle me."

"Could he have seen you at one of those addresses you were checking out?" Rebecca asked.

"Maybe. It doesn't much matter, though, does it? I was an idiot for taking the risk I did, and it almost cost me my life."

"Then focus on the positive."

"What on earth is that?" Nicole muttered. She put down her glass to massage her throbbing temples.

"You were right all along. There was a cover-up."

Nicole grimaced. "I might be able to feel a little vindication if I could find the baby."

"Maybe he's being held as a bargaining chip."

"Then why not state their demands?"

"You haven't stayed still long enough for them to know what they have left to protect. One thing is cer-

tain, though—you can't risk your safety again. Even
if they're willing to surrender the child, I'm not sure
they would let you live.''

"I have to learn what they are trying to cover up,"
Nicole said, her anger building anew as she thought of
an innocent baby being used as a pawn. And to discover whether Jay was a victim or accessory. ''When
I do, I'm going to buy a full-page ad in the *Dallas
Morning News* and expose those bastards for what they
are.''

Rebecca sighed and turned to her husband. ''Until
Roman returns you're going to have to see to it that
she's never alone.''

Max didn't agree immediately. ''I'm not sure we
shouldn't look into hiring a full-time bodyguard after
all. Who knows if McKenna will be in any shape to
help himself, let alone her?''

Although Nicole knew he meant well, she knew the
only person she would feel safe with was Roman. She
squeezed Rebecca's hand in thanks and forced herself
to her feet. ''I'm going to find myself a few aspirin
and call Houston.''

30

Great sorrows cannot speak.

—*John Donne,*
Elegy on Death

The funeral was on the first Monday of September and it rained. That didn't keep anyone away, though.

Roman didn't mind the rain; he thought the least heaven could do was weep for his baby, since it had taken away his ability to. He didn't, however, like being surrounded by strangers. He supposed they were decent people—he recognized several as staffers at the hospital, and some were sobbing as hard as Glenda— but he would have preferred to be here alone with his daughter. He hadn't even been allowed that at the hospital after the life-support machinery had been switched off. Glenda had clung to her until they'd come to remove her body to the funeral home. There'd only been a moment for him to kiss that soft white forehead that would never grow wrinkled, let alone warm again; too brief seconds, to stroke that too small hand—and then Glenda had stolen even that from him by shrieking that his gestures were useless, just as he'd been useless throughout Meggie's illness.

"It's too late, you bastard!" she'd screamed. "You think showing up for five seconds makes you a good father? You may have fooled her into believing you cared, but not me. I wish I'd never met you, do you hear? Then I would have had a healthy baby, one who wouldn't have suffered so. I hate you! *I hate you!*"

She'd only stopped because Super Doc—for once looking apologetic and even embarrassed at the outburst—had dragged her away. What's more, Roman understood what shock and grief did to people, had been on the receiving end of its worst sides a number of times throughout his career. He even sympathized with the warp in Glenda's psyche that made it necessary to find fault in others to assuage her own bad life-decisions. How the hell she thought she was ever going to have a mature relationship with anyone was beyond him.

The one thing Roman couldn't deal with was the vacuum inside him. Like a cadaver that had been split wide and hollowed out, there was nothing left anymore. That's why he stood in the rain apart from everyone, including and especially Meggie's tiny white coffin. He wanted the bruising pelt of each drop, the weight of the water soaking him because he couldn't feel anything else and that was terrifying.

As soon as the minister finished his last prayer, Roman left, walking to the rental car before anyone could approach him to offer condolences. Not that he expected anyone would, aside from the minister and funeral director. People had been casting him wary, secretive glances throughout the service as though he had *Loser Father* tattooed on his forehead. Oh, yes, Glenda had obviously been creating some interesting fiction during the short time she'd been down here.

The trip to the airport was a blur, like the windshield whose wipers couldn't sweep the flood raging down and sometimes across it fast enough. The tropical depression in the Gulf of Mexico had reached Houston, and this was only the first wave.

His flight took off on schedule, though, and the irony of that didn't slip past him. Modern technology couldn't keep one precious little girl alive, but it sure could defy nature and the laws of gravity by safely thrusting thousands of pounds of metal and hundreds of human souls up into a cauldron of wind and rain. It was all fucking nuts as far as he was concerned.

He found himself both hoping and dreading that Nick would be waiting for him at Love Field. He knew she was worried by the tone in her voice when he called to tell her his flight number, and knew she'd be more concerned once she saw him, so he asked her to just meet him out front. He did look a fright. Even the stewardess had kept an eye on him throughout the trip up, and probably didn't like what she saw because as soon as they landed, she had the copilot come out and pretend to make small talk in the forward galley just in case he went off the deep end. Roman ignored them and strode off the plane and through the concourse like a well-trained zombie.

The clouds from the impending weather system had yet to reach Dallas and he stepped out of the terminal into blazing sunlight, and stifling heat and humidity. The traffic situation at noon was a nerve frayer, but he spotted Nicole's white sedan in the mess and quickly wove through the solid stream of cars and trucks to reach her.

One glance at her as he got in and he knew he couldn't risk another. Her eyes had flooded at the sight of him, and she looked as though she'd gone twelve rounds with Glenda herself.

"Thanks for doing this." His voice sounded strange even to his own ears, and he tried to avoid further conversation by shoving his canvas bag between his feet and securing his seat belt.

"I told you that I would." Her voice was soft, tender. "How are you?"

"Fine. Your lane is moving."

He knew she was watching him and he nodded ahead.

They didn't say more than a half dozen more words to each other after that. As she pulled into her driveway, it struck Roman that he didn't have any clean clothes and should have asked her to stop at his apartment. Once there, though, he would probably have asked to be left there—and he knew she wouldn't. Not without staying with him. She'd been through enough without suffering that dump.

But he didn't want to follow her up into her apartment, either. The urge to flee built as she locked up behind them.

"Let me take that." Her touch as gentle as her tone, she relieved him of his bag, setting it beside the side table. Returning, she stood studying his face. "You're exhausted. Have you been able to get any rest at all?"

"Did you?"

"Roman."

As she put her arms around him and laid her head against his shoulder, he closed his eyes. She smelled as delicious as ever, looked like an angel in her ivory suit, but the hands he raised to take hold of her waist and ease her back might as well have belonged to a robot.

"You'll ruin your suit, and I need a shower." Almost strangling on the words, he escaped to the bathroom.

He was rough on the water taps, and they protested as he wrenched them as far as they would go. His clothes received equally unkind treatment. And once he was naked, he was least kind to himself, stepping into the stall not caring if he froze or burned himself before adjusting the spray.

Then he just stood there as the steam built, stood there with his hands against the fiberglass wall. Water pounded at him. It didn't hurt enough, though. It didn't reach the frozen pit inside him, and it sure as hell didn't stop his mind from images of the past—Meggie weeping in his arms after losing her hair, waving to him bravely as they carted her off to a treatment, or her finally peaceful angel's face once the machines were turned off.

Don't you cry, you son of a bitch. You don't have a right to cry.

But it was finally coming, the storm of grief. As with a tornado raging across barren plains, it had plenty of room to grow in the shell he'd been reduced to; consequently, the sobs that slowly rose from deep within, shook him until the whole stall shuddered with his pain.

God, he wanted to break the place apart. His outrage was as powerful as his hurt, and it went on and on. Even when his throat was too raw to make any audible sounds, he continued to shake.

He supposed that's why he missed the sound of the stall door opening, but he tensed when the air stirred, and a groan tore from him when Nicole's lips brushed against his back.

"Don't. Please."

"You didn't walk away from me when I begged you to."

She would remember that. She had to be gifted with a touch that burned through the wall of ice that was his grief and drew him toward a place of warmth and life.

Life…as she stroked the length of his back, a yearning for it flickered and grew despite himself. He recognized it immediately, but didn't want it. Life hurt. There were too many choices, obligations, ways to make mistakes. But the yearning grew worse as Nicole wet and soaped a washcloth and began bathing him.

Her nurturing touch stirred him awake…his shoulders, his thighs, his chest. For the first time in days he began to feel his blood pumping through his veins again, but with it brought guilt, so much guilt and doubt about himself. What if Glenda had been right? What if he had been a lousy father? What if, by some miracle, his being down in Houston more often could have saved Meggie's life?

"Damn it, Nick." His voice barely more than a rasp, he tried to tell her to quit by rolling his forehead against his upper arm.

"I know. I know."

She whispered that over and over as she washed him, massaged the stiffness out of muscles held tense for so long that he ached to the bone. Until he began to move with each rhythmic stroke. Until he began to lean into each stroke like a starving dog following the scent of a morsel of food.

Needing her to understand what she was inciting, he spun around and captured her head between his hands. "This isn't a good time. I'm feeling..."

"What?"

"Too rough."

Golden eyes shadowed with their own secrets and mysteries caressed his face. "You don't scare me."

"Why not? I'm scaring the hell out of me."

She didn't get to answer because the truth was, he didn't want her to. He wanted to kiss her regardless of his protesting. And he did.

Filling his hands with her hair, he drew back her head until her throat was a taut but graceful bow, and ran his lips down its length, up, and down again, sipping at the water and her essence, warming himself with her heat. Finally, on a shaky sigh, he whispered, "Ah, God. If anyone could... Would you?"

Her fingers traced slow circles on his hips, skimmed to his thighs. "Tell me."

"Save me from the dark. The cold. Myself."

She didn't give him promises, she gave him what he needed, closing her soapy hand on him, rising on tiptoe to press her mouth to his. With a groan, he thrust his penis deeper into that sudsy, feminine vise, and his tongue into that sweeter orifice.

As he'd warned her, unleashed, his hunger lost all restraint. He angled his head and hers and began feasting on her, devouring her with a fervency that could have been called angry if it wasn't so pitifully desperate. He recognized that, and in some corner of his mind was ashamed. But he didn't stop. You didn't watch the gates of Eden open to you and turn back to the ashes.

Her hand worked him, gentle as a whisper one moment, scoring him with her nails the next. She aroused him with the rest of her body, as well...her breasts drawing his hands like magnets, those hard little nipples piercing his palms from the instant of contact...her saucy butt teasing his throbbing flesh when, smooth, like a dancer, she turned around and rubbed against him that way...and her mouth, sweet heaven, her mouth, wholly involved with his no matter which way she faced, no matter what he asked of her.

She made him want again, and then made sure he'd never wanted a woman more fiercely. Every move she made—and she never stopped moving—spoke of her preoccupation with him and what pleasure it gave her. That pleasure had a voice when he streaked his hand down her front and found the slickest, wettest part of her.

The sound of her gasp, the velvety moan as she flowed with it was almost as erotic as the way she tried to turn in his arms and climb onto him. But his need was even more urgent and he stayed her, bent her and drove into her from behind.

As moist and willing as she was, the shock of it stole the air from his lungs. He couldn't find words either, and the hand that touched her slick hair shook.

He could only grip her hips and whisper thickly, "Hold on."

The shower spout could have pummeled them with rocks, he wouldn't have noticed after that. There was only this passionate storm to ride out, the need to accept what too often had remained elusive, but what burned hotter between them with each thrust. And there was the music of it all that was also theirs alone—that of water sluicing off their bodies, flesh connecting with flesh, air rushing from behind gritted teeth and parted lips.

Then, even as he saw her fingers curling into her palms as she pressed them against the wall, he felt the shock wave of wild release coming, and wanting to savor every tremor that raced through her as much as his own, he bent over her, wrapped his arms around her, and gave in to the ragged groan that erupted from him at the same moment she cried out.

As with the rush of water he eventually raised his face to, the tremors continued...even after he drew her against him and her head fell back against his shoulder. The wonder of it, the perfection had Roman abruptly shutting off the faucets.

What they'd just shared couldn't have been better if she'd been made for him. Maybe that's why his eyes burned again behind his closed lids. Sure, he knew he would go on. Survive. But if he'd learned one lesson, it was that love had never and would never be his to keep.

31

*In trouble to be troubl'd
Is to have your trouble doubl'd.*

—Daniel Defoe,
Robinson Crusoe, The Farther Adventures

It was dusk when Roman woke from his deep sleep. Nicole heard him moving about in the bedroom and bathroom and gave him his privacy, deciding that when and if he wanted to come out, he would.

For her part, the hours since she'd eased out of bed had passed quickly enough because she'd been busy— the best thing under the circumstances. And from the sound of approaching footsteps, she was about to find out his reaction to what she'd been up to.

"We need to talk."

Looking up from the lettuce she'd been shredding, she found him standing in the entrance of the kitchen wearing the new jeans she'd bought him, and nothing else. The barefoot, bare-chest look was definitely sexy on him, but not necessarily great news.

"You needed something to wear, Roman," she said anticipating his mind-set. "Your other suit is at the cleaners, but they can't guarantee that after the abuse it's taken that it will ever be the same again. As for the rest...you had to be able to put on something when you woke.''

"What if you'd been grabbed or worse while you were out? Where the hell would I have begun to look for you?''

That's exactly what she thought he would worry about first. Her. It was touching since he still looked as though he wouldn't get farther than the bottom of the stairs before collapsing from exhaustion.

"I didn't go out. I made a few phone calls and had everything delivered. It's no big deal.'' She hoped that would relieve his mind. But if the temperature drop in his bloodshot blue eyes and the grim twist of his mouth were anything to go by, she'd guessed wrong—and, belatedly, she knew why.

"Maybe it's no big deal to you,'' he said softly, "but it is to me.''

Pride. Not male pride. Roman's. An entirely different thing.

Nicole gave up on the lettuce. She wondered if she was about to have to give up on everything. If what they'd shared earlier couldn't count for something— oh, not a commitment or anything like that, but...a real friendship? An honest acceptance of each other?

"I just wanted to help,'' she replied, choosing her words carefully. "I wasn't showing off or flaunting my connections. Yes, I have them, but I've never taken advantage of that before. However, I knew how upset you would be if I went out by myself, how dangerous it is now. So I guess you could say that I did what I did for both of us.''

Not wanting him to see how deeply his rejection was going to hurt, she carried the sieve of lettuce to the sink and began rinsing. Seconds later she saw Roman's reflection in the kitchen window. He swept her hair, which she'd left down, from the back of her neck and kissed her nape.

"I'm sorry. For jumping to conclusions, for not giving you the benefit of the doubt...for everything."

Heaven help her, but she was growing more sensitive to his touch by the minute. Even now, her body still hummed from the lovemaking that had continued in her bed. As a delicious shiver swept through her, she shut off the water and leaned back against him. "Don't apologize. Just hold me."

He wrapped his arms around her waist and touched his lips to her hair. Their gazes met in the reflection in the window, and her heart did something wild and strange in her chest. God, she hadn't wanted to fall in love with him, but just that vague image of his shattered face in glass was so dear to her.

"How are you doing?" she whispered.

"Holding on to my sanity. Thanks to you."

She covered his arms with hers and stroked his biceps, his forearms dusted with hair as dark as what matted his chest. "I wish I could have been there with you."

His hold tightened, but he shook his head. "We have enough strikes against us without you having to have witnessed that."

Nicole decided he should have been a mason; his talent for putting up walls was second to none. "Want to talk about it?"

"I can't, Nick."

The words were barely audible, but the kiss he placed against her temple eased the stab of pain that came when he let her go and picked up her glass of wine. As he took a swallow, she cleared her throat and said, "Chardonnay. Want me to pour you a glass?"

"To be honest, I'd prefer a scotch instead."

Turning back to the sink, she gestured to the cupboard beside the refrigerator. "Help yourself." She better than most knew what he was dealing with, and that he knew she knew. She just hoped he didn't forget that in his eagerness to hide. "Any appetite yet? I'm guessing you didn't eat more than a bite since you left."

She saw him glance at the counter beside the stove where she had two filets marinating, then continue filling his glass with ice and pouring the liquor.

"I'll give it a try. Thanks. But don't...overdo, okay?"

You couldn't get more basic than a small salad, smaller steak and a baked potato. Glad that she'd guessed right, she returned the lettuce to the salad plates and began mixing her own Caesar dressing, very aware of the deep drink Roman had taken.

"Guess I'd better call Tucker," he said.

Here we go, Nicole thought. "He doesn't expect to hear from you until morning."

Roman had crossed to the phone and now turned to her. "He called? I didn't hear the phone ring."

It hadn't, since she'd pulled the jack out of the wall for the extension in the bedroom and turned down the ringer on this one. "He stopped by. First to see how you were, of course, but...also to check on me and return the notebook.''

''I see. Maybe you'd better fill me in on how your weekend went.''

''Food first.''

''Nick—''

''You're going to be angry and then you won't eat at all.''

He didn't argue with her, he simply went back to the phone and started punching in numbers. Nicole rushed over and depressed the plunger.

''Let him have tonight with his family. I pretty much ate into their weekend together.''

A muscle flexed in his cheek, but until he took hold of her upper arms and moved her around the counter to one of the bar stools, she couldn't quite tell how upset he was. When he sat her down and leaned into her face, she knew.

''Talk.''

So she told him. Everything except how terrified she'd been when Willard tried breaking in. However, she supposed the way she avoided his gaze and her spare commentary in certain areas exposed a good deal.

''God,'' he whispered when she was done.

Before she could begin to decipher what that really meant, he wrapped his arms around her and buried his face against her hair. His hold was so tight, she could barely breathe, and yet she didn't care. She'd been needing this since Willard's reluctant retreat.

''Didn't I tell you to stay at Max's?'' he muttered. ''What was I thinking—I might as well have been talking to myself. I should go over there and throttle him, then go after Ralph!''

She let him purge. He went on about danger and risk-taking and outright stupidity…some of it applicable, a goodly amount not. That told her how necessary this was for him. Except for those few moments in the shower when he'd lost control, and now, she suspected he'd been keeping himself tightly contained. How healthy could that be?

What she didn't expect was when he released her was how bright his eyes were, and the telling way he pressed his palms into their sockets. That told her how much he cared, and how well he understood what had happened. Even so, she was somewhat startled when he frowned and lunged over to the dinette area window, twisted shut the blinds, then repeated the process with the kitchen and living room windows. It was as he lit the candle on the counter and switched off all the lights that she had to ask.

''What are you doing?''

''Trying to make you less of a target. From now on you leave them shut and except for the bathroom where there is no window, you try to function with that.'' He nodded to the candle. ''You don't stand directly in front of windows, you don't open the front door without first checking to see if anyone's—hell, what am I saying? From now on, you don't step out of here without me or Ralph ahead of you. Is that understood?''

Perfectly. ''You think they're definitely after me.''

''Six affluent men have some private I-don't-know-what going on…two people are dead…a cop is stalking you, and his partner is taking the nearest exit door to get away from him. Yeah, I think it's a good bet that someone wants you out of the picture.''

"But it's too late. Killing me wouldn't end the investigation, not now that you and Ralph know, too. Then there's Max and Rebecca.''

"Let's not advertise that you've told the Van Dorns. As for me, well, I'm not bulletproof, and Ralph's got a wife and six kids, which makes him vulnerable in a number of ways. No, there's still room to stop us—and I think we're going to hear about the most likely way soon.''

It took Nicole a moment to understand. ''The baby!''

"That's my guess.''

Once again Nicole dealt with a new wave of revulsion. To hide behind an innocent child was beyond despicable. And what about her guilt in all of this? In the end, her mistrust was putting too many people in jeopardy.

"I know what you're thinking, but don't,'' Roman said. ''It's the shortest route to losing your mind.'' He glanced around as though looking for something. ''Show me what Tucker found.''

Nicole reached for her purse by the phone and drew out the infamous leather notebook. Within it Ralph had tucked a few sheets of paper from his own notebook. The identity of the other three men—Donald Belcher, E. E. Starrett and Jerry Fishman. Of the three, Fishman was the easiest to recognize, thanks to his fame as the owner of the largest number of video franchises in the state. Nicole had heard of Starrett, but oddly enough couldn't place him until she saw Fishman's home address, which Ralph had also managed to find.

"That's where that young model died a few years ago!" she cried. "Supposedly there'd been a wild party, she got drunk and stepped off the second-story balcony at Fishman's Cedar Hills ranch. He was celebrating—"

"His fourth divorce, now I remember." Roman tapped his index finger on Starrett's name. "The dead girl was his date and her parents sued him and Fishman after the autopsy revealed other bruises not necessarily in keeping with what one would expect after a fall like that. The D.A.'s office didn't feel they had enough of a case to take it to trial, and there were allegations of a cover-up. It was a mess, but in the civil suit both Starrett and Fishman settled out of court with the family, and like everything else in this news-hungry world, public focus moved on."

Nicole nibbled at her lower lip. "What's Starrett's profession, do you recall? I was thinking that the settlement must have made a considerable dent in the family coffers."

Roman made a rude sound. "I doubt it. He's in general contracting. I just saw another of his company signs in front of some site off Central."

A contractor! Over the weekend she'd sadly concluded that Roman had been right about Cameron being involved. But Starrett would have been a relationship Jay would openly want to nurture.

"I'm still going to have to call Ralph," Roman said breaking into her thoughts.

"You have all the information he does. What more can he tell you tonight?"

"His hunch about what Isaac knows. How to get the guy to talk to us, and to get three of us in with the lieutenant without Willard finding out."

This was what he'd alluded to before about the relentless demands of the job. She could even see how Glenda had loathed it because she would have tried to compete, and in trying, lose. She also understood that this was why he thought *they* were unsuitable for any long-term relationship. But if he was willing to dive back into Jay's case, despite his own personal tragedy, how could she not do everything in her power to make it easier for him—including keeping her concern for his emotional well-being to herself.

She slipped off the stool to give him room. "I'll finish getting dinner ready."

As she started around him, he stopped her by cupping his hand around her cheek. "Do you understand that I need this, Nick? Maybe, just maybe, if I can find your little guy, I can get a piece of my soul back."

As he spoke, there was something in his eyes, a fatalism that filled her with the most awful sense of foreboding. Those haunted, yet determined eyes told her that if it came down to it, he would do anything, including sacrifice himself, to achieve that goal.

And he wasn't going to ask if that was an acceptable option.

Wanting to throw her arms around him and make him promise heaven knew what, she pressed a kiss into his palm and whispered again, "I'll get dinner."

32

*If you cannot take things by the head,
then take them by the tail.*

—Arab proverb

Isaac Newman had been a man of routine for all of
his professional life. The ongoing joke in the department was that he'd been born with a pocket-watch
chain instead of an umbilical cord; but on Tuesday
morning, all that Roman and Ralph cared about was
that he left his house on the south side of Hillcrest
Memorial Park Cemetery at his usual time—six-
fifteen, by their best estimation—and drive down to
the convenience store on Hillcrest where he'd been
stopping for years to purchase his egg sandwich and
tea. That is if Ralph had remembered the name on the
sack correctly.

Parked across the street, they both sighed in relief
when the familiar old Pontiac pulled in at six-twenty-
two. They had at best twenty-three minutes to achieve
their goal.

"Move it," Ralph said.

Roman started the pickup's engine and shot across
the four lanes, barely missing being broadsided by a

delivery truck, and almost taking off the taillight and bumper of a Mercedes-Benz. Ignoring the angry horn blasts, he slid into the empty space on the left of the Pontiac before Isaac could get his door open.

One look at the older detective's face and Roman knew their hunch was right. He looked sick...or ready to cry. Roman would have felt sorry for him if it wasn't for the amount of suffering he'd been allowing.

Ralph climbed out and leaned on the roof of the navy Pontiac. "You know why we're here, don't you?"

Isaac's long face sagged like a melting rubber mask. "All I want to do is retire. Why can't I be allowed to do that?"

"Because every time we turn around the body count rises." Roman had rounded the back of the pickup and joined Ralph at the window. "And I'll be damned if they're going to add a baby to the list."

"Baby?" Startled, Isaac looked from one of them to the other. "I don't know anything about a baby. I don't—oh, shit." He rubbed his hand across his thick eyebrows. "Are you wearing a wire?"

"We don't need wires, old son," Ralph drawled, patting his shoulder. "We have you. But what we don't have is much time. McKenna's right about a baby's safety being on the line."

"I swear, I don't know about any baby."

"But you do know that the AEA death last month wasn't legitimate?" Roman watched Isaac close his eyes and nod.

"From the beginning. Wes had called me saying he'd had an appliance problem at his place and was running late. Next thing I know he's the one to answer that 911 call. The address was out of his way, but I still might not have thought anything about it, except he later told Braxton that he'd been rechecking some facts with a witness on another case and had been barely a block away when he heard the call on the radio. That means he had driven into town, taken a car and gone out again. But he'd told me he was at home worrying about food spoiling in a busted refrigerator.''

"Did you call him on it?" Ralph asked.

Isaac's laugh was bitter. "You know Willard. Unless you're the sergeant or lieutenant, he sees any kind of questioning as a personal attack. We don't say two dozen words to each other all day that aren't work related. Then I saw his report on that Loring guy, and I didn't want to learn more."

"You knew it was crap, too."

"When I was in the navy, there was a guy who was into that shit, and while on leave in the Philippines, he got a bar girl to help him. Problem was she'd seen his wallet, so sure she tied him up...so tight that there was no way he was going to get loose without help. Then she grabbed the wallet and took off. A buddy of mine had shore patrol duty at the time and he saw the room afterward. Said the guy nearly destroyed the place, not to mention his face trying to get that bag off his head.''

Roman gave Ralph a what-did-I-tell-you look before adding to Isaac, "Are you saying that you know Willard was responsible for Jay Loring's death?"

"I'm saying that he was excessively solicitous of the family, suggesting he would work on the media people to back off if they told friends and the press that their son actually committed suicide to avoid the embarrassment an AEA tag would cause if it got out. And the truth? Willard never gave a damn about a victim's feelings let alone the family's. In our first rape-murder together, the girl was lying there with her dress pulled over her head, and here comes the girl's father forcing his way into the room. Now I know I can't contaminate the crime scene by laying anything over her, so I'm trying to block his view. Willard? He stands there almost smiling as the guy pukes his guts into his hands. I think that was the beginning of my first ulcer.''

"Well, let me help you with your latest," Roman said, certain that he would have decked the prick himself. "There was a baby in that room the night Loring died. And now that baby is missing."

"Holy Mother of God." Isaac covered his face with both hands. "I didn't know. I swear it."

"No one knew at first, because Nicole Loring was smart. She smelled something rotten about Willard right away. But she didn't realize how on target she was. Ever since, she's been subjected to his cat-and-mouse games as he tries to stop her from proving that Loring's death was a murder. But she stopped being an amusing annoyance to him when he learned that Jay Loring left behind some insurance in case the worst happened. Names and addresses of six men somehow linked to Willard. Does 22k C mean anything to you?"

Isaac looked away. "I think he was blackmailing somebody...or blackmailing for someone, I don't know. I do know that when that Mexican boy showed up dead, I overheard him say over the phone that their 'wetback problem' had been taken care of.''

It wasn't as much as Roman had hoped to get from him, but the lieutenant would be able to request a full investigation based on what they had. He checked his watch. ''You know what you have to do now, don't you?'' he said to the older detective. ''You have to go straight to Lieutenant Waldrop and tell him everything you know.''

''I can't do that. A cop ratting on—''

''Scum,'' Ralph interjected. ''Hell, they'll probably give you a citation.''

''They'll take away my pension. Dolly doesn't have six months left. The emphysema's got her on a respirator full-time now and she needs constant monitoring. I can barely afford to cover what our medical insurance won't pay.''

Ralph bent low until he and Isaac were face-to-face. ''Listen to me, you spineless deadbeat. Your wife enjoyed every goddamn cigarette she ever put between her lips these past sixty years—probably a helluva lot more than she enjoyed having you between her legs. But there's a baby out there who's less than sixty *days* old, and he's never even sucked on his mama's titty. What's more, if Willard stays true to form, that may be the upside of his life. So do you think that McKenna here, who's just put his baby into the ground, or I give a rat's ass if you're solvent or not?''

Drawing a deep breath, he straightened. ''Crank up this jalopy, mister, and let's see if you remember how to be a cop.''

Moved by his partner's impassioned speech, Roman

drew a deep breath himself. He already knew that Tucker was a good guy, but what he'd witnessed told him that Ralph was probably a terrific father, as well. He planned on telling him so and thanking him again for all he was doing for Nicole as soon as they were back on the road. But as he reached for the door handle, his gaze looked past Ralph who was about to get in on the passenger's side of the truck. To Isaac. Isaac lifting his automatic...

"Tucker!"

33

Something was dead in each of us,
And what was dead was Hope.

—Oscar Wilde,
The Ballad of Reading Gaol

"I should have your badge."

Roman stood before a furious and disgusted Lieutenant Waldrop and almost handed it over. He was disgusted, too, and sick from having seen too much death. Christ Almighty, he'd seen more of it in the past month than in all the years he'd been a uniformed cop. And none of it had been necessary, that was the pitiful part. What a stinking waste.

"Where's Tucker?"

"Calling his wife, sir. They had a parent-teacher meeting today and he's asking her to reschedule."

"Where's Willard?"

"He's not in yet."

That was both the good and bad news. While he was relieved that Willard had yet to show and apparently didn't know that his partner had blown out the back of his skull, no one had a clue as to where he was or what he was up to. Concern for Nicole had

Roman itching to get to a phone to check on her. Sure, he'd felt fairly confident about dropping her off early this morning at the Van Dorns before rendezvousing with Ralph, but she and Max would be at the office now. It would be easier for Willard, Carstairs, anyone to get at her. Of course, if Waldrop's mood was anything to go by, he might soon be able to keep an eye on her himself—that was if he and Tucker were forced to take leave while Internal Affairs conducted their investigation into Isaac's suicide.

He waited as Waldrop circled his desk and went to the door. "Tucker! Get your ass in here, *pronto*." As he returned to his desk, he added to Roman, "I know you've been through hell these last few days, but considering what we're dealing with here, I can't allow you to use that as a reason to disobey department policy."

"I didn't plan to, Lieutenant."

"Sorry, Lieutenant." Ralph hurried into the office and at Waldrop's signal closed the door.

He looked equally gray-faced, Roman thought, who knew better than anyone what must be going through his partner's mind. Had he pushed too hard? Was there anything else he could have said? What do you say to Isaac's widow? What did this do to their case?

"All right, let me have it," Waldrop said when they were all seated. "In detail this time."

Twenty-some minutes later there was a knock on the door and then Willard stepped inside. He took one look at Roman and Ralph and snarled, "You bastards!"

"Freeze, Detective," Waldrop snapped as Willard

started toward them. He nodded to the door. "Back outside. Get yourself a cup of coffee and pull yourself together. I'll be with you in a few minutes."

As Willard left, Waldrop rested his elbows on his desk and ran his hands over his hair. "I swear I had better days in Nam. Do you know what you have now? Nothing. And for what? A good detective is dead."

"If he was an example of good, maybe we need to redefine our role to the community. Sir," Ralph added at his superior's sharp look.

"Shut up, Tucker, or Dolly Newman may not be the only dependent about to suffer a loss."

Hoping to deflect some of the heat off his partner, Roman leaned forward. "Lieutenant, we have the notebook Jay Loring kept, the money and Nicole Loring's testimony."

"Which we all know is irrefutable, despite the fact that you're sleeping with her." Waldrop had demanded Roman answer that question the moment Roman had admitted he was staying in her apartment. "As I said, you have nothing. Except the witness at the complex—what was her name again?"

He looked down at his notes at the same time Roman and Ralph said, "Binnie Wagner."

"Who isn't any more sure of what she was seeing than you are of what Willard's crime is supposed to be."

Wondering how much of the lieutenant's resistance had to do with their jumbled bag of half-conclusive evidence and how much with the distaste of having to deal with a dirty cop, Roman replied, "She can testify that Willard had been to Loring's apartment on previous occasions, that it wasn't *chance* that it was Willard who answered the 911 call."

"Then get her in here and let her say all that to me."

Ralph squirmed in his seat as though getting an electric charge. "Lieutenant, you can't ask her to do that. You might as well send Willard out to go pick her up. Let us get her into a safe house, then we'll take her deposition. From what she told us, she can identify Carstairs, Starrett—all of them as having been at Loring's at the same time as Willard was. What if we're looking at another Cedar Hills case? What do they know about Angelo Aguirre's murder and the disappearance of Nicole Loring's nephew?"

Waldrop's face grew bright red and he leaned forward pointing repeated at Ralph. "Every time you open your mouth you remind me of an intentional disregard for and break in department procedure and policy. Get out of here, both of you, and don't leave this building until I've spoken to Willard."

Ralph followed Roman out of the senior detective's office and shut the door. "We're gonna get screwed," he muttered.

"Wish I could disagree," Roman replied.

Across the room Willard ended a call and stood, having seen them emerge. As he approached them, Ralph growled deep in his throat. "Whatever happens, you have to keep me from ripping out his throat. I can't let my boys grow up with a jailbird as a father."

"Done. But it may only be because I'm beating you to his ass."

Close enough to be heard without being overheard,

Willard smirked. "Hello, assholes. Finished kissing away your careers?"

Ralph stepped toward him. "Why don't you kiss my—"

Roman drew him back. "That's right, Willard, laugh," he said, far calmer if only on the outside. "Who cares if your partner's lying on a slab of cold sheet metal."

"You put him there not me, *Cowboy.*"

"Uh-uh. You did. And you'll pay for that, just as you'll pay for everything else—you and the rest of the 22kers—whether it costs us our badges or not."

Willard didn't so much as flinch at the drop of that name. "Oh, I guarantee you, you will lose those." He closed his hand on the door handle to the lieutenant's office. "What remains to be seen is what else you'll be stupid enough to gamble away."

As a last insult, he reached out and felt the lapel of Roman's suit, the suit Nick had bought him. And Willard knew she had, it was in his eyes and his mocking smile.

As soon as the door shut behind him, Ralph peppered the smooth walnut with a string of crude expletives. When he was out of breath, he settled for kicking the nearest chair.

Roman ignored the looks they were getting from the other detectives—the news about Isaac had traveled fast and so far no one seemed to know whether to come over and commiserate or to treat them like piranha—and nodded toward their desks. "Go call the Wagner woman and give her the cheerful news. I'll check in with Nicole and do the same."

"While you're at it, ask her if they have an opening for two ex-cops with flexible hours."

Funny thing was, thanks to Nick's generosity, he finally looked like someone who wouldn't stick out like a sore thumb at Van Dorn's.

And hadn't Willard noticed.

Hearing Nicole's voice helped him get centered again. Also to yearn as he relived last night and the memory of going to sleep with her in his arms.

"Did Max agree to get the security people for the next few days?" he asked.

"Yes. Someone should be here by noon."

"And you'll go to the Van Dorns' home after work until I can pick you up?"

"Roman, you sound strange. What's wrong?"

He was right; she already knew him too well. "Our attempt to get at Willard through Isaac didn't quite work out as we'd hoped. Newman committed suicide."

He heard her gasp, and then nothing as she processed the shocking news as well as she could. Roman hunkered over his desk, pinching the bridge of his nose. It was, he figured, the maximum privacy a guy could get at the moment.

"I'm sorry for laying this on you over the phone," he told her. "It seems I do nothing but."

"How are you holding up? How's Ralph?"

"He'll be touched that you asked about him. We're…ah, honey, we're not so good."

She took a moment to respond. "You saw him do it, didn't you? Oh, Roman. Why?"

He knew she was asking a multilayered question,

and because he was still answering the same one for himself, he took his time sharing his conclusions. "Because he'd had enough. He was disillusioned, depressed...ashamed."

"Who's going to break this to his wife?"

"The lieutenant. We just came out of his office."

Something in his voice must have worried her. "Don't tell me that he's blaming you?"

"Some would say he has grounds. He thinks we left Isaac with only one option—although we disagree."

"Has Willard heard? How did he react?"

"Like a snake shedding its skin."

"Why am I not surprised? Odious man."

"Speaking of sweethearts, any more contact from Carstairs?"

"No. But maybe he's been warned not to try again."

Roman appreciated hearing her sounding hopeful about that. The closer they came to some resolution with this situation, the more he regretted having said anything to hurt her, as he had when discussing the attorney. "That does raise the question of who's calling the shots."

"I just want it over. Goldie will be coming home a bit earlier than expected. I don't see how I'm going to be able to explain all this to her, let alone ask her to let me continue living on her property. If anything happened to her as a result of my problems, I couldn't bear it."

"One day at a time, Nick. That's all any of us can do."

She took a deep breath and purged it. "When you find out anything, will you let me know?"

"As soon as I can."

"Roman?"

"Yeah?"

"Are you...are you really all right? Will there be trouble because you were there when...?"

He didn't want to lie to her, but the truth would leave her with little hope. "It comes with the territory, Nick. Don't worry about me."

But he knew she would and he adored her all the more for it.

Ralph had ended his call shortly before him and Roman met his gaze as he replaced his own receiver, a question in his eyes.

"The bad news is that she has no faith in us," his partner said, rubbing his temples. "The worse news is that she's definitely not coming here, and might not be *there* if and when we come by to pick her up."

Roman looked at his hands. This morning he'd believed it was all coming together: that they could carefully squeeze Isaac and get a confirmation out of him, that Willard would see a lost cause and start plea bargaining, that he and Ralph would present Binnie Wagner to the D.A. like some prized golden goose. And now he had the worst feeling that it would be a miracle if, on their way out this evening, their vehicles didn't blow up the minute they keyed the ignitions.

"We need her, Tucker. We have to tell the lieutenant that it's imperative to get to her immediately."

Ralph tapped his fist to his mouth as though about to start bird calls, but knew the big guy was really tempted to put that fist through the nearest wall. "You don't know Waldrop. He's the most easygoing guy on the planet—until you don't take one of his directives seriously. Thank God," he added on a different note.

As Ralph all but leaped to his feet, Roman swung around his chair to see what was going on. It was Willard coming out of the lieutenant's office. He kept walking across the main room and then turned left into the reception area and out of the department, shoulders squared, head high. Roman couldn't figure it.

Waldrop signaled them over. "This is how it goes," he said upon shutting his door again. "Wes is on his way to pay his respects to Dolly—"

"Oh!" Ralph bent as though suffering a sudden appendix attack. "And you believed him? Lieutenant, the only reason Willard would go anywhere near Isaac's wife would be if he suspected she had something on him, and then he would shut off her oxygen bottle before he said 'hello.'"

"You will stand down, Tucker." The former marine glared from him to Roman. "Both of you."

Ready to reach into his pocket for his shield, Roman clenched his teeth and waited. Ten years, he thought, ten damn years.

"Give me a little credit for having a reason to occupy this office," Waldrop continued sternly. "As I was about to say before the theatrics, I did ask Willard about everything you brought up, and a few other things like his standard of living which, despite appearances to the contrary, I haven't turned a blind eye to. And, no, I'm not satisfied with every answer that was given, but it's not enough to send IA after him.

Yet. But that still leaves me with a dead detective, a cop who hung on all this time, had announced out of the clear blue that he was retiring, and then just as abruptly blows his brains out.

"Go get your witness," he said in conclusion. "When you have her safe, call me."

Roman and Ralph left so fast they didn't realize they hadn't thanked Waldrop until they were in the hall. Opting for the stairs instead of waiting for an elevator, Roman checked his watch.

"How much of a head start do you think he has?"

"Too much. You'd better let me drive."

34

Chaos is come again.

—William Shakespeare,
Othello

When Wes Willard left the municipal building, he didn't head for one of the unmarked cars, but returned to his BMW. He knew he would need something with horsepower, not one of the tired pieces of crap dribbled down to Homicide through the budgeting office. As he depressed the remote that unlocked the sturdy vehicle, his mouth curled into a sneer. Respect, that's what it all boiled down to anymore. No one had any respect for the real talent. But he wasn't going to waste his time worrying about the pedestrian mentality of the number crunchers. It was time to cut his losses and move on.

As he shot across downtown's wide interchanges, he was forced to keep swallowing against the bitter taste of defeat determined to rise up his throat. Throughout his life he'd hated to lose, reviled it almost as much as he despised losers. The premier one had been his father, who had managed to screw up not one but two businesses in his lifetime. Thank goodness the

fool had finally seen the light and had the good sense
to drive down to the Gulf and walk into the piss-warm
sea. At least that's what the evidence had suggested,
since all that had been found on the beach was the
family VW and his father's Florsheim shoes. But Wes
knew it was true based simply on his study of the man.
His father had always looked behind him, at what was
done, never to the future—which would also explain
why there was no suicide note. The turkey probably
hadn't remembered that fine point until he was neck
deep in water. By then the changing tide would have
made it impossible to return to shore. He certainly
hadn't possessed a trickle of the imagination it would
take to plan something like running off to Mexico.

Losing his father had left Wes and his mother in an
economic bind, since Mr. Wizard had also forgotten to
consider that the insurance companies weren't going
to pay on those policies once he opted out of his life.
Again, a failure. If only his father would have *asked
for advice;* even at eleven Wes could have pointed out
the greater wisdom in finding someone to murder him.

Fortunately, Wes's mother had been made of a better weave of brain matter. No sentimentalist, either,
she'd done okay for them. Almost succeeded reaching
the big time when the CEO of a budding oil explora-
tion company where she'd worked as a secretary took
notice of her. The guy had actually promised to leave
his wife and kids and marry her. But the wife was a
sharp cookie herself and had put a quick stop to those
plans by getting pregnant with their third child. Wes
never did understand how a guy could be willing to
abandon kids already born, but never the one that was

still in the oven. Maybe the shrewd wife whispered into his ear as he slept, told him that they would be the parents of the new messiah or something. In any case, the two-timer suddenly experienced a moment of conscience, which in turn forced his mother to marry the company's accountant. Another jerk, Wes thought, although he'd admired his mother for not putting all her money on one horse. Floyd never figured out that his wife continued her affair with the CEO. Wes had enjoyed telling him after she succumbed to cervical cancer. The prick deserved it after Floyd told him that he didn't like Wes's condescending attitude.

At least he'd gotten his bachelor's degree out of the relationship—only it hadn't been at a name school like some people.

Reaching for his phone, he dialed Carstairs's number. Good old Carstairs and his five frat buddies from UT were about to be left to their own devices again—after they helped him get out of town. He already knew where he wanted to go, too, although he wouldn't have minded staying if the environment had remained hospitable. But when you traded in commodities and that commodity was people, you had to anticipate things going wrong, the tides of fortune occasionally changing. Like Isaac, poor dumb schmuck. How the hell could he have let himself get cornered by the cowboy and the hillbilly?

At any rate, what was done was done and, like that cat in the White House who kept landing on his feet, he had someplace to go; in fact, he'd checked out California on his last vacation just because the president was spending so much time there. He'd liked what he'd seen, too, and had even made a few initial contacts. He was a true believer in emulating people you admired. Now wouldn't it be a hoot if he and the prez's paths crossed one of these days.

"Marlene," he said upon hearing the sultry voice of the firm's receptionist. "Willard. Put me through."

"I'm sorry, Mr. Willard—" she'd been trained early on never to use his title "—Mr. Carstairs isn't in."

Wes sighed, accepting that it was going to be a day of petty annoyances. He checked his Rolex watch instead of the dash clock, simply because he liked the look it presented to anyone observing him—successful and important. "When do you expect him back?"

Marlene hesitated. "I'm sorry, Mr. Willard, but...I don't. What I'm trying to say is that he's out of town. He flew to the Caymans last night with the family for an extended vacation."

He what?

The light on McKinney directly before The Crescent turned green but Wes continued to sit there until someone behind him honked. Disconnecting without another word, he struck the phone against the steering wheel.

"You conniving slimeball!" he screamed as he passed the majestic building.

Of all the ones to have turned yellow, why did he have to run? Carstairs was the leader of the group, and always had been. For all their outward success, the others were mullets in the stream of life without Cameron's direction.

Wes had spotted the high-profile attorney entertaining a client for lunch at an upscale topless bar almost two years ago while questioning the girlfriend of a suspect who was working there. Although intrigued with the concept of building business relationships while openly using the panacea of sex, he didn't actually initiate contact until he'd studied Carstairs thoroughly. Only after ascertaining that the attorney was the image of the conservative business and family man on the outside, and a wolf with an unquenchable appetite for the exotic just below the skin, Wes waited for the right moment—Carstairs's birthday to be exact—and sent over a girl he'd met during his brief time in Assault. Out of gratitude for helping her permanently unload an abusive deadbeat husband, Feliciana Arroyo posed as someone from a singing telegram service delivering greetings from one of Carstairs's clients. Once she'd gained access into Carstairs's office, Feliciana gave him the birthday greeting of his life. As she'd left, Wes had her leave his business card behind as an open invitation should Carstairs ever be interested in some real excitement.

And that's how his little side business had begun. Carstairs had taken the bait, and the rest of The 22karat Club had quickly signed on, glad to have a "safe" way—as he'd pitched it to them—of satisfying their considerable appetites for the innovative and experimental. After all, he'd pointed out sympathetically, did they want to risk another near-catastrophic fiasco like the one that had occurred at Fishman's ranch?

"Hell no," they'd all responded.

Those were the good old days. The boys had been enthusiastic, giddy as teenagers who'd figured out you could use a condom for more than a water balloon. When the boys were in a mood to party—whether solo or as a group—they simply contacted him, and he made all the arrangements, culling the talents of his ever-evolving stable of aimless souls and general fuck-ups, people like Feliciana, Angelo Aguirre, Jay Loring, and a few others. People not all that different than his old man—losers, who had little to offer society and who just didn't know how to function without direction, or the misfits like Loring, who needed to live on the edge occasionally to feel alive.

The operation could have gone on indefinitely if Loring hadn't gotten religion or domestic fever or whatever it was that had made him think he could change…and if after Loring's death, Aguirre hadn't seen a way to make some money on the side by biting the hand that fed him. There was Nicole Loring, too, damn her meddling soul. She had proven to be the biggest pain in the lot. If he did anything before he left town, it would be to teach her a lesson about poking her patrician nose where it didn't belong.

The first rush of anger overcome, Wes dialed Roy Benedict's number. Roy was the next closest, location-wise, and after Carstairs he was the most intelligent.

"Is he in?" he asked as soon as the receptionist answered. "This is Willard."

"Mr. Willard…oh, hello." The woman sounded as though this was the last call she'd wanted to answer. "I'm sorry, but he's not."

Wes narrowed his eyes, beginning to suspect something underfoot. "Let me guess…he's decided to take a spontaneous vacation with Mom." This fat pervert still lived with his invalid mother of all things. It hadn't taken much imagination to figure out how and why he'd turned into what he was or why his specialty in law was sexual harassment, job discrimination and wrongful discharge. Most of Roy's clients were women, and he liked to cop a feel by hugging up the victims in a show of fatherly support.

"Er, no. It's business that's called him out of town. A complicated case. I'm not exactly sure yet what day to expect him back."

"I'll bet."

"But I'll be sure to let him know you called, Mr. Willard."

"Don't waste your breath."

Wes disconnected again.

So that's the way the bastards were going to play it. Despite his assurances to Carstairs the other day that he still had things under control, that witnesses were under control and if worse came to worst could be silenced, and that diaper-dirtying evidence would soon be removed from the scene as well, they were all going to act like rats abandoning a sinking ship.

He knew better than to bother phoning any of the others or bother with sanitizing now. The only wise course of action at this point would be to pack, get to the bank and haul ass. As it was, he would be smarter to drive to Houston or New Orleans before catching a flight west.

But he couldn't let himself go anywhere before taking care of one last thing. He owed himself this little present.

Finally able to smile again, he dialed Feliciana's number.

35

The first four acts already past,
A fifth shall close the drama with the day.

—Bishop Berkley,
On The Prospect of Planting Arts and
Learning In America

"What did he say?"

Nicole wasn't really in the mood to listen to Carlyn's continuing headaches with her live-in boyfriend when it was clear to everyone but the parties involved that the relationship had ceased to work. But she hadn't been concentrating very well on an article she'd been asked to write for *D Magazine* that they'd already subtitled, *Art For The Public Good.* What with all that was going on, and the news Roman had hit her with less than an hour ago, she'd only managed a rough opening paragraph when Carlyn walked in with coffee for both of them. Hoping that her protégée meant what she'd just announced and was finally making some solid progress one way or another, she sipped her drink while waiting to hear the rest.

"I don't think he believed me at first," Carlyn said, apparently still a bit bemused by her broken engagement. "Heaven knows, I couldn't have been more explicit. I said, 'Dennis, I realize now that I'm not ready to marry you or anyone else.' And what does he do? He pauses and gives me that what-planet-are-you-from look that always tells me he's in his anal mode. Then he continues talking about the china his parents want us to have that were his grandmother's and how I had to phone his mother immediately to thank her, even though I'd seen the stuff the last time we were at his folks' for dinner and I *hated* the sickly colors. It was as if I'd spoken in a foreign language. But what it did was finally convince me that my opinion didn't matter to him."

Nicole leaned back in her chair and warmed her chilled hands on the firm's Noritake china, thinking that either Max had been fiddling with the thermostat again, or she was more run down than she'd imagined. "How did you make him finally take you seriously?" she asked automatically.

"By going straight to the guest bedroom closet and digging out my luggage."

"My. Is this the demure young thing who sat right in that chair last May and said she had found 'Mr. Perfect'?"

Carlyn swept her hair behind her shoulders and attempted a haughty look, but there was no hiding the laughter in her eyes. "I'll forgive you for that because of all the pressure you've been under, but behave, will you? We all have to learn our lessons as best as we can."

"Well, you've got that right. Where did you spend the night? With your folks?"

"I may be a slow learner at some things, but crazy I'm not. No, I went to Rena's. My airline attendant friend? She's going to be out of town until Thursday and offered me the use of her place. In fact, I may move in with her and share expenses rather than look for my own apartment."

"Not a bad idea, at least for a while. It does take a while to find your bearings regardless of how wise the split was. And who knows? Dennis may surprise you yet by offering to try changing in order to reconcile."

Her assistant wrinkled her pert nose. "I hope you won't think me shallow by saying this, but I think I can do better. I don't mean status-wise, but in character. And I want *romance*. It struck me as I was staying with you those few days and watching Roman, how attentive and concerned he was to your needs. The look on his face when he talked about you..." Carlyn sighed wistfully before growing serious again. "How's he been since returning from Houston?"

"It's been devastating for him. I know Meggie's on his mind all the time, but he won't talk about her or the funeral. He's trying to make work his balm." But that was difficult, too, especially when every day brought a new catastrophe like this morning's. She couldn't, however, tell Carlyn about Isaac.

"You have that in common."

The observation jarred Nicole out of her private brooding. "Do we? Maybe so." As many missteps and wrong conclusions as they had made with each other, it would be nice to remember once he walked away that there had been more than sex between them.

"That's an awfully sad look, my friend."

"Believe it or not, I was just realizing that I would like to be able to talk to my mother about him." She laughed dryly. "Then I realized not *my* mother, but *a* mother."

Carlyn mimicked her laugh. "I'd lend you mine, but you'd only be trading Big Mama for Holly Golightly."

"What an accurate analogy…and why do gay sons understand mothers better than daughters do?"

"They're probably breast-fed longer."

Groaning, Nicole finished her coffee and shoved the cup and saucer across her desk. "That does it, get out—and take this with you!"

Carlyn left, an impish smile on her face. "I'll buzz you when lunch arrives."

Already bending over her work again, Nicole waved. Catered daily lunches were going to be another standing order from Max since Roman talked to him.

She was shaking her head over the strange protectiveness she seemed to bring out in some men, and the lack of compassion in some women when the phone rang. She thought she was hearing things when her mother announced herself. Talk about ironies, she mused.

"Well, this is a nice surprise," she said. "I was just thinking of you. Is everything all right?"

"There you go again. You know, Nicole, just once I'd like to call without you assuming that we can't function here in Hicksville without you. For your information I've kept my distance to give you time to get out of whatever mood you were in the last time you were over. But apparently I haven't waited long enough."

Dropping her head into her hand, Nicole wondered if this debilitating cycle would ever end. "I see. Excuse me for not phrasing myself properly. How are you?"

"I'm not so sure now."

Hearing the pouty note in her mother's voice, Nicole wished there was a Big Daddy in her family, so he could shake some sense into Big Mama. "Are you planning on deciding anytime soon," she drawled, "or are we supposed to simply gnaw at each other until one of your bridge friends triggers your call-waiting?"

"Actually, I thought you'd be interested in knowing that Foley's is having their Red Apple sale this week. It wouldn't hurt for you to check around your area and see what's available. Considering what you wore here, I'd say your wardrobe is in dire need of polishing."

When all else fails, attack appearance. It was her mother's stock weapon to try to control her, and Nicole wasn't going to fall for it, either. "Consider the message delivered." Loud and clear.

"I'll see what they have in your size here. If I find anything—"

"No, no." God forbid they start that again. "Thank you for the offer, but I'm perfectly capable of shopping for myself."

"It's no bother if you need my help, Nicole."

But I don't! I need you sober, or sane, or whatever it is that you're not!

Nicole cleared her throat to purge her exasperation. "If I change my mind, I'll let you know."

"Well, you know, I really do have other things to do than sit by the phone and wait for you to call."

"Then by all means *do* them."

She hung up and covered her face with both hands. Why on earth was she hoping to find Jay's son? No one deserved to wind up in this basket case of a family.

Less able to concentrate than ever, she rose thinking she might go out to the warehouse and look for inspiration from the treasures out there, but she was stopped by the ringing phone.

"Please," she whispered, reaching for it. "Give up, Mother."

"Miss Loring?"

It wasn't her mother, it was a young woman. "Speaking."

"Miss Loring, I don't expect you to believe me, but you have to come quick. It's all falling apart."

That voice...she had heard it before. Where? "I don't understand, who is this?"

"Don't you remember that night at Velvet's?"

How could she ever forget it? "Yes. And you're right, I don't think I'm going to be able to believe anything you say, Mrs. Arroyo."

"Look, I'm sorry for the way things turned out, but I have to protect myself, too. You're not the only one who lost a brother."

"Why don't you tell me why you're calling?"

"Do you want the kid or don't you?"

Nicole gripped the phone tighter, even as she told herself that it couldn't be this easy. "You have him?"

"For a few minutes more, but he's about to be taken away from here and then I don't know what's going to happen to him."

Dear heaven. "Give me the address. I'll notify the police."

"Are you nuts? I'm not about to go to jail for kidnapping or anything else that wasn't my fault. I had nothing to do with this. The kid was thrust on us."

Us. How many were involved? "Look, I didn't mean to suggest otherwise—" she tried to think fast to reassure her "—it's just that you sound worried and upset, and I wanted to reassure you that the police can protect you."

"Yeah, right. Lady, we both know they're the ones who caused all this, so forget it. Just tell me—are you coming or not?"

Put that way, there was no question. "Give me the address," Nicole replied.

The woman hung up before Nicole could ask her for directions or be sure she had the correct house number. As stunned as she was exhilarated, Nicole hung up thinking of six things to do at once. And she had to hurry. Willard was headed for the Arroyo home, as well.

"Carlyn!" She raced out of her office and almost ran into her assistant in the hallway. "Where's Max?"

"In the back of the warehouse. What's wrong?"

"I've found Jay's baby! Use my office. Call Roman." She shoved his card with all of his numbers into her hands. "A copy of the address is on my desk. He'll recognize it. Tell him that Willard is planning to take him and that I'm sorry, but there's no time to wait."

"Nicole!" Carlyn tried to grab her hand as she rushed for the exit. "This isn't smart. Nicole!"

* * *

Ralph had just pulled in below Binnie Wagner's apartment and he and Roman were looking around. "Any sign of him?"

"Not that I can see." Roman twisted both ways in his seat for any indication that their hunch was right and that Willard had beat them here. "At least her car's not gone."

"Let's go find out if that means anything."

They climbed the stairs to the second story apartment and knocked on Binnie Wagner's door. When she failed to answer, Ralph swore.

"I knew it. She probably called a cab and hooked 'em. If things turn any more our way, I don't think I'll be able to stand it."

"We knew she was afraid. We can't blame her for that." Roman knocked again, and called, "Mrs. Wagner? Are you there? Please open up, ma'am. It's Tucker and McKenna."

"What do you want to bet she's on her way to Love Field or DFW?"

"I am not," Binnie Wagner snapped from the other side of the door. Chains rattled and locks turned, then the door opened just wide enough for her to peer through and scowl at them. "I had to make sure it was you two, that's all."

Ralph tapped the security hole. "Believe it or not that's why they put these things in the doors."

"Use your own eyes, Mr. Smarty Pants. I'd need a ladder to see out of that. Besides, I was deciding whether to trust you or not. I never did cotton to boys who use nasty language."

Roman rubbed at his upper lip to hide a smile. "Ralph didn't mean it, Mrs. Wagner. Sometimes our commitment to our work makes us too intense, that's all. As a matter of fact, that's why we're here. We've talked to our commanding officer and he's given the authorization to place you in a safe house. Once we get you settled, Lieutenant Waldrop would like to interview you regarding what you saw going on next door."

"Do you think I was born yesterday? I watch all the cop shows on TV like everybody else. Wesley probably has the location of each one memorized the same way you do. No sooner would you leave me, and here he would come. No, thank you. I'm going to my brother's in Lancaster, and I'll take myself there. As a matter of fact, I was just finishing packing."

"It's Weston, Mrs. Wagner. And we can't guarantee you'll be safe there."

"You can't guarantee anything, period, which is why I'm not talking to any other police until that Detective Weston fellow is in jail."

Crossing his arms over his chest, Ralph leaned back against the balcony railing giving Roman a look that said, "You resolve this."

"Mrs. Wagner, the detective's name is Weston Willard. If you don't get that part right, his lawyer will have a field day telling the jury that if you can make a mistake with his name, you might also have made a mistake with what you saw. As for arresting him, we can't do that until we have your deposition."

"Then you have a problem, don't you?" She opened the door wider and nodded to the luggage beside her. "You want to make yourselves useful, you can be gentlemen and carry these down to my car. I called my brother and sister-in-law and told them I was on my way. If they don't hear from me in a half hour, their son, my nephew, told them to call him. He's with the Lancaster Police Department."

"No kidding?" That gave Roman an idea. "Do you think he would agree to stay over at his parents' home evenings to keep an eye on things?"

"Of course, he would. That's where he lives. Rodney's a good boy."

"Then I tell you what we can do. We'll get your things downstairs, follow you down there, and introduce ourselves to your family. This way they'll know that if anyone else approaches your house, something is wrong. Do we have a deal?"

Binnie Wagner beamed at him. "I think we can do business."

"You've got us turning into damned valets and chauffeurs," Ralph muttered, once they were back in their car. "Next the old biddy'll want us to deliver pizza."

Roman had taken over driving again and followed Binnie Wagner out of the parking lot. "Hey, she's willing to cooperate now, and you know this is as good an arrangement as any we'd come up with. Cheaper, too. And not only will she be surrounded by family, but you tell me what farmer doesn't own at least a shotgun?"

"No, the best news is that she'll have overnight protection. You remind the lieutenant when he bitches about the hour long round-trip this will take."

"That's closer than where she would have ended up if she'd gone to Love Field or DFW."

"Yeah, yeah, yeah."

In actuality it took only twenty minutes to get to Binnie's family's farm, thanks to her tendency to drive like a NASCAR racer. But the farm was also located conveniently close to the I-35 interchange.

After introductions were made and a bit of small talk was indulged in to reassure the family, they were going over precautions with Stuart Potter, Binnie's brother when Roman's beeper sounded. He checked the number and immediately asked to use the Potter's phone.

"Something's wrong," he said quietly as he passed Ralph. "This is Nicole's number but the message is from Carlyn."

The moment he got through to her, he learned the news was far worse than he'd feared.

"I couldn't stop her!" Carlyn cried. "I'm so sorry, Roman."

Despite the dread that made his stomach roll, Roman quickly assured her. "It will be all right. Just give me the address." But when the girl started reading it off, he had to gulp air for the second time that day. Before Carlyn was finished, he slammed down the phone and was running for the door.

Spotting him, Ralph demanded, "What?"

"Nicole's headed for the Arroyo place. Feliciana had the kid all the time!"

36

*Come not between the dragon
and his wrath.*

—*William Shakespeare,*
King Lear

Muttering about her incompetence, Nicole pulled into an abandoned gas station and once again reached for her Mapsco map book. Thanks to her nervousness, she'd forgotten the directions she'd looked up twice already. At the rate she was going, Willard would get to the Arroyo home before she did!

"Come on, come on…" She thought she had figured out where to turn off Military Parkway, but unfamiliar with this part of town, she'd obviously passed it and had now gone too far in the opposite direction. Then she'd turned into a road that sounded similar to the one she really wanted and lost several minutes before she'd found her way back to the parkway.

"Ah." Her finger stopped on the right spot. As she thought it was only two, no three streets up from where she was. Somehow she must have missed it the first time around.

Her nerves were a mess, her stomach one large knot,

her hands damp and trembling. She'd waited so long
for this moment that she couldn't believe it was about
to be over. She only hoped that Carlyn had gotten hold
of Roman and that he wasn't far behind her. She would
feel safer if he and Ralph were present through this.
In fact, she would never have come alone if not for
Feliciana's anxiety that had warned loud and clear that
there was no time to waste.

As soon as there was a break in traffic, Nicole eased
back onto the road and into the left lane looking ahead
for the turnoff. This time, instead of trying to read
street signs, she counted—a good thing, too, since the
third road had a sign completely covered by an overgrown hedge.

She coasted down the road trying to read house
numbers and instead found herself appalled by the conditions these people lived in. She also couldn't help
noticing that she and her car stuck out like a dime in
a handful of pennies, and the number of people openly
staring at her added to her unease. But what had her
braking was noticing that she had gone too far. The
house numbers were descending from the one she
wanted.

Shifting into reverse, she realized that the address
Feliciana had given was for the first house. Relieved
that there was no sign of Willard's car, she quickly
parked, slung her purse over her shoulder, and hurried
to the front door.

The Arroyo house was as poor and untended as any
of the other residences. Nicole hoped the baby had
been treated better than some of the children scurrying
around like stray pups.

"Hello?" she called through the screen door. She knocked on the wood frame and peered through the dirty webbing.

Feliciana Arroyo and two other people emerged from around a corner. The girl lingering back the farthest was very pregnant and yet holding a tiny baby, naked except for a diaper. A young man noticing her reluctance returned to put his arm around her as Feliciana unhooked the latch to let Nicole enter.

"What took you so long?" the Hispanic girl demanded.

"I took the wrong turn, I'm sorry." Nicole smiled to reassure the frightened-looking group. Unable to resist asking, she nodded to the infant. "Is that him?"

"Yeah. And that's as close as you're going to get to him," Wes Willard said, suddenly appearing behind the young couple.

As she looked down the barrel of the automatic pointed at her chest, Nicole clasped her hand to her throat. *Why?* she thought looking first at Feliciana, then the other two people. One by one they lowered their eyes.

"We didn't have a choice," Feliciana told her.

Nicole wasn't sure if she sounded defensive or resentful.

"Shut up," Willard snapped. Then he pushed the younger man's shoulder and tugged the girl by her arm, directing them back down the hallway. "Vamoose, you two. And don't let me see you poking your heads out of your room, unless you want to lose them."

Satisfied that they were gone, he motioned with his

gun for Nicole to step toward the left into the cramped living room, then moving beside Feliciana, he smacked her on her bottom as a signal to do the same.

"What do you want?" Nicole decided that terrified or not, she couldn't let him control her as he had in the past. "If it's money—"

"I'll be doing all the talking this time." Sneering, he shook his head. "You are such a pain. If I'd had a clue as to the trouble you'd cause me, I'd have finished you off that first night."

The admission had Nicole curling her fingers into her palms. "It was you."

"Surprise! The only satisfaction I've had since then is knowing that you've been driving yourself nuts thinking about me walking right past you that night while you slept. So close," he said stepping nearer. "I could have done anything I wanted. Scary huh?"

"More like repulsive."

"Ha! You rich bitches are all alike. I wonder what McKenna sees in you."

"You'll get to ask him. He's on his way here."

"No, he isn't. He and Gomer are probably sobbing into their beers at some bar right now for losing their badges. Do you know what they did?" he asked Feliciana cheerfully. "They put the squeeze on my partner and the dumb jerk killed himself. What a pair."

"How can you ridicule Isaac like that," Nicole said. "Didn't he protect your back, support you, *look the other way* for you because of a code you both were supposed to honor? No, excuse me, it's obvious that was all one-sided. You don't know the meaning of moral fiber." Nicole gave him a pitying look. "You had to have been such a disappointment to him."

"Ask me if I care." But Willard was clearly unhappy with what she'd said. He waved the gun at her again. "You think you're so superior? You didn't even have a clue as to what a deviant your brother was, what a wild card he could be. Hell, even I never knew what he would be willing to try."

It was all Nicole could do not to grab something and throw it at him. "Jay might not have been perfect, but no matter what you think he did, what you might have *forced* him to do, he was a dozen times better than you are."

"Forced. Maybe only because he liked being forced." Willard gestured to Feliciana. "I think it's time for her to see how wrong she is."

"Please, Wes," the girl replied, nervous fingers tugging at the fringe of her tight cutoffs. "Just let it go. What if she's right about the cops coming?"

"Whine, whine, whine. You want your sister and her wetback husband sent back to Mexico before their baby is born? You stop yacking and do what I say. Put the tape into the machine. Let's show Miss Mighty Mouth what a saint her pretty boy brother was."

He'd drawn a video out of his jacket pocket, but Feliciana continued to hang back. "Is that one with me in it? Wes, c'mon. My sister doesn't know, man. Don't do this to—"

"Put the fucking tape in the player!"

Sweat broke out on Willard's face. As soon as Feliciana accepted the cartridge, he tugged at his tie and unbuttoned the top button of his shirt.

"What the hell, do you have to give yourself a blowout just to get anything done around here? And why isn't the air-conditioning on? You make enough money!"

"I send it all home. You know that."

"Home. That's about right with you people. You come here and mooch off the country, despising it and us, but you're happy to take our cash."

Her movements as stiff as her expression was vengeful, Feliciana shoved the video cartridge into the player and turned on the TV. Seconds later Nicole saw Jay facing the camera. If Feliciana's expression was disturbing, Jay's broke her heart.

Staring in disbelief at the camera, then to the side, he abruptly lunged at whatever disturbed him. "Are you nuts? Hey!" he cried. An instant later the camera swept to a baby lying on the pallet in the corner...and the gun aimed at him.

Nicole pressed her fist to her mouth to keep from crying out. She refused to give Willard the satisfaction of seeing how upset she was, but she watched in horror as the camera went back to Jay.

As the gun was pointed at him again, he backed away. "Okay, okay. One last time. But then we're done, right?"

There was no response from the cameraman. With a defeated sound, Jay began undressing.

Realizing what was about to happen, Nicole turned her back to the screen. "You can't ask me to watch this. I won't!"

Willard replied, "Feliciana, go get the kid. Maybe Miss Priss needs the same motivation her brother did."

"No!" Nicole shook her head at Feliciana. Then to Willard, she added, "You're a monster."

"Just keep your eyes on the screen."

She thought the morning she'd found Jay had been the most horrible she could imagine, but now as she was being forced to watch his last minutes of life, she knew she'd been wrong. Tears flooded her eyes; however, there weren't enough to mercifully blot out the mortifying images on the screen, nor did they mute Jay's fragmented pleas not to have to continue debasing himself. And when he turned around and offered his hands behind his back, she saw the camera angle moved as the camera was placed on the dresser so Willard could fasten the handcuffs on Jay—intentionally fasten them backwards—before pressing the key into his hand and pushing him back onto the bed.

Nicole broke into helpless sobs as Jay realized what evil trick had been played on him and panicked, at how he tried to lunge off the bed to seek help, only to see Willard aim at the baby again. Then there was that awful groan...that first groan she had heard after arriving at his apartment that night...the groan she now saw was her brother's despair as well as his ultimate decision to end this as quickly as possible.

Shattered, she covered her face with her hands and wept uncontrollably.

"Look!" Willard whispered into her ear.

"No!"

"He loved doing this. He was quite the adventurer, our Jay was. There was almost nothing he wouldn't try for a sexual high, and the money made it all the more exciting."

Squeezing her eyes shut, she clapped her hands over her ears to block Willard's voice as well as his whisper on-screen to Jay to stay on the bed or else.

Willard grabbed her wrist and jerked it down. "Look, I said! See what people pay ridiculous sums to experience. What kind of guys do you suppose get their jollies from watching other people's perversions? Can you guess? Your esteemed buddy Carstairs was one. In fact he was my best customer. Imagine him chasing after you and being unable to resist seeing more of your brother."

"Stop!" Nicole screamed.

It was too much and, in that instant, she knew if she didn't get out, get help, she would lose her mind. It triggered something wild and feral in her and she erupted, flinging herself into Willard, her elbow connecting with his jaw one instant, her knee finding his groin the next.

Then she ran.

She burst through the screen door, the force of her escape slamming it against the outside of the house. She meant to run into the yard, to scream for one of the people that had been out in the neighboring yards to call for the police. But blinded by tears, she misstepped and her high heel got caught between the boards on the stoop. Thrown off balance, she lost a shoe and went flying off the porch.

She hit the sidewalk with her hands and knees simultaneously, and as she skidded, she cried out as skin was torn away. Nevertheless, driven by hysteria, terror and pain, she screamed, "Help! Somebody—*help!*"

She couldn't believe it, through the distorting veil of tears, people were simply standing there.

"Please! Call 911! *Ahh—*"

Suddenly she was grabbed from behind by her hair. Willard had recovered and followed, and he was dragging her back up the stairs into the house.

"No!" she screamed again. She knew if he succeeded in getting her inside it would all be over. It was probably all over anyway. The searing pain as he threatened to tear off her scalp made surrender almost an appealing choice. But she just couldn't do it.

Desperate, she twisted around and raked her nails at the hand in her hair.

Willard cursed and wailed. No, he wasn't wailing, she realized an instant later. That was a siren.

Then he was beating at her fingers with the butt of his gun.

The pain from his blows was excruciating, but she hung on—because of the stealthy approach of Feliciana bearing a long kitchen knife in her hand.

"This is for my brother, you murdering bastard," the girl snarled. She drove the knife into Willard's back.

He howled like a wild animal and released Nicole to reach behind him. Drawn too far off balance, Nicole dropped backwards striking her head and spine hard on the steps and then repeatedly as she bounced down each step until she landed on the ground.

Through the ocean roaring in her ears, she heard the blast of gunfire...Roman shouting...another shot.

And finally the insanity stopped.

37

*Blood that is to flow
will not stay in the veins.*

—Turkish proverb

As the world grew silent again, Roman heard Ralph whisper behind him, "Good God Almighty." He couldn't agree more. If they'd been seconds later…

Not allowing himself to finish that thought, he straightened and, continuing to hold his gun on Willard, he hurried to the prone trio, glad that Nicole was nearest. Seeing her being assaulted by that creep and then that fall had been one torment too many in a day, a week of endless heartbreak.

"Nick," he whispered through the ache in his throat. When she didn't move, didn't so much as open her eyes, he stooped beside her to press unsteady fingers to her carotid artery. Relief swept through him when he felt the faint but steady fluttering against his fingertips. "Hold on, sweetheart," he murmured, caressing her cheek. "Help's coming. Hold on."

With no small reluctance, he moved over to Willard, first picking up his gun and shoving it into the back of his waistband. As he was checking for the detective's pulse, Willard's eyelashes fluttered then lifted.

"Hey, Cowboy. Glad you can at least...shoot straight."

Roman didn't say anything. What did you say to the Willards of the world that would make an impact with them? Besides, he was dying and that was justice enough. He waited for the glazed look in Willard's eyes, and moved up the stairs to Feliciana.

Their situation reported, Ralph joined him. The girl was sitting, using the house as a backrest. Blood was oozing out from between her fingers as she held her side, and from the fear in her eyes, it was apparent that she thought Willard had mortally wounded her with the one round he'd gotten off.

Ralph was the one to remove her hand and check the spot. "It's your lucky day. This looks like mostly a flesh wound." He paused to listen to sirens approaching on Military Parkway. "Hear that? At least one of those should be an ambulance."

"He...killed my brother," she said as though he hadn't spoken.

She closed eyes that Roman noted were empty of tears. One tough lady, he thought. Her grief and shame were her private business. He could only imagine what journey she'd made to come to this point, and why she'd made some of the choices she had. Things could have been resolved sooner if she'd been straight with them. Roman couldn't forget that, but her actions had also saved Nicole's life, and probably that of Jay's baby. It allowed him to find compassion for her.

"I'm sorry," he said, touching her shoulder. "I

wish things could have turned out differently. But we'll see what we can work out for you.''

Glad to be able to leave her to Ralph, he hurried back to Nicole. He was growing increasingly worried that she hadn't regained consciousness yet, but because of the fall she'd taken, he was extremely reluctant to move her in case she'd suffered a skull fracture or spinal injury. He settled for taking her bloody hand within both of his.

"Stay with me," he whispered. "Please. Don't you go, too."

First he felt a tremor in her hand, then her lashes fluttered. When she opened her eyes, he exhaled a pent-up breath.

"That's my girl."

"Haven't we done this…before?"

"And hopefully for the last time. You want to see stars, you should ask me."

She winced as though suffering a spasm, then groaned softly. "Comedian."

"Ah, Nick…when will you learn to wait for the cavalry?"

"Didn't think there was time." She moved the fingers he held. "I need to get—"

"Whoa." He released her only to take hold of her shoulders and keep her still. "Don't move until they get you in a neck brace."

"But the—"

"Hush now. Help's here."

As the squad cars began arriving, followed by two ambulances, Roman continued to reassure Nicole until the emergency personnel squeezed him out of the way.

Although unwilling to let her out of his sight, he did check how the people tending to Feliciana were doing—and that's when he saw the couple standing in the doorway holding a baby.

The girl was big with child, so it was unlikely the one she held was hers. Could it be...?

He stepped closer to them. *"¿Es señorita...muchacho?"* Because he knew how bad his Spanish was, he also directed one index finger from Nicole and the other from the baby and brought both fingers together.

"Sí, señor."

He knew he should say something, but suddenly he couldn't find his voice. He glanced back at Nicole who was now fitted with a neck brace and being readied for transporting.

"Please," she mouthed.

But his feet wouldn't budge. In the end it was Ralph who said something to the couple and took the infant.

"Hey, big guy," he drawled. "How'd you like a ride in Uncle Ralph's police car? I'll flash the lights for you." As Ralph approached Roman he muttered, "I know this stirs memories, but he's a baby, damn it. It's not his fault."

Roman stiffened. "I know."

"Then take him. He needs to go in and be checked out, too."

"Why can't they put him in one of the ambulances?"

"They have Nicole and Feliciana going in one. Where do you want him to ride? With Willard?" Ralph eased the baby into his arms. "Relax for crying out loud. She's watching. This is not the time for you to burst her bubble. Sit in the back seat and I'll follow the ambulances.''

Roman did as Ralph directed because his partner was right, he didn't want to upset Nicole. But the truth was that he wasn't ready to be this close to another child. It was too soon, and the grief that it stirred sliced too deep.

His unease must have transmitted itself to the baby because he soon started wailing.

''Jeez, Mac,'' Ralph said, eyeing them in the rear-view mirror as he started the engine. ''You're scaring the little fella to death.''

Before he could reply, he heard, *''¡Señor!''* Then he saw the young Hispanic man hurry to Ralph's side of the car and handed him an envelope through the open window. *''El niño.''*

Roman recalled that *niño* meant child and suspected the way the guy was gesticulating that inside the envelope was the infant's birth certificate.

''Gracías,'' Ralph replied, and handed it over the seat. ''Why don't you look inside and see what his name is?'' he asked Roman.

He'd managed to get the baby to stop crying by rocking and patting him, but Roman wasn't willing to go any further. He slipped the envelope into his pocket. ''That should be Nicole's privilege.''

''Oh, brother,'' Ralph muttered.

The rest of the day raced by as Roman and Ralph delivered the baby, learned of all the tests Nicole was going to have to endure, waited until Feliciana was resting comfortably in a room to question her about what happened, and returned downtown to make their reports. Because he'd used deadly force, Roman was also reminded that he would have an interview to explain his actions there. It was typical procedure, but it was just one more thing added to an already overwhelming day.

He almost forgot to phone Binnie Wagner to give her the good news and thank her for her cooperation. Her spunky attitude won the first smile he'd managed in hours. But it vanished as he and Ralph walked to their vehicles.

"Going back to the hospital?" Ralph asked.

"Yeah. But I hope she'll be asleep."

"She won't be—unless they had to drug her. She's gotta have too many questions to be able to rest yet."

What they'd learned from Feliciana had been grim, and Roman had stolen a half hour to race back to the Arroyo place and get the tape. It was in his car now, and he planned on burning the thing as soon as possible. Not that he had any hope that it was the only one with Jay Loring on it; however, it would be the start Nicole would need to begin healing.

"Will you tell her 'hi' for me?" Ralph asked.

"Sure." That would be the easy part.

Ralph stopped.

After two steps Roman paused and glanced back at him. "What?"

"It's none of my business, I know, so I'm only going to say one thing. Don't break her heart. I like her. She deserves to be happy."

"All the more reason to give her a chance to get on with her life."

"You deserve to be happy, too. And you're nuts about her. What's also nice is that she's pretty crazy about you."

"I thought you were limiting yourself to one thing?"

"Don't go all stiff on me, and don't do it to her when she talks about the kid. I know you're dealing with a huge black hole inside you right now..."

"No, you don't know." Roman appreciated Ralph's intentions, but he'd had enough of people telling him that they knew what he was feeling. "You don't know. And Nick's life is in transition. She's a mother now. I'd as soon rub salt in my open flesh than have to watch her play house."

Ralph looked away for several seconds before nodding. "You're right. She deserves better than someone determined to make her pay for what she can't help." He held up his hand in a goodbye salute. "I'm going home to my family. How are you going to get through the night, let alone the rest of your life?"

Roman didn't reply because he had no answer.

Nicole was drowsy but awake when he entered her room. It was less frightening to look at her without the brace around her neck, but it tore at Roman's heart to see her latest injuries, the bandages on her hands. But most of all he hated seeing the pain in her eyes. Because he knew it was born not from any physical injury, but from the kind of emotional trauma only a human being can inflict on another human being, he went straight to her and enfolded her in his arms.

She held him as tightly as her sore body allowed. "I didn't think you'd come back."

"Didn't the nurse with the zillion freckles tell you that I would?"

"Yes. I didn't believe her."

"How do you feel?"

"I'm telling myself it doesn't matter because it's over. It is over, isn't it?"

"He's dead, and we have a pretty good start on piecing everything together thanks to what Feliciana's been telling us."

"She saved my life. It's strange to want to hate someone and be grateful to them as well."

"I got the tape, Nick."

She leaned back and her eyes filled with tears. "Did you…?"

"No. Willard is dead. I wouldn't look at it unless you asked me to."

"Don't. Burn it."

"I will. Right after I leave here."

She went back into his arms. "I don't know how I'm ever going to forget. He filmed it, Roman. He made Jay do such awful things, forced him by threatening to kill the baby. He made me watch it all. My own brother."

Roman gently rocked her as he had soothed Jay's son hours earlier. Behind his closed lids, his own eyes stung. He understood violence, but he would never get used to the evil done against innocence. Never.

Somehow Nicole was going to have to forget that there was a side to her brother that was not healthy. Whether his "syndrome"—if that was the right word—was biological, a result of his dysfunctional childhood or what, no one would ever be able to tell her, so she would never know if he *could* have been helped or cured. Nevertheless, she was going to have to look at Jay's son every day from here on and give the child the best of who his father was. The magnitude of that responsibility—Roman didn't know how she was going to do it.

"Cameron Carstairs saw it. Paid to watch!"

"That's what The 22karat Club was. Carstairs and his other perverted friends had created their own mini fraternity, where even the tongue-in-cheek name made it clear that they weren't as *pure* as their 24 karat images and public lifestyles would suggest. There was a big meeting this afternoon," he told Nicole, hoping to reassure her. "Based on the little testimony we have so far, along with Jay's notebook listing everyone involved, the D.A.'s office is going to try to go after the group. They may also be able to reopen the old Starrett case."

"I've been thinking about why Jay kept the book in the first place. I think he did it in case I changed my mind about Cameron. It was his way to keep him away from me."

And he must have suspected the worst the night Willard came to his apartment, which was why he'd stuck the notebook into Nicole's purse. How naive to think that a man like Willard would let someone who knew as much as Jay obviously had, go. But to Nicole he murmured, "Could be," and gently kissed her forehead.

"What will happen with Feliciana and her sister and

brother-in-law? I don't want them charged with kid-napping. They took as good care as they could of the baby. And paid a terrible price of their own with the death of Angelo.''

If only Aguirre had been clearer with what he'd been trying to communicate to them, whatever his motives. Then again, once Willard found out, the kid had never stood a chance.

''Feliciana has agreed to be a primary witness for the prosecution,'' Roman said. ''As a result, anything she might be charged with down the road should have a reduced or probated sentence. As for her sister and brother-in-law, I don't know. Even if the authorities want to return them to Mexico, there may not be time. The girl is pretty close to term and what with the added stress…'' Roman cleared his throat. ''Here. I meant to give you this.''

He reached into his pocket and handed over the envelope.

''What is it?'' she asked, holding it awkwardly in her bandaged hands.

''I haven't looked inside, but I would gather it's his birth certificate. It must have been among his things when Willard took him out of the apartment.''

Nicole offered it back to him. ''Open it for me. We'll find out what his name is together.''

He wished he could, but once the child had a name Roman knew he would feel more of a connection, and he didn't have the energy left. Not tonight.

He placed the envelope on the table beside the bed. ''You're exhausted, and the head nurse told me that she was going to wake you regularly because you did suffer a concussion this time.''

"Not a severe one. They're discharging me in the morning.''

"So I heard. I'll check the time on my way out and be here to drive you home.''

She searched his face. He knew she was gauging something.

"You've done so much, already, and now your department is short two detectives. Max and Rebecca have offered. So has Carlyn.''

He allowed himself one more kiss before beginning his necessary retreat. "I'll do it.''

"All right. Thank you.''

"Sleep well,'' he murmured.

But as he risked one last look and saw how alone and vulnerable she looked lying in that bed, he knew that she wouldn't get any more sleep than he would. Because like him, she would be thinking of tomorrow and the inevitable closure that was going to be as painful as anything else they'd had to deal with.

Epilogue

That virgin, vital, fine day: today.

—*Stéphane Mallarmé,*
Plusieurs Sonnets

"His name is Joseph," Nicole said as Roman drove them away from Baylor Hospital. "Joseph Loring. I'm going to call him Joey."

Roman didn't need to glance over to know she was gazing down at the tiny, dark-haired bundle in her arms. She'd barely taken her eyes off the child since he'd arrived to take her home. For that matter, the big-eyed tyke seemed fairly preoccupied with her, too. Maybe he was seeing something that Roman had noticed himself, specifically how, except for their vastly different coloring, there was a similarity in their facial construction that strongly announced a genetic connection.

"Joey's nice for a little boy," he managed.

"The mother is listed as Lucy Loring, but you know the odds of that being legitimate. The head nurse checked St. Paul for me and said that Lucy Loring paid cash for her delivery. What does that tell you?"

Roman lifted his eyebrows at that news. "That she

was probably from a well-to-do family. Maybe she's a diplomat's daughter.''

"That's much nicer to imagine than a drug lord's offspring.'' Nicole sighed. "I like the name Lucy, though. No matter what, she had a sweet side to her.''

As do you. Roman had been bombarded with signs of a new softening in her since yesterday. He knew it was that maternal thing that happened when women held an infant, and in Nicole it enhanced what was already a pretty damn mesmerizing package. Dangerous reactions for the realist he needed to be.

"Oh, by the way, Stan says hello,'' she said breaking the silence that had fallen between them. "He stopped by just before you arrived. He told me a few things, and showed me a breathing technique that I think will help when the panic attacks set in and I'm not able to con myself that I can cope with all this. But I am going to take him up on his offer to visit him. At least for a while.''

Roman liked hearing that. Stan would watch over her. "He's a good guy.''

"How was going in this morning? Everyone in the department must be terribly depressed.''

"Yeah. Mostly for Isaac's sake. But they're disappointed in him, too. And God knows they're disgusted with Willard.'' Not wanting that name to dwell in her mind, he added, "Ralph sends you his best. He said Shirley would like to help you with any baby things you might need until you feel up to shopping yourself.''

"How sweet. I'll take her up on that. What with Goldie arriving tomorrow, I should spend what extra energy I have making sure everything is ready for her at her place. I've neglected things over there terribly."

"For good reason," Roman replied, frowning at the thought of her working herself to exhaustion. "Promise me you won't overdo?"

"I'll need to stay busy, Roman."

Quiet words, but they held enormous meaning. Because he understood that meaning too well, he didn't protest any further.

The closer they came to her apartment, the quieter they both grew. When he finally parked beside her car that he and Ralph had driven back here yesterday, he knew his heart was pounding as though he were midway into a marathon through Death Valley.

He was almost grim as he helped her and the baby up the stairs and inside. And by the time he made the next three trips to carry up all of the gifts and flowers her friends had sent, he was sure sweat was soaking through his jacket.

"Can I get you anything before I go?" He glanced around the small but welcoming apartment that had also been an oasis for him through his darkest hours.

"I don't know what. You're probably eager to get back to the station anyway."

He finally let himself look at her. Bruised and underweight, she was still the dream he'd always thought her standing there in the white top and slacks Carlyn must have picked up for her. "Not eager," he said thickly. "But…it's time, Nick."

"I understand." She moistened her lips. "Go."

He didn't budge. He couldn't when she was looking as though he was stealing something from her.

"Honey, it wouldn't work. Apples and oranges and all that."

"You're right. But thank you. For everything. I mean that from the bottom of my heart. And take extra good care. Please."

He pretended he didn't hear her voice crack and forced himself to get as far as the door. "Listen...maybe after a while, once things calm down and I get my head screwed on straight, you won't mind if I check in on you? See how you and the little guy are doing?"

"We'd like that."

Her smile was brilliant, but her golden eyes were quickly flooding with new tears. Or maybe it was his own that made him think so. In any case, he suddenly found himself propelled across the room and wrapping her and the baby in his arms.

"God, Nick, who am I kidding? I want to stay. I *need* to stay." He punctuated each brief sentence with an intense kiss. "So you're stuck with me, until you wise up and throw me out."

"You'll have a long wait, Detective McKenna," she replied when he let her speak again. "Because I happen to love you."

He rested his forehead against hers. "You're going to have to put up with my dark moods, the lousy hours, the unimpressive pay..."

"What's that compared to what we've already been through together?"

She could be right. He prayed that she was because he knew he would forever be only partially alive without her.

"Okay," he said, exhaling shakily. "Then you're stuck with it."

"It?"

"This damaged heart," he replied, taking the hand at his nape and pressing it against his chest. "And all the love that's in it."

"It's a great start, McKenna."

Yeah, he thought, bending to kiss the forehead of the little boy watching them so seriously. A pretty amazing one.

Bibliography

1. *The Handbook of Forensic Sexology*. Edited by James J. Krivacska, Psy.D. and John Money, Ph.D. Amherst, NY: Prometheus Books, 1994.

2. Hazelwood, Robert R., Park Elliott and Ann Wolbert Burgerss Dietz. *Autoerotic Fatalities*. Lexington, MA: Lexington Books, 1983.

3. O'Halloran, R. L. and P. E. Dietz. "Autoerotic Fatalities with Power Hydraulics." *Journal of Forensic Sciences JFSCA* Vol. 38, No. 2, p. 359–364.

4. Wiseman, Jay. *SM101: A Realistic Introduction/ The Medical Realities of Breath Control Play*. (Taken from the Internet.)

Would Rhy Baines
recognize his wife?

New York Times Bestselling Author

LINDA HOWARD

Sallie Jerome, a.k.a. Mrs. Baines, had picked up the
pieces of shattered dreams after Rhy walked out seven
years ago. A news reporter for one of the nation's
leading magazines, she'd become the independent,
self-possessed woman Rhy had always wanted. Only,
now *she* didn't want him. Or did she?

An Independent Wife

"Howard's writing is compelling."
—*Publishers Weekly*

On sale mid-April 1999
wherever paperbacks are sold!

Let bestselling author Candace Camp
sweep you away in this delightful
and sensuous romp...

SWEPT AWAY

Revenge was never so sweet....

His eyes met hers, and for a moment they were
frozen in time. She detested this man with a fury that
threatened to swamp her. And tonight she had to
make him want her more than he had ever
wanted any woman....

But is it the thrill of taking revenge, the duel of wits or
even the fear of exposure that accounts for the heady
exhilaration she feels at Lord Stonehaven's nearness?
Or is it the man himself?

On sale mid-May 1999 wherever paperbacks are sold!

MIRA

New York Times Bestselling Author

CATHERINE

THE ARISTOCRAT

COULTER

Football star Brant Asher loves his "American-as-apple-pie" life. Until he learns of his inheritance. Suddenly he is the heir to an English estate...and to his ugly duckling cousin, Daphne. Brant must marry her, or he'll lose everything. Marriage is the last thing he wants—until he meets his bride-to-be. The ugly duckling has become a swan...and she wants nothing to do with an arrogant American. But Brant isn't about to give up his legacy. Or his beautiful cousin....

> "Catherine Coulter has created some of the
> most memorable characters in romance."
> —*Atlanta Journal-Constitution*

On sale mid-May 1999 wherever paperbacks are sold!

MIRA

Also available by
award-winning author

HELEN R. MYERS